Heart of a Goon
Series One

ISBN # 978-0615649221

I0642586

Contact Information:
Make Checks Payable To:
Jeanne Thomas
C/o Danny Trevathan/UnderGround Elite
P.O. Box 2122
Bristol, TN 37620
Phone (304)997-4577

Printed in the USA.

UNDERGROUND ELITE PUBLISHING PRESENTS

HEART OF A GOON

(Series One)

DANNY TREVATHAN

(The Don of Underground Fiction)

I'm the Don

I'm the Don
Of everything that was and everything that is
I will drown water and kill death
I'm a certified go-getter, a bonafide wig splitter
I'm the itchy finger that stay ready to pull the trigger
I'm the Don
The underground street Don, I'm married to the game
Writing books is my wife
An I fuck that bitch morning-noon-and night
I'm the reason the sunsets and hides from the darkness of night
I'm the Don
I'm an untamed beast
I roam, rule, and conquer these streets
The fiction, arid fantasy that you visualize is my reality
I'm addicted to the life
I'm addicted to money
Fuck you pay me
If you don't like it so what
I'm eternal life
You can't slay me
These are words of wisdom for the wise
You can't kill me
Death already tried
This is my life, my legacy, my truth
So remember your fiction, your fantasy is my reality
I'm the Don
Of Underground Fiction
(Now kiss the pinky ring)

Thank you & Acknowledgments

First I would like to give blessings and thanks to the Almighty High (God) for giving me this talent to produce and write stories so vividly. Without you I wouldn't of made it this far. Especially the life I was living. Ducking and dodging the police, bullets, haters, death, jealousy, deceit, and love that was real from some. (Sorry to those if it was)

To those who read my first books in rough draft and gave me the encouragement and inspiration to keep striving because they seen my talent in raw form. Oh, I got's to make this quick and short. Leodius, my dawg you pushed me to get these books out there, so here they are. I got nothing but love for you. 50/50 (Craig) good looking, Big Bridgeforth, Coop, L.C. (Warren), White Tim, Scoody, Chuck Jones, Tone. P, Click who been down over 25yrs, Wade, Jermaine. G, White Craig, Rell, T.Y., Deion, Bridge from Cleveland. Tony (Peanut) Brown, you gave me some solid words. Dante J (Chop), Tye (NYC) much love and respect. Deno, stay pure. Dewey (NYC) thanks for staying on me about part three. D-Bell (Farrell's Finest) you let me know my shit fire! Saeed (Philly). Gary Booth. Kenny. R (Clev). Wink (VA). Gezzy (Chi) keep Andrea. Lionel Meredith (Kinfolk). M.0. (VA). T-Mack (DC) get that book out. Taye B (Painesville) stay real homeboy. Jamel Williams (Trouble) you get your job back? Regina. Mims (Sunkist) thanks for and love, I still got that belt. Adrian Hudgins (Detroit) stay solid. Garry Haile (PA) Get them books out. Fly Tye (PA) author of Money Hungry, thanks on the insight. Londa (Akron), who bought my first book and loved it, thanks. To NiNi: I haven't forgot about the love you showed me in Akron, get at me. Wayne W. P. Vincent Shirley (KY) thanks on the solid words Pimp. Moose (DC) stay up player. Marv (BX) stay real and thanks for the encouragement. Swendoe, you like a little brother to me and I gots nothing but love for you. Billy, you stay out the way homeboy. Arte from down the way (Clev). Maurice Trammell (Bone), much love. Monty (Yonkers). Ill Beale (DC). T-Baby (NYC/PA) good looking out. Ta da Party, Deangelo, L.C. (Warren), Hasson, what's up player. Bruce.H, stay real. Lil Red. Steve Gore and Tyrelly.

Stiem, what's good old man? Shawn Rankin. Peewee, see you in a second player. Deangelo, AJ Kennedy Sr., thanks for the words.

To my Family: Mom, you took care of all three of us by yourself for years and I love you for that. But somewhere down the line you forgot about being a mother and grandmother.

Aunt Diane, you been a mother to me and I can't tell you how much it means to me. I love you and appreciate the love and caring.

To my blood sister Tanya and my nieces and nephew: I miss and love y'all. We had some good times and laughs. And I plan on having many more with all y'all.

To all my kids: Never think I don't love or think about y'all. I love y'all all the same and unconditionally.

To my aunts and uncles: Janice, Carolynn, Diane M, Sandra, and Shawna. Love y'all. Uncles David, Perry, and Bobo who's been a father to me since mines wasn't around. To my uncles that passed, Butch, Penny, Donny, and Bernard you gave me some of that pimp juice when I was young. Tony, you taught me how to hold my own and have heart in them cold ass streets. To my Grandma (Mother side): The family hasn't been the same since you've passed. It's like everybody don't even know each other. No more get together's. It's sad. Charles (Step Dad), you stuck around I see. Cousins: Damon, Tye, Toot, Shawn, Brenda, Man, Shelly (Can I get a haircut?), Lenny, Leroy, Tomorrow, Tone Tone, lil Tony, Andre (Dre), Spunk, Chuck, Eric, Tito, Carla and Bernard.

To my cousins who passed: Jack. M. Warren Wright (Bimo), you told me to get my books out there and here it is. Wish you were here to witness this. Mikey, we had some wild times together, miss you.

To my only full-blooded brother Sanicka, who was killed by a coward he grew up and called a friend who shot him over 18 times. I'll always come to your gravesite and pour out a little liquor for all of y'all. Yours and many others death goes to show you that even your worst enemy could be your so called best friend's hiding his true intentions and feelings towards you and yours. I wish I could of took them bullets for you. I hated and wondered why it wasn't me that died like that. I was the one out there living for that drama like it was normal and loving it. NOT YOU! Hope your proud of me for turning my life around and doing this legit book thing.

To my kids mother, I'm sorry I got locked up and left y'all to take care of things I should of been there to do and help with. Y'all did good with the kids. I mean this from the bottom of my heart, and hope y'all let me throw a party for y'all.

To Jeanne, you've helped me believe there are true sincere partners in this world that are women. You've been the angel when the dark side was calling. I love you with a love so pure that not even the government could stop or penetrate! You and the kids my family. I gots nothing but love and respect for you. Thanks for believing in me. I'm blessed to have you in my world.

To a few ladies from the past and present that I've encountered in life: Oashea (stay sweet), Rochelle. W (Star), stay positive. Sabrina W, I got nothing but love for you. Thanks for hooking me up with them jobs. Mechee (Red Bone), I'll never forget the love. Ebonee (Chocolate Princess), they don't understand. Tisa Y. Steph (R.I.P) you taught me something valuable. Trish, thanks for the job.

I thought about who I would put in this section because I know how most think and talk. But I really don't care! This my s$#t! Some didn't even deserve to be mentioned. But since your fakeness gave me a little tiny motivation, I gave you that. And to those who doubted me, my grind, story producing, and belief. I know y'all prayed for my downfall for years. Too bad. I'm like the air you breathe, so inhale. You can hate and despise all you want, but you got's to respect my grind to never lay down. Thanks for the hate and talking about Danny Trevathan.

I've been trying to do this book for a while now because I know I'm good at it. It's been a hard grind and hard work. Alot is needed and put into my books. But I still kept pushing these bad babies. Not a week went by that I didn't work on my books. I never gave up on my dreams. Now I'ma push these muthafucka's like a whole brick of hard on the first of the month cause I know I'm the truth! I'm a real ass mu'F*#ka from the street who feels what I write deeply because I've then seen it, lived it, and breathed it. I'm not proud of it, but it has taught me how to take these characters and breathe life into them and make stories that are so intriguing that you feel like your there. But, I'll let you be the judge of that.

Oh, and I want to give another big thanks and shout out to those who helped me get my first book in print and out. Y'all made it happened for me and I got's nothing but respect and appreciation for all of y'all at Crystell Publications and Big Flex. Look forward to working with y'all on many more.

Enjoy readers, and I'm open to any comments and statements you may have pertaining my books you read. God Bless you and yours…

FROM THE DON OF UNDERGROUND FICTION
DANNY TREVATHAN....
Email address: d.treva99@yahoo.com
Facebook address: Danny Underground Elite Trevathan

Prologue

The cold blade of the straight razor sliced like a sharp knife across hot butter against the Mob Boss Ramond "Porky" Carbaina's throat with ease as his blood gushed out like a shaked up can of soda pop and his eyes got big like he hit a fat fifty piece of crack rock. He tried to call his attacker a few nigger's, but he choked on his blood sounding like he was gurgling a mouth full of mouthwash.

"Good work, Lenny," Cris praised the black man who just killed Ramond Carbaina as he gazed at him with cold black eyes.

Lenny looked at the Italian white man with the dark hair and saw the gun in his hand, and knew shit wasn't right. He knew Cris was thirsty to climb to the top and would kill who-ever for it. He was supposed to do this hit and take claim at the table amongst the other Mob Bosses, and Cris was to tag along. He was the only black man in the Mob at this time and this would make him a "made" man and very powerful.

"I'm sorry my friend. I can't have you taking my glory and position," Cris told him with a sinister smirk on his face, like he was going to enjoy this.

"You dirty piece of shit!" Lenny barked, wanting to use the blade he was gripping that was still dripping with fresh blood on Cris badly. Lenny had just slaughtered and mangled three Mob men with ease like the professional killer he was.

"BUCK! BUCK! BUCK!" The slugs slammed into Lenny's chest and stomach knocking the wind out of him. Lenny tried to slice Cris one good time and saw the gun rising towards his head as he got a swift slice across his left hand and the gun went off. He saw flashes of his life zipping past and smiled at the ones of his son Lenny.

Cris saw the smile upon his face and noticed the bullet had only graced him, and didn't penetrate his skull. "You sure was a trooper my friend," Cris uttered, aiming again. "BUCK!"

Darkness evaded Lenny's world, as he died with a smile on his face thinking of his son.

This book is dedicated to my brother Sanicka Trevathan (R.I.P)

and

Jeanne Thomas

Chapter 1
"From the womb to the streets"

As the cold pellets of raindrops beat down on him as he walked up McGuffey Street, in Youngstown Ohio, it intensified the emotions he was smothering in as if he was getting shot by a BB gun. He could not believe what had just transpired with him in the Plaza in front of everybody. He wondered why he was so different. Why the constant pain and suffering seem to shadow him. He was fourteen years old and tears of anger blended with the rain ran down his young face.

"I could of just let it ride and acted like it wasn't shit! Nah fuck that! Angie was supposed to be my girlfriend and was being all shady, flirting all up in big Roy's face. So I had to pull up on they asses! Fuck they thought!" Lenny mumbled to himself, thinking of what just happened.

Everybody was hanging out after school in the Plaza, because the stores there and the weather. He was there alone because he didn't have any friends he was tight with like that. He always felt different, and was treated as such. He saw Roy with his hand on Angie's lower back close to her ass, and she was all giggling and cheesing at Roy. That had got him heated (mad). Roy was a junior football star at their school, who weighed a solid 190 pounds at six feet tall. Lenny was only five foot eight and still growing, 145 pounds, with a light skinned complexion.

When he walked up on Angie and Roy, he told Angie to "come'on," and grabbed her arm. She jerked away and yelled so loud everybody heard it and turned around to look. "Get off me Lee! Leave me alone!" She yelled. He was so stunned that his eyes got wide in disbelief and his mouth dropped. It felt like his heart had been stepped on and splattered as sweat broke out on his forehead and hands.

Roy stepped to Lee looking down at him. Then he grabbed him up by his t-shirt lifting him off the ground. "Get yo punk ass outta here!" Roy shouted as spit sprayed all over Lee's face.

Lee snatched Roy's hands off him and growled, "Bitch, get off me!" and sucker punched Roy in the eye, making him see stars. The other football players saw what was going down and ran over to them then started throwing punches at Lee. He couldn't tell who all was hitting him, it was so many. He threw a few punches back, but it was too many of them, so he covered up protecting his face as best he could to save his teeth. When they stopped he heard Roy say, "Watch this," and felt someone pull his underwear up trying to give him a wedgie and turned around to stop him.

"Get the fuck off me!" Lee yelled swinging. The other football players held him down. Roy lifted him off the ground and you could hear his drawls ripping. The people around started laughing and making jokes and Lenny felt a rage shoot through his body and coldness settle in his heart. The taste of his own blood triggered something in his system and stimulated his membrane.

Lee heard someone holler, "Let him go chumps!" He was let go and dropped to the ground. He got up to attack them and seen it was Bobo who yelled out to let him go. Bobo was from the same housing projects as him, the Victory (Vic's). He was six feet tall, seventeen, and a shade lighter then Lenny and skinny. People didn't fuck with him cause he was known to shoot and fight, plus he had did Juvenile time a few times. "Go home!" he told Lee.

Lee glanced around at everybody and yelled, "Fuck y'all!" then started swinging on one of the football dude's fucking him up. Bo stopped him because the security was coming. So he ran out to where he was now. He was soakin wet as he got to his projects where lived with his two younger brother's, and single parent mother. His mother Jerry was in the living room with his aunt Paula when he stepped inside the apartment.

"Boy you all wet, you gon' catch a cold," His mother said, then noticed the look in his eyes, and knew something wasn't right. She got up off the couch and said, "Come'mere baby," and took him up stairs. His two brother's Kevin who was ten, and Otis was eight, were up there in the bedroom they all shared watching TV, so she took him in the bathroom. "Take that wet shit off and tell me what's wrong?" Jerry was 5"2", 150 pounds, with a Tan complexion.

Lenny felt like she was treating him like a baby, but knew that she loved him to death! She treated him and his brother's all the same. Her love for them was strong. She didn't sugar coat nothing when it came to what was happening in the real world, and in life. She knew she had to be real and hard raising three boys all by herself. She didn't want them in the dark when it came to things.

"It wasn't nothing Ma," he mumbled, looking down to avoid eye contact.

"Boy tell me what happened, and stop playing all shy with ya mother," she told him staring him dead in the eyes. She lifted up his chin, and he told her what happened. She went crazy! "Come'on!" she hollered, "You going back down there to fight that punk and who-ever else want some or I will!"

"But Ma," he started to explain, but she cut him off and he knew she wasn't playing one bit. Come on, I ain't trying to hear no soft shit! I ain't raising no girl's in this muthafucka!" She told his brother's, "Get dressed cause y'all going to help y'alls brother fight."

"Shit, let me grab my coat," Aunt Paula said, standing behind her sister Jerry and running back down the stairs for her coat.

They left the apartment and got into Jerry's raggedy Sunbird, and drove down the street to the Plaza. It had stopped raining by the time they parked and got out the car. Lee saw Bobo as they walked into the Plaza. Bobo knew some shit was about to go down by the look on Jerry's face. He knew she didn't take no mess and had witnessed her beat down a few females, and a couple dudes, so he followed behind them. Everybody was still there Lee noticed, as all eyes zoomed on them.

"Now which punk started it first?" Jerry asked, frowning at everybody with one hand on her thick hips and waving with the other. She didn't look her age, and could of passed for a teenager.

"Him," Lee replied, pointing at Roy who was still talking to Angie.

"So you the chump fuckin with my son, huh?" Jerry asked, walking up on Roy. "You can't even fight him by yo damn self! Got these flunkey's helping yo punk ass! Well fight him now!"

That was Lee's cue to get at Roy, so he rushed him. Roy threw him off and Lee fell to the ground and he was about to kick him, when Kevin busted him upside the head with a rock he got from their projects when they were leaving their apartment on their way there. Blood was leaking out of Roy's big head. Lee started swinging all wild on him connecting on some crazy shit! His two brothers followed him throwing their own blows. Roy fell down and they started stomping him all over.

Angie tried to push them off Roy, but Jerry stopped her.

"Bitch!" Jerry hollered at her, slapping the spit out her mouth. "Now go tell yo mother that!" Angie ran out of there scared and embarrassed.

One of the football players grabbed Kevin up, and another one was about to grab Lee when his mother sucker punched him straight in his mouth hard as hell! He stumbled back dazed with blood pouring out. Jerry kicked the one holding Kevin in the privates squashing his nuts like grapes. He screamed like a hog letting Kevin go. Another football player put his hands up in a boxer stance on Jerry.

"All you want to fight a girl like a man, huh?" Jerry taunted getting in her boxers stance.

"All hoe ass nigga!" Bobo shouted, about to get with him.

"Nah... I got this pussy baby," Jerry told Bo as she bobbed her head, "Watch out!" Everybody was staring in awe at her. She had turned the whole get together out. Rick, the young cat she was squaring up with had second thoughts now, but couldn't back down now because everybody was looking. Rick threw a one two punch and she dipped it like a pro, and came back with a upper cut and over hand right on his chin that rocked his world and put him to sleep on his feet as he crumbled to the ground like a bag of stones.

"Who else want some?" Jerry shouted out. Two other football dudes stepped up. "Come'on, I got enough ass whooping fo you too!"

"All you nigga's want to fight her? Fuck with me!" Bobo yelled. They looked and saw the gun in Bobo's hand. "Don't nobody fuck with the Vic's!"

Somebody yelled out the police was coming and everybody ran. Low's mom was like a little kid with his aunt as they all ran back to the car. They all drove off with Bobo in the car with them laughing up a storm on the way back to the crib.

"Thanks Bo," Jerry said to Bobo when they got back to the Vic's.

Once everybody had chilled for a while outside in front of Jerry's spot,

Bobo was standing with Lee by themselves and told him, "Man, you got to start letting loose on these busters!"

Lee didn't fully comprehend exactly what he meant by that, but he had a good feeling.

Lee's brothers were hyped after the fight. They were running around the house play fighting. His aunt had gone home that stayed out there. And his moms was in the kitchen cooking chicken and rice for them. Lee couldn't remember his dad because he was a baby when he left. His mother told him he was killed by some robbers. His mother had a boyfriend she had been seeing for two months now. The last boyfriend she tried to have, Lee and his brother's chased off. Every young kid wants their parents to be together or without another that ain't their parent, even if they don't know the circumstances. Lee was past that, but his brother's weren't. When she was done, they all sat in the living room eating and watching TV.

"Y'all did good today," Jerry told them. "Never let nobody fuck with y'all. I don't care who it is! Get they ass before they get you! Y'all hear me?" She asked. They all nodded their heads soaking in what she was inbreeding in them.

"You see how I hit that boy Mama?" Kevin said, putting his plate down and standing up to show how he did it. He quickly sat down picking his plate up. You couldn't put your plate down for too long around there without watching it because the roaches would be on it quick.

Lenny knew his mom loved them, and she always made sure they knew how much by the things she would say to them and do for them.

Before they went to bed that night, her boyfriend Sal came over. He stayed fresh. Sal was a major drug dealer on the East side of town where they stayed at. He drove a brand new do-do brown 1990 Fleetwood, was 36 years old, and had done prison time before. He walked inside their apartment looking brand new in his Puma jogging suit and shoes. He was dark brown like the caddy he had.

"What's up kids?" He spoke, sitting down next to Jerry. "How you doing today?" he addressed Jerry. She explained to him what happened today, and Kevin helped demonstrating.

"Oh, y'all handled y'all biz, I like that," Sal told them nodding his head smiling in agreement. "This calls for a treat." He reached into his pocket pulling out a roll of money so thick it made the kid's mouth drop. Sal peeled off three crispy fifty dollars bills and gave each of them one. That was the most money Lee had ever seen besides his mother income tax money she received and put in the bank for them every year.

"What about Momma?" said Jerry, with her palm out.

"Shit, fo you sweet woman, you get this here," he answered, handing her a hundred dollar bill.

"Shoot, I put in my work than her. I should get all those. For real!" Kevin said. They all busted out laughing. "Shoot, I ain't playing," said Kevin, making them laugh even harder.

Sal stayed for a few hours and left. He never spent the night, but he took Jerry out all the time. He was the only man who had lasted this long that the two younger brothers liked.

The next morning Lee had to go to school. He went to East High and attended the 9th grade. When he got outside a few kids from their hood ran up on him all excited, talking about what happened and that they couldn't wait to hear what went down.

"You an yo family crazy," one of the kid's named Bobby said.

"I think you were real brave," said this little cutie named Tina, batting her big brown eyes at him. She was 5 feet and 115 pounds.

"You just like him," said this boy named Fatcat that was too big for his age.

When they all got to school, they saw Bo hanging out front with the so-called, roughneck dude's, and some girl's.

"That nigga crazy," Bobby commented, talking about Bobo. Lee just nodded his head at Bo and kept going.

When they got inside, some kids were staring at Lee. He felt their stares and saw the look in their eyes, and knew why they were acting so differently...the drama from yesterday. He never felt like he did at that moment. It was a feeling of being noticed. It made him stick his chest out more and walk with a limp. Bo saw him during lunch and laughed to himself. He liked the little dude, and he had alot of heart.

Lee saw Roy at lunch sitting with some dude's, girls, and his old girlfriend Angie. Roy's face was all beat up. He ice grilled them as he walked by. He thought Roy was going to start something, but he just frowned his face up and rolled his eyes like a girl at him. This gave Lee more confidence and heart, and between classes he would holla at the honeys and walked his little pimp walk.

School was about to be out and Lee had just left his last class. He was going down the back stairs when he saw Roy with three football players named Rick, Sammy, and Ben. His survivor organism kicked in, cause he knew it was trouble. He took this way all the time after his last class, and they were never back there. He was going to turn around but said, "fuck it!" Two of them got behind him.

"So what's up now lil nigga?" Roy muttered poking his chest out.

"This!" said Lee and landed a solid right to Roy's jaw that threw him off. Before Lee could follow up with some more blows, the other three players started hitting and kicking him when he fell to the cold tiled ground. Lee blacked out from the beating. While he was out all kinds of dreams of how he was played in the past flashed like a motion picture in his mind, and anger built up inside him like an inferno.

Two hours later.

At the hospital, Jerry, his brother's, and Aunt Paula sat by Lee's bed crying and worried. His Grandma (Jerry's mom) entered the room with his uncle Pete behind her.

"What the hell happened?" Grandma Faye asked, going to his bed and rubbing his face. "Who did this to my baby?" Jerry told her what she heard from some kid's that stayed in the Victory. "Them lil bastards gon' pay for this! Touching my baby."

An hour later, Lee woke up and saw everybody. His nose was broken, eyes black, lips swollen up, and he was in a lot of pain.

"Oh, my baby woke!" His mother cried leaning over him. "I'ma get them bum's for this!"

Lee was let out the hospital the next day. When they drove up in front of their apartment, they saw the regulars out doing their usual, selling drug's, drinking, talking shit watching the ghetto scenery. Bo was on the block with some of his sidekicks selling stones (crack) when he saw them drive up and Lee get out the vehicle with his Aunt Paula and mother.

"What's up lil nigga?" Bo asked. "I see you made it outta that bitch lil soldier."

"We gon' be inside," Jerry told Lee. "Hi Bo."

"Hello Ms. Jerry, Paula," Bo spoke, and they waved and went inside. "Check little homie, if you want pay back holla at me. Fuck them chumps."

"Al'ight." Lee knew it was code and law on the streets to get back at the ones who did this to him. His mom even said it herself. So he knew it was a must that he went at them. He couldn't let it go without inflicting some kind of pain back, being raised, and taught this. 'Like a pit bull that's trained to kill.

Chapter 2
**Things we inbred and say to our kids grow in them, stick with them,
and ring in their heads while young and growing up...**

Lee stayed home for a week and then went back to school. The first time he saw Roy, he walked up on him in the hallway in front of everybody, and they were all anticipating a fight because of what happened to Lee before and his mother showed up.

Lee got up in Roy's face and said, "It ain't over fat bitch!" and strutted off.

Roy couldn't believe this little nigga's heart. He just shook his head and played it off like it wasn't nothing as he looked around at everybody.

Lee went in the bathroom later on, and saw Bo and Prince smoking weed. They had the whole bathroom cloudy as fuck.

"Aye lil soldier, hit this," Bo said handing him a joint. Lee wasn't a smoker, but he hit it anyway and felt mellow as fuck. "Now take these here. They bring out that dark side in ya," Bo said handing him two small blue pills. Lee looked at the pills all crazy.

"What is this shit here? I ain't trying to be no dope fiend," he replied, not wanting to be like his father who was strung out on drugs his mother told him.

"Man, they V's (valiums). You won't be no fiend, just check them out. Here, wash it down with a beer lil nigga," Bo told him giving him the quart of Colt 45 beer he was drinking on. Lee took them and washed them down with the beer.

"Man I don't feel shit!"

"Oh, you will in like twenty minutes," Prince told him laughing.

Lee didn't like the way he said that laughing, and went to lunch.

Lee got his food that was on a tray and went and sat with Tina and some other kid's from the hood. Tina and Lee had started going with each other when he got out the hospital, and they had become close. Tina wasn't nothing like Angie, she was slimmer and prettier. She lived with her mother, Helen, and her little brother Reno. Her dad was killed out there where they lived in the Victory years ago. Lee started eating and all of a sudden the valium high kicked in. At first he was wondering why he was feeling different, then he remembered taking them pills. He leaned back in his chair cause he started feeling relaxed and calm. He glanced over at Tina and licked his lips, letting his eyes roam over her body. Then he reached out and put his hand over hers on the table.

"Damn baby, you look pretty as hell today. You know that?" Lee told Tina, as he rubbed her hand.

Tina was caught off guard by his sudden approach and bluntness. Lee had never been so up front and bold.

"Thank you," she replied blushing.

"I know that's right. I've been trying to fuck her for a year now," said one of the boy's at the table named Bobby. Lee hopped up out the chair and smacked the shit out of Bobby.

"Don't ever disrespect my girl buster!" He barked.

It happened so fast that everybody didn't believe it until they saw Bobby getting off the floor looking shocked. Tina's eyes were wide open stunned as if she got slapped too. Everybody at the table just shut up and went back to eating. Bobby walked out glancing back at Lee ass he mumbled to himself, crushed. The bell rang and lunch was over. Lee was walking Tina out saying things to her that she never knew he could or would. He was popping boss shit to her. When Lee saw Roy and his crew about to leave, he walked over to them and slapped Roy's tray all over all of them. They were fucked up by his action. Roy was about to charge him when two teachers rushed over to see what was the commotion.

"I'll holla at you hoe ass nigga!" Lee told him, and walked out squeezing Tina's ass.

During class he just chilled out. He was high as hell. He was in a whole different world of his own, and it felt good.

After school when he was walking with Tina on their way home, Roy and his crew jumped out a car on them. Everybody crowded around being nosey. Bo was two cars down sitting on the passenger side in Prince's ride, when he saw Lee and Tina surrounded. He jumped out of the car with his

38 snub-nose. Lee was so high he didn't give a fuck.

"Come'on! Fuck all you muthafucka's!" He shouted to Roy and his crew with his fist up standing in his boxer's stance. Tina had her' little dukes up to ready to fight, when they heard a gunshot go off making everybody jump.

Bo stepped through the crowd and blasted in the air again making all the people around being nosey hit the ground like bricks were in their pockets.

"Ah bitch, y'all want to fight a nigga huh?' I done told y'all before bout fuckin with the Vic's hoe! Now y'all done fucked up!" Bobo yelled aiming the gun at Roy.

"BOOM!" He shot Roy in the leg and he went down screaming. His crew took off running knocking people out of the way. Bo started to bust on them but there was too many folk's in the way.

Lee tried to grab the gun out of Bo's hand. "Let me do this bitch! Let me do him!" Lee hollered.

"Naw watch out!" Bo said, pushing Lee back. He stood over Roy pointing the heat (gun) at his face. "Didn't I tell yo ass? Now look at cha, I should just kill yo hoe ass."

"Please don't! Please! I'm cool man," Roy pleaded, scared to death.

"Shut up bitch! I ain't trying to hear that hoe shit!' replied Bo.

Tina was trying her best to hold Lee back, but he got loose from her and ran up on Roy and started kicking him. When they heard a police car siren coming, Bo ran an got in prince car, and Tina and Lee hit the back of the woods that was behind their school that led to their apartment complex. They were breathing hard as hell when they stopped in front of Lee's crib.

"You got blood on you," Tina said pointing towards Lee's pants leg and shoes. "Do you think he dead?" She looked worried and scared thinking about it.

"Hell nah! I wanted to do his ass too!" He looked disappointed. "Let's go inside."

"I can't, I gotta go home. But I'll be over later on. Love ya," Tina told him and walked away. Lee went into his crib. Jerry was in the kitchen cooking and Lee walked in and sat down at the kitchen table.

"You hungry baby?" She asked, turning around. She could tell right away something was wrong by the look in his eyes and by the way he was looking. "What's wrong?" She walked over to him and noticed the blood on him. "You bleeding?"

"Oh no Ma, it ain't my blood. Bo shot Roy cause he was messing with me and shit." Lee didn't cuss in front of his moms, but he almost slipped up he was so hyped.

"He didn't kill him, did he?"

"Nah ma."

"Then why you got his blood all over you like that?"

"Cause I started kicking him after Bo shot him."

They heard police sirens outside and rushed to look out the window, and saw Prince's car turn the corner speeding hitting cars as it came down the street flying. Prince drove up on the grass and sidewalk then wrecked into a pole. Prince and Bobo got out and took off running. The police jumped out their cruisers and chased them. Lee and his mom went outside to watch the action going on. The police came back ten minutes later sweating and breathing hard, mad as hell they didn't catch them. They had the car towed away after they searched it good.

That night when things chilled out, Bo, Prince, and everybody else was out in the hood kicking it. Lee came out to hang with them while they sold dope, smoked, and drank. When the cops rolled through everybody would get ghost and come back when they left. Lee was checking out all the money that came through there and how they made transactions with their products. He went with Prince to see this other dope dealer named Potpie, to re-up, who stayed out there with them.

"What's up Prince my nigga? I see you and Bo ass still doing some wild shit!" Potpie stated, talking about the incident that happened today.

"That wasn't nothing big boy. Let me get some hard. What you want for a quarter?" Prince smiled.

"It's tight out here right now. So I'm letting them go for $325 homie."

"Damn nigga! That's high," Prince responded. Everybody called Prince by this name cause he looked like the musical genius alot.

"That's how it is lil nigga."

"Let me get that then."

Potpie looked at Lee. "What's up little nigga? You want to get down? I'll front you a eight ball cause I know you stay out here."

"Naw man, he Bo's lil dude so be cool," Prince told him.

"I hear ya," he replied not wanting to fuck with Bo cause he was to shiesty. He had fronted Bo one time and he never paid him back. And always came up with an excuse to why he didn't have no money. Potpie knew Prince be copping for Bobo through him. As long as they kept spending with him he didn't care. "Tell Bo what's up with that money he owe me."

"Al'ight," Prince told him, getting his dope and leaving. When they got back on the block, they gave Lee three V's and some wine. He was fucked up.

"You cool little nigga?" Moose asked, cause he knew this was Lee's first time hanging like that getting fucked up with them. Moose was dark brown and fat, but he stayed freshly dressed.

"He cool fat ass," Rat cracked, standing at 6"4" and weighing 230 pounds, average looking, 17 years old and was built from doing a Juvie bid not long ago.

"He alright clowns," Bo told them. "Little nigga here's three hundred worth of stones," Bo handed Lee some rocks. "Now these ones are twenty dollars and these ones are fifty," Bo explained. "I'm bout to go fuck this bitch real quick, I'll be right back."

"You a snake ass nigga, hope yo ass get caught digging in her stank ass," Prince joked.

"Whatever hater."

"Hating... Nigga I already hit that two times a few months ago," Prince shot back. "You know how I do," Prince smiled. Bo didn't reply, he just walked off.

Tina walked up on Lee and asked him if he wanted to come over and watch TV.

"Nah," Lee replied high as hell.

"Are you drunk or something?" Inquired Tina with her face frowned up staring at him.

A car pulled up and a fiend got out wanting a fifty-dollar rock. Lee rushed him beating everybody out. After the deal was made, Tina asked Lee about what just went down.

"I know you ain't selling that shit?"

"Yeah, this Bo's dope." He showed her the rocks that was in a pill bottle.

"Don't get in no trouble. I'll be at home, ok?" She told him, and walked off switching her little tail feather.

"I see you got a lil tenderoni, huh? You hit that yet?" Prince asked.

"Nah."

"Homie you better handle yo biz."

Lee sold all Bo's dope in less than an hour. Prince saw how he grinded Bo's shit, and asked him could he sell his while he ran to the store with Moose fat ass.

"What you got?" Lee asked him, pocketing all Bo's money in one pocket so he wouldn't mix theirs up. He had made a little profit off of Bo's product.

"This two hundred worth and take this gun too." It was the same pistol Bo used earlier on Roy.

Lee felt the steel of the gun and the warmth it gave him made him feel different. It was almost like getting your first piece of pussy. Your first car when you drove it all by yourself. Bo came back and Lee handed him the money he said all his dope was worth. Bo counted it, and peeled off a fifty and gave it to him.

"Good looking out. You still got more?" He asked, seeing the dope he had.

"Naw, this Prince's." He went to the store with Moose. Bo saw the gun in his waist and smirked to himself.

Ten minutes later some dude's came through in a beat up Regal shooting at them. BUC, BUC, BUC! Everybody hit the ground fast but Lee. He pulled the pistol out and ran up on the car blasting like he'd been doing this shit his whole young life. The nigga's in the car was surprised and shocked at the young boy running up on them as they fired, like he was bullet proof shooting back. The car skid off and Lee ran after it shooting. He was steady pulling the trigger and wasn't no more bullets.

"Click, click, click." Bo got up from behind a car and took the gun from him reloaded it.

"Little nigga you got a lot of fuckin heart!"

"Man I didn't know you was crazy like that! You off the hook!" Rat told Lee, laughing and patting him on the back. Everybody that was out that had ducked and hit the ground came over to praise Lee. His mom came out to see what happened and if someone got shot. She saw Lee was alright, and wasn't nobody shot out there and went back in.

"Nigga we gonna have to give yo ass another name. Fuck that Lee Lenny shit dawg," Bobo told Lee. Lee liked that idea. He never liked his name because he was named after his father, and felt he had ran out on them not giving a fuck about him and his brother's.

They were trying to figure out another name for him when Prince and Moose came back.

"Here you go," Lee said, giving Prince his money from the dope he sold for him.

"Good lookin out little nigga. Where the gun at?" said Prince.

Bo told him what happened, shocking Prince, "Lil nigga got balls huh?" Prince said giving Lee a thug hug.

"Well check, peel me some of that scrilla (money) fo helping you out playboy," Lee told him. They all busted out laughing.

"Lil cat thirsty too. I like, I like," Prince stated, and handed Lee seventy-five dollars. 'We definitely gotta change this cat's name."

It was just getting dark out when Tina came back out. "Lee, I'm bout to go lay down, you taking too long, ok?"

"Alright baby, I'ma holla at cha in a second," Lee replied slapping her on her booty, and bending down watching her butt as she walked off.

"I got it! What about Lowdown or Low?" Said Bo. Everybody said that was it agreeing.

Lee thought about it. "That's cool. I like Low."

"Good. Come'on y'all, let's hit my pad up," Bo told them. Two other dudes that was part of their click, Jay, and Alvin, told them they were going to sit out there a little longer and get that money.

Bo stayed out there in the Vic with his twenty-six year old girlfriend named Cathy, who was pregnant by him. Plus his mom and sister Pattie lived out there. Cathy was dark skinned, 150 pounds, big tits, and a fat ole ass. He had three other kids' already by two other young girls. Missy had two, Dana who stayed there had one, all boys. The door was already opened when they got there, so Bo just opened the ragged screen door and they all stepped in. The hot air smacked the shit outta all of them. She had cooked and that had brought the degree's up. There were two other girls' in there with Cathy, and they were listening to Keith Sweat's "Make It Last Forever" song. Bo squeezed next to Cathy on the couch.

"Dang boy, it's hot while you all up under me," Cathy told him smacking her lips and frowning her face up at him. Lee sat down next to Brenda. Prince, Moose, and Rat went to the kitchen table that was practically in the living room, and started rolling some weed and counting their money. The other girl named Kim saw the money and went to stand by Prince.

Prince saw the greed in her face. Sit yo fine ass on my lap," she obliged with no hesitation.

"What you cook?" Bo asked Cathy rubbing her back.

"I made you steak and fries like you said nigga, it's in the oven," she answered, getting up to go fix his food.

"Make my lil nigga Low a plate too," he said, indicating with his head who he was talking about.

She blew her breath. "I ain't gon' be serving yo little home boy's," she commented as she went in the kitchen shaking her behind with attitude.

"Shut yo smart ass mouth an fix them plates:" Bo shouted out.

"Low... Why they call you Low?" asked Brenda.

Low looked at her up and down and stopped at her pussy, that was poking out in the thin cotton short shorts she had on and said, "Cause I get low like that, down like that," and turned his head as if wasn't no need to explain no more, like she wasn't even there.

"Excuse me then," she remarked smacking her big lips and rolling her head on her neck.

Bo cracked a smile, he couldn't let her know that he was cracking up inside.

"That lil nigga bout his biz. Watch, he about to blow up out this bitch," he said japing Low's image up for her.

"Oh yeah, Well he need a down hoe by his side, don't he? What kind of ride you pushing Low baby?" Brenda asked batting her eyes at him.

"Bitch, I'm pushing these Nikes right now," Low told her with a mad dog look on his face. Brenda's face changed real quickly. Then she thought about what Bo just said about him blowing up, and smiled.

"Well we can still work something out boo," she replied, thinking about the potential Bo had confessed he had.

Cathy brought Bo's and Low's plate out and sat down. Low and Bo smashed the food while they drunk and smoked some weed with the girl's. Bo called Low to the back room an hour later. "Look, you can fuck her in this room here, and make sure you fuck the shit outta that hoe," Prince, Moose, and Rat walked into the room.

"Fuck y'all nigga's up to?" Rat asked.

"Letting him know he can fuck Brenda in here," Bo told them.

"Let's fix him some potion fo that hoe dawg," Prince grinned.

"Man he don't need shit to hit that freak," Moose said, girl was all over his ass slobbering an shit."

"Give me four of them V's," Bo told Prince, who handed them to him. Bo crushed them up and dropped them into a tall glass and poured some beer and wine in it. "Give her this here dawg, and I bet her pussy get hot."

Low took it and gave it to Brenda. "Boy what's this?" she asked.

"That's a little potion I hooked up for those who know how to kick it." rolled out of Low's mouth.

She took it and drunk some. "Uumm...damn its good."
Prince chuckled. Kim was walking to the bathroom and thought he was laughing at her.

"What's so funny boy?" She smiled, thinking he was liking her.

"Yo wig. Naw, I'm just playing with cha."

Twenty minutes later Brenda was high as fuck. She started getting all loud and dancing freaky. She was a nice looking twenty-two year old light skinned broad, 135 pounds with thick legs and a nice firm ass. Her hips were wide because of the baby girl she had two years ago. Her and Kim shared a house right up the street from the Victory together. She sat on Low's lap grinding and wiggling her ass all over his private part. Low was hard as a project brick! He felt like he was going to bust a nut if she kept at it. He had only fucked three times in his life. Bo winked at him. Low whispered something in Brenda's ear, and she got up and took his hand and led him to the back.

"Come'on, we can use this room," Low told her. He shut the door behind them and turned around and Brenda had stripped ass naked that damn fast on him. When he saw this grown woman's body, he almost came on himself. Her muffin was so hairy, she had an afro down there. Low ain't never been with a grown woman so it made him want to fuck her even more.

"Comere an let mommy take them clothes off ya," Brenda said in her sweet baby voice. Low walked over to her and they kissed, her hand went straight for his dick as she shoved her tongue down his throat. Then she dropped down and took his shoes off, and unbuckled his pants, pulling his Fruit of The Loom underwear down with his pants. His dick smacked her in the face. "Oowwee...see ya got a nice hard big dick for me," she purred, grabbing it and she shoving it in her mouth moaning. She tasted the pre-cum that was on the tip and took his wood out her mouth and said, "Uumm...you taste good," lips wet from his pre-cum and her spit. She put him back in her hot mouth and started going faster as she sucked him like a cherry "Now A Later." Low couldn't hold back and his legs were getting rubbery, so he stepped backwards towards the bed and she trailed him never losing her rhythm and suction. Low sat on the bed and braced himself, because he felt it coming from his scrotum hard as hell. His legs started shaking and locked up on him as he busted.

"Gaawwdd...ddaammnn!" Low groaned out releasing as she sucked and swallowed his nut down. She raised up licking her lips.

"Uumm, you got some good ass dick. I know you gonna fuck me."
Hearing that made Low's dick pulsate and get hard again. "No doubt," he said.

She saw his wood pulsating growing hard and hurried up an got on the bed and spread her legs like jelly on a peanut butter sandwich. The hairs on her pussy was so thick, it was hiding her goods. Low started rubbing his joint between her Vulva lips and she went crazy. He had watched some porno's and gotten some pointers.

"Ooohh...fuck me...fuck me Low," she begged, wiggling her hips. He shoved it in and started pumping like a jackrabbit on her ass. "Get this pussy nigga! Uumm...hell yeah!" she hollered throwing it back. Low had to raise up off her cause she was throwing it hard, and it was feeling so good he almost busted. "Let me get in the doggy," she moaned. Low pulled his jimmy out and she got on her knees and all pussy and asshole was in his face in 3D. He started fucking her and she was yelling out all kinds of nasty shit. She was wearing his young ass out, so he had to lay down so she could ride him. "Oohh shit! I'm...c...cumming!" she screamed coming all down his dick and balls.

Low nutted again while she was screaming out getting hers. "Ah... uuhh..." She kept grinding and hopping on his dick, so he pushed her off. They laid there sweaty as fuck catching their breath. "You gon come spend the night at my house?" She wanted some more dick from him, and to lock him down.

"Nah, not tonight."

It was getting late so Low got dressed. "I'ma be over yo house tomorrow," he told her. "Come'on, get dressed. They came out the back room and Low told Bo and the crew he was about to leave. They all gave him some dap (hitting fist) and told him they would see him tomorrow.

It was twelve midnight when he walked into the crib, and he knew his mother was going to trip. She was on the couch with Sal eating a Staples breast shrimp dinner. They had one of the best soul food spots in the city. You had Fosters on the East side too, but they closed early. Garland had some bomb grub to that was right up the street from Staples, and The Eat Shop was right next to Garland's. You also had the Soul Kitchen on the South side.

"So, I see you made it back home little man. Where you been?" His mother asked.

"Over Bo's house, I'm sorry Ma."

"Want something to eat?" She slid the styrofoam with food to him.

Even if you wasn't hungry, smelling Staples made you so. "Yeah, thanks." Low sat down, surprised she wasn't tripping and mad.

"Here mom," he said handing her a hundred dollars.

She looked at it, then at him. "Keep it baby. Thanks," she knew one day he would come to her with money. It was in his blood. His daddy was not only a hustler, he was a stone cold killer. So she wasn't surprised when he offered her some money she knew he got hustling off the land. "Put that up an stack your paper honey."

"So you getting money huh?" said Sal. "Well if you want to step your game up, and yo mom's don't mind. Holla at me lil Bra, and I'11 look out fo ya."

Low looked at his mother to see what she was going to say. She just shrugged her shoulders as to say, "she didn't care" at him. "Al'ight," he replied, knowing his mother gave him her blessing and permission to get in the game. Her doing that made him realize that she saw him as a young man, and believed he could do whatever he wanted to do.

He ate and got up to go to bed when he was finish. His mom gave him a hug before he left and went up the stairs. Out of all the times she hugged him, this one was a strong tight one, and she held him longer than usual. She let go.

"Good night Ma."

Jerry smelled the sex, alcohol, and weed on her son. Plus, could tell he was high. She knew this day would come when he would hit the streets. She didn't want him to, but she knew he had to grow up and learn things on his own. She didn't want to shelter him and try to hide him to the realities of life. If she tried he would be in the blind out in the world, and ain't no telling what would happen to him then. So she made sure she kept him up on his young toes and didn't fabricate shit in life to him.

Chapter 3
Things that shape our character, mode us, and make us...

The next day was Friday and Low got up with his brother's to go to school. His mom made sure they had clean clothes and new shoes. After he got dressed he grabbed an egg sandwich his mom had made him and hit outside. He saw Tina, Moose's brother Fatcat, who was on the heavy side like his brother, Kelly, Angel, and Fred.

"Have a nice time last night?" Tina asked all funny and rolling her eyes at him.

"No doubt and y'all can call me Low or Lowdown for now on," he told them. Tina just stared at him like he was crazy.

"Okay Low," Fred said. "That's a fly name there."

As soon as they got to school Low was called into the Principal's office. When he walked in two police were in there.

"Sit down," the one white cop told him. "I'm Malley, and this my partner Jackson," he said pointing to the tall black cop. "We heard you were involved in the incident that lead to Roy Phillips shooting yesterday. Can you tell us what happened?"

"Yeah," Low said." All I know is that I was being jumped and somebody just started shooting. I don't know who it was cause I was on the ground. The next thing I knew, Roy was screaming he was shot. So I took off not wanting to get shot too."

"So you can't tell us who shot him?" asked Jackson, knowing he was lying from the report they got and statements.

"Naw, I don't know who it was for real," Low answered nonchalantly. Which pissed them off.

"Listen you little punk kid, we can take you to jail, or you can be smart and don't piss us off!" Malley barked.

"Man, I told y'all I don't know!"

"Okay, have it your way," Jackson told him shoving him up against the wall and putting the handcuffs on him. "Little shit!"

"Hold on gentlemen," the Principal got up saying. "Let me talk to you officer's out here." He led them out of his office.

Ten minutes later they came back in and told Low he could go. "We'll see you again, bet that!" said Jackson.

"You can go to class now," his Principal told him. "And stay out of trouble."

Low went to his class that already started. Everybody was peeking at him during class. After class Moose was waiting for Low at his locker. Moose was seventeen and in the 12th grade.

"You alright? What them pigs want?"

"To tell like a bitch. Tell Bo to chill out, alright?"

"Yeah, he know. He know you a solid cat too. Ah, I'll see you after school."

After school Low was outside talking to Fatcat, and Fred, when the high class dudes and girl's rode by in their rides with their noses in the air. Cindy, the leader of one of the most popular girl's group just drove by in her Trans Am with her girl's, and rolled her green eyes at them.

Moose drove up in his 79 Cutlass and asked Low if he needed a ride?

"Naw man, I'm straight."

"Yeah," said Fatcat.

"I didn't ask yo fat ass, but come'on," Moose told his brother. When Low and the other's he was walking with got to the Vic, everybody was just hanging out. Low saw this short light-skinned dude he thought he remembered from somewhere. When he got up close he saw it was his rappie Pep, who had gotten sent away a year ago for stealing cars. He had gotten bigger now and Low didn't recognize him at first. "Whuz up Pep?" Low said, as he gave him some dap.

"Ahh...ain't shit my nigga. I just got out of Tico this morning so I'm trying to see what's popping in the hood," Pep told him.

Low saw Bo and said, "Hold up right quick, let me go holla at Bo right fast." Low went and told Bo about the cops asking about Roy getting shot.

"Good looking out on the heads up," Bo said.

"Ain't nothing... You were looking out for me," Low told him really meaning it. Low hollered at Pep again, and then went to put his books up and let his moms know he was back from school. Jerry was in the kitchen preparing their dinner, and told him that the Principal had called informing her about the incident and the cops talking to him. She told him it was cool, and to just be careful. Low took her advice in, nodding his head yeah.

"Be back in an hour cause the food will be ready by then," she told him.

"Alright Ma." His little brothers were outside riding their bikes playing chicken, so he kicked it with them. After an hour went by they went in and ate. When Low was done he rushed right back outside. His mom noticed he was all hyper lately, and knew it was the streets and him getting older. He would be turning fifteen in another month on the twenty first of June. Low had been kicking it with Bo and them the whole week, and had gotten real tight with Pep. They were the same age, and in almost all the same classes. Low had spent the night at Brenda's a couple times and had hooked Pep up with her girl Kim, who was dark skinned, 146 pounds, with a nice body and some 36 D's. He and Pep made a little money by selling Prince and Bo's dope. But Pep wasn't into it as much as Low. Low loved getting that money.

The next day after school, Low and Pep walked over to Brenda's and Kim's crib. When they got there they saw a clean as fuck, dark blue Eighty Five Cutlass, sitting on gold Truces and Vogues with blue guts, and a blue ragtop.

They stepped on the porch and saw the front door open and you could see through the screen door. Brenda, and Kim were hugged up with two nigga's with a lot of gold on, and some other dude was on a cell phone. The nigga Brenda was with, and the one on the cell, both reached for their heat (guns) when they saw them come on the porch. Low snatched the screen door opened and they stepped inside the house. Low felt some kind of way seeing Brenda all under dude that was pointing a Nine at him frowning.

"What's up Kim?" Pep asked.

Why nigga's always ask "What's up?" on occasions like this, when it be clear as day what is up!

"Yeah," Cal said to the one with Kim. "Well what's up Kim?"

"Cal, I'm with Tito. I don't know what this boy talking bout," she said.

Pep went to slap her and Tito put the gun to his head, so the dude with Brenda up pipe on Low to.

"Nigga you got a problem with me? Huh?" Dirty gritted.

Low ain't never had a gun stuck to his face before. He was so high that it made him calm, even though he knew he could die right at that moment too. Low glared down at the nigga holding the gun.

"Nah man," said Low feeling his heart pounding out his chest.

"Don't kill him Dirty!" Brenda pleaded jumping up off the couch. "They only fourteen!"

"Damn hoe! You fuckin little nigga's that young?" Dirty said, "Y'all lil nigga's get the fuck outta here before y'all get fucked up punks!" Low ice grilled him. "Little nigga, you think I'm playing wit y'all?" He muttered, tapping him on the forehead with the gun.

"Get outta here chumps!" Cal told them looking at them all crazy.

They were mad, hurt, and felt played. They walked out of the house and when they got outside they started running. As they were running Low was yelling, "I'ma kill them nigga's!"

When they got to their projects Bo and the rest of them were all hanging out doing their thing. Low and Pep ran up on them breathing hard, hype telling them what just happened, the dude's names, and what they were driving.

"Oh yeah, them bama's from the South side. I'm hip to them, let's go get our heat!" Bo said.

They grabbed their weapons and gave Low and Pep guns too. Then Prince, Rat, Moose, Alvin, Bo, Pep, Jay, and Low all ran to where they were at. Dirty, Cal, and Tito, were on the porch talking to the girl's about to leave when Brenda yelled out, "Aw shit!" panicking scared. They all turned around and saw them coming towards them and pulled their pistols out. Bo and Prince was ahead of everybody, so when they saw them on the porch they stopped running and started walking.

"What's up with you nigga's?" Bo hollered out, "Y'all got beef with my lil nigga's here or something?" He pointed to Low and Pep.

"Naw, them cats to young fo a nigga like me. But, if they come wrong I don't discriminate who I lay down!" Dirty replied, frowning his face up all ugly at them.

"Well I'm coming wrong!" Prince yelled out.

"Man gon wit that shit!" Cal said, not wanting nothing to go down.

"Naw nigga, y'all gon!" Bo shouted, raising his burner (Gun).

Brenda and Kim ran in the house when they saw Bo raise, then Dirty and them raised their weapons up to. Bo let the first round off and Low started busting like crazy and then ducking behind a parked car. Dirty and Tito cut loose as they ducked behind the porch wall with Cal. There was gunfire blazing everywhere. Bo was behind a tree next to the car Low and Pep was at shooting. Prince, Moose, and Alvin were behind another car. Everybody was yelling, talking shit and shooting. Low glanced over and saw Rat on the sidewalk bleeding from what looked like a gunshot to the shoulder.

"Fuck! Bitches shot me!" Someone on the porch screamed out. It was Tito, he had been shot in the arm.

After about three minutes went by of gunplay, they heard the police coming. Everybody ceased firing and they grabbed Rat up and took him to the hospital. Dirty, Cal, and Tito hopped in their ride and took Tito to the hospital too. They had to lie about how they got shot at the hospital. They saw each other there and couldn't do nothing, because it was packed with security and police who asked them a thousand questions on how they got shot.

Some neighbors told the police it was some boy's from the projects and described them. Jackson and Malley knew from their descriptions of the individuals that it was Bo and the rest of them from the Victory, so they cruised through the projects hoping to see them out, but they were at Bo's crib smoking weed, getting high off V's, drinking, and listening to N.W.A.'s album "Straight Out Of Compton" talking about how they were gonna ride down on them nigga's hood tonight.

The phone rang and Cathy answered it," Guurrll, I ain't got nothing to do with that mess and you know it Brenda!"

Low heard her name and jumped out his seat. "Let me holla at that hoe!" He said taking the phone from Cathy. "Bitch! See what yo stank ass did?! Don't let me catch yo hoe ass!"

Bo grabbed the phone from Low. "Look Bren. We know you ain't mean for this shit to happen today," Bo nodded his head putting his finger to his mouth to tell Low to be quiet as he let Brenda talk. "I hear you...I might need your help. Ain't nobody gon fuck with you," Brenda was telling him alright, and that she was sorry about Rat being shot. Bo told her alright and hung up getting the information he wanted. He looked at Low and said, "Man you never let a hoe know you got beef or a problem like that! She could get yo ass locked up, feel me?" Low nodded his head yeah.

Tito was released from the hospital later that night. He was at their dope house on the South side on Glen Haven with their other comrades talking about the dudes from the Victory. It was ten of them at the time as they plotted, but their real leader, Dirty's big brother, and Tito's cousin, Victor, who was twenty-four, was at his house counting money doing business. He had told them to go handle them wack ass nigga's. Vic had a little money and fronted his brother and cousin, and they fronted their crew and sold them dope. Victor considered the dudes in the Vic lightweight to him. He knew Bo, and had sold him dope a few times, so he wasn't one bit worried about him. Big bank take little bank, was his motto and belief. Most believe this here on the street. But in all reality, it's what's in yo heart. Just imagine this. One man with a rusty 22 up against an army of 20 who got high powerful weapons and money to back them, right? If that one man got the heart to get up on them at the most unexpected, and vulnerable times. Who will win the war in the long run? We talking streets here, not political wars, but small level wars.

Chapter 4

**Gun smoke and the power from the blast fills my nose and heart with
serene, and I know who I am.
GOON...**

Tina came over Bo's crib looking for Low, and he told her to go home.
She was salty and left mumbling.

"Let's roll," Bo told'em, grabbing his gun. Low, Pep, Moose, and
Prince grabbed one of the guns lying on the bed. "Moose you sho you want
to roll? You know we might get chased by the police."

"You know yo fat ass can't run," Prince cracked, picking up a shotgun.
"I'ma take this here."

Jay was looking at a 44 Bulldog. "Let me roll. You know you ain't
trying to get caught."

"Fuck both you nigga's! I'm rolling!" Moose told them getting mad.

"We all can fit in the car. So let's go then," Bobo said.

Pep, Bobo, Prince, Low, and Moose all got into an old four door Chevy
they got off a fiend and drove off. It was 11 p.m. and the night breeze felt
good hitting Low's face as he sat in the back seat. The Tec nine he was
clutching was getting cold so he put it between his legs. The Ghetto Boys
was playing out the speakers, and the music put him in the mood for what
he was about to do even more.

"Make sure y'all got your gloves on and y'all bullets clean," Prince told
them. "Can't leave no prints on them shells an shit."

When they got to the South side, close to their destination, Bo turned
the music down some. "Yeah, we got these hoes now. They ain't looking fo
this shit here! I want everybody busting on they hoe ass too! This the street,
Brenda said look for a broken down truck on the grass in front of the
house," he told them as he turned on Glen Haven. He flew down the street
and they peeped people out front. "Yeah, that was it." He bent a corner
down another street. "Everybody blast at they ass! Prince, you two shoot out
the passenger side, and me and Pep will shoot out my side."

Low's heart was beating fast as fuck as they came back down the street getting closer. This was his first time bringing this kind of drama, and violence that could bring death. He didn't have no second thoughts about what he was about to do at all. This was payback and the way he was raised to get justice.

"Now!" Bo yelled out hitting the brakes and lights. Fire from their weapons lit the area up as they released on people. Low saw two people fall from his gunshots that he was aiming at. You could hear screaming and yelling between gunshots, then shots were being fired back at them hitting the car making sounds as if someone was playing a piano. Bo stepped on the gas as Prince and Low kept shooting. Bullets busted out the back window and hit the trunk as they sped away from the scene.

Low's gun was hot in his hand. He felt revitalized. The ramification of what he just did didn't even bother him. If anything it awakened more of that internal demon that was lurking within.

When they got back to the Victory, they all went over Bo's house to chill and watch the news to see if their actions and work left anybody breathless and wounded.

The ambulances left Dirty's house and the cops were still their getting statements from witnesses. Two people who was shot died, some girl and Dirty's and Tito's partner Philly. They were mad as fuck! Dirty called Vic and told him what went down, and Vic told him to bring Tito with him and meet him at the crib on Warren in an half hour.

"Damn! Two gone!" Moose was stunned. He never was no murderer.

"Good! Fuck'em!" Bo expressed.

"I'm bout to go over Tina's spot, cause she tripping," said Low.

"Dang nigga, you ain't hittin that?" Prince asked.

"Are you in love or something?" asked Bobo.

"Nah man, that's my girl brah," Low said knowing he had feelings for her for real.

While Jackson and Malley were at the scene where the shooting just occurred over Dirty's, they noticed a car that was described in the shooting on the East side that day. They already had gotten Bo's real name, Brain Brown, from the police reports and knew him and the little posse he hung with had something to do with this incident that took two lives and was steaming mad and upset. They cruised through the Vic's right after that hoping to see Bo or anyone of the dudes he hung with outside. Lil Shawn, their look out went and told Bo and them they were out there asking where they were.

"Fuck them bitches," Bo said, but was really worried.

Tina was on the porch with her girl Kelly listening to music when Low walked up, "What's up y'all?" He spoke sitting down.

"Nothing we heard Rat got shot," Kelly said being nosey, waiting for a response.

"Yeah I heard," Low replied, like he didn't know about it.

"Dang, that's yo boy and you don't know what happened? Anyway, where yo boy at?"

He knew who she was talking about but played like he didn't. "Who?"

"Pep silly," she told him rolling her eyes.

"Oh, over Bo's house I think."

"Dang, y'all act like y'all stay over there or something," she replied, getting up off the fold up chair, "Well I'ma leave you two alone. Tell yo boy I asked bout his cute self."

She left so Low took her chair. He was about to say something to Tina when he saw the police ride into the Jets (projects).

"Let's go in the back, to many poe-poe out here tripping," he told Tina noided.

"Oh, okay." They went on the back porch and Low took out a fat joint of sticky.

"You got a light?" He asked.

"Boy you know I don't smoke around my house you tripping!" She glanced around to see if her mom's was watching.

"Well let's go over Bo's house."

"No way!" Tina said twisting her cute little brown face up at him.

"Come'on, my mom gon with Sal, and my brothers are spending the night over my aunt's house in West Lake."

"Alright," she replied.

When they got there Low checked the mailbox for the apartment key. He got it and opened the door cutting the lights on. Roaches scattered everywhere for cover. "I hate these nasty lil muthafucka's," Low thought, but wasn't embarrassed cause Tina has them too. He opened the fridge and got two cans of Old English beer while Tina went and sat on the couch. Low sat down next to her and cut the stereo on to Levert's slow jam.

"That's my song right there," Tina started dancing in her seat as Low lit the joint and they sat there smoking, sipping beer and talking.

After a while they were tipsy and started kissing. Low pulled her firm titties out and licked and sucked them making her gasp. She had on short shorts, so he put his hand up under her shorts and slid her panties to the side and fingered her pussy. This was the first time he felt her pussy and it was so tight it wrapped around his finger like a hot Taco burrito wrap.

"Oohhee…shoot Lenny," she moaned.

He started finger fucking her slowly, and she laid back opening her legs. "Let me take these shorts off," he said.

"Um, okay. You sure your moms and them ain't coming back right now?"

Low didn't want to stop what they were doing and about to do, so he said, "Yeah, but let me lock the door and put the chain on it just in case." He got up with a boner and locked the door. He came back and got on his knees and started pulling her shorts down.

"I don't know Lenny, I never done this before," she panted.

Low knew he had to keep her hot, so he started kissing her and easing her shit off. When he had her shorts half way off, he glanced down and saw her fat lipped pussy with soft black hair around it. He rubbed her clit that was peeking out at him.

"Oohh Lee…," was all she could get out her mouth.

"That's right baby, feel good don't it?" He mumbled.

"Uhuh…shieeet Lenny…yes," she moaned. He eased up on her as her legs were wide opened and both her feet planted on the floor as he removed his hand and tried to put his dick in her, and she jumped, "Owwhh…that hurt Lenny, take it out."

"Alright," he groaned, and tried again pushing harder this time and feeling something give, as he slid into her tight ass wet coochie "Aaww…Uumm…" She hollered out trying to scoot away, but Low held her tight and pumped. "Oh my...Gawd!"

She wiggled and raised up trying to push Low off but he wrapped his arms around her waist as he pumped like a dog in heat. A couple humps later, Tina was feeling a tingling sensation in her loins and all through her tummy down to her coochie, and it felt marvelous. She started wiggling her hips in sync with him moaning, enjoying this first time pleasure. "Muumm...yeah...that feels good. Don't cum in me Lee baby."

Her nana was so tight, wet, and good that Low nutted quick and strong. "Oh shit! Fuck!" He started shaking and all like he was going into a seizure or some shit! He laid on her chest as his dick shrunk up some still inside her.

"Boy, I know you didn't cum in me! I told you not too!" She felt some hot liquid in her and knew he nutted in her. She pushed him off. "Boy! I ain't trying to get pregnant, are you crazy?"

"It felt so good I couldn't help it.

She was grabbing her clothes and putting them on. "Whatever! Let me put my clothes on so yo ass can take me home." Low crawled over to her still half-naked and kissed her on her butt. "Boy stop!" she laughed, pushing him back.

When they got to Tina's crib she told him she loved him, and he knew she meant it. That "Goon Life" was calling him in, and when it's in your blood you go to it full speed. After he took her home he stopped over Bo's house to see what was up.

The next day Victor and his little soldiers sat in his crib on Warren on the South side of town. Vic was telling them how to handle this weak situation with the dude's from the Vic, and couldn't believe them broke niggas had enough nerve to fuck with him and his crew. "I want y'all nigga's to hit them bitches up in the afternoon while they still out there and ain't expecting it till night time," he told them, pacing the room with his fat, but solid body. "Here, take these." He dragged two big suit cases from under the closet and opened them up, handing them all fully semiautomatic assault weapons. Their faces lit up like a Christmas tree. "Take two hot (stolen) cars and light that hood the fuck up! Y'all hear me? Light that bitch up!"

Chapter 5

Molded from experience, made from experience, because of experience...

That afternoon in the Victory projects, there were kids out playing and people sitting on their porches. Rat had got out the hospital and was back on the block with Bo and them doing their thing.

"Man, I'm bout to flip this hog (ride) on these hoes fo my birthday," Bo said, knowing his birthday was two days after Low's, "Nigga let's throw a block party out this bitch since our b-days are a few days apart, it will be both our shit. We can have it on the twenty second," Bo said to Low.

"Hell yeah, that sounds cool man," Low replied feeling that.

They were standing around discussing it, and didn't see the two car's creeping around the corner until Moose yelled out, "Watch out! Here they come!" and hit the ground with his fat ass.

Low saw so many big guns sticking out the two car's windows that he couldn't move, it seemed like he was paralyzed. His eyes were big as fuck! Everybody reached for their heat running for cover but Low.

Dirty was riding shotgun hanging out the window when he saw Low and aimed the AK-47 at him firing. Other people out started running and screaming, but Low just stood there staring as slugs flipped by his head and body. Dirty let off seven shots and Low was still standing there as the car got closer to him spitting mass bullets. Low saw Prince go down right in front of him as he tried to shoot back and three slugs tore into him blowing chucks of his flesh off. That snapped him back to life. He ran behind a car as bullets from Dirty's gun trailed him. Bullets hit the car making it rattle. Low saw Bo shooting from behind a car parked next to the one he was behind.

"Nigga where yo shit?" Bo shouted, as he ducked from some bullets. Low felt for his pistol that had fell down his pants leg. He grabbed it and started shooting as the two cars were on their way out. He got up and ran after them busting one of their back windows out as they bent the corner out of sight. Low turned around to see who got hit, and saw bodies lying around and people crying, yelling, and screaming. His blood was steaming as his nerves jumped he was so mad. He couldn't believe what them nigga's just did.

Bo jumped up and went and bent down over Prince's motionless body as his life flowed freely into the street, soaking the earth with his genes. "Muthafuckin…bitches!" Bo hollered.

As Low ran over there to where Bo was he saw an eight year old girl with half her face blew off, and three more people shot but still alive. He stopped in his tracks looking down at the little girl as her mother came out crying trying to pick her up and her brains fell out her head like rich lasagna with everything in it. Some people had to get her because she was hysterical. The police and ambulance sirens could be heard coming, so everybody dirty took off behind Bo to his spot. Bo went crazy while Low just sat there silent. Moose had got grazed too and was there trying to stop the bleeding. Rat was breathing hard still in shock as he watched Bo rant and rave talking shit. Low was mad and still trying to get over the little girl's death. They heard someone knock on the door and Cathy answered it letting Tina in.

"Oh Lenny, I'm so glad your alright. Your mother been looking for you," she said hugging him. Low told Bo and them he would see them later. He took the back way home with Tina cause it was swarming with police and he didn't want to see the soaked bloody pavement. On the way he gave Tina his gun and told her to hide it for him. When he got to the back door of his crib he heard someone inside talking to his mother, so he looked in the window and saw the cops Malley and Jackson. His heart started to pump fast cause he was thinking they were here about the murders he partook in yesterday, but you couldn't tell it when he entered the apartment. His face was blank.

Jackson jumped up, "Put your hands up against the wall son!" He patted him down. "He clean."

Malley stood up and said, "Lenny, I know Bo got all this killing started and you helping, you going down with him if you don't talk boy!"

His mom hopped up. "What the fuck y'all talking bout? Y'all got me and my baby fucked up! Get the fuck outta my house!" She yelled mad as hell as she snatched the door opened, "Out!"

"We'll be seeing you later," Jackson told Low as him and Malley walked out of the door staring at him.

Jerry slammed the door on them. "Lee you getting grown but I hope you don't get caught up in no bullshit! You hear me?"

"Yes Ma, I hear you."

"Trust no one...them streets ain't got no friends honey. Yo friend is a dog, cause a dog can't talk. Get what I'm saying?" Low nodded his head. "Now go chill over in "West Lake" over your aunt Cookie's for a couple weeks till this shit settle down."

On the way to his aunt house he stopped at Bo's. When he went in, Pep, Rat, and Jay was there. Pep was over this chick house in some apartment complexes close to the Victory when shit went down.

"Man we're going to chill till after our block party," Bo said. "So everybody lay low." Bo didn't like the fact that the cops kept asking about him, he was annoyed.

Pep went with Low to stay over his aunt Cookie's on the North side. When they got there, they sat on the porch with his aunt and her girl Marsha, watching the ghetto life, nigga's shooting dice, slanging, drinking, and just hanging out. These projects were way bigger than the Victory, so it was much more action with a lot more people. While they was sitting there they saw two little nigga's pull up in a clean ass eighty-two Buick Regal, two toned black and brown with metal flakes, sitting on deep dish chrome Dayton's, banging N.W.A's shit. They hopped out in Nike jogging suits and sat on their car playing music and serving dope. They had mad clientele too, cause most the fiends skipped over all the other drug dealers and came to them. One of them laid a Tec 9 on the hood as the other one served and he watched. Some young honey's stopped to holla at them while they got money.

"Them young goons need to gon' somewhere else, selling that mess as if they got a license," aunt Cookie stated, with her high yellow self, sipping on a wine cooler.

"I know that's right child," Marsha added. "You know they killed old man Boo last week gurl."

"I heard, they never bothered me though," Cookie replied, "They gave me money a few times fo nothing. I'll say that. But that Nut a wild one, ain't he child?" She said shaking her head looking at them sell dope and do their thing.

"Umm..., I don't know, Roe just as bad and crazy," Marsha added.

Lee and Pep looked at who they were gossiping about, then got up and walked up the street to see what was going on up at the little park there. They stopped at a Arab store right next to the park called Falls Playground. We already know there is always a liquor store next to the hood, so ain't no need to elaborate this. They started drinking the 40 ounces of Colt 45 they let them buy when they noticed the three girls that were just talking to Nut and Roe approaching their way.

"What's up wit y'all?" Low asked.

"You," said the one girl named Sandy. She was short, dark skinned, cute as hell, and thick as a brick house at 5'11.

"That's what's up. My name Low and this my nigga Pep here." Low dug what he saw a lot as he gazed all over Sandy's body.

"What's up?" Pep spoke. They all greeted them and gave their name.

"Where you guy's from?" The girl named Rhonda asked. She was the one all over Roe when they saw them down his aunt's. She was a petite little thing with pretty green eyes, and a ripe banana complexion.

"From the Vic's on the East side," Low answered.

"What's popping wit you?" Pep asked stepping up on the girl named Shawn. She was dark skinned, but a shade lighter than her girl Sandy, with big thighs, ass, and long black hair.

"I got a man," Shawn told him, putting her hands up, palms out to him.

"Oh, my bad hot mama. What's up with you then?" He asked the green-eyed wonder Rhonda.

"Tooken," she replied.

"Damn, a nigga can't get no play around here?" Pep remarked.

Low was talking to Sandy as the other two girls' went inside the store. When they came back out and was about to leave, Nut and Roe drove up. Roe was driving because it was his ride. Nut had one just like his but a different color.

"Yo what's up?" Nut yelled from the passenger side window over the loud music bumping out of the car. Shawn sha-shaded up to him and leaned over into the car rubbing his shirtless chest, as Rhonda went around to the driver's side.

"Where you nigga's from?" Nut asked, turning the sounds down.

"East side," Pep answered.

"Oh yeah... Y'all get money?" Nut inquired.

"Light weight," Low spoke up, with Sandy still standing by him.

A car drove up and a fiend hopped out and Nut started serving him, when all of a sudden the fiend snatched the dope out of Nut's hand while he was sitting in the car and took off running.

"Bitch!" Nut hollered out, trying to get out of the car.

Low pulled his 38 special out and ran after the fiend catching up with him and shooting him in the leg before he could get in the car waiting for him with the door opened. The car drove off seeing what happened and Low shot at it busting the back window out. Pep started kicking the fiend who was on the ground hollering like a pig in agony.

"Nut and Roe ran up with their Tec's in their hands. "Aw bitch, you tried to play me like a sucka! Huh?" Nut yelled pointing his burner at the fiend. It was around 2:30 P.M. in the afternoon so everybody was outside, but Nut and Roe didn't give a fuck.

"Hoe!" Roe hollered, then him and Nut unleashed six times together into the fiend, making his body jerk as the bullets hit and entered him. Pep and Low just looked at them nigga's like they were off! They never saw nobody get killed so close up like that without a care as to who was looking and around. The fiend laid in the street as his life drained into the cement.

Nut glanced at Low and Pep and said, "Good lookin out."

"Yeah, that was good looking playboy," said Roe. They were still standing there like it wasn't nothing. The girls were quiet as they stood waiting on them by their ride as they walked back.

"Y'all want to kick it?" Roe asked Low and Pep.

"Yeah, that's cool," Low answered as he glanced around at the people in the park who started walking back to what they were doing before the incident. Wasn't many who care for another's life if it wasn't their kinfolks or friend. Death was as common as the government welfare check that was received within the projects.

"Ay we'll get at y'all later," Nut told the girl's.

"See ya later," Low told Sandy, letting her know he was at her.

They got in the ride and drove off. Nut turned the music up and "Above The Law's" shit came on. Low and Pep ain't never been in nobody's ride who had bang like this. Roe had four twelve inch woofers installed that had the bass making them feel each beat. They hit the Drive-thru and Roe got four Strawberry Hill Boones Farms and a six pack of Old English. Nut pulled out some light green weed and they got smoky an nice.

Low took out a bottle of V's and handed them to Nut in the front seat. "You nigga's take V's?"

"Hell yeah!" Nut answered, looking at the V's like they were pussy. "We gonna be cool as fuck! Y'all some cool ass nigga's."

They rode around the North side and then hit the East side up. They seen some girl's and Roe stopped. "What's up with you hoes?" Roe asked the three young girls.

"Nigga who yo ass calling a hoe?" One of them shot back at him rolling her head around on her neck, as the other two put their hands on their hips with attitude and their faces twisted up.

"You bitch!" replied Roe. The girl's cussed him out and kept walking as Roe cruised following them talking shit. Then he drove off.

"Hit my hood up," Pep said. Roe drove to the Vic's and they saw Bo out with Rat and the rest of them. Bo had pulled his strap out when he saw a car full of nigga's riding deep coming through. He saw Pep stick his head out and tucked his burner like everybody else who had took their heat out. Dirty and Tito had them on their toes since they lit the hood up.

Low jumped out the ride. "What's cracking nigga's?"

"Man, y'all fools almost got shot the fuck up!" Rat stated.

"Rat you wasn't gon do shit!" Low joked, and introduced them to Nut and Roe.

Bo liked Roe's car. "Y'all cats getting money over there in the Lake? What y'all working with?" Bo asked, nosey as hell.

"No doubt killa. We get that paper," Nut told him. "We fuckin wit four an a half player."

"Damn, I'm still on one punk ass ounce. I gots to step my game up," Bo thought to himself.

They chilled out there for two hours. Low went to holla at Tina, and then his moms, giving his brothers a couple dollars and leaving.

Low told Roe and Nut about the beef with Dirty and Tito while were in the car.

"All them nigga's some hoes," Nut stated. "They ain't no killa's fo real! They do drive byes, not walk byes. Me and my nigga's get right up on a bitch and do they ass proper like. Fuck that missing shit. Our old school homie taught us that."

They got back to West Lake when it was dark. Pep was leery coming back because of the fiend Roe and Nut had killed earlier. Low realized Roe and Nut didn't even mention or seem worried about the murder they did. So it didn't bother him either. They all was high fuck. Roe pulled into the bottom of the projects and parked. It was pitch black there because someone had shot the lights out, and when they got replaced they would get shot out again. So now they didn't even bother putting them back up. You could see some folks because of the moon's light that shone.

"See that nigga there," Roe said pointing at some tall skinny older black dude. "That nigga straight up bout that 187, that's our big brah Smoke."

They got out the car and Low and Pep followed them as they approached Smoke, but before they could get ten feet near him four dudes up pipe on them.

"It's cool," Smoke told'em holding the guns, "That's the lil homies with some other cat's." Smoke had a soft voice like a whisper. When they got close to Smoke, Low saw the reddest eyes he ever saw on a person. This nigga's shit was blood shot red and he looked like a fucking frog. Pep and Low had to strain to hear him. "What y'all little brah's up to?" Smoke asked them.

"Aw shit, just kicking it with our two new nigga's here, Low and Pep," Nut answered.

"What up O.G.?" Roe said.

"Where you little nigga's from?" Smoke eyed them suspiciously.

"From the Vic on the East side," Low told him.

"Oh, I got a lil hooker out there I fucks with. Sit down an have a drink wit a nigga." They all sat down and chilled with Smoke talking and learned alot from him that night.

"Let's go get some pussy," Roe said, "I'm high too."

"We gotta see who Pep gon fuck wit, cause Low trying to get wit Sandy black ass. Might have to get a fiend fo this fool," Nut joked, making them bust out laughing. "This one got some good pussy too."

They got to Rhonda's crib out there, and she was outside with four girl's listening to music smoking weed. Rhonda and Shawn was happy to see their men and gave them a hug. Sandy even gave Low one.

Pep stepped to the other girl with them.

"Hey how you? My name Pep," he said to the short chocolate girl with the red lipstick on her fat lips, just rolled her pretty brown eyes. Pep looked down and saw her nails and toes were polished in red, and she had some wide hips, nice titties in a halter-top, rocking a mini skirt that hugged her curves tightly and nicely. "Oh, you can't speak?"

"Oh that's our girl Amy, Pep," Sandy told him.

"Yeah, Amy huh? You a fly cute lil thing," Pep eyed her saying. "You got a man?"

"Sho do. I mess with Joe," she replied, like his name held weight.

"Fuck Joe," Nut stated. "He a hoe nigga, Pep."

"Uh, he takes care of me," she puffed, putting her hands on her hips.

"Smart mouth hoe," Roe said.

"Let's go to our spot," Nut told them, talking about the apartment they sold dope at and kicked it at, they rented from a fiend for some crack while she stayed with her boyfriend.

Nut opened the heavy front door when they got there and they all stepped inside as Nut cut the lights on. Roaches ran for cover like muthafucka's rushed the mailman on the first. Nut turned on the music and Sir Mix A Lot came on. Their fridge was full of beer and wine. They were already nice (high) but took some more V's and smoked some sticky with the girl's. The girls got all giggly and goofy, so Pep took advantage of the moment. He was freaking all over Amy. He sat next to her with his arm around her rubbing her thighs.

"Boy stop," she told him, but he could tell she was liking it cause she was smiling at him and not removing his hand, so he let his hand fall down to her chest and rubbed her titties. Her nipples got hard as a penny. "Stop!" She hit his hand sliding over.

"Ay, let me holla at you nigga's right quick," Low told them getting up from next to Sandy and walked into the kitchen, with them behind him. "Check, this how you going to get that funny acting hoe." He put four Valiums on the table and crunched them, then put them in a tall glass of beer, mixed with wine. Nut and Roe was cracking up on this move.

"Nigga you Low down fo real killa," Nut said.

Pep gave the drink to Amy, and a half hour later she was all over him. "Let's go upstairs," she told him, rubbing his wood through his pants. Pep didn't hesitate jumping up off the couch following her.

When Pep got inside the bedroom with Amy, she shut the door and kissed Pep, putting her tongue all in his mouth while she undid his pants. His pants fell to the floor and she pulled his drawls down grabbing his pipe stroking him, he was rock hard. She dropped down all of a sudden so quickly and put him in her mouth, that it shocked him.

"Oooooeee..," Pep sighed, standing up as she worked him.

She stopped and told him to get on the bed. He laid on the bed and she got between his legs sucking him even harder. "Damn...you got some...good head...," Pep groaned, about to cum.

"Ummm...cum in my... (slurp)...mouth... (Slurp)...give it to me," she moaned and said. That made him cum blowing her wig back, and she swallowed it all moaning.

This hoe a boss freak, Pep was thinking as he laid back and let her play with his dick.

"Eat my pussy baby," Amy purred.

Pep ain't never ate no pussy before but he was down to find out how, he was so horny. She laid back and opened her legs wide, then put both hands down there and opened her goodies. Pep was stuck gazing at her pinkness that winked at him. "Fuck it," he said to himself, and dived in. He started licking and she moaned, so he figured he was doing it right.

Amy started throwing her hips, smashing the pussy in his mouth smothering him. "Oh lick it baby...ummm! Lick it good!" She grabbed his head rotating her pussy in his mouth as she climaxed. "Oohhh, I'm cum...cumming!" Pep tasted his first pussy and liked the flavor. Pep's dick was hard again after tasting her candy so he fucked her.

Down stairs Nut told his girl to get naked. "You too," Roe told Rhonda. The two girl's stripped without no hesitation. Rhonda had a pretty little tight body and perky lil titties, and Shawn had mass ass on her chocolate frame, with a nice size chest. Nut and Roe came out of their clothes and their girls went to kissing on them from head to their pipes. Low just glanced over at them trying not to be oblivious, but seeing them two bad chicks naked had him bone hard.

Roe looked over at Low and said, "What's up nigga, you fucking or what?"

Low looked at Sandy and was about to tell her to strip too but got a glimpse of Shawn's fat ole ass when she turned around. Sandy was waiting for him to tell her to take her shit off cause her pussy was on fire from looking at everybody else get down, and her digging Low's swagger. She had caught emotions the first time she saw him. Low glanced at her and said, "You know what it is," she stood up and took her clothes off and Low saw the nappiest pussy he ever laid eyes on, even in the porn movies he saw. Her body was nice as fuck, he was thinking. She didn't have a blemish on her Hershey colored thick body. Her nipples were big and hard and looked like tasty chocolate M&M's on her grape fruit size chest.

Low got up and took his shit off. His dick sprung out of his boxers at attention. "Dang baby...you hard already?" Sandy said eyes full of lust as her pussy tingled.

Low sat down and she got on her knees between his legs and took hold of his dick with one hand, and gently massaged his balls with the other as she stared at him with admiration. Then Roe bent Rhonda over the couch he was on facing him and started beating the pussy up. Her green eyes were watching Low as she screamed out all nasty shit with a fuck face. "Fuck...fuck...me! Ooohh shit! Damn!"

She had the prettiest green eyes, which turned Low on even more making him bust a nut down Sandy's throat choking her. "Gawd damn!" Low hollered out.

"Damn killa, you trying to kill that hoe," Nut joked, hearing Sandy coughing, as he was getting rode by Shawn.

They freaked all night and kicked it. Fiends kept knocking on the door for product all night too, and Nut had no problem answering the door butt naked serving them. Only a few men fiends said something, but a lot of the woman ones tried to get with him and offer their services for some product. Shawn had to cuss their asses out a few times cause some reached for his swipe.

The same night Bo got chased by the police but got away. "Man them bitches sweating a nigga. I gots to lay low an stay out the way. That buster Roy musta have pressed charges on me, soft ass!" Bo was telling Moose, Rat, Jay, and Alvin.

Chapter 6

Getting that first piece of dope to sell is like getting high off it, because an addiction is formulated with what comes with it.

The next day Low and Pep woke up, got cleaned up, changed clothes, and went back over Nut and Roe's dope house again. They had left late that night to go back over Low's aunt crib. When they got there one of their workers let them inside named K.K. Another one called Joker was on the love seat cutting up rocks of crack cocaine on a plate with a needle you sew with. They all spoke to each other. Roe and Nut was in the kitchen weighing up dope they were buying from Smoke who stood by with his partner Hank.

"This shit A-1, shit, I can smell it," Smoke said, as he broke off a piece of cain off a kilo weighing it up. His ugly ass was licking his fingers that had cain on it like it was BBQ sauce an shit. "You nigga's want the same thing, right? Four and a half?"

"Nah, let's us get nine ounces Smoke. That way we can get a deal like you said," Roe told him. Low and Pep ain't never seen so much dope and money at one time before.

"Ok, now y'all talking bigger. Y'all can get it fo fifty two hundred."

"Cool killa," Nut said, pulling out a knot of money. He peeled off two hundred dollars and threw the knot on the table. Right then Low knew he wanted to get down. His heart skipped a beat and it was love at first sight. Money and dope, dope equaled money.

"Did you bring them works man?" Smoke asked his dude Hank.

"And you know this, maann," Hank replied, holding a plastic baggie with needles in it. Hank took a needle out and gave it to Smoke. Smoke then put some powder cocaine in a spoon and adding some water. Then he stirred it around mixing it good and took out some cotton and drained the dope through the cotton, so it would keep the imperatives out. Meaning it would get mostly all pure cocaine. Low was looking and knew what Smoke was doing, but when he put the needle in his arm he was shocked.

"Yeah, this "D" good as shit," Smoke drooled from the mouth.

Low glanced at Pep and he just shrugged his shoulders like "Whatever." Low couldn't believe this suppose to be killer was getting high like that.

Smoke had spit dripping out of the side of his mouth. He looked up at Low and Pep with them big frog blood shot red eyes and said, "You two nigga's want to buy some work?"

"Naw," Low replied, "We cool right now."

"Well holla at me when you do. Don't be buying and selling nobody else shit around here," he told them in a better not type tone. "I'm outta here. You lil nigga's stay up and get yo paper." He got up and walked out with Hank tailing behind.

Nut and Roe weighed their dope up that they fronted K.K. and Joker and they hit the block to grind.

"So what's wit y'all? Y'all two nigga's want to slang some dope or what?" Roe asked Low and Pep.

"Hell yeah," Low answered, already with it full fledge.

"Yeah," Pep replied, just wanting to get a little money and roll with his partner.

"Here, take an ounce apiece and bring us back two G's," Nut told them, throwing them each an ounce. "Get money killa's."

Low was japed up now that he was fucking with an ounce like Bo. Him and Pep broke the hard crack ounce down, and bottled some of it. They took the rest and hid it over Low's aunt crib and hit the block. It was one O'clock in the afternoon and they stood in front of the Arab store to slang their stones, but customers kept going to a group of young cats twenty feet away.

Roe walked up and said, "how y'all doing? Y'all getting play?"

"Naw man, they all going over to them dudes over there," Low told him nodding in the direction of where them six young dudes were standing serving.

Roe frowned his face up. "Aw, that's hoe ass Joe and his pussy ass boy's."

A customer was on their way to Joe's crew, but saw Roe and rushed his way instead. "Hey Roe, let me get a nice fifty piece," the skinny man said.

"Check, these my two muthafuckin nigga's here, Low and Pep, and they got them boulders fo yo shoulders. Tell everybody," Roe told the fiend. Pep served him and the other fiends and custies saw this and bum rushed over to them. "You nigga's good now. I'll holla at y'all later." Roe walked off, telling all the fiends to go to them.

Joe didn't like Roe at all, and sure wasn't feeling the two nigga's trying to take all the ends that was coming his way. Joe whispered something to his partner Will. Will walked over to Low and Pep.

"Fuck up with you nigga's blocking the cash flow?" Will barked.

"Man, get the fuck outta my face!" Low said.

Pep sucker punched Will and he fell. Joe and his crew up pipe and lil Rob started shooting at them, making everybody scatter. Low and Pep ran behind a car parked in the parking lot and took out their 38 revolvers. The other dudes had automatics. They saw Smoke running towards them with five dudes strapped with big ass 45's in their hands.

"What the fuck going on? Who y'all shooting at?" Smoke asked, not seeing no out the way ass characters in the vicinity.

"Some lames that ain't from around here that's trying to cut into the action!" Joe told him. Low and Pep jumped up from the car Joe was pointing at.

"Aw man, that's Nut and Roe's partners," said Smoke, shaking his head. "They with them so cut the dumb shit!" He ordered.

Roe and Nut came running from behind an apartment with M-16's in their hands. "Fuck jumping Smoke?" Nut asked Smoke as he ice grilled Joe and his crew.

"Just a misunderstanding, that's all lil brah," Smoke replied talking with his hands. He knew how Roe and Nut felt about Joe and his rappies and wanted to murder them, and Joe felt the same way but didn't have the heart to do it. Nut and Roe had bodied a few already with no problem. But, when you got a scared nigga with a gun ain't no telling what he might do when his back is up against the wall. Smoke knew Joe wasn't no killer, but Roe and Nut were. "They didn't know these two nigga's were with y'all. It's straight now," he told them trying to decipher the situation pointing to Low and Pep before it got out of hand, knowing the animosity amongst them. Plus he was selling dope to Joe and his crew and didn't want to lose money over Joe being murdered, so he tried to diffuse their beef all the time and keep the peace flowing.

Nut raised his M-16 up to lil Rob's head and said, "Bitch ass nigga, y'all want beef?!" Roe did the same with his at Joe's dome. Low put his to one of Joe's dudes, and Pep followed suit, making Joe's partners draw theirs, making it look like a standoff at the OK Corral in some old western movie.

"Don't nobody pull a muthafuckin trigga! I then done told y'all nigga's it was cool, so let it go!" Smoke grumbled, looking like a devil with them flaming red ass eyes. "Everybody put they shit down now!"

They all respected Smoke, and had seen him kill many folks while growing up, plus doing a lot of other crazy things. They respected his road dawg Nate too, but he didn't come around like he use to. Nate was the brains behind everything and had the real dope money. They put their guns down.

"Hoe ass bitch," Roe muttered to Joe, and walked away with his nigga's behind him.

"Don't fuck with them two nigga's," Smoke told Joe and them, and walked away salty they had blew his high.

Low and Pep went back to their hood the day before his birthday. They came back with their pockets fat from slanging in West Lake, so they helped the crew get shit for the party for him and Bo. They bought all kinds of drinks like pop, beer, wine, and got mass food to grill. The next day, some girls out there cooked the food for them. Bo's sister Pattie helped make and cook the food. She looked like Nia Long but lighter and not as thick. Little kids were everywhere, running around with food all over their little faces and hands. It was jam packed out there. Black folks didn't pass up no good free food and drinks, especially no grilled grub at that. Low's mom was cooking talking shit about two badass lil boys running around feeling on girls behinds.

"Where that boy lil Danny's mother at? He just running round here like he ain't got no damn manners an sense," Jerry said, watching his little dark complexion ass smack a older lady on the butt and take off leaving his BBQ handprint on her ass. Jerry took off after him. Lil Danny and his side kick that everybody called Doe-Boy, was laughing at their antics when Jerry walked up on them. "You two think you're funny, huh?" She asked, grabbing both of them by their ears.

"Oowwee!" Lil Danny shouted. "Let go of me!"

"What's wrong with you old lady!" Doe-Boy yelled.

"I will fuck both you lil bad fuckers up if I catch your asses do anything else out here!" Jerry hit both of them upside the head making them yelp out. Jerry walked away and kept her eyes on them.

"You know both their mothers on that stuff child," Low's aunt Paula told Jerry after she sat back down, sighing.

Jerry felt sorry for them when she told her that. She was watching them when Low came up behind her and hugged her.

"Hey Ma," Low said.

"Boy, I almost elbowed yo butt in the mouth. Don't be sneaking up on me like that," Low laughed. "Alright, do it again an see if you be giggling," she looked at her oldest son still laughing and couldn't help but to laugh too.

"I see you over there spanking lil Danny and Doe bad lil butts," Low told her, seeing the two young boys that were like two years younger than him glancing their way.

"Somebody needs too," She puffed. She thought about her sons manners and said. "Go over there and talk to them. Especially, that lil mannish one Danny."

"Okay Ma, anything for you." Low did as she asked, and really liked the two younger boys. Him and lil Danny clicked like blood brothers off rip.

Tina could see the change in Low, and hoped it was for the better. He had given her two hundred dollars and it was his birthday party. That touched her. Nobody never looked out for her like that. He hasn't been back to the hood since the first time we had sex, I wonder if he fucking someone else? She was thinking as she watched him talking to lil Danny and Doe Boy. "I love his ass I really do."

Pep walked up with Kelly, Tina's friend. "Hey girl," Kelly spoke. Pep spoke to Tina and walked off. "This a nice party, ain't it?"

"Um huh," Tina answered, mind on Low.

The party was a blast, and the police only came through twice, Roe and Nut showed up with they crazy asses and was on all the honeys out there.

For some reason Bo was starting to dislike them. He peeked at them every chance he got. The party went swell, and Low really enjoyed it.

Two days later him and Pep came back to the hood selling their work. They had bought an oz from Smoke for nine hundred and was getting most of the money from customers that were out there and coming through. Bo had bought him a car, a 79 El Dawg. Low was happy for Bo cause that's all he use to talk about. Low thought Bo could've gotten something a little cleaner, but it was alright, just needed a paint job and a few new things. Low chilled with Bo and them for a second then went home. When he got home his brothers were outside and his moms was in the living room waiting for Sal to come over, so he went in the kitchen to break his work down to what every size broke off the crack rock, then estimate the price of it. When Sal got there he walked into the kitchen and saw Low cutting his dope up. He smiled thinking about the days when he did the same thing.

"I see you getting a little money now huh?" Sal said grinning. "What you fucking with?"

"An ounce," Low replied, like he was balling out of control.

"Well that's cool an all but let me holla at cha," Sal told him sitting down. "I like you lil nigga, and I want to put you all the way on. And I heard how you bust yo gun. You wit that?"

"Getting money...yeah, but what you talking bout?"

"Let's take a ride and I'll show you," Sal replied, getting up. They walked into the living room and Sal told Jerry they were about to take a ride and would be back in an hour.

"Alright," she said looking puzzled.

They got in Sal's Fleetwood and drove off, getting on Oak Street on the East side. Sal had Al Green music on as he was telling Low he did time for murder and had been out the joint now for six years. Low was surprised to find out that Sal supplied most of the East side, like the nigga Pot Pie who Prince had gotten his and Bo's dope from. They pulled in the driveway of this nice house in Campbell where mostly whites lived. You had to have a little money at this time to stay out there at this time. They got out and Sal opened the door and two big ass black Doberman Pinchers came running out barking.

"Sit down, sit down!" Sal commanded. They sat down still growling at Low so Sal took them in the back room and locked the door.

"Sal, is that you?" yelled some woman.

"Yeah Wanda, and I got company," Sal yelled back. He told Low to have a seat and walked to the back.

Low sat down in his plush ass living room that was all black with a big screen TV and glanced out at the freshly cut lawn and flowers through the window. It smelt like some kind of incense in there. Low looked up cause he saw some movement from the corner of his eye, and saw a bad ass girl who was five foot six, brown paper bag skinned, with a fat ass that was in stretch pants. She had on pink fluffy house shoes and a t-shirt that was tied up in front. She came out the kitchen and looked him up in down.

"Hello," she spoke.

"What's up?" Low replied looking into her big brown eyes.

"Girl take yo butt in the back," Sal said.

"That girl getting too fast for me, I'm gonna have to put a watch dog on her tail. She just like her momma," Sal said after she walked out. Low thought she was his girl at first, but it sounded like she was his daughter by the way he was speaking about her. Sal had to drop something off so they left, but Low kept picturing Wanda sexy ass. They drove to the Lincoln Knolls that was next to Campbell, and was a small neighborhood with houses. Sal drove up into this driveway and some fat dude was on the porch with two white girls and one black one smoking weed and drinking.

Sal told Low to "Come on" and they got out the ride.

"How you living my nigga?" The fat dude asked Sal.

"I'm good player," Sal answered, as the fat dude got up and opened the screen door, and Sal walked in behind him with Low.

Two other older dudes were in the living room watching boxing.

"Bring me nine whole ones out hard," Sal told them. When one of them got up to get it, Low saw the Uzi that was tucked in his back pants. The other two dudes looked at Low. "This my little rappie here, whenever he come thru give him what he ask fo. He will be with another in the car, but he will be the only one to ever come inside. You hear me?" They all nodded their heads as dude handed Sal the nine in a brown paper bag. "Alright, I'll get at you nigga's later."

When they was in the car Sal said, "You heard what I said?"

"Yeah," Low replied nodding his head.

"I want you to have someone in the car with you, just in case the poe-poe try to pull you over, they can run with the shit." Sal gave Low the bag. "That's you playboy. I want fifty-six hundred back. Can you handle that?"

Low's heart was calm as he held the package, and that was really unusual for a first timer with that much product in his possession. Dope boys that have been doing it for years, adrenaline still pumps when they got a package. Low's palms itched, and he believed the old saying that said, when your palms itched, you about to get money.

No doubt," Low replied.

Sal dropped Low off back in the Victory and drove off. Low saw Pep and yelled out to him. "Pep, come on!"

They went over Low's crib. "We bout to blow up out this bitch my nigga!" Low said, as he took out the dope that was in the bag and in a zip lock baggie, and threw it on the kitchen table.

"Damn homie, what's this?" said Pep, eyes wide as he lifted up the dope looking at it.

"That's nine there, and we're gonna split it up nigga. Sal fronted me and we gotta bring him back fifty six hundred. That's four and a half a piece, and we pay him twenty-eight hundred back apiece. Now that's love!" Low was hyped thinking of the cash flow and income.

"Hell yeah that's love! That's enough to get me a nice car an shit!" Pep stated. Pep wasn't feeling selling dope, but the money was good. His mind wasn't thinking outside the box. He was thinking and doing like mostly every black does, thinking on the smaller scale, when you're putting your very life, freedom, and those who love you life in existence over a car.

They split the product up and hit the block. "I'm selling all stones," Low said, cause he wanted to double his money.

"Me too," said Pep, as they slung they shit.

For two days they made a killing in the Vic's. Bo was getting salty cause all the customers were going to them. Low sensed his hate, so him and Pep went to the lake. It was bigger and dope sold faster out there at the time. They told Nut and Roe what they had, and they told them to go ahead and get their money, they would just tell Smoke they were buying from them. They was on the block all day and night, it took them only four days to get rid of all their work. They had seven thousand apiece when they were done.

Low asked Pep, "What you gonna do?" He knew what Pep was going to say, "I'm going to go buy me a ride, cause that's all he had been talking about."

"I'ma re-up with you and buy a car with the rest."

"Man, you don't got no driver's license."

"I'ma have my dude and somebody in my family take the test, and I'll just go take the picture. That's how Roe and Nut did it."

They paid a fiend to use their car to go re-up and drop the dope off at Low's crib. Then they went and hit the car lots up on Market Street. They stopped at three of them, then Pep spotted a 82 green Cadillac, it was clean. He paid twenty-two hundred for it then took it straight to Jakes Customizing car shop for a paint job, gold kit package, wheels, and system. He had them do a metal flake money green paint job on it, crushed velvet seats with gold button trimmed in gold all around, and gold Truce and Vogues. It all added up to five-thousand. Pep gave them his last two grand and told them he would be back in a couple days with the rest. They told him it would be done in two weeks.

An hour later they were back on the block with Bo and the crew grinding. Pep was telling them how he just bought a Lac and that it was in Jake's getting hooked up. Moose said, "Yo shit gonna be fly as fuck when it come outta Jake's." Bo didn't say shit. Moose continued talking. "Man y'all fuckin wit weight now?"

"Nigga, we fuckin with nine of them things," Pep boasted.

"Y'all nigga's doing yo thang," Moose told'em, giving them some dap.

Bo couldn't believe they had nine ounces of dope, when he been fucking with an ounce at the most for a while now. It was his own fault for blowing his money on bullshit, he never gave himself a chance to get past an ounce. Now these little nigga's that he gave part of the game he felt, was getting more than him, he thought. He was salty and jealous at the same time.

"Y'all doing it like that, huh? That's cool," he commented, giving them some daps.

Bo and them left while Low and Pep stayed on the block til four in the morning grinding. They was wondering why wasn't nothing mention about Dirty and Tito since they came through their hood busting not giving a fuck who got shot. Bo ain't said nothing, and Prince was suppose to be his best friend. Low had even caught Bo slipping out of Prince girl's spot two days ago. That shit wasn't cool at all, he thought and told Pep. "Man that nigga's a dirty mu'fucka," Pep said.

They rented a fiends car to re-up with Sal's dude six days later. Pep was japed up because he had just paid the bill on his ride and it would be ready in five days. "When you gonna buy a car?" Pep asked Low as they chopped their work down to size to serve.

"Man, I'm cool for now. I'm trying to do something."

Pep had left and Low was in the kitchen counting his money when his mom came in and sat down. Low had fourteen thousand now.

"Boy I want you to invest your money wisely, everybody always buying cars trying to show off! That ain't shit when you got to go start over again with the same amount. Dumb nigga's."

"You need anything Ma?" Low asked.

"Naw boy, save it for something that will last."

"I'ma buy you a house in a couple of months," Lee told her.

Jerry smiled. "That will be nice. I'ma go start a saving account for you. Only you and me will be able to get the money out. I've been saving all my income tax and putting it in there for a while now. My income tax money for last year should be here next week, so we'll do it then. I'll just pretend I put my money in the bank, you gotta watch the Feds in this dope game, that's how they got yo uncle and alot of these big shot callers. Flossing their money like they legit an shit."

Low soaked every word in like a sponge.

Later that evening Low and Pep went over Nut and Roe's house and the girl's came by. Amy had been sneaking off with Pep since that night they fucked.

"Let's go to the drive in, they showing some Kung Fu shit at Ski Hi tonight," Nut told everybody.

Everybody agreed, and they all hoped into Roe and Nut's Regal's and bounced. They stopped at the store and got some Tops (rolling papers), drinks, and some ice. They parked next to each other when they got there. Fifteen minutes into the movie, Roe asked Low to change seats with him and Rhonda so they could get in the back. A few minutes later Low heard Rhonda moaning and looked in the back seat seeing Rhonda in the doggy getting her goods beat up. Low got horny and took his pipe out and Sandy started sucking his shit like a Lemon Head. Low leaned back closing eyes enjoying the cap he was getting.

"KNOCK, KNOCK, KNOCK!" Someone knocked on the window scaring him. Low jumped and saw Nut grinning with his face pressed against the glass,

"What's up?" Nut asked still grinning.

"This cap, nigga!" Low replied, mad he was interrupted from the nut he was on the verge of releasing.

"My bad, when y'all freaky nigga's get finish, we're sending the girl's to go get something to eat."

Roe got finish and you could smell sex in the car. Low shot his load down Sandy's throat and Roe was in the back tripping by telling Sandy to hurry up hoe.

"Man roll the window down, smell like fish in this bitch," Roe said.

"Shut up boy." Rhonda hit him, "Foul ass mouth."

Amy and Shawn were outside the car waiting on them when they got out to go get the food, so Pep and Nut hopped into Roe's car.

"Man it stank in here, smell like pussy an shit," Nut cracked.

"Damn, you nigga's got right into the ass," Pep said, putting his head out the window. Low and them busted out laughing.

Low had thug love for these three nigga's. He felt closer to them than he ever did anybody else. They had a good time at the movies and when they pulled back up into the projects, Joe and his crew was standing right out there. Nut had seen them and drove right there on purpose, ice grilling them as he parked.

Amy tried to duck down and Pep grabbed her by the hair, "Hell nah, bitch get up!" Pep told her in the back seat of Nut's car. Nut put one in the chamber of his forty-five, and Pep put one in the nine milla he was gripping. Roe drove up right next to them and saw the deal, so him and Low cocked one into their burners. Low felt the vibe and welcome it.

Joe saw Amy and his whole facial expression changed. "This bitch must be crazy!" Joe muttered stepping up to Nut's car with his crew as they were getting out. Amy was scared to death it was late at night, and many people were out enjoying the night air because it be burning up in the daytime. Nut and Pep had their guns in their hands, as Low and Roe walked over.

"Bitch you crazy or something!? Get yo dumb ass over here!" Joe spat, pointing at Amy. He went to grab her and Pep got in front of her.

"Nigga gon' somewhere, she ain't going nowhere!" Pep gritted saying.

"What the fuck you say nigga?" Joe uttered, glaring at him.

"You heard me! You ain't deaf!"

Joe glanced down and around, and saw the gun in his hand and all the rest of his rappies strapped too, and knew he was off guard. He looked at Amy and uttered, "Hoe this how we doing it, huh?"

Amy studdered, "I… I…know you gonna beat me up so I'm not coming with you right now Joe," she was hoping she didn't fuck up the money Joe be giving her, cause Pep wasn't giving her nothing but dick and a good high. He bragged about having a car that was getting fixed up but she haven't seen it, or his money.

"Hoe you ain't got to worry bout fuckin' wit me again, bitch!" Joe yelled, and walked off really wanting to put his hands on her.

"Soft ass chump," Nut commented mad Joe didn't try something.

Things were going sweet for Low. He had a nice little piece of change saved up, he would have around twenty-one thousand in a second and was thinking about copping a whole chicken (kilo) or at least a half of one. Pep was out there kicking it with his money and today they were going to go get his car out the shop. Pep had went and bought a all blue new suede Nike jogging suit, shoes, and some gold. The big fat ass gold chain had his name swinging on the emblem.

Low's mom took them to get Pep's car, "Boy, that's a nice ride you then bought," Jerry said when she saw it parked out front of the shop and Pep pointing it out. They got out the car and she looked at it good. "Oh. I see you got the inside done too." He had the gold buttons with his name in them. He turned on the CD changer and the music bumped out of the four twelve inch woofers were hitting hard, "Ok boy that's enough. I'm going back home, y'all be careful."

Low and Pep had both obtained their license illegally, so Pep was ready to floss his shit. They drove off bumping E.P.M.D. song Strictly Business. Honeys and nigga's stared at his car and tried to see who was driving it as they drove up McGuffey. Pep was leaning feeling good. Low glanced over at his nigga and just smiled. It felt good to see his nigga doing alright feeling good riding around the hood in something clean that was his. Pep stopped in front of the girl's house that had got the beef started with Dirty and Tito. They came outside to see whose music was beating loud as hell in the clean Caddy, when they saw Pep leaning in the cleanest ride in their hood their mouths dropped. They came down the steps to holla and Pep cruised off, leaving them there stuck.

They drove into the Vic's and Moose and them saw who it was and was surprised. Moose started jumping in the air with his fat ass screaming, "Gawd damn, yo Lac fly!"

Bo was fucked up. Pep shit was killing his. People in the hood came to look at his ride. Tina was there with Kelly, Pep's girl, who was all inside the car bobbing her head to the music.

Sal drove up and saw Pep's ride and got out. "I see you bought you a clean ass hog," he told Low, thinking it was his.

"This ain't mine," Low said, "this Pep ride."

"Oh, I see. Most young dudes buy a car as soon as they get some money."

"Let me holla at cha," Low said. They went and leaned on Sal's car. "I'm trying to buy a bird or a whole one, what can I get it fo?"

"I thought you was spending yo money tricking or getting high, since I ain't see you buying no ride an shit. But I see you smarter than I thought you were. You moving up faster than anyone I've been fucking with, I like that in ya." Sal put his hand under his chin like he was in deep thought, then said, "Eleven thousand five hundred for a half, and twenty-four thousand for the whole thang."

Sal was fucking with three birds and getting them himself for eighteen thousand.

"Let me get a half fo now," Low told him.

"Alright, I'll let them know you coming."

Pep was buying his own shit but Low always went and got it. He could've sold it to him out of his own package but he was going to sell rocks and ounces, so he could flip his product, and gross more revenue. Pep usually got a couple ounces or four in a half, he didn't give a fuck, he just wanted a little ends. "Yeah, I gots to get this paper out this bitch!" Low said to himself, as he walked back from making the deal with Sal, on his way to go get his re-up money for the half of brick. He saw Pep was busy talking and showing off his ride to roll with him. He saw lil Danny and called him.

"Ah…lil Danny! Comere!" Low shouted.

Lil Danny was bent down admiring the rims on Pep's car with Doe Boy. He heard someone call his name and glanced around, seeing it was Low. Sweat was running down his dark skin face as he walked towards Low with his lanky built frame.

"Yo, what's up, you call me?" Lil Danny asked.

"Yeah, I need you to roll with me to take care of some biz."

"Alright, I'm ready." He didn't even hesitate about rolling with Low. It was just a bond there with them.

Low told Pep he would catch up with him later, his mind was on his money, and money was on his mind. Money was in his mind and his mind was in money.

Bo, Moose, and Rat jumped into Pep's ride and they drove around kicking it. Pep pulled into the West Lake projects and nigga's and chicks were like "Damn yo shit slick!"

Joe and them saw his car and had to give him props. "Yeah, yo shit ice nigga," Joe told Pep.

Pep went to get Nut and Roe. "Damn killa, I gots to flip something new on yo ass now, straight up," Nut said when he saw the new car.

"Me too, shining on a nigga," Roe said checking out the inside.

The girls came out and Amy was all teeth, smiling. She knew he had a lil money now. "I know he got some money now," she thought, gazing at the gold shining around his neck, picturing it being around her neck.

Chapter 7
Blood on my hands and they can't understand how I can kill...

Two days later, Bo got chased by the police and caught when he crashed his car. They took him to the County Jail because he had just turned eighteen and was already on probation, so he couldn't make bond. He called Moose and told him to go get his stash from over his girl's house Cathy. He only had seventeen hundred dollars when Moose recovered it. So the crew put together some money for his lawyer, because big Roy had pressed charges on him. Jackson and Malley had pressed Bobo to tell them all about the shooting and the murders, but Bo knew that would hurt him even more, so he didn't say zip. He knew he was going to do some time anyway.

Sal had been feuding and beefing with these two dudes from out of the Kimmel Brooks projects named Tim and Bruce. The Kimmel Brooks was the worse projects on the East side. The beef was over some bullshit crap game that then moved and escaladed over turf. Bruce and Tim had been riding round all day searching for Sal, when they noticed Sal's car turn into the Vic's.

"Man there that chump go there!" Tim shouted excitedly, as he drove pointing as they drove up McGuffey. He was a skinny short brown-skinned dude around 35 years old.

"Hum huh, that's him," Bruce muttered, cocking a bullet into the Tec Nine. Tim turned the corner after Sal, seeing him stop, so he parked down the street. "Yeah homie, we got this buster now," Bruce said. "Pull right up next to him. I want to make sure we don't miss this time."

Sal was sitting in his car with Low Moms. They had just got back from going out to eat and was chilling, listening to the Jays talking. Sal was just telling her he would be back later, when a car with two nigga's drove up beside them. Bruce looked right into Sal and Jerry's face with his mug twisted. He wanted to kill Sal so badly that he didn't care who was in the car with him. Sal saw who it was but before he could do anything Bruce pulled the trigger of his Tec Nine over and over again, making sure he got him. He blew Sal's face off and hit Jerry in the head twice and once in the neck, making blood squirt out like a fountain. They died instantly at 10:23 P.M. Bruce and Tim skidded off into the night back to their hood on the East side.

Some of the people in the hood saw the gunfire and others heard it, so they came outside to see what was going on. Moose and Rat had seen it all and ran to the car as soon as Tim and Bruce skidded off. When Low's little brother's came outside and saw everybody surrounded by Sal's car, and noticed their mothers outfit she had wore that day with blood all over it, they pushed their way through the crowd and dropped to their knees crying touching her. It was a sad and ugly sight. Pep and Low had just drove up and saw everybody surrounded around Sal's car, so Low jumped out of the car before Pep could even park. He pushed through the crowd and saw his brother's on their knees crying with blood all over them. His heart was already beating fast when he saw them like that, but when the realization of what they were mourning and touching stabbed him in his heart, soul, and spirit, sweat popped out on his forehead and it felt like his heart had burst.

The car door was opened as half of Jerry's body was hanging out and Low saw the shirt that looked familiar but her face was nothing but blood with brain matter hanging out like oodles and noodles. He stopped in his tracks not wanting it to register. Everything went silent in his world for thirty seconds, which felt like infinity. Then he heard his brothers screaming and it snapped him out of it. He dropped to his knees with them over their mother's body as her warm blood soaked them, as if they were being born from her womb again. Low cried and cried for so long in pain, that he didn't realize that the police and people were trying to pull him away so they could examine the body and go over the crime scene. Jackson and Malley looked on in amazement cause it was an awful bloody saddening sight. Low felt his mom was the only person who really loved him and been there for him no matter what. This incident changed his life forever. What was already in him and running through his veins, was now out, fully awakened like a wild grizzly bear that hibernated in the winter. But the pain he felt right then kept him in a zombie like trance. His family came over that night and washed the caked up blood off him. They had to give him a sedative just to get him to calm down and sleep. However, no amount of dope could erase the nightmares and pain he endured while he slept.

The next day he woke up and just laid in bed for thirty minutes, His mind was clocking and his heart was heavy with sorrow and he felt numb. He got up and got dressed then went downstairs. His grandma and aunts were in the living room with his brothers and other family members. They looked at him and saw the pain in his eyes. He had a look that they had never seen before and they had to turn away.

"You hungry?" asked his aunt Paula.

"Naw," Low answered then sat down with them. Everybody started crying and mourning. His brothers were in their grandma's arms crying as she held them.

Low couldn't take it and walked outside. He saw Moose and them and asked them what happened? There was an intense look in his eyes that wasn't there before they all noticed. They really didn't want to tell him about the incident, but felt it was only right to let him know just how things went down that night.

"Whateva you want to do nigga, I'm with you!" Moose said mad as fuck about his mother getting killed. Jay, Alvin, Rat, and even lil Danny and Doe-Boy agreed in unison.

"Them bitch ass nigga's gone' pay triple fo this," Low said so calmly and vehemently, that it scared Moose. Low walked over to Pep's house and his mom let him in. Pep mother didn't know what to say to him, so she just told him Pep was in his room.

Pep was in his room high as fuck with twelve guns out loading them up. When he saw Low he jumped up and hugged him.

"Nigga its war out this bitch! We gonna do them hoes real good," he said crying grabbing guns off the bed. "Let's go, fuck this shit!"

Low stared at him and said, "No doubt, but we gonna wait till tonight to handle this shit dawg."

Low saw nothing but whoever killed his mother death. He saw some V's in a pill bottle and took five of them, and washed it down with some Wild Irish Rose Pep had on his dresser. They sat there an hour getting fucked up, then got up and put three guns in their waist and left. Pep's mother saw the guns and just shook her head knowing her son wasn't going to listen to her. And wasn't nothing she could think of or phantom to stop Low. She felt his pain dearly and the guy's that did it too, cause she saw the look in Low's eye's.

When they stepped outside Roe and Nut was out there in front of Low's crib talking to Moose and them about the shit.

"Nigga it's on an popping," Roe said with a frown on his face giving Low some dap.

"We wit you killa," said Nut dapping him. "Let's roll."

They were about to get into a friends ride Nut had, when Tina appeared from around the apartment building. She walked right up to Low and looked him dead in his eyes. All Low could do was grab her in his arms, and she cried on his chest.

"Ah, I'll see ya later. I gotta go," Low told her, in a hurry to shed his mothers' killer's blood.

"What's up? Y'all need me to come?" Moose asked.

"Nah, we cool killa," Nut said. "Y'all nigga's chill."

When they got in the car Roe asked them did they know what the dudes looked like.

"Hell yeah!" Pep answered. He had sold them some stolen car stuff a few times.

"Bet. Look in that bag on the floor and take that shit out," Roe told them.

Pep reached for the duffel bag on the floor by his feet and pulled out some leather gloves, duct tape, and some ski masks. Roe told them the plan as they rode. When they got close to where them dudes be at and hung out, Low started putting on the ski masks and gloves without being told.
Nut drove around the back of the red brick Kimmel Brook projects and parked.

They got out the car and Roe scoped out the neighborhood. "Go see if you see them pussy ass chumps," Roe told Pep. Pep ran around the apartment buildings. It was so quiet you could hear crickets and other kinds of bugs out. You could even hear people in the projects. Where they were parked wasn't no traffic because it was a dark wooded area with no lights on the telephone poles.

Pep came back breathing hard. "They out there playing dice wit some others cats."

"Bet. Let's handle these bitches," Nut said rolling his ski mask down over his head and face. Everybody did the same and slipped their gloves on and the jumpsuits over their clothes. They looked like Swat.

"Let's do this shit!" Roe uttered, and they all got back in the car.

They rode right up on the dice game and jumped out like Swat shooting in the air. "Everybody hit the fuckin ground!" Nut yelled waving a pistol grip pump at everybody there.

"Don't nobody fuckin' move! Nobody!" Roe shouted aiming his nine millimeter.

Low pointed his 44 bulldog Magnum at Bruce and Tim. "Y'all two muthafucka's put yo hands behind yo backs!" He muttered, blood boiling he wanting to kill them so badly.

"Here, take my money," Tim pleaded, as he went to go in his pocket. "I got."

"Bitch!" Low yelled kicking him in the face so hard his head lifted up off the ground and blood flew in the air landing on the dude next to him face and eyes. "Shut the fuck up!" Roe taped them up. They were suppose to put them in the trunk of the car but Low flipped out. He pulled a big ass hunting knife out and said, "You hoes remember that lady y'all killed last night? Huh? This fo her bitch!" He bent over Tim and grabbed his hair pulling his already bloody face up and ran the knife across his neck cutting his throat, as he slammed his head to the cement letting go. It sounded like a watermelon being squashing to the ground. Tim thrashed and wiggled on the ground choking on his blood gurgling like a fish out the water. Then Low stood over Bruce and uttered, "Bitch, that's how you bitches get done up!"

Bruce was crying up a storm, "Please man... I...didn't do nothing. Just let me go." Tears were running out his eyes and he didn't care who heard and seen him begging for his life. You could smell death, and that Tim bowels had been released.

"Shut up hoe! Ain't no saving yo bitch ass now! Didn't I say shut the fuck up!" Low yelled as he shoved the gun in his mouth knocking his front teeth out. Bruce tried to talk mumbling, "Bitch!" BOOM, BOOM, BOOM!" Chucks of the back of Bruce's dome flew off. "I said shut the fuck up! Didn't I?" Low snarled, then shot him three more times in the chest.

The other dude's that were on the ground started throwing up and begging for their life, but Nut and Roe held them down.

"Let's go!" Roe hollered.

Tim was still shaking, so Nut shot him in the head, then Low shot him three more times.

"Come'on, let's be out!" Roe yelled, and they ran back to the ride and sped off.

Nut parked the car next to a wooded area a block up from the Victory. They got out and Nut went to the trunk of the car and took out a can of gas. He poured it all over the inside and outside of the ride, then lit it on fire. Then they ran over Pep's house.

"Give me the guns and the jumpsuits y'all two used," Roe said. "Here put it in this bag." They did what he asked, and then watched Roe as he took all their jumpsuits and the two guns outside to the dumpster and burned them. He told them he was going to get rid of the two guns and knife when they left. Low sat there in silence.

"You did good killa," Nut told him, "We about to bounce so we can get rid of this hot shit, but we'll be back tonight."

"We'll have Moose take us to the pad," Roe told them. They dapped one another and left.

Low left and went home to get things ready for his mother's funeral. His mom had an insurance policy that covered her expenses for everything, and left him and his brothers some money. But he paid for a lot of things out of his own money because he wanted her burial and funeral to be right. He bought his brothers and family clothes to wear. He stayed high trying to kill the pain, but nothing could diminish what he felt and lost. The day of his mother's burial everybody that knew Low and his family came to pay respect. Some people came just because they knew a lot of people would be there and they wanted to be seen and others just because they prone to as if this was a place to meet others.

Low sat in the front row with his brothers and family. From that day on Low made a promise, to always bomb first on who ever no matter what, and make his moms proud, while she was in heaven gazing down on him. She had always told him not to take no shit, and to be smart about everything he does, whether it be right or wrong. He was so angry that she died the way she did, leaving him and his brothers all alone.

However, he knew he had to go on like she always told him, "Never give up, or let them see you down. They will prey on any weakness they see you have. So stay strong and dish out whatever they tried to you triple." So he vowed to take all her words and put them into effect. He watched as her body in the casket was lowered into the grave and tears fell freely from his blood shot eyes, as a part of him was buried that day too into the cold ground six feet. Three days later, he and his brothers moved in with their aunt Paula that stayed a building over.

Pep and Low was back on the block selling dope as usual, but there was a change in Low. He was more thirsty for the dollar and his grind was twenty four seven. Low took all the dope sells from Pot Pie and he was getting salty as fuck! He had all the little nigga's out there slanging for him until Low came along showing them love with cheaper prices and hanging on the block with them taking all the customers. When a customers would come out there to the Victory to get dope from Pot Pie, they were cut off and sold dope to by Low. When they came for weight, Low would serve them. Pot Pie got mad as fuck when he saw Low serve his best customer and rushed outside to confront him.

"Ahh little nigga...you crossing the line now dog!" Pot Pie barked, pointing his finger to the back of Low's head.

Low turned around from serving the customer and Pot Pie's finger was inches from his nose. "Bitch, I been crossed the line." Low gritted as he went for his gun in his waist. He was about to pop Pot Pie right there on the spot, but Moose grabbed him. "Get the fuck off me!" he shouted to Moose, as Pot Pie took off running and he pushed him off.

Low chased after Pot Pie gripping a German Ruger Nine Milla in his hand. Low caught him just as he was opening the door of his house and shot him in the back two times. Pot Pie yelped out feeling his spine being entered by the slugs freezing him as he fell. "Now who crossed the line hoe, huh?" Low uttered as Pot Pie looked up at him shocked, and shot him in the face blowing half his face off. Low walked away with the burner still smoking.

Pot Pie's dudes Rally and Mark were in the house where their friend Pot Pie just got killed right in front of them on the couch watching the game. They had saw him open the door when the shots rang out and he fell right in the doorway five feet from them. When they were about to hop off the couch to see if he was alright, they saw Low step to him with the gun smoking, and froze. Low shot him dead in the face after saying what he said, and Rally threw his guts up. Rally and Marc couldn't believe what just happened. Marc sat there stuck, not saying a thing. Rally was mad as hell about his boy getting gunned down like that. Mookie, Pot Pie baby mother came running down the stairs in the apartment and rushed to her baby daddies body kneeling over him crying till the police arrived.

Low and them had left cause they knew the police was coming. Before they left Low had walked right back to where they were and made a few sells right after he killed Pot Pie, like he ain't did shit! Moose and the crew couldn't believe how cold blooded Low just gunned Pot Pie down right in front of everybody not caring, and coming back making some sells as if it was nothing.

Jackson and Malley had just made high rank Homicide detectives and showed up talking to everybody to get some information on who did this and what happened. On the sly Rally told them he would tell them who did it but not in front of everybody, so Malley gave him his card with a number on it to get in touch with him later today. Low and the crew sat over Moose's house out there getting high.

"Fuck that nigga," Pep said, talking about Pot Pie. By the way they all saw Low murder just now, they knew he wasn't the same little cat as before, and wasn't to be fucked with.

Tina had heard that Low killed Pot Pie and her love for him couldn't let her believe he would do it like everybody was saying it was done in front of everybody like that. Her girl Kelly was running her mouth about it, but she was in deep thought. She already knew he wasn't the same old shy Lee.

That night Low and Pep went to the Jets (Westlake) and hooked up with Amy and Sandy. They went to the hotel called Wagon Wheel and spent the night.

"No!" Low shouted out swinging, knocking the hotel's lamp over as he had a nightmare. He was dreaming about his mother. In the dream he was right there when the bullets came sparking out the gun at her and he tried to jump in front of his mother to take the bullets but he was too late as her blood splattered in his eyes and face.

"You alright baby!" Sandy shook Low out of the dream.

Low woke up in a cold sweat. "Um hum," he replied wiping the sweat off his face thinking of the blood.

They got up the next day and dropped the girls off and went over Nut and Roe's crib. They wasn't there and found them on the block, so they kicked it with them for an hour, then went back to the Vic's. Rally had gone down to the police station at 10 AM and made statement to testify on Low. Malley and Jackson couldn't believe what they just heard, this fifteen year old boy just murdered a person so heartlessly. They knew he was involved in the other killings around the projects as well, but they never thought he would be such a killer himself. Malley pictured the day he saw him crying over his mother's bloody body and saw a helpless kid that day. But now, he had a whole different picture. And it wasn't a pretty one at all.

Low and Pep went to their cribs to change clothes, and an hour later the cops were at Low's aunt apartment banging on the door to pick him up.

"What the hell you want with my nephew?" Paula questioned them, looking just like her sister Jerry but big boned. Low stood right behind her not even scared or nervous.

"Murder!" Jackson stated, pushing past her. "Put your hands up!" He told Low frisking him and reading him his rights.

"Aunt Paula, go get me a lawyer. I got some money upstairs and over grandma's house," Low told her as he was getting dragged out. He had fourteen thousand over his grandma's, ten thousand upstairs, and a nice sum in the bank. They told his aunt they were taking him to the Juvenile Justice Center (JJC or Juvie).

Pep and the crew with the rest of the hood saw them bring Low out hand cuffed, and Pep started talking shit mad. "Bitch ass nigga's always telling shit! Hoe muthafucka's!" He yelled while standing on the corner. Pep went an talked to Low's aunt Paula and she told him about the Lawyer.

"Alright, you ready to go?" Pep asked.

"Hold up, he told me to go get his money for the lawyer." Paula ran into the apartment and came back out with her purse stuffed with money. "Tina watch the boys till I get back please!" Paula yelled out to her, and Tina nodded her head okay. They were at school at the time.

"Stop at my place so I can get some money," Pep told her when they got in her car.

They went to the lawyer that they had gotten for Bobo. A thirty-six year old Italian man named Sammie Burner. They walked into his office and asked the secretary to speak with him. She called into his office to inform him he had some clients, because he was talking with a client at the moment.

"He'll see you two in a few minutes." Ten minutes later, a white man walked out with two black men.

"Hello, may I help you folks?" The white man asked Paula and Pep.

"Yes, we need to hire you," Paula told him.

Sammie could see and hear the desperation. "Alright, step in my office please. And we'll see if I can assist you two." They walked into his office and sat down. "Now how may I help?"

Pep started telling him the situation, and then threw two fat knots of money on his desk. "I can get more, just get him out as quick as you can."

Sammie looked at the rolls of money with a rubber band around them and picked them up. He counted it by flicking through the corners, then looked at Pep and said, "Don't worry, my friend is a judge there in Juvenile. Write his name down and y'all phone number so I can contact y'all when I need to. They wrote their information down and left.

Chapter 8

You don't look ahead at the consequences when you into that GOON LIFE. You only live for that moment...that money...that thrill.

Sammie drove to the JJC and went straight to the clerk's office. He was a well-known lawyer with a lot of clout and pull, therefore when the lady clerk saw him she was all smiles.

"Hello, what can I do for you today Mr. Burner?" she asked flirtingly in a sexy voice. Sammie stayed in the finest suits and had looks that could be graced in GQ magazine.

"I'm fine, thank you. And I see your looking mighty splendid," she blushed. Sammie sometimes used her to get information that he wasn't suppose to get and know about. She would even rush whatever paper he needed done before anyone else. "I would like to know what all you have on my client Lenny Trevor."

"Oh, the young murderer. Let me get his file for you," she got up making sure he got a good look at the tight skirt she was wearing as she went into the back room.

"Thanks," he said. She came back and gave him the file touching his hand lightly. "Appreciate it. Can you call the guards and let them know I'm on my way to see my client."

When he got there, he was put in a holding room to wait for his client. While he waited, he took the time to read his file. Only one witness that wrote a statement, not bad to beat at all, Sammie thought on as he read what evidence they had. Nevertheless, he would easily buy this case with the kind of pull he had, if the money was right. It wasn't a high profile case. And it wasn't a white person that was killed.

Low couldn't believe he was in this bitch! He was in deep thought thinking about how much time he would do, when the guard came and told him his lawyer was here to see him. The guard cuffed him and escorted him down the hall.

Sammie looked up and saw this young, skinny, so called killer he was just reading about as Low was let into the room and shown a chair to sit in.

When he saw him, he remembered that he had given him money to represent another client he had in the County right now.

"I remember you. Looks like you're in a jam, huh? Your aunt and friend gave me some money to help you, so we got's to see if we can get you outta here."

"Cool," Low said, "How much you want?"

"I was paid already."

"Man, fuck that. How much you want right now to bounce me out tomorrow?" Low had a serious look on his face.

"Well, it will cost you ten thousand for my services," Sammie replied, not believing this young black boy had any more money than what he had already serviced."

"You got it," Low told him.

"Okay, well let's see what we got here on you." Sammie opened the file. "They only got one witness. Do you know some kid name Rally Jackson Jr?"

"Yeah...I know the lame," Low said calmly as he felt the killer mode kick in his blood.

"I will be back to talk with you tomorrow and you should be out of here either tomorrow afternoon or the day after." Sammie gathered his papers together and got up. "See you tomorrow." He put his hand out to shake Low's, they shooked and he left.

Low was steaming mad as fuck as he was taken back to his cell. He was stunned that Rally hoe ass told on him, and he spared his life when he gunned Pot Pie. He asked the guards could he use the phone and called Pep's house and cell and didn't get no answer. So he called his aunt Paula and told her to tell Pep that Rally was the one who got him locked up and he would be out soon. His aunt was worried about him and told him she would tell him. After hanging up on her, he called Tina. She was crying and he really wasn't trying to hear that, so he hung up on her and called Roe and Nut's house. Roe answered and told Low him and Nut were there chilling with the girls eating, kicking it. Low told him about Rally being the reason why he was locked up.

"Don't worry bout shit. We got cha dawg. Call me back later so I can go handle this lil shit."

"Is that my baby?" Sandy asked.

"Yeah," he told her. "Here talk to yo girl Sandy I gotta go." Roe gave her the phone. Roe took Nut in the back and told him what Low said.

"Oh, it's 187 time," Nut said ready to body something.

"Fo sho, it's on an poppin," Roe stated.

Pep came back and they told him the deal. "I'ma kill that bitch ass nigga," he said walking off to do it.

"Hold up Pep," Nut said grabbing his shirt.

"Fuck that!" Pep uttered, pulling away from him.

"Listen, we gonna do this shit an not fuck it up!" Roe told him with a frown on his face that made Pep stop and stare at them. He knew they were killers and had done it more than he had. So he just nodded his head agreeing. They told the girls they had something to go take care of and they could stay if they wanted.

"Here, serve this while y'all here," Nut told them sliding a big plate with crack rocks on it. "The powder right here." His girl jumped right on it.

"I know I better get my cut this time to, nigga," Shawn told him. Nut laughed going out the door. "Laugh if you want to, fuck around and get chalk."

When Low hung up, he had all kinds of thoughts running through his mind as he went back to his cell to think. One thing about being locked up, you have time to think about things more clearly. Especially things you never thought of before, because on them streets your mind be racing hundred miles a minute. Low dozed off after chow and dreamed about his mother's murder, jumping up out of his sleep in a cold sweat. He sat up in the dark cold cell with his back against the cold brick wall, and thought about times with his mother.

Roe drove the fiend's car up the street of the projects, up the street to Delaware Street, and pulled into this driveway and parked, Roe and Nut got out and told Pep to come on. They went to the back door and a dog started barking. Nut knocked on the door. Pep was looking around and noticed a clean ass Benz in the open garage. Someone peeked through the peephole in the door and said, "What's up?"

"This Nut, Roe, and my nigga Pep."

"Hold up," the dude behind the door said, and you could hear him walk away. Two minutes later he was back and unlocked the door. He was a big bald headed nigga with a 357 in his hand. They stepped in and he told them to go down the steps in the basement. When they got down there Smoke was there with three other nigga's. It looked like they was just chilling, getting high and watching Super Fly on a big screen TV.

"What's up wit you lil nigga's?" Smoke asked blowing on a fat blunt.

"We gotta holla at cha," said Roe.

"Who that?" This one brown-skinned dude with braids asked, pointing at Pep.

"He cool," Smoke said. "He that little nigga I was telling you bout partner, Pep, and the other one that just got a 1-8-7 the other day Low."

"Oh, so this one of them young killa's, huh?" he said getting up. He stood about five foot eleven. He walked over and shook Pep's hand. "I'm Nate," he said. Pep had heard about him a lot through Nut and Roe, plus other people around there. All he knew was that he   didn't hang around to many people, and if you did get a chance to see him he would be with two down fly ass females that stayed strapped watching his back, front, and sides. Or he would be with Smoke.

"What y'all wanna talk about?" Smoke asked.

"It's serious," Nut answered.

Smoke nodded his head, "Come'on," he said, and got up and started walking up the stairs. Nate followed. When they got upstairs Roe told Smoke and Nate the deal.

"Yeah, that's fucked up little nigga's," Nate stated.

"Y'all gotta do him and do him right, you can't slip or miss. You hear me?" Smoke told'em.

"Give me the run down on where he at and who all was there," said Nate. Pep told him everything he could remember. "Now listen, this how y'all handle this...." Nate mapped out for them how to take care of the problem and free their road dawg. This would be a major turning point in Pep's life. He wouldn't just be a killer, he would become a murderer.

That night, Nut, Roe, and Pep cruised the streets of Liberty, an upper middle class section next to Youngstown, looking for a car to steal. When they spotted one, Roe and Pep hopped out. Roe glanced around while Pep used the screwdriver to pull the window back and slid his arm in to unlock the door and get in. Pep put the screwdriver in the steering column and broke it open, then broke what is called the horseshoe to release the gadget to start the car. The car started and Roe jumped in and they drove off with Nut following. They dropped the fiends' car off around the corner from the Vic's and drove straight to the Vic's with their gloves and ski masks on.

They pulled right up in front of Rally's building, hopped out and ran to his apartment door with gats in hands. Pep tried the knob just in case it was opened, and it was. Pep turned to look at them as he eased the door open. Nut pushed past him and bum rushed inside with Roe behind him, and found Rally and Marc chopping up some crack rocks. Marc and Rally eyes got big as fuck when they saw them come in ski-masked up waving gats yelling, "Get on the floor!" Nut ran up the steps to make sure no one else was inside the apartment, then came back down.

"Nigga, you told on my nigga Low?" Pep hollered at Rally with his 38 snub nose in his face. Rally peed on himself right then, cause he knew he was busted and in deep shit. He knew it was Pep's voice. You could see the steam from the hot piss coming from him on the floor.

Marc looked over at them and said, "Man I ain't no snitch!"

"But you fuck wit one!" Roe told him, and shot him in the head two times and once in the heart.

Pep slugged Rally in the head with the 38, and then over the heart three times where Nate had told him. "Heart and dome shots are the best way to kill someone when you're up close on them," Nate had told him.

"Let's go!" Nut said, peeking out the window. They ran out the door as people got out their way outta the jets to the hottie (stolen car). No one tried to stop the three gun totting ski-masked nigga's. They went back to Westlake and chilled with the girls. Pep's heart was thumping, but settled down after he got drunk and high.

Malley and Jackson arrived on the murder scene standing over the fresh two dead bodies, not believing their witness had just been killed.

"These murders are starting to center around this young Lee kid,"

Malley said, as they both looked around for any evidence and questioned potential witnesses. They had gotten nothing to go on. People standing around when the murdering happened wasn't talking.

"This fuckin' punk kid is going to be trouble. We got's to get him now before he grows up and gets to smart," Jackson told him.

"Yeah, I know," Malley replied shaking his head as he watched in older lady crying and screaming over Rally's corpse.

Nate and Smoke saw the news that night. Nate laid back in his king size bed with his two girls Jessica and Rena watching the big screen TV. He had a feeling about them young nigga's that he liked a lot. They just needed some guidance he thought to himself.

Low didn't sleep to long that night, he kept having crazy ass nightmares, and the noise from other young dudes talking and rapping all night kept him up. He stayed up till 4 AM until they called breakfast. After breakfast he called his Aunt Paula's house. His brother Kevin answered the phone, and the first thing he said was, "Lee, Rally and Marc got killed last night. The cops been out here asking questions early this morning."

Low didn't feel no pain or sadness for Marc, especially none for Rally. Low talked to his brother for a few more minutes, then hung up and called Pep. He wasn't home, so he called Nut and Roe's crib. Nut answered.

"What's up Nut?"

"Aw shit killa. You should be out any day now."

"Yeah, I know. Tell Pep when you see him to talk to my lawyer so I can bounce."

"I got cha. Hold up doe, he upstairs," Nut yelled upstairs for Pep.

Pep came down to the phone all happy an shit. "What's up my nigga? It's all good, you should be out soon."

"Yeah, I heard. I'm supposed to go to court at nine this morn. Call that lawyer and tell him the good news, just in case he don't know and didn't catch the news this morning or last night."

"I got cha, you cool?" Pep asked. They talked for a couple minutes and hung up.

Pep called the lawyer and told him about the witness. "Ok, that is real good for my client," said Sammie. "He should be out later on after court, thanks." Sammie hung up and leaned back in his chair thinking about how this incident might have occurred. He had dealt with plenty cases and people, but these young guy's he felt were something different. He called the judge that would be hearing Low's case. "This Sammie, Ms. Ellen, is Judge Whitley in?"

"Yes, hold on Sammie dear," she clicked over and then put him through.

"Hey, how you doing Sammie?" Judge Whitley said coming on line.

"I'm fine, just fine. Listen, I got a case in front of you this morning...well, better yet, I'll be there to speak with you in a minute, ok?"

"I'll be here," he answered, hanging up thinking of the money.

Sammie left out the door to go talk to the judge.

Moose, Rat and Jay were still sleep over Bo's girl's house when the phone rang. Cathy answered the phone. "Hello," she said with attitude.

"Get yo lazy ass up!" Bo laughed, knowing she would get mad.

"Boy, it's too early fo yo dumb shit! You must be bored. You know I don't get up this early."

"You up now, with yo pregnant ass. I see Rally got smoked last night."

"Um huh, that fool got in that young crazy ass fools business, and got smoked," she said, smacking her tongue against the roof of her mouth and blowing air.

"Who you talking bout?" Bo asked her.

"That fool Lee, Low or whatever y'all call that crazy fucker!"

"I thought he was locked up fo killing Pot pie?"

"He is. But them other fools still out, and everybody knows Rally told on Low. Mookie told me he wrote a statement an shit. She telling everybody with her big mouth." Mookie was Potpie's baby mother.

Bo was tripping off what he just heard. He couldn't believe those little nigga's could murder shit like that.

"Where Moose at?"

"He over here with Rat and Jay. They sleep."

"Hoe, you fuckin with my nigga's? I'll beat yo ass, I ain't playing!" Bo had did time before and knew how things went down when a nigga was on lock. Their so-called woman would get weak if she wasn't already, and set the goods out to a nigga. Even to the homeboy. Only 1% out of 10 kept their legs closed and loyal.

"Nigga you crazy! You ain't gone do shit to me! Let me get Moose before yo ass get hung up on!" Cathy said smacking.

"Bitch, I wish...," she dropped the phone down before he could finish. Bo was heated. Women knew how to piss a brother off real good when he was in this predicament. They had no problem throwing salt on a open wound.

"How you, brah?" Moose asked when he got on the phone.

"Nigga which one of you nigga's fuckin' my bitch?"

"Man you trippin, you know we don't get down like that!"

"My bad," Bo said. "So what's poppin?"

"Man them little nigga's off the hook, I tell ya. They killed Marc and Rally ass! Them lil cat's ain't playin out this bitch!"

"Damn, that shit crazy! I didn't know Marc got killed too. Damn!" Bo was stunned by this. "Both of them?"

"Yeah man. You shoulda seen how calm an shit that fool was afterwards. Acted like he didn't do zip but spill a lil milk. So when you go to court?"

"Tomorrow. I gotta do a year and I'll be outta this hell hole."

"That's cool," Moose told him.

"Put that freak hoe of mines back on the horn. Much love nigga."

"Much love brah," Moose replied, and called Cathy.

When Sammie got to the judge's office he was let straight in his chambers. "So what's the deal?" Judge Whitley asked, getting right to the point knowing it concerned dividends.

"I got a client here for murder that goes before you this morning," Sammie told him sitting on the end of his desk, as the judge sat back in his big leather chair. You couldn't tell the judge was over fifty with his short black hair and baby face.

"Oh, that's a serious one there, huh?" says the judge, and smiled, cause he knew some dead presidents was coming his way for sure because it was a murder case. He was adding up in his head how much at that very moment.

"Well, the only witness has been killed, and there isn't no other evidence," Sammie explained. Whitley's smile faded quickly now, because he knew he wouldn't get paid like he was just hoping. He would have to let him out without the funds.

"But, I got a feeling this one is going to be getting into a lot of things, and his money is good," Sammie said, and slid five thousand dollars in an envelope to Whitley.

Whitley's smile reappeared back like a crack head at the dope house door and he nodded his head. "I'll see you in court Sammie."

"Alright," Sammie replied getting off the desk. "Let me go see my client."

Before court Lee made a deal with his lawyer, he would pay him five thousand more and give him a retainer for future incidents if they came. Later on that morning Low saw the Judge and was released. Jackson and Malley were in the back of the courtroom during the hearing and was pissed off that he got out so easy and quickly.

"We'll be seeing you real soon," Malley told Low when he walked past them out the courtroom. Low just glanced at them and kept walking with his lawyer.

"Let me give you a ride," Sammie told Low outside. They got in his fire red Mustang and sped off up McGuffey to hit the Vic's. They pulled up in front of the apartment building Low told him to. A few dudes rushed the car trying to serve Sammie some rocks, weed and whatever they could. Some saw Low with him and backed off. All Sammie heard was "What you need?"

"Good lookin," Low told him getting out.

"You take care. And stay out the way for a few days," he said shaking Low's hand.

"Aright." Low got out the car and shut the door. His brothers were happy to see him and came running up to him. They went in the crib and he chilled with them and his aunt. Tina came over when she heard he was out. Two hours later he was dressed, and went to check out the crew and see what was jumping.

It was 11:30 AM and the dudes he was fronting were out on the block posted, serving stones. They all gave him some daps and was glad to see him out. Low showed them more love then anyone had, by fronting them, and selling them product for cheap.

"Where everybody at?" Low asked.

"I think Moose an them over Cathy's house," Lil Danny told him.

Low walked over there and knocked on the screen door.

Moose answered. "Awe nigga you out?" He said looking like he saw a ghost.

Low didn't even answer his stupid ass question and just walked in seeing everybody laying around sleep. "Damn, y'all must of been out all night getting money."

"Hell yeah, we ain't crash till like six this morn," Moose told him.

"Where the phone at?" Low asked looking around. Jay, Alvin, and Rat all spoke to him still groggy and sleepy.

"Cathy got it in the back in her room," said Moose. Low went in back and knocked on her bedroom door.

"Come in," Cathy hollered. She was talking on the phone when he stepped in. "Oh girl hold on," she said. "Oh Lowdown, what's up crazy ass?"

"Ain't shit, just wanted to use yo phone right quick."

She put the phone back to her ear. "Girl let me call you back, this crazy boy Low wanna use the phone. OK, I'll tell him," she hung up and gave him the message from Brenda. "Brenda said she miss you too."

Low screwed his face up at her like she smelt like dodo. "Fuck that bitch!" He took the phone and started dialing.

"Excuse me then," Cathy retorted, blowing air smacking.

Low called Roe and Nut's crib. "Who this?" Roe answered.

"That nigga who gone fuck yo ass up when I see ya," said Low making his voice different.

"Muthafucka I ain't hard to find! Just bring it when ya see me!"

Low busted out laughing. "All Low, stop playing. Where you at?"

"Nigga come scoop me, I'm in the Vic."

"We on our way." Roe hung up and told Pep and Nut that Low was out, and they hopped in Pep's Lac to go get him. Low was outside when they drove up. They jumped out and hugged him like he been gone for years. They got in Pep's ride minutes later and drove off.

They was high as hell off V's, weed, and drinking when Pep pulled into the car wash on Oak Street to wash his ride. Low looked down the row of cars people were washing and saw the girl that was over Sal's house that day he first went there with him, his daughter Wanda he recalled. She was washing a clean ass red Iroc-Z-28 with some other girl. She had on short jean shorts bending over and her light brown paper bag color ass cheeks were hanging out. Low boned up right on the spot. This hoe bad as fuck, he thought to himself. Pep turned around to see what had his nigga's mouth open.

"Nigga let's go holla," Pep told him.

"That's Sal's daughter," Low told him.

"Which one?" Asked Pep, getting on his toes trying to get a better look being he was short.

"The one bending over with the jean shorts on, "Low was licking his lips.

"Damn, she got a fat ass!" said Pep. Low started walking over there and Pep trailed behind him.

Low walked right up on her and stood behind her staring at her ass as she cleaned the rims. She turned around putting her hands on her hips.

"Excuse me, is there.... You Low?" she asked. They stared at each other for a second, so Pep went to holla at her girl. "I'm sorry about your Mom."

"Yeah, sorry bout your Dad." Low looked away cause he heard a car.

"I've been meaning to come talk to you, but my cousin Morgan told me you were locked up."

"Yeah, I was. I know him. What you want to holla bout?"

"Just some things. I'll tell you what, let me give you my number and you call me later today so we can talk, ok?"

"Alright."

She got in the front seat of the car and wrote her number down. Low was staring at the print of her pussy that was poking out when she sat down. "Here, make sho you call me," she handed Low the number and got out the car. While they stood there talking, Pep was leaning on her car getting her girls hook.

Nut came over and said, "What's crackin with y'all fine honeys? Y'all lookin fo a killa to tame ya?" The grease he had in his hair had his waves shining as the sun beamed on him. Nut wasn't no bad looking young nigga by far. The girls saw the gat tucked in his waist and his demeanor let them know he was gooned out.

"Nah killer, I'm cool," Wanda said, making Low laugh.

"Well where yo girls at? They can't pass this up here," Nut said pointing at himself, making them all crack up.

Nut passed a fat joint to Wanda. "I'm cool killa," she told him, so he passed it to her girl.

She took a hit and started coughing. "Damn, what is this shit?"

"That's Dro," Pep told her.

Roe walked over seeing they were into these honeys. "Damn, what's going on over here? Can a nigga get on?" he said looking at Wanda.

"Yeah, with that joint," she shot at him all fly. They all busted out laughing.

"Ok baby, I see you fly. I like that."

Low introduced them and told them she was Sal's daughter. They all had a different outlook on her then. They all talked for a few more minutes, then pulled out.

"Man, that hoe Wanda a dime piece cuz, straight up," Roe commented.

"Yeah I dig her man, she got a fat ole ass too," Nut added. "Her girl Linda tight too wit them big ass titties," They all laughed. "I'll fuck the shit outta her."

They drove to the Westlake projects and stood on the block sipping beer and Boones Farm while Roe and Nut served. That Benz Pep had saw behind that house where Smoke and Nate was at came cruising down the street at a snail's paste. It was a 90's big body, all chromed out with the tinted windows. "That's Nate," Roe said, and waved him down.

The Benz halted, and the windows in the back came down. "What's up young playa's?" Nate spoke, leaning deep to the left in the back seat. Only Roe could see him because he was up on the back window.

"Good lookin out on that too. This Lowdown here," Roe told him, talking about how he put the plan together for them to free Low by croaking Rally last night. Roe was motioning to Low to come over.

Nate told whoever was driving to pull into the parking lot. When it stopped, two girls got out the front seat and glanced around. They were some bad looking muthafucka's, Low and Pep saw. After they gave Nate a head nod saying it was cool, he stepped out the car.

"So this Low, huh?" he said putting his hand out to shake Low's. Diamonds were gleaming on every finger. "Excuse my clothing, we just got back from a wedding."

Pep and them told Low how Nate had instructed them on the problem they had.

"Good lookin out," Low told him. Low could tell he was nothing like his partner Smoke.

"That wasn't nothing," he replied. "Roe an Nut, y'all already know my girls. Low and Pep, this Jess and Rena." Pep and Low said what's up to them.

"Y'all some cute little thugs," Jess told'em.

Nate sat on his Benz chopping it up with Low, while the others stood around fucking with girls. Low told Nate he would be needing some work since his connect got killed.

"Yeah, I heard," Nate said. "I'll tell you what, I'ma have you fuck with me personally since you fuckin with a whole one, and I feel you tight. I will have whatever you need dropped off to you whenever you need it. Cool little player?"

"Now that's love. Can I come holla at cha tomorrow?" Low asked ready to get on his grind full fledge.

"No doubt. Better yet, let's take a ride right now."

Low told the crew he would be back later, and got into the back seat of Nate's ride with him. When the girl's got in the front seat, they both laid gold pearl handle 25 automatics on the seats next to them. Nate saw Low looking. "You strapped?" Nate wanted to know.

"Nah, but they is," Low remarked.

"They got licenses for theirs," Nate replied. They drove off. "Put some funk on." Rena turned the Funkadelic's on. "Let's hit the Lounge," he told the girls, talking about a bar he owned on South side. "Yeah Lowdown, I like yo grind an heart. You got the skills to get paid out here, so I'm gonna let you in on some major shit you must know out this bitch off rip. Don't trust shit! Not a fuckin soul playa. Stack your paper and be about yo biz out this bitch! Never let no one you don't got some kind of trust for know where you lay your head at, and where you stash big figures and dope at. I know some nigga's who rob and kill for pennies. Invest your money wisely so you can always have something to fall back on...." Nate talked the whole time, giving Low a lot of game and science to surviving in this hustle. Low was feeling the inspiration he was giving him too. They pulled up to a club. "This my little bar here."

"Oh yeah." Low was seeing what dope money could get him.

"Come'on," he said, after the girls checked around and stood by his car door with their hands on their gats.

They went to the door. When they got inside Nate walked to the front and was greeted by all kinds of people like he was a star. They sat down and chilled for a few. Low had never been in a bar and Nate ordered them some Gin and orange juice. Low was feeling good as he watched the grown women shake their moneymakers. Then they left there and Nate showed him a music store he owned as well, on the North side.

He told Low he owned a few other things and he could too. Low was seeing the big picture. "You can get the bird for eighteen."

"That's love," said Low.

It was getting late, so Low told him he could drop him back off in the Lake. When Low got to Nut and Roe's spot, they were on the porch kicking it with about six dudes and eight girls.

Sandy bum rushed Low and hugged him, "Oohh baby I'm glad your out," she pouted, kissing him all over his face. Low palmed her fat ole booty and stuck his tongue in her mouth, tasting Old English beer. Low greeted everybody and sat down.

Pep pulled him to the side. "Yo homie, ain't you going to hit Wanda up?"

"Oh yeah, let me go call her." Low got up and went in the crib and rang her phone. She answered on the second ring.

"Hello."

"Can I talk to Wanda?"

"Boy this me," Wanda said, knowing his voice that quick. She had been thinking about him all day. Plus she needed him for a reason.

"What's up?" Low asked, hearing the excitement in her voice.

"Can you come over? I'm still at the house in Campbell," she was happy she had bumped into him today. She knew her father liked and trusted him because he had bought him to their home. He had told her that his little ass was getting money quickly for his age. Plus, she heard he was dangerous and had murdered the guys that had murdered his Mom and her Dad. When she first saw him she thought he was cute anyway. Right now she needed to talk to him to see if she could trust him.

"I'll be there in like twenty minutes," Low told her, and hung up. She sounded kinda anxious, he thought. He told Pep and them the deal, and got Pep's Lac to go holla at her. He stopped at the corner store on the way and got a quart of colt 45 beer. He pulled into her driveway and got out. He heard dogs barking. It must be them Dobermans he remembered. As he came up the walkway to the door he saw someone peak out the big front window. Before he could knock Wanda opened the door for him.

Damn! Lee said to himself when he saw her in them short ass cotton shorts, big fluffy white house shoes, hair pinned up, lips glossed and shining, and tight t-shirt that was cut up and showing off her flat tummy.

"Come on in Lowdown," she told him in a sweet voice.

"Where them dogs at?" Low asked, glancing around the front room.

"Oh, I put them in the basement, it's cool," she told him laughing. She turned on the TV and Low's favorite movie was on. And he got a good look at her ass when she cut the TV on. Nigga's you know we gone look. And women, you know it too. Don't play like you don't do it unintentionally.

"All shit, Juice on. That's my shit," Low said.

"Mine too. You want something to eat?"

"Hell yeah, girl," Low replied dropping down on the couch like it was his crib and picking up the remote turning the volume up.

"I got some chicken I fried, you want some of that?" she asked.

"If you can cook...hell yeah. I'm hungry as hell."

"Funny," she turned around to go to the kitchen and Low checked her ass out good this time, seeing it jiggle. This hoe got some class and ass, umm, he thought. Nails done, feet done, and hair hooked up. He leaned back, sipping the colt 45 beer he bought in with him.

She came back with two plates that had chicken and French fries on them. "I heated it all up," she said sitting the food down on the coffee table in front of him. "Here's a glass for yo beer."

Low took the glass and put it on the table and said, "I drink my shit out the bottle."

"Okay, thug nigga," Wanda said smiling at him. She sat down next to Low as he grabbed his plate. "Low, I don't know if you did it, but if so, thank you fo taking care of them busters that murdered my Dad an your Mom." He just nodded his head chewing on his food. "So how is business?"

"It's alright. Who's staying here wit you?"

"I stay by myself, why?"

"How old are you?"

"Eighteen and grown."

"My bad baby girl. This chicken rubbery."

"Oh no you didn't," she said looking at him with her face all twisted up.

Low smacked on the chicken showing no emotions on his face, then cracked a smile. "Nah, just playin... This shit slamming."

"You got jokes, huh? I was about to say." They talked during the movie and Low found himself liking her. Their parents had gotten killed together, so there was a strong bond between them already.

"Low, I feel I can trust you, and I don't trust many. My father's old friends and his connect keep stressing me about some dope they say my father had just got." Low glanced at her right quick. "Well, between me and you, I got it and I want to sell it to you wholesale. My old boy always showed me where he kept his stuff at, and what was what. I ain't giving them fuckers shit my father put in work and died for. Fuck them."

Low saw the serious look on her face and the way she said it, and felt her. "Don't worry. I got you baby girl." He wouldn't of gave nobody shit either that his Mom had left, fuck that! Thought Low.

"So I'm your baby girl now?" She asked, sucking meat off a chicken bone, making Low's dick stretch.

"That's on you," he replied. She put her plate down and scooted closer to him.

"I was talking to somebody," she told him, not even thinking about him at the moment.

"Well it's over fo him."

"Oh yeah."

"No doubt baby girl."

Wanda leaned in. "Make me know it," she purred. Low kissed her and her mouth was hot and soft. She reached down grabbing his dick that was boned up. She stood up and told Low to come out his clothes after feeling his pipe. They started taking their clothes off together.

She had some pretty light brown skin and little hair around her pussy, with firm grapefruit sized tits. Low started sucking her tits making her moan out as they stood up, and she reached for his dick and stroked it, rubbing pre-cum all over the head.

"Oohh baby, you got a fat dick," she told him moaning. She sat on the couch and pulled his dick towards her mouth. When it went in Low almost busted from the heat of her mouth and the way her tongue slid across his shit. He couldn't believe this badass hoe was sucking his shit and was about to put him down with some money.

He looked down and sighed out seeing her pretty eyes gazing up at him with lust in them while his dick slid in and out of her tight pretty ass mouth. He couldn't help it, he nutted.

"Gaawwdd damn! Low groaned, blowing her wig back.

She took him out her mouth cause Low's cum was drowning her, and let him cum all over her chest. "Oohh... yeah, cum all over me baby," she purred as she jacked his dick on her. She drained him and Low had to sit down.

"Let's go take a shower," she told him, getting up. When she walked away, Low got hard again that quick looking at her fat booty jiggle. They got in the shower and Low started fucking her from behind. "Oh my...god...you...you far in me...shit!" she cried out as he beat the pussy up and her ass vibrated every time he slammed into her.

"I'm...cum...cumming! Fuck!" Her pussy was so tight it was sucking his dick in every time he pulled out. He fucked her there and in the bed that night.

As they laid there all sweaty in bed, she gazed at him and said, "Baby you did it to me so good. I ain't never came like that before." Low didn't trust shit after his Mom got killed, but he liked Wanda a lot for some reason other then their parents being together and dying together.

"So who this connect that keep pulling up on you?" he asked sitting up in bed.

"Some crazy ass Jamaicans, named Waun and Ramon or something?"

"You know where they stay at?"

"Yeah, my pops took me over there one time before."

"Alright, show me tomorrow. Now tell me what you got and want back from this shit you got?"

"I got three birds and I want back what my father charged, but since we tight and all...," she said giggling grabbing his wood gazing down at it and him. "And I'm trying to get rid of the stuff. You can give me back forty thousand for all three of them."

Low added it real quickly in his head. "Bet, you got a deal," she said putting her hand out to shake his. "I'd rather you shake this snake," he told her. She punched him and they wrestled in the bed. He fell asleep next to her in bed and was soon woken up by a nightmare. He was waking up now three or four times a night now. The last time he woke up, he was thinking about all the money he would have after he sold all this product. I'll be a young hood rich little muthafucka, he thought. I'll front Pep one for twenty thousand, and make like thirty thousand apiece...he fell back to sleep thinking.

Chapter 9

Wasn't nothing like knocking a bad chick, getting the gushie, and her throwing you some weight. Makes your swagger climb another notch...

The next day, Low woke with a piss hard on. He looked over at Wanda as she slept on her back, and his dick got harder as his eyes trailed down her back all the way down to her feet. He rolled out of bed to go take a piss and she woke up.

"Where you going baby?" She asked, then saw his dick sticking straight as he stood up ass naked. She thought his light-skinned complexion gave his dick the ripe Banana look. And she loved Banana's.

"To use the bathroom," Low answered dick swinging, and having no shame.

"You need some help with that?" She asked sweetly, batting her eyes gazing at his joint.

"Yeah," Low said over his shoulder going to the bathroom. He wanted to let her handle it right now, but didn't want to take a chance on when he nutted, he would piss too, because he had to piss bad.

She got out the bed butt naked and went in there with him. She turned on the shower as he stood over the pisser. Low was trying to piss when she got behind him and reached around and removed his hand from holding his hard dick down to piss, and wrapped hers around it and aimed it for the toilet.

"Girl you crazy," Low mumbled, trying to concentrate.

"Oh my gawd, your dick is so hard. Uumm..." Wanda wished it was in her twat right now. She felt the warm piss come up through his dick and out.

Her hands felt damn good wrapped around this dick, Low was thinking as he peed. She shook it for him to make sure it was all out.

"You a pro at this, you do it all the time?"

"Hell nah! Don't play me boy," Wanda told him, and bit his ear.

"Watch it girl."

Low got in the shower and Wanda sat on the toilet. Low started laughing at her.

"What you laughing at?" she asked.

"You pissing."

"Ain't no shyness with me, you seen it all already now." They took a shower and fucked, got dressed and went downstairs to the kitchen to get something to eat. "Do you want me to have the stuff brought over here now?" Wanda asked, as they sat eating. "You know I don't keep shit where I lay my head, my pops taught me that."

"Nah, I can't roll out with it in that flashy car. Can you get it brought to me in the Vic's? Better yet, call whoever you was gone have bring it and they can follow me back to the Vic's."

She got on the horn (phone) and called Linda. "Hey girl, what's up? Yeah I know it's early, but check this, I need you to bring my baby here okay? Alright, later girl." They chilled for a few talking and playing with each other.

Linda drove up and came in. "Hey girlfriend, hi Lowdown." They all spoke back to her.

"We going to follow Low to the Vic's, so we can give him the stuff there," Wanda told her, picking her purse up off the table.

"Let's roll," Low said.

Linda and Wanda got in Linda's Sunbird and followed Low to the Victory. When they got there Moose and the crew was outside kicking it and getting money on the block. Wanda and Linda stayed in the car when they pulled in front of Low's aunt's crib and parked. Low's little bad brother Kevin ran over to him as he got out the car and followed him.

"What's up brother, I see you got some honeys following you, huh? I'll take one of them for you," Kevin said.

Low smiled at him. Low bent down at the door where Wanda was sitting. "This my lil brother Kev, baby."

"Hi cutie," Wanda said, winking at him.

"What's up with yo girl? She fine," said Kevin.

"You fine to, and handsome," Linda said.

"What's up then? Step out the car," Kevin replied. They busted out laughing.

Wanda handed Low a grocery bag and he told her he would call her later. He went straight to the crib with the bag, and took it out.

"Yeah, this three things," he said to himself. He put two up and tucked one up under his shirt, and headed over to Bo's girl house to use the triple beam scale, and to break it down. He told Moose and them to come with him when he saw them outside. Cathy was on the phone as always, when they entered her spot.

"Yo boys just came over. Low and them," Cathy told Bo.

"Ah, we gon' use the back right quick, alright?" Low told her.

"Mm huh, go head. Bo want you," she said handing him the phone.

"What's up nigga? You cool? I'm gonna drop you off a "G" right now with Cathy," Low told Bo.

"Good lookin out. I'm glad you out. Stay out there Low, this shit lame as fuck! I'll be out in like eight months, so this ain't shit."

"If you need anything just let me know."

"Alright, good lookin out."

"No doubt."

"Much love," said Bo.

"Much Love," Low responded back, then gave the phone back to Cathy. They all spoke to Bo and went into the backroom. "Shut the door," Low told them, knowing how nosey an much Cathy ran her gums.

Rat locked the door. Low took out the scale out the closet along with a big plate and placed them on the dresser. He lifted his t-shirt up and pulled out the kilo. Everybody was looking like "What the fuck is that?" Low put it on the plate and popped the string around it as all eyes looked on. The aroma from the kilo of cocaine hit their senses.

"Damn nigga, it's like that?" Moose asked with eyes big as boiled eggs.

"That's a fuckin key there!" said Jay in awe. Rat and Alvin gazed at the fish scale key of dope like it was a winning lotto ticket.

"Man I need thirty thou (thousand) from this one. I want to give this to y'all right down the middle. Y'all can cut it and get more outta it too," Low told them, looking into all their faces. "So what's up?" He asked. He wanted everybody to eat. "Y'all want this work fo thirty or what?"

"Hell yeah!" Moose said, jumping on it. "Let me see how much I can cut it with first." He got some B-12 out the drawer and they weighed up an ounce, then a half ounce of B-12, and took it to the kitchen to cook up. It came back to an ounce and a half.

"Shit," Rat said. "Put it in the microwave and we might get two back."

"We'll take it, right?" Moose said, looking at everybody else to see if they agreed. Everybody confirmed. Rat was happy as hell. Ain't none of them ever had that much before.

Low left and called Nate. Nate told him to meet him at his Music store on the North side around two o'clock. Tina came over and Low told her to hold the bag of dope for him. She took it and asked him when he was going to spend some time with her? He told her he had shit to do, but he would be back later tonight. They kissed and he left heading for Westlake. Low was on a paper chase and didn't have time for quality spending, like ever hustler trying to build his grip up.

Nate had talked to his connect and found out it wouldn't be any dope for weeks. He had just gave Smoke his last brick too. He had another connect in Cali, but didn't feel like fucking with that crazy nigga and having to go through setting up the trip to get the product here. So he said to himself that he would just chill for three weeks until his connect got right.

Low told Pep he had a bird for him and he went crazy. "Nigga's its on now!" Pep shouted at Nut and Roe.

"Damn that hoe had three of them things!" Nut said. "You musta beat the guts up killa fo real to get that."

"I laid pipe on her dawg. Straight plumbing!" Low told them, making them crack up.

"Hoe better be glad I didn't get to her then, bitch woulda signed her car and house over too," Nut cracked, grabbing his joint. They all laughed.

"Nigga you'll fall in after me," Low told him. They sat there joking for a while kicking it.

Low and Pep went over Tina's house to get one of them birds for Pep. She was in her room talking to Kelly when they walked in.

"Why the fuck you ain't call me?" Kelly jumped up in Pep's face with attitude asking.

"Girl you better get out my face, acting all crazy," Pep told her pushing her in the chest on the bed. Kelly hopped up about to swing on him, but Tina broke it up.

"Ah hell nah!" Tina yelled getting between them. "Not in my fuckin house y'all don't! Get yo boy!" She told Low.

"Chill man," Low told Pep. Pep sat down shaking his head.

"School starts in two weeks," Tina told Low.

"Yeah, I know. Let's go get som'em to eat," Low told them.

They went through the drive thru at Burger King and parked in the lot across from the Lincoln knolls Plaza on the East side. Some dudes in two clean ass short body nine eight's pulled up on side of them, talking loud and drinking.

"Who the fuck is these nigga's?" Pep said.

"That's them cats from New York. They mess with my girl," Kelly said. Pep turned his sounds up and the New York cats glanced over. Two of them got out of the car and came over.

"What's up?" Pep asked turning his sounds down.

"Yo son, yo shit knocking kid. My name Fresh and this Manny." He introduced himself and his rappie.

Pep nodded his head and said, "what up?" While Low gripped his burner.

"Where you get your sounds hooked up at?" Manny asked. Pep told him and drove off. "We gots to get them sounds kid," Manny said.

"I hear ya B," Fresh replied, watching them drive off.

Chapter 10

Just because I took you away from yours, don't mean I'll take from mines...

After Low dropped everybody off, he meet with Nate. When he got there, dude working the cash register told him where to go. "Go through that door right there, he waiting on you already."

Low walked into the office and Nate was at a pine wood desk sitting behind it in a leather chair watching the security cameras.

"Come on in and shut the door," Nate told him without looking up his way. "So how you doing?"

Low told him the deal and how he came up on the three bricks.

"You got hustlers luck. So what you gonna do with the ends you making?" Nate wanted to know, seeing where his mind was.

"I wanna invest in some shit, but first I want to move my lil brothers outta the projects and buy them a house."

Nate looked at him, liking his idea and way of thinking. "That is a good idea. Let's go look at some houses right now. I ain't doing nothing," said Nate. "But you got to put it in your name somehow. You don't want the Feds on yo ass. You said you got a bank account, right?"

Low nodded yeah, remembering what his Moms said about the Feds.

"Well, you can make it like you paying payments on it. I know this cool real estate agent dude. Let me call him for you." Nate got on the phone with him and set it up. "Alright, he gonna meet us at this house he got in Campbell right now for sale."

Lowdown liked the way Nate got right to business with ease. He jumped to the point and made shit pop. On the way there, Nate told him he would be the first young nigga he knew at fifteen years old with a nice crib he owned himself. When they got there Low couldn't believe how huge the house was. It was brick red, with a two-car garage and a pool in the back. "How much?" Low asked before going to even look at the other homes.

"Cause you with Nate, you can get it for forty-seven thousand," the white man told him.

"Alright, let me go look at it some more," Low replied. It had four bedrooms and a big attic that Low could make his room cause it was big as 'hell he thought. But when they got to the guesthouse over the garage, he chose that instead. Low liked that spot, and tried to buy it right then.

Him and Nate talked to the white man for a few minutes to work out the sale. "It would probably be best if you put your aunts name on the paper work too," the agent said.

"That would be cool. I'll bring you twenty two thousand later on today," Low told him. The white man grinned and shook his hand, making the deal.

"I got some other houses too, so if y'all want to go see them you can?" he told them. They went and checked out the others, and decided the first one in Campbell was the best one. His family would be out the way and his brothers could grow up in a nice home and go to a nice school. His mother would be proud. Now I gotta get all new furniture, he was thinking.

"You made a good choice. I dig that," Nate told him in the car. "Now don't take nobody out there. Keep it private. Feel me?"

"I feel ya."

Nate dropped Low off back at his music shop to get the fiends car he was using. Low drove back to the Vic's to get the money and go meet the real estate agent at his office. Low handed the real estate man the money. He counted it then showed Low where to sign the papers, then handed him the keys to the house. Low felt so good, he wanted to yell. He did something he told his mother he was going to do, for the family.

"I need your aunt to sign these papers too."

"Meet me at the house tonight, at seven. She'll be there." His aunt would be surprised as fuck, Low thought smiling. She stayed out there almost all her life, now it was time for a change. He went to get his family and told them it was a surprise for them. He drove up the new house driveway and got out, "Come'on," he told them.

"Boy who house is this?" His aunt Paula asked, looking at the freshly cut grass and flowers planted all over.

"Just come on," Low said, walking in using the key he had, and saw it was empty, "it's ours!" Low told them. They all started jumping and hugging him, then ran around the house looking around. "I'ma give you the money for everything, so throw that other stuff away. We don't need no roaches coming with us," Low laughed.

"I know that's right!" Paula stated, tears in her eyes. She was full of joy. She knew her sister would be happy. The real estate agent walked in. "Here come the cops," Paula said.

"Naw, he the man we bought the house from, you gotta sign the papers with me for the house," Low explained.

"Oh, I'm sorry," Paula said nervously, not use to white men. She signed the papers and they stayed an hour looking around. Wasn't another house within a 100 feet.

"I'ma give you ten thousand tomorrow to get started on getting the new stuff for the house, plus they got to enroll in school here," Low told his aunt. His aunt hugged him real tight.

"You did good baby," she cried on his shoulder. "Your mother would be happy and proud of you."

"Thanks. Let's go."

"When they got back to the Vic's, Moose and them was on the block. There were more cars than Low had ever seen before out there pulling up to get dope. Low walked over to his homeboys.

"Damn, it's jumping out here, what's going on?" Low asked, as he glanced around at all the traffic flowing in and out. They were killin'em.

"Man it's a drought out this muthafucka, and we the only ones that got work. Nigga's coming from all sides of town," Rat told him as he served a old dude an ounce of crack. "They want ounces and we slanging them for twelve hundred, nothing else but ounces nigga! We done got rid of twenty of them thangs already. We'll have yo paper later on."

"We got an extra half and some grams off of each ounce too, so we tight. We got that powder too, cut it up, and it's going like hot butter pancakes," Moose said giving Low some dap.

A week later, Low had sold his bird and the rest of the guys had got rid of the brick he had fronted them. Pep still had some and was killing them out there with it. Low had all Wanda's ends and was about to go give it to her when Roe and Nut drove up all hype.

"Yo where Pep at?" Nut hollered out the car window looking all crazy.

"He down the street clockin his shit," Low answered, seeing Roe had a frown on his face too.

"Fuck that, let's roll. We got beef!" Muttered Nut.

"Let me go get him and my heat!" Low said.

"Fuck that, just grab yo shit!" Roe told him. Low ran to grab his burner. On his way back Pep appeared seeing him clutching a 45 in his hand as he ran to the car.

"Ah, what's up?" Pep asked, as Low jumped in the back seat.

"These hoe ass nigga's up pipe on us and shot up Roe's car on the South side at this party." Pep got in the back seat. Nut drove off and Roe handed them two Tec-Nine's.

"These busters don't know who they fuckin with," Roe gritted.

"Slow down nigga, before you get us pulled over before I get a chance to wet these lames."

When they got to the South side on the street the party was on, Nut cruised at a snail's pace. It was still packed out with nigga's and honeys. The music in the car was down low playing Ghetto Boys. "That's them bitches!" Nut uttered.

Low saw Cal with his crew Nut was talking about, and gripped his gat putting one in the chamber. He wanted Cal bad. Nut pulled up on the side on them and Roe started blasting on them. Low hopped out the car shooting. Some people dropped from being hit, and others ran. Cal had ran and Low had ran after him being that his aim was directed only at Cal from jump. Roe and them looked at Low wondering what the fuck he jump out the car for, shooting and running after a nigga. Roe had to pull off cause they were getting shot at from all over.

They turned the corner and saw Low running from the back of a house chasing Cal. He jumped a fence right behind Cal, Low's heart was thumping and he got a rush he never felt before. He was like a wild animal stalking his prey. Cal tripped and hit his head on a car bumper, and got up to run when Low opened fire and caught him in the leg making him fall. The 45 blew a hole as big as an apple in his thigh making him roll around on the ground in agony. He got up and tried to stand holding onto the car for support so he could run, but Low ran up on him and hit him over the head with the butt of the gun dropping him.

"Ooowwweeee!" he screamed out, blood   leaking from his head now to.

"Bitch you know who this is!?" Low yelled, as he lifted his mask up real quick and put it back down. Low wanted him to see and know who had his life in his hands now, he had Low's before, now shit then changed deeply and he wasn't going to let him get away.

"Ah man, I don't got no beef with you!" Cal cried. "Shit man!"

Someone came out the back door from the house who's yard they were in an the driveway. "Hey, get the fuck outta here!" The black man hollered at them. Low turned around and shot at him, making him duck and fly back in the house slamming the door.

"This for Prince and that lil girl you killed bitch!" Low said shooting Cal two times in the head and three times in the heart, then ran, leaving him to a close casket.

Roe and them didn't see Low nowhere, and heard the cops coming so they had to bounce. "Where the fuck he at!?" Pep shouted mad as fuck.

Low made it six blocks up the street called Ravenwood, where his uncle Pete stayed. He ran through the neighbor's back yard, jumped his uncle back yard fence and ran to the porch laying down as a search light from the police cruiser shined all around the back yard. Dogs were barking like they were trying to dry snitch. He was breathing hard as hell from dipping and dodging the poe-poe . He took the mask off and put it in his pocket, then tucked the gun in his waistband, because he was still clutching it in his hand. He crawled to the back door and tried to open it but it was locked, so he knocked.

"Who is it?" His uncle Pete yelled.

"Lenny!" He answered, glancing around.

The door opened. "Boy, why you didn't you use the front door?"

Low rushed in. "Took a short cut Uncle Pete."

Pete had heard the police outside and on his scanner. He shut his door and looked at his sister's son.

"You need a ride somewhere?" He didn't see no car when he looked outside. Pete looked just like his sister, Low's mother. He was just taller. He was 35 years old and had been working at General Motors since he was 18 years.

"Nah Unk, I'm cool. I'ma call this girl to come get me." Low went to the fridge and took out a Pepsi pop. His family always had Pepsi pops around. He didn't like them but his mouth was dry as cotton and wasn't nothing else he saw in the fridge.

"Ok, well let me know if you do," he told him, looking at him knowing something was up. "I heard about the house you got your brothers and aunt too. You be careful out here. I'm going to go look at it tomorrow since Paula bragging.' You did a good thing, I'll be upstairs, got a lil chick up there," he told Low walking up the steps.

Low got on the phone and called Pep's pager. Then called Wanda and told her to come pick him up.

Pep called right back and Low answered. "Man where the fuck you at?" Pep asked, "This Low here," he told Nut and Roe.

"I'm cool. I'll holla at y'all later. Wanda bout to come scoop me up."

"Alright crazy ass nigga, later," Pep said hanging up.

Wanda came and Low had her take him to go get her 40 G's he had put up over his aunts crib. He made her park around the corner because he had saw Tina and Kelly outside when they drove by. He handed her the loot and she smiled a cover girl smile.

"Thank you boo," Wanda sweetly said.

They went back to her house and fucked hard and long that night. Killing and getting money seemed to stimulate Low and give him more of a drive. It even made him sexually more passionate. All his senses were more in tuned and clearer.

Chapter 11
The more deeper I get, the more pussy and murder I get…

The next day when she dropped Low off in the Vic's, Tina saw them kissing before he got out the car. She was so hurt, that she ran back home and cried in her room for an hour. Low was her first love, and first ever to pop her cherry. Low was counting money when his aunt yelled up the stairs and told him Tina was there. He put his ends up and came down stairs.

"Hey, what's up baby?" Low said.

She just looked at him.

Low could tell she had been crying and something wasn't right. He took her outside and asked, "What? Somebody been fuckin wit you or something?"

Tears came out her eyes. "I saw you kissing…that…girl," she sniffed.

"Oh, that's it? That shit wasn't nothing," Low frowned at her saying.

"Oh, it wasn't nothing, huh Lee? Well it's something to me," she spat angry he was acting like it wasn't nothing.

"Look, I ain't trying to hear that shit!" Low told her and went back inside upstairs.

Tina stomped her feet hurt and salty. She couldn't believe he just acted like it wasn't shit. She was in love with him, and it felt like he just shitted on her.

Later on Low was riding around with Roe when Wanda paged him. They stopped in front of Nate's music store and he used the pay phone outside to call her back. She was upset and scared, talking so fast he couldn't understand her.

"Slow down," Low told her, holding the phone away from his ear she was so loud.

"Them fuckin Jamaicans pulled a gun on me and told me I'd better have their shit in a week or their going to blow my head off!" She cried.

"Where did you see them at?" Low asked. "They came over my house!"

"Alright, I'll be over there in a sec," Low told her. He told Roe the deal.

"I'ma roll wit you man, but first let's go get some CD's. They got some new shit out nigga." When they walked in they saw Nate with his two girls putting CD's and tapes on the rack. "What's up y'all?" They said.

"Ain't shit little players, just working my nine to five life like everybody else," he said laughing. Low told him he needed to talk to him right quick. "Let's go in the back. Put these last CD's up," Nate told the girls. Roe went with them to his office. "What's the deal?" Nate asked. Low told him what was going on. "Ah, I see. That's where you got that work from huh? Yeah I know them punk ass, sucka ass lames. I tell you what, if you with it. This what we can do...." Nate began to run the blueprint down to them.

Low drove up in Wanda's driveway, got out the car and went in the house. "Low I'm glad you here," she told him looking sad.

"Listen, this what I want you to do alright..." Low ran it down to her.

"Anything you say baby," she replied after he explained to her what he wanted her to do.

It was 10 PM and Wanda was inside Jitso's bar on the East side. She had called the Jamaicans and told them she didn't want to be alone with them cause she was scared, so meet her at Jitso's. It was Friday night so the bar was packed. To be a little bar it stayed packed and full of honeys, rats, and vets. Nigga's loved it there cause they knew they had their selection of either one. Mostly East side cats frequented there. Low, Roe, and Nate sat in a stolen Chevy Blazer with dark glasses on even though the windows were tinted. They had been waiting for 40 minutes.

"I wish these hoes would come on," Roe stated, eye balling a light-skinned chick shake her ass as she walked into the bar. "Uumm... I'll eat that."

"There they go," Nate said. They were in a clean ass Lincoln Mark 8. They put their masks on and slid out the car ducking behind the cars. There were people out, but they got out their way and minded their own business.

Ramon and Waun had just got out the car and started walking towards the bar door, when all of a sudden Low and them jumped up with guns and a pistol grip pump to their faces. "Lay the fuck down!" They demanded. The Jamaicans hit the ground as people scattered like roaches. Nate and Low patted them down taking their guns.

"Now put yo hands behind yo back," Nate told them. They tied then up real quick with duct tape, snatched them up, and threw they asses in the back of the Blazer and peeled off.

"What the fuck you want? What the fuck you blood clots want?" the Jamaicans kept yelling in their accent.

"Shut the fuck up!" Nate told them. Ramon said something else so Nate took out a big ass Bowie knife and stuck him in the leg making him holler out. "Where you got that shit at!" Nate yelled, knife dripping with blood.

"We got nothing! Nothing!" Waun hollered.

Nate took one of Waun's shoes off and held his ankle, then cut his baby toe off. It looked like one of them pork reins out of the bag. Waun was screaming out crying now.

"Now bitch, you think I'm playin!? Yo life next muthafucka!" Nate yelled.

"All the stuff at the house!" Waun screamed. "At house!"

"What street bitch?" asked Nate, with the knife to his throat.

"Oak street!"

"Who at the house?" Nate asked choking him.

"Just my girl," Waun coughed.

"Hit Oak Street," Nate told Low, who was driving. When they got to Oak Street, Nate had him point out which house. "Pull in the driveway. Where yo house key at bitch?" He told Nate in his pocket. Nate took them out. "Which one bitch, I ain't whodini?" Alright come on, grab him too," Nate told Low and Roe, talking bout Roman.

They went in through the back door dragging Waun bleeding ass and Roman. They heard a TV on in the front room, "Is that you Waun?" some girl asked. They entered the room where she was and Roe shoved the pistol grip pump in her face. "Oh my god!" she screamed.

"Shut yo fuckin mouth before I blow it off!" Roe grunted.

"Lay down! All of y'all!" Nate told them. "Now where the shit at?"

"In the attic, in a chest box." Waun confessed. Roman was staring at him like he wanted to kill him for telling where shit was at.

"It better be," Nate threaten him. "Tie that hoe up," he nodded to Roe, never using their names. "Let's go look," he told Low. They went in the attic and found the chest with a lock on it and Nate shot it off. When they opened it, they saw money and cocaine. "Grab a bag or something." Low saw a bag with clothes in it and dumped the clothes out. They put the lick, (dope and money) in the bag and went back downstairs. "Let's roll!" Nate said, standing over Roman, then shot him in the head two times and once over the heart. Blood and brain matter had splattered all over his pants legs. The girl fainted. Low did the same to Waun and they rushed out of there.

They got back in the Blazer and drove to another car they had parked down by the freeway, then got on the freeway and got off on the North side and went to Foster street to a house Nate had there. They got out the car and Nate said, "Take them clothes off and put them in this bag," Nate told them while he was putting his in the bag. He gave them some shorts and shower shoes to put on as they stood in the garage. "Come on," he told them walking them into the back yard holding a can of gasoline. "Put yo hands out," he told Low, and poured the gasoline over his hands and his. Then he sprayed them down with the water hose.

"What was that for?" Low asked.

"To get rid of the gun powder residue because you used the gun. They got back into their regular clothes that they had Left. Nate grabbed all the clothes they had just worn and they drove down to Westlake and burned them in the dumpster, then went back to the house on Foster. "Y'all can count the ends out while I clean these guns and file this shit off of them."

They counted one hundred and twenty two- thousand in cash, and had five birds. They split it down the middle giving them forty thousand a piece, and let Nate keep the extra two grand. They split the cain up and sat back and chilled.

"Low," said Nate, "it's on you if you want to kill that hoe Wanda."

"It's cool," he told Nate.

Nate looked at him hard. "Always be sure playa, never forget that."

Around 2 AM Roe and Low left in Roe's ride. While riding in the car Low thought about what Nate mentioned. Nah, he thought, all is cool with her. He called her at Nut and Roe's crib and told her to go home. It was still a drought out so they made a killing with the dope from the lick.

Chapter 12
Being Recognized Can Change You

A week later, Low's aunt and brothers had moved into their new home. Low had fifty thousand left from the lick they did to play with. He had already paid his lawyer what he had told him he would, just to have him on retainer. He was hanging out with his crew thinking about flipping with a ride and putting it in his grandmothers name. Moose and Rat had flipped new rides alike, just different colors, 88 Mustangs.

"I'm tellin ya, we getting so much pussy now it's crazy." Moose was boasting as he held a forty ounce of Colt 45 beer, talking to Alvin, Jay, Rat, Low, lil Danny and Doe Boy. "I had a young fine hooker walk right up on me last night at Wendy's, talking bout she want me to fuck her brains out."

"What you do my nigga?" Alvin asked, juicing him up, enjoying how Moose was all hype and getting his shine on now.

"What I do? Nigga I smashed my hamburger and took that freak right around the corner and parked right there, and tore that ass up! Fuck you thought I did," They all laughed as Rat went and served a customer.

"All nigga, yo fat ass ain't hit no hoe that fine in yo car like that. You too damn fat to be fuckin a bitch in that Mustang an shit," Jay cracked.

"Nigga fuck you. And you right. All I did was set my seat back and let the hoe ride this muthafucka!" Low spit his beer out laughing.

"Ahh shit, you better be quiet. Here come yo girl Sofia," Alvin warned him seeing her and Rat's girl Pam approaching.

Moose turned around quickly. "Oh what's up boo?" The look on Moose face made everybody bust out laughing.

Sofia looked at all them laughing like they were crazy and rolled her eyes. She was dark brown, cute, with a ghetto booty and a small chest, with a short haircut that had different shades of color in it. She was rocking the new gold Moose had bought her. Her and Pam stayed out there.

"Fuck you goofy nigga's laughing at? Moose, I fixed your food and put it in the oven. Me and Pam about to go to the Mall, so I need some money," said Sofia with her hand out.

Moose didn't want to say no to her, because he knew she would make a scene. "I hope you cooked the shit right," he told her going into his pocket.

"Don't I always baby?" Sofia said sweetly, because she knew he was putting on a big daddy front.

Pam walked right up on Rat and stuck her hands in his pocket. Pam was light skinned with a fat ass and big titties, and looked like a young Pattie Labelle.

"Girl get yo hands out my pocket. Fuck wrong with you?" Rat asked Pam, but didn't remove her hand because she was playing pocket pool with his joint.

"I need some money too," Pam moaned.

"Take some out my pocket," Rat told her, loving how she was massaging his balls.

Sofia and Pam left, and they started clowning Rat and Moose.

"Man I gotta get me a ride before school start," Low told them.

"Let's hit the car lot's then nigga!" Pep said.

"Hell yeah!" everybody said. So they all jumped in Rat and Moose's car and left, leaving lil Danny and Doe Boy to serve.

Low saw some raw rides at the second car lot they was at, but didn't want to spend that much cake. He was about to flip a newer 5.0. Mustang on Moose and Rat ass but decided not to.

"I want something different than all these rides we see in the hood all the time," Low told'em as they checked out cars.

"Shit nigga, what you want a spaceship?" Pep joked.

"Fuck it, I'ma get a Benz or something," Low said. Then he saw a Midnight black, drop top Corvette gleaming.

"Damn This bitch hurtin'em out here," Rat said checking the Corvette out.

"Let's go see what they want for it," Low told them.

The white sales man didn't believe this young kid really had the money to buy the Vette, and just wanted to joy ride in it or steal it, until Low killed them thoughts by pulling out knots of money with rubber bands around them and dumped it on his desk. Low made the deal under the table with him, and called his uncle to tell him the deal. His uncle Pete came up there and put his name on the title, and Low drove off the lot with his nigga's following him to the sound system shop. He wanted four twelve inch woofers put in, but it would be tight, so he got two instead, and two ten inch ones put in the doors, with the ten disc CD changer. Then he took it to the paint shop and left it there to get a gold metal flake paint job, trimmed in gold, with Lowdown at the bottom of the gold siding on both sides, and gold Dayton's. He paid them extra to hurry his shit up and make it top priority. His ride would be ready by the time school started they told him.

Low felt so good about buying his first ride, that when they got back to the Victory he had Pep take him to his mother's grave site for an hour.

"It's all going good Ma. It's hard without you, but I'm making it. I got Kevin and Otis outta the projects too. It's a nice house, you'll like it," Low said talking to his mother's grave as he leaned against the tomb stone and tears rolled down his face as he talked When he was done, he got up and walked to the front gate to wait for Pep.

Pep drove up fifteen minutes later, seeing the look on Low's face. Low got in the car and he didn't say shit. He just turned the music up and drove to Westlake. Wasn't nothing you can really say at times like this if you ever been in this position and place. Sometimes leaving a person at peace is the best thing you can do.

Low sat back in the car seat and an incident that occurred when he was young popped (entered) in his mind.

"Yup, he over there right now honey child," the coffee bean brown completion man with feminine ways told Jerry.

"Let me get my shoes on, this muthafucka think he slick!" Jerry huffed, as she looked for her tennis shoes.

"Guuurrrlll, his sorry ass ain't even worth it! Time to move on honey child," he gestured with his hand broke down at the wrist. "Let them two ugly lookin maggots have each other baby."

Jerry was tying her Puma's up tight, not even trying to hear what he was talking about, as Lenny 10 years old looked on. He had seen his mother whoop three women and one man in his young life, so he knew she was about to kick this girls ass over her boyfriend Ralph. She the one that homosexual Cupcake had mentioned, who stayed out there in the projects.

His mother stormed out the screen door with Cupcake following. Lenny being nosey went out the door right behind her. His two brothers were in the front yard playing with some other kid's, making clouds of dust and dirt kick up, cause wasn't no grass where they played tag.

"Y'all stay right here till I get back, I'm just going up to the next building," Jerry told his two brothers, Otis and Kevin. Jerry knew Lenny was following her and felt he was old enough to realize how things went down in life.

Lenny wasn't tryin to hear what his mother told his brothers, so he lagged behind wanting to see who was about to get a for sure beat down from his mother. Jerry stepped in front of the apartment door and started banging so hard on the door the windows shook, causing a scene and everybody to be nosey and get in her business, wanting to see what this incident would bring on the excitement side they could talk about in the hood. The door swung opened and some skinny red boned sister yelled out with attitude.

"Fuck you beating on my goddamn door fo like that hoe?"

Jerry didn't even answer her, she just grabbed her screen door opening it with one hand up more and "BAM", sucker punched her making her stumble backwards with a busted lip dazed. Jerry walked right into her apartment. "Nigga you think you gone' play me like I'm dumb! You got me fucked up!" She shouted at Ralph who was laying on the couch half-naked till Jerry barged in with only some tight red bikini briefs on shocked.

"Jerry what the hell you doing busting in this girls place like you crazy! You… (CLOCK!) Oowwee!"

Jerry had picked up a quart of Old English beer on the table and busted Ralph up side his head with it. "Fuck yo sorry ass."

The girl Michelle grabbed Jerry from the back and the t-shirt she had on rode up her back exposing her yellow panties and tiny butt cheeks as she screamed.

"I'ma kill you bitch! Eeehhh…I'll kill yo ass!"

Lenny was about to help his mother but she flipped the girl over and started stomping her into the carpet. "Next…time…pick...the right...one! Whore!"

Ralph snatched Jerry off of her yelling head leaking, "Are you fuckin crazy? Get out of this girls house!"

"Oh, I know you better get yo nasty hands off my guurrll!" Cupcake hollered getting all dramatic with his hands and neck.

Ralph was dragging her out and Jerry looked over at Lenny and yelled, "Get this bitch off me!"

Lenny knew he had to do something, so he picked up a big leather belt from the floor with the steel buckle. Lenny swung it just as they got to the door, and it wrapped around Ralph's head with the steel buckle popping him on the cheek making him scream out like a little girl letting Jerry go as he fell outside half-naked. Jerry started stomping him when he went down.

"Come'on boy!" she yelled to Lenny to help. His little feet tap danced all over Ralph's ass.

Low started laughing to himself as he thought about that time with his mother. Pep glanced at him, hearing him laughing. He didn't know what he was laughing at, as long as he was feeling better he didn't care.

Chapter 13
"Money moves everything around me!"

The day before school, Pep took Low to go get his ride. They had been at the Mall all day buying clothes. This year they were coming in right, with all new fresh shit, jewelry and all. They parked in front of the car shop and went in. Low's whip was in the garage part shining like a muthafuckin new Quarter in there.

Low drove out that bitch banging Too Short (Freaky Tails) sitting pretty, as Pep followed and they rode through the North side hitting streets where a lot of people hang out on, especially on Elm Street. Nigga's were staring at Low's Vette, and chicks were shaking their asses and getting in provocative stands. Low peeped game and smiled feeling good. He drove to the grave sight to see his moms as Pep waited on him. When they were about to leave he saw Wanda coming in to see her father, so he stopped her and hollered at her.

"I love your new car," she told him, sitting in it checking it out. "This sweet baby...Well, call me later okay? So you can take me fo a ride."

Low replied, "Alright, I'll holla at cha later," she got out and Pep beeped his horn looking at her butt and she waved getting back in her car.

When they got to Westlake, everybody was checking his car saying, "Damn my nigga, we ain't seen no nigga flip no Corvette yet!" Girls, hoes, rats, and a few women were standing around never paid Low attention before, was now eye balling him up and down like a pregnant chick who ain't ate all day and he was a cheeseburger with the works. Roe and Nut came and took his shit for a ride up the street and back. Sandy thick chocolate ass got in and begged for a ride, so Low took her to the store and to get something to eat.

"I wish you were going to our school," she told him as they were sitting in the parking lot. Sandy would be in the 12th grade this year and Low and Pep the 10th. Sandy was horny and begged him for some, She didn't have to beg cause Low was fully into her. He took her over Roe and Nut's spot and beat the pussy up, and bounced. He jumped in his whip and stopped at the house on Delaware cause he saw Nate's Benz outside the crib him and Smoke be chilling at. He parked his ride and knocked on the door. Someone peeked through the peephole and then opened the door. The big bald headed nigga they called Body bag for some reason Low didn't know stood there in the doorway butt naked with a 357 he always came to the door with and carried.

"Damn nigga! You ain't got no fuckin clothes an shit? Fuck you tripping on! Where Nate at?" Low asked keeping his eyes away from him.

"Down stairs," he waved with the gun, letting him in. "I hope he ain't naked too," Low stated as he went down the stairs hearing some old school music playing. He saw a big booty white girl with a Rican one freaking Nate on the floor, while Smoke and his dude Hank cheered the girls on. "You nigga's freaked out wit y'all old asses!"

Low never had no white pussy, so when Smoke said, "Fuck you all staring at this white hoe like that fo? Get naked an hit it since you standing there all googy eyed an shit." Low was in a daze looking at the white chicks ass. When Smoke said that, Low started stripping quick. Nate tossed him a rubber.

Low looked at it like what the fuck is this, cause he never used one before.

"Better strap up and put that on brah," Nate told him. "Sick him," Nate told the white girl, and she crawled over to Low and started suckin his dick while putting the jimmy on at the same time.

"Slurp, uumm...slurp," the white chick moaned on his joint.

"Shhiitt," Low called. He couldn't take it no more and bent her over and fucked the shit outta her. Nate and them were laughing up a storm at Low attacking the pussy like a wild man.

After they finished, Low told them to come outside so they could see his ride he just bought. Sweat was dripping all down his face from fucking. They sent the girl's on their way and stepped outside.

"Aw lil nigga this bitch raw!" Smoke said. They all gave him props.

"Take me fo a spin right quick," Nate told him, wanting to talk to him about some business.

They jumped in and drove off. While they were rolling around Nate was telling him about some dope houses he was getting because it would be more money faster and better. Low told him it sounded tight, and wanted to know more. Nate ran it down to him, and Low liked it. Low dropped him back off and went to the Vic's to floss his shit in the hood. When he drove up Rat and the rest of them were out.

"Damn, yo shit on point!" Moose hollered.

Everybody was giving him props and checking his whip out. Tina showed up with Kelly and her cousin Misha, who always was fighting and kicking somebody ass. She was thick for her young age with short hair and a light brown complexion. Kelly was a pretty girl with a slim build, big brown eyes, and a little nice booty.

"Gurl, yo man car nice," Kelly told Tina.

"You going to take me fo a ride, or what Lenny?" Tina asked Low, with her hands on her hips. She was the only one besides his family that still called him by his real name.

Low looked up at her as he sat in his car with Jay and said, "Yeah, come on."

"Ah Low you got anything on ya?" A fiend name Roc asked who use to get money and looked out for Low.

"Nah," Low told him.

"I got cha. What you got?" Jay told him getting out the ride.

"I got 10 dollars, but I want a twenty. I'll pay ya back when my check comes this week," Roc told Jay.

"Naw, I can't do it."

"Here," Low told Roc going into his pocket, and taking out a fifty from a knot, as Tina got in the passenger seat shutting the door. "Go get you a cold bottle on me."

"Thanks Low," Roc said, taking the money.

"Later y'all. Alright Roc," Low said, and drove off.

Tina was smiling at Low's good gesture. He always did something good for people. That's why she couldn't figure out why everybody was saying he killed the two dudes that murdered his mom like they were saying they were killed. And the incident with Pot Pie really had her messed up, cause a lot of people seen him do it. So wasn't no way she could deny he didn't do it.

"You going to school tomorrow?" Tina asked.

"Yeah, fo sho."

"Well, you going to take me to school in the morning?" she asked, looking at him with them big pretty brown eyes.

He didn't want to, but he was stuck like a nigga on camera robbing a bank without a mask, on a busy day when the police was cashing their checks. Damn, he thought, I should of bought her ass a Hooptie an shit, he was thinking.

"Well?" she said smacking her tongue up against her upper gums.

"Yeah, I got cha."

When Low dropped her off, he sat outside with the gang and some others. He saw them girl's Brenda and Kim who initially got the beef started with Tito and them nigga's from the South side, leaving with Bo's girl Cathy. He felt like doing something to them but didn't want to spoil the good spirits he was in. They were checking out his whip, giving him sexy looks as they walked by, then drove by in the car.

"Fake ass hoes," Low whispered to himself, "I ain't forgot about y'all bitches." He left there and went and fucked Wanda and laid back at her spot that night.

The next day he got up to go change for school. Wanda didn't stay to far from his crib with his brothers and aunt, since they both stayed in Campbell. He picked Tina up and saw Pep waiting for Kelly to step out because he was taking her to school too. Both girls had set this up. Tina looked good in her Nautica jeans, Reebok women Classic tennis shoes, and matching red Nautica shirt. Low was rocking all blue and white Polo down, White Nike Cortez sneakers that were called dope boys, Polo shades, a fat gold chain with Low as the emblem and razor sharp crisp jeans. Pep was fly also.

Moose and them were waiting to, so they all headed to the school in their new shit flossing on folks. They had the whole school checking them out as they bent corners and gangstered their whips all in the street and parking lot blasting their sounds, making a crowd gather around like it was a party, dancing and shit. Security came and made them turn their music down, but they ignored them until they started talking about calling the real police and kicking their asses out of school before they even got to go.

Some Rican dude named Puncho that went to school with them drove by them hitting switches in a clean ass 70 Catalina, steel grey, chromed out with 100 spokes. His ride was water, he was banging some Rican rap shit with this other big Rican on the passenger side of him, and three gorgeous Rican chick's in the back dancing.

Low and them parked in the back parking lot of their school East High, and got out and chilled like everybody else before it started. Honey's that never paid Low no attention made it their business to strut by switching and saying hello, even though Tina and Kelly were there, Low and his boys were checking them out from head to toe.

Tina wasn't feeling that, and her and her girlfriends posted up behind Pep's car glaring and rolling their eyes at the girl's, making comments about them loud enough for them to hear'em.

"Thirsty ass bitches," Tina uttered, rolling her eyes at two girls with fat titties and ass that winked at Low as they went by shaking their moneymakers.

Low had gotten a reputation cause of them murders. Even his boy's names were spreading around the city like mayonnaise on a project bologna sandwich. People heard all about what happened to Low's Moms, and how he had did the dudes that did it in cold blood. It was things even made up that didn't happen or even occur. But, that's how folks talked when there was drama to be gossiped about.

Low saw Roy drive up with his dudes. Then Angie came in her little car with three of her girl's and hung out. She kept glancing over at Low giving him the sexy eye and face thing.

"Bitch must be crazy," Low mumbled shaking his head thinking.

Puncho pulled up next to Low and hit his switches, making the whip drop down. He rolled his window down and mass weed smoke escaped out the car like it was a fire inside. "What's up essay?" Puncho said to them. "I see you got clean ride essay," he said in a funny accent. He had long black hair and hair up under his chin.

"Yo shit clean," Pep told him, looking at the rims.

"I like this," Low told him. "This killin'em out here."

Puncho hopped out his ride with weed smoke trailing behind him and shut the door. He was short and stocky. "My name Puncho," he told them putting out his hand for a shake.

Low looked at it for a second, and then shook it. "I'm Lowdown."

"I like essay, that's slick name," Puncho said with broken English. The other dude got out the car with a blunt in his mouth with Loc shades on, huge, with tattoo's all over him, and one side of his neck. "This my partna essay's, Big Dawg. He mean son of a bitch! But he cool."

Low and them just looked at him nodding their heads and saying, "What's up" to his big crazy looking ass.

"Say what's up," Puncho told Big Dawg, and he nodded his huge baldhead and hit the blunt. "Oh fuck essays, here come pigs!" Puncho grabbed the blunt from Big Dawg hand and threw it on the ground stepping on it.

Security guards came and told Puncho to either park his car or leave the premises. Big Dawg stood in front of Puncho like he wanted to work (fight) with the guards.

"It's cool Big Dawg, I'll park," Puncho told them, and parked his car right, and came back over to them. "Ah essay's...y'all smoke killa?" he asked Low and them.

Moose answered, "Hell yeah!" Puncho handed him a blunt lit, and Moose took two puffs, and started coughing hard.

"Easy essay, that there Cali green. My home boys grow that killa funk down there." Pep and them were cracking up.

"Let me hit that bitch!" Pep said, and took a long hit and started coughing and hitting his chest. "Damn, this shit strong!"

"Got's to be use to that funk essay to hit it hard," Puncho told'em. Big Dawg had a small grin on his face.

The girl's got out of Puncho's car wearing short miniskirts giggling, as they went inside the school. Low and them stayed out there 20 more minutes talking before school started, then they all went in high as shit. This was Moose and Jay's last year in school. Rat and Alvin just didn't attend and want to go.

They all went and got there schedule, and while in line with everybody, Low bumped into Angie coming out the line, which she did on purpose.

"Oh, hi Lee," Angie spoke, smiling.

Low knew she had planned it like that, and looked at her like she spit on him in his face. "Bitch hoe, keep moving!"

Angie was shocked, as she hurried away eyes big in disbelief.

Pep was hip to her cause Low had told him the deal about her, so he yelled out, "Bitch you heard my nigga!" and spit on her leg. Angie really rushed away scared and crying. Everybody just looked on tripping, but not saying nothing to them about it. Tina had saw the incident with her girl Kelly, Pep's girlfriend.

"That boy off it. (Crazy) You see how she ran outta here like a track star? Damn shame," Kelly commented.

Tina replied, "That's what she gets, trying to talk to my man after she played him like that."

"I know that's right," Kelly added laughing.

That day in school was different for Low and Pep, because they never got attention like they were receiving now. Low had only saw Roy from a distance so far cause Roy was keeping it like that it seemed, so Low didn't sweat it. But deep down he was anticipating it, and knew he would encounter him again and it wouldn't be nice at all, the way he felt.

Roe and Nut had a ball in school. They had skipped half their classes and was now by the girl's bathroom feeling on their asses with some other dudes they knew, until this one guy approached them with three other cats asking, "Which one of y'all pervert ass nigga's felt my girl's butt?" The girlfriend was behind him peeking and they saw her.

Roe said, "Oh, that's yo bitch? She got a soft ole ass on her!"

"What you say?" Dude asked, like he didn't hear him.

"Bitch nigga, you heard me! Her ass soft as fuck!" Roe shouted. Dude charged Roe putting his hands up, and Roe and Nut up piped on him and his three buddies. "Now bitch what's up? I just might fuck her now, buster ass nigga!"

Dude cried he was sorry. "Please man, I don't want no trouble. You can feel or fuck her all you want." The girlfriend heard that and got mad and stomped away.

"Call me, you heard yo man!" Roe yelled out to her. "Now get out my face chump, fo I ask bout yo mommy." They saw the security coming from someone telling, and ran out the school to their rides and left. They drove to the East side to see what was up with Low at school because they were about to get out in a few minutes.

After school Low and his crew clowned again in their whips in front of everybody. Puncho joined them with his partna Big Dawg. Girls were staring and trying to hook up, and nigga's were hating, except the players. Tina had bought a camera so she was taking pictures, until Pep got the camera from her and started taking pictures of all the chick's an shit. Then Low joined him with the rest of the homies, telling the girl's to lift their mini's up and show some ass an shit. Some girl's did, and their boyfriends got salty as fuck. Tina and Kelly was upset and couldn't believe the shit, they were looking mad as hell! Tina snatched her camera back.

Nut and Roe pulled up in their two clean Cadillac's that was the same year but different colors. Roe's 81 Fleetwood was the same color as his Regal, black & brown. Nut's was the same as his Regal too, blue & grey. They joined in with them clowning and getting on the honeys. Moose and the rest of the gang had gotten some girl's in their cars. Tina and Kelly wasn't having that shit! They all hit the hood up, the Victory projects, and got out while they sent the girl's to the store to buy some drinks. Moose and Rat's girl Pam went to a different school called Chaney, that was supposed to be better and had alot more whites going there. So the close was clear for them.

Low was sitting on Nut's Lac when Bo's sister Pattie walked up on him. Pattie looked like Nia Long, but a shade lighter and not as thick. She had a nice body on her and was 19 years old.

"Hey Low, how you doing? Is this yo car here?" She asked, all up on him close.

"Naw, that's mines there," he indicated nodding with his head to the Vette gleaming in the sun. It was something about seeing that Vette shining in the projects like that.

"Oohh that's a sweet ride," she said, putting her hand on his knee. Tina had went home to change clothes, upset at how Low had acted after school with his comrades. "You gone take me for a spin one day, right honey?"

Pattie asked, eyeing him up and down flirting.

Low stared at her yellow petite cute ass and replied, "No doubt, whenever you ready." The heat from her delicate touch on his knee felt good. "Oh yeah, here, give these to Bo fo me." He got off the car and went in his whip and came back with a stack of pictures that they had just taken. "Give him this too." He dug in his pocket and pulled out a knot and took out eight hundred one hundred dollar bills. "Send him five, and you keep the rest for you and your Moms."

Pattie was taken aback by his generosity. She was already digging his little goon ass. "Alright baby, thank you. I'll tell Bo you sent this too, Bye," she walked off shaking her little plump derriere hard, giving him a good view as he gazed at her heart shaped butt.

"Who that killa? Damn!" Nut inquired, staring at her work it.

"That's my nigga Bo sister," Low answered him, eyes still attached to her rump.

"Oh she got's the hot's fo ya killa," Nut laughed, hitting him.

Bobby, the boy Low had smacked in school last year about Tina at the lunch table, just stared at Low as he drunk some beer and hung out there with them. He still had a grudge and resentment about the incident and hid his feelings about it.

Chapter 14
Even if it took days and years, I never forgot!
I put that on my Momma, word is bond…

Two days passed and Pep and Low were fucking with different girls and getting much play. They were at their locker in school about to go to class when Roy and Angie walked past smiling and laughing. Low's blood started pumping to his heart like gas thrown on a fire, and he reached into a locker next to his that they kept heat (guns) at and Pep peeped him and grabbed his arm.

"Hold up man!" He told Low, looking at him like he was crazy. Looking at Low at that minute in his face, he didn't know him. His eyes held something so intense that it even shook Pep up some.

Roy and Angie had heard Pep and turned around, not realizing their lives were being put on hold.

"Bitch what you looking at?" Low grumbled, mugging (frowning) Roy, who didn't want no trouble with Low one bit after hearing the things he had done. Roy stopped smiling and pulled Angie getting out of Low's sight.

"We'll get that lame nigga later," Pep told Low.

"Yeah, you right," Low replied, "I'll catch cha later." Low went to class.

During school Low had seen Tina and told her to take his ride home, and gave her the keys. Tina didn't think nothing of it, and was happy to be seen pushing her man's whip.

When the bell rung for school to be over, Low told Pep he would see him back in the Vic.

"What's up nigga?" Pep asked, seeing the look on his face.

"Ain't shit, I'll see ya in a minute," Low told him hurrying off. Low went to their stash locker and took out gloves, mask, and two pistols and ran out the side door of the school that nobody used, with the stuff up under his shirt. He had been watching which way Roy came and left school on the sly since school started, so he been plotting this move on the low any ways. He just couldn't take it no more! It was killing him inside and he had to feed the hunger. He ran through the wooded area next to the school and came out on the street the school was on, that was named the same as the school, East High. He leaned on a tree pulling the mask down, then peeked out watching the cars coming and going from school. People were cruising in their rides, so it was a line of cars moving slowly, just like he had hoped it would be.

Roy had Angie and his dude Sam with his girl Shannon in his car. He was feeling good smiling and shit, when all of a sudden someone jumped in front of his car with a ski mask on waving a big ass gun pointing it at him. He couldn't speed up or go backwards, cause he was sandwiched in, so he tried to run the masked person over but he jumped out the way and ran to his side of the window shoving a 45 to his dome yelling, "Bitch, you know what time it is!" Roy knew the voice, but it was too late to put a face to it as the 45 slug entered his temple, blowing his brains out the other side all over Angie like Spaghetti as his body flew on her, and she screamed. Then the masked person stuck the gun in the car shooting him four more times as the car rammed the back of another in front. Then he turned shouting, "Bitch I ain't forgot you!" and shot Sam two times in the face making him unrecognizable as pieces of his face flew all over, and then Angie in the back as she tried to get out the car and run. She turned around hollering when the bullets hit her and he shot her in the face, over the eyes and two times over the heart.

The girl in the back was screaming and kicking Sam's dead body off her trying to get out when he pointed the gun at her. He looked at her and didn't shoot, he had a flashback of his mother's death. He jumped out the car and took off running through the woods. People in cars had seen it and heard the shots rang out and tried to get the fuck out the way, driving their cars up on the sidewalk and grass.

Low saw Roy coming, and his heart felt a calm. This is what he been waiting for. His heart was beating fast till he saw Roy, then it got still like. When he jumped in front of Roy's car he wanted to see his face and look on it as he looked into his eyes and knew it was the end. He jumped out the way to avoid Roy from trying to run him over and got mad cause the fool didn't know it was over for him and for trying, so when he stuck the gun to his dome, it felt so right, so good. "Bitch, you know what time it is!" And put one in his left temple splattering out the right side all over Angle as she screamed out with his fresh blood and brains on her and he slumped over on her. To make sure he was dead, and to see Angie more terrified, petrified, he stuck the gun in the car and shot Roy four more times. Pointing the gun at Sam next cause he made a move. "Bitch I ain't forgot you!" and shot him for putting him in the hospital, and for his mother never getting that revenge and payback she was talking about, blasting him two times in the face making him have a close casket as chunks of him flew all over, then Angie tried to get out the door so he shot her in the back making her scream out more and turn around.

When she faced him crying out, images of that day she played him flashed in his head real quick and he shot her in the forehead and over the heart. The girl in the back seat was kicking and screaming trying to get Sam's lifeless disfigured body off her. Pointing the gun at her he had a flashback how his mother died. The girl had nothing to do with the beef, so he hopped out of the car, not even realizing that the car had ran into the back of the one in front of it. He ran through the woods in the back of the school that lead back to the Victory. He felt a relief go through him now as he ran and the air entered his lungs about what he just did.

Low got to the end of the woods and stopped to look out. He saw Pep and them outside. He took the mask off and tucked the gun, and snuck around to where Pep was. Pep didn't even see him until he said something.

"Pep, come'on," Low told Pep, who jumped at first startled. They hopped into a fiends car that every one of them used, and Low told him to drive to the water. The water was McKelvy Lake on the East side, not far from them. Pep just drove and didn't ask shit. When they got there Low threw pieces of the gun in the water after he wiped it down and beat it down with hammer as they drove by, then he told Pep to go behind the Plaza. They got there behind Lincoln Knolls Plaza and Low stripped down to his drawls and threw his clothes in the dumpster there, and got a can of gas out the trunk and poured it all over his stuff in the dumpster. Pep got out the car looking around to make sure no one was around. Low set it on fire.

"Yo, pour this gas over my hands fo me," Low told Pep, handing him the gas tank. Pep wasn't hip to the gas thing and looked at him funny but did it anyway. Then they left and Low had him stop at the store and go in to get him something to wear in the Plaza. They stopped at Wendy's and Low went inside to wash his hands and forearms. Low ordered some fries and a burger while inside, and came out smacking as he walked to the car. He felt hungry as hell for some reason. He thought about the look on Roy face and smirked.

Detective Malley, and Jackson house nigga ass, came to the murder scene at the school as soon as they found out the one victim was Roy Phillips. Then they drove straight to the Victories. What they just saw made them sick to their stomach and despise who done it.

"Ain't no way this little fucker didn't do this!" Jackson stressed to his red-faced partner.

"Yup jack, we gots to get that little prick before he kills even more people! I knew it was coming too, you can just feel someone like that is about to go all out an is just ruthless, and cold hearted."

Jackson replied, "Yeah, he done went too far this time. Three young fucking kids! And one a girl! Fuckin bastard!"

They drove up fast into the Victory, and Moose, Alvin chipmunk looking ass, Jay, and some others saw them coming. Some dudes that sold dope for them ran. "Shit," Moose mumbled. Word had already spread about the murders, and Moose already knew in his heart it was Low who did it. He had saw Low and Pep leave in a hurry in the fiends car.

"Where's Lenny at?" The Detectives barked to the group when they jumped out of their vehicle.

Rat Said, "Shit, we don't know. Probably went to the store right quick," all smart.

Malley slammed him on the car hood and shook him down. "All you punk's drop to the ground!" Malley shouted, with his gun out. Jackson called for backup as two other officers went and knocked on the apartment door where Low use to live and getting no reply. They saw wasn't no curtains when they peeked inside.

As the cops were doing all that, Pep and Low drove up and parked, as two cop cars came behind them. Pep got out and tried to walk the other way when he noticed what was going on. But Low walked right up on the

Detective's, speaking.

"What's up?" Low said, like he had no idea what the fuck was going on and up.

Jackson and Malley glanced at each other, and got off the two guys they had on the ground. "Watch them!" Jackson told the other officers there. "Put your fucking hands in the air!" He ordered Low.

"Fo what? I ain't did nothing!" Low replied, with a smug on his face.

Malley tackled him to the ground. "Little fuckin devil, you know what the hell is going on!" He screamed, trying to break Low's arm. "You murdering bastard!"

Tina and some other people out there started shouting, "Let him go! Get off him!"

"Get back, before all y'all go to jail!" Jackson yelled to them.

"Punk, where the gun you just used?" Malley demanded twisting Low's arm while the cuffs were on him.

"What gun?! You crazy white man!" Low grunted out.

"Watch that with your smart ass!" Jackson told Low, helping his partner lift Low off the ground. "You're going downtown."

"Fo what?" Low asked all cool and calm and that really pissed them off more.

Chapter 15

It's not always in the eyes of a person. It's what lies in the heart...

The killings were all over the news and everybody was talking about them. Low's name was ringing and the girl that he let live said she didn't know who it was, and didn't want to be involved. She didn't tell them what she heard the killer say before he murdered them. The cops and Detectives Malley and Jackson tried their best to get her to talk, but she was scared to death and didn't see who it was anyway she told them. They even tried to get her to make up some fictitious story to incriminate Low. But she wasn't going for it at all! They were mad as fuck! Low was taken to Juvenile on suspicion, but they had nothing at all on him, and knew that they were going to have to release him.

Pep had called Sammie right away and Sammie flew to the police station to see what they had his client on. When he found out three homicides he was drunk, but didn't let it show in front of the police that told him the charges. He left there to go see Low in Juvenile.

When he saw Low come in the room with cuffs and a big orange jump suit that was two sizes big, he couldn't picture this young kid being a stone murderer like that. But when he looked him in the eyes, it was something there. And the way he carried himself with such confidence even now, Sammie knew he was dealing with a young killer in the making. A young boy with the "Heart of a Goon."

"Hey Lenny, what's going on?" Sammie greeted him with a big smile saying, covering his thoughts.

"Aw shit Sammie, they got me here on some bullshit!" Low sat down saying.

"Well Lenny are you sure they got the wrong guy? To me, it seems like they always do," Sammie said, seeing if he would bite, but Low's face revealed nothing.

Low said, "Hell yeah, just get me outta this bitch! Fuck you even ask me that dumb shit for?" Low grilled him, staring into his face to see if

Sammie was on his side.

"Had to ask just in case they had anything. Never worry about me being on your side. You'll be out tomorrow after I talk to the judge, okay? Just hold your horses." Sammie started putting his papers up to leave feeling a little uneasy with Low's mugging.

"Alright, that's cool," Low replied getting up to go, then turned around and said, "They ain't got shit on me Sammie," and walked out the door.

Right then, Sammie knew he was dealing with a stone cold killer and his heart stopped.

Pep, Roe, Nut, Moose, Rat, and Jay all sat at Alvin's house talking about their nigga Low. "He'll be out in a minute, watch," Pep told'em.

Moose was fucked up about the murders. That little nigga crazy as fuck! He was thinking, fuckin insane as hell!

"It's hot as a mug out. Police been rolling through all day trying to catch a nigga," Alvin stated.

Wanda drove out to the Victories to see what was up with Low, and saw some young dudes selling dope. She asked about Low and they told her the cops took him, she asked have they seen her cousin Morgan and they said, "No!" They told her Pep and them were over Alvin's spot out there. Wanda went over there and knocked on the door. Roe and Nut reached for their heat pulling them out, making some of them nervous.

"Who is it?" Alvin asked, as he went to peek out the window.

"It's Wanda, is Pep over here?"

Alvin opened the door after he looked over at Pep who nodded his head to let him know it was cool. "What's up Wanda? Come in." Wanda stepped in and saw everybody.

"What's up y'all? What the world is up with Low?" She asked looking worried.

Pep said, "it's cool, don't worry about it. He'll be out."

"I hope so. If he needs anything let me know. And tell him to call me if he call any of y'all."

They all told her "Alright" and she left.

Tina was on her porch when she saw Wanda come out there in her Iroc. She was already in shock by what was being said that Low did, and seeing

Wanda ass made her so mad and hurt, she threw the glass of Kool-Aid she was drinking and ran in the apartment crying. She loved Lowdown and hated him at the same time now.

Nate was sitting at his music store waiting for his pager to go off so he could send his soldier to go pick up his dope from the connect, when his cell phone rang. "Yeah, what's up?" It was his girl Jess.

"I thought you should know your little buddy, Low, supposed to had done that on the news. Them triple murders at the school."

Nate wasn't shocked or surprised, and took it as part of life. The life he always been into. Deaths, money, jealousy, hate and sometimes love, which was rarely. All this comes with the life and you must add it to staying on top of the game. That means evading the police, Feds and all kinds of hate boys. You got jealous niggas, jackers, snitches, and those that just can't stand you cause they don't got the heart or brains to put their own shit into effect. Then you got girls and some hoes that wish they had you, but don't, so they tell lies, trying to set you up, or take you down. This "GOON LIFE" was a muthafucka, so nothing surprised Nate. He had did time before and seen all kinds of nigga's that got taken out over little mistakes. So he tried his best to lay low and keep it tight. But that "GOON LIFE" is hard to get out of once it's in your heart. So he knew what Low was going through, he had done so much shit that he couldn't remember himself. That's why he liked Low and them little cat's so much. Nate hung up with Jess and called Roe to see the deal on Low.

Roe called Nate back. "You hit me up brah?"

"Yeah, is my lil rappie cool?"

"Yeah he straight. He'll be out in a second big brah, its cool."

"Alright, stay up," Nate told him, and hung up. He didn't use the phones a lot because he knew how they got a lot of nigga's cased up. He leaned back in his chair to think.

The next day the lawyer Sammie was on his job early at the crack of dawn. He had talked to the Detectives Jackson and Malley and found out that they would be releasing his client today. So he flew to tell Low he would be getting released in the afternoon. Low was like, "Cool, I told you they had the wrong guy." Sammie didn't even reply because he knew the real. He just told him he was going to the clerk office to make sure his release papers was taken care of, and would give him a ride back.

Pep and them had went to school and everybody was giving them weird faces and whispering. In this town it was like the more shit you did, like killing and all, the more females you got. Until this day it's like that. Even in other Towns and States too. Sad, but true. Hoes and girl's flock to killers and Goons that are about their business and bloodshed. They loved Goons, or should I say niggas with the "Heart of a Goon."

The most popular girl in school Cindy walked up on Pep at his locker. "Hey, how you doing boo?"

Pep looked at her mix ass with the hazel eyes and said, "You, and anything you want to be up."

She smiled and replied, "You, that's what's up."

Pep grinned like the big bad wolf did to little Red Riding Hood. "Well it's on then. I'll tell ya what," he said handing her a pen and his tablet. "Write yo digits down and we'll hook up later."

She wrote it down and said, "Make sure you call me," and switched off.

Pep watched her ass as she switched away and mumbled, "You damn right I'ma call, I'ma beat that pussy up!"

Puncho walked up on him while he was dazing at Cindy's butt. "Ah essay I see you check out the ass on that Mamie, huh? Nice A?"

"Man I'm bout to dig in that hooker an show her all she's been missing, by acting like me and my homeboys wasn't even alive last year. Fuck that fake ass bitch!"

Puncho laughed, then said, "What's up wit my dude Low getting out essay? That clown keep me cracking up gringo."

"He'll be out this week, I hope."

"Okay essay, let me go puff on this killa before class start an shit. Come'on Big Dawg!" He yelled down the hall. "Let's get lifted."

The lawyer Sammie was mad as hell. The two Detectives had not sent the paper work to have Low released. So he had to go see their supervisors, and he told Sammie he would have to wait until tomorrow now because it was too late. So Sammie had to go tell Low he would have to wait till tomorrow.

Low didn't trip at all. "Alright, just make sure I'm outta here tomorrow then."

"I got cha buddy," Sammie told him.

Low felt good as he went back to his one-man cell and laid down on the thin bed matt. Getting Roy and Angie with the other dude who had jumped him felt good as hell. He remembered his Moms words and the last time he saw her alive, then fell to sleep. In his sleep he had dreamed, and they were all nightmares. He tossed and turned all night. He woke up three times in a cold sweat out of a nightmare sweating, and just stared at the ceiling until he fell back to sleep. He had a lot of anger inside, so he was motivated by revenge, get back, and how he use to get played. But he was driven by money, power, fuckin honeys, and combined all together made what was in the "HEART OF A GOON."

Nate's pager finally went off with the code from his connect saying it was alright for him to send his worker to pick his supply up. Nate called his girl's and told them he'll see them tonight, then hit his soldier on the hip with their code to go get the supply.

Sporty got the code from Nate, and hopped into the rental and went to pick the product up. When he got there he parked in the back of K-Mart store and got out and pushed the buzzer.

He was let in by some Italian man. "Hey buddy, how's it going?"

"Aw, it's going alright, "Sporty replied.

"Well let me see if the Boss is in so we can get you your order and you can be out of here. Come'on." He took Sporty to this office and told him to "Hold up" and went in. An older Italian man was in the office with a suit on and a younger version of him was standing up in a jogging suit with long black hair. "Ah um, Nate's pick up guy is here Mr. Throlinne."

The older man replied, "Good, good...Tell him to be careful cause its police everywhere because of these kids murder at the school."

He nodded his head and went to tell Sporty.

Sporty said, "I'm hip. Good lookin out. Well come'on so we can get this stuff loaded, I got things to do."

He told Sporty to go pop the trunk and his guy's would bring it out as always and put it in the trunk.

So Sporty sat in the car while they loaded the goods, and then drove off when they were done. He used his cell phone and put the code into Nate's pager to let him know he was on his way and would be there in a few minutes. When he got there he knew Nate was there because both Pit Bull dogs were inside the 6 Ft picket fence outside running around when he got out the car to open the gate and drive the car inside. Nate came out the house as he was closing the gate with a scanner in his hand.

"Let's unload this shit," Nate told Sporty. "So you can get this car outta here." Nate didn't like cars in the spot to long cause it had just left the Mobs spot in the back Plaza. So they unloaded the 10-kilo's, half brick of heroin, and 130 pounds of weed. Sporty pulled out, Nate hit his two girl's up to come move the goods to another location, and then he would front some workers and sell the rest to only four people that he fucked with, Roe, Nut, Smoke and Lowdown on the weight side. But he would have his girl's drop it off to them and the ones he fronted. This was the only time he saw the product. Two more times like this and he had plans of getting out the game. Smoke was his ace boon coon and he loved him, but he didn't stack his chips like he did. Smoke didn't give a fuck about stacking his money. Nate didn't give a fuck that Smoke got high, but he was starting to do too much now and it was affecting him and his cash flow. Him and Smoke grew up together and did a number together for a robbery that went bad, so their bond was deep.

Pep had went to pick that girl Cindy up later and fucked her. Her pussy wasn't all that like she betrayed and acted. He took her to the Motel and fucked her Goon style. He beat the pussy up so thorough on her square ass, she was saying she loved him afterwards. "Man wait till my nigga hear about this shit here. He gonna trip," Pep was thinking. He had called the Lawyer Sammie to see what was up with Low and he told him he would be out tomorrow, so Pep was glad of that. It was as if he lost his motivation to be out there selling dope with Low gone.

Low got out the next day and got dropped off in the Victories by his lawyer. Everybody was in school except Alvin who was on the block drinking and clocking (selling) with the old heads. He was serving some dudes a eight ball of powder when Low showed up.

"What's up my muthafuckin nigga?" Alvin shouted, happy to see Low giving him a thug hug. Low saw his ride sitting in front of Tina's pad and remembered he had given her the keys and told her to take his whip.

"Shit player. Is Tina home?"

"Nah, she went to school with the rest of them nerds nigga," Alvin replied, tossing his 40 ounce up taken a drink, Alvin looked like a chimp monkey, ears and all. "I'ma need some more work too."

"I got cha. Let me go see if her Mom's got my car keys." Low dapped him and spoke to the old heads and walked over to Tina's apartment and knocked on the door.

Tina's Moms answered the door. "Oh Lenny baby you out…that's good. I knew you didn't have nothing to do with that awful mess they claimed. You okay honey?"

"Yeah, I'm alright. Naw I didn't have nothing to do with that ma'am. Did Tina leave my car keys with you?"

"Yup...they on the kitchen table. I told her not to be driving your car around like it was hers. Let me get them," she got them and gave them to Low. "Here, you hungry?"

"No ma'am, thank you. Do you need anything?" Low asked her, knowing times were hard.

She squelched her face up and replied, "Well, a couple dollars if you got it."

Low went in his pocket and took out a grip, and peeled $200 off for her. "Here ma'am. Tell Tina I'll see her later."

"Thanks baby, I'll tell her. Be careful out there."

"I will. Bye."

Low drove straight to his mother's gravesite, and sat by her tombstone with his back against it. "Ma, I paid that punk back and that hooker. I let loose like you told me, and bombed first. I wish you could be here. I miss you so much and love you," he whispered as he felt heat go through his body. He sat there for an hour zoned out. He got up and wiped his eyes with his forearm, as he looked down at his mom's grave. He took a deep breath and held it in for a second before he released it, then walked away. He got to his whip and called Nate up on his celly.

"Yeah," Nate said when he answered, not knowing the new number. He had told Low to always switch cell phones up after two days when you were doing dirt and was wanted by the poe-poe bad.

"What's up Brah?" Low said, starting the car.

"You out, huh? That's good playboy, come holla at me. I'm at my bar, I'm on my way."

When Low got there and drove into the parking lot, he saw a clean ass 89 Nine Eight with the you can't see me dark tinted windows, white rag top, with gold buttons trimmed in gold all around, gold grill, and trimmings. Truce and Vogues with a power hold. Low was like "Damn that bitch water" to himself as he walked into the bar. It was a lot of people there for it to be early. He walked to the back where Nate kept a private booth. When he got there he saw Nate and his girl's with some brown-skinned dude in an all-white silk short set on, and two badass white bitches sitting with Nate's women.

Nate saw Low coming and yelled, "Over here, lil ... Brah, sit down." Then he introduced Low to dude. "This my nigga from the land (Cleveland) Chism. He reached out to shake Low's hand, and Low noticed all these diamonds on his fingers, watch, and bracelet.

"What's up player?" Chism said.

"What's up?" Low replied back.

Nate said, "This little nigga solid here, and he about his paper."

"Oh yeah nigga, that's all I need to know if it's coming from you." Chism stated. Then he looked at Low. "My dawg here speaks mighty highly of you my man, so I know you bout yo biz and paper."

They started conversating and Low found out Chism owned a couple clubs and car shops up there to cover up his dope and hoe money, cause he was pimping too. While they were talking, two black chicks approached and tried to holla at Chism, since he was a new face in the establishment.

"Look here, chocolate treats," Chism told them, making them giggle. "Y'all got to many war wounds, and I only sponsor polly pure breads." (Meaning white girls)

The two black girls glared at him like he was crazy and replied with attitude, "What nigga?"

"Yeah stank hoes, that's how I get down," he told them.

They both snapped their necks and stomped away yelling. "Sell out ass nigga!"

Low asked, "What is polly pure breads?" Looking at Chism for an answer.

"White bitches only, my young player."

They busted out laughing. They sat there and kicked it for a while till Chism said he had to roll, had trap money to check up on. So they walked him out with his two bad bitches that matched his cocaine white ride. He handed Low his business card and said, "Stay down for yo crown young player and come chop it up (Talk to) with me in the Land." They shook and he got in the back seat of his car while one of the girls drove and the other held the door for him to get in the back and then got in with him. Low and Nate watched him drive off.

"Come'on, let's hop in yo car. I got something to show you," Nate told Low.

Chapter 16

Deep in the game, ain't no shame,
and shit sho ain't the same. It's all then changed...

Low drove his car while Nate showed him where to go. They were on the East side going up a street called Republic that was around the corner from one of the most violent projects in the city, the Kimmel Brooks. But Low and them were cracking up their hood with the recent murders and steady drug flow.

"Pull up in this driveway here," Nate pointed. "This one of yo new spots you run, lil nigga." It was a red wooden, one floor, two bedroom house with a garage in the back and two big trees. Low parked and they got out. Nate took some keys out his pocket and unlocked the back door and they went inside. "Yeah Low, my girl's already furnished it an all." It was nicely furnished with TV's and all.

Low didn't picture a dope house looking like this. This was a nice livable spot. "This bitch laid out!"

"You got another one too, let me show you. It's in La-La Land on the East side on Truedale by the store. Oh, here yo keys."

Low felt like he got the keys to a gold mind when Nate handed them to him.

They went to the one on Truedale and went inside. It was much bigger than the last one. It had a basement, three bedrooms upstairs, attic, and two-car garage and was already furnished.

Nate said, "Roe and Nut got two new spot's too. Smoke said they were getting too big and greedy, so it's best we expand and get money all around the city. Just hip your customers onto the new spots and watch'em jump!"

Low had the two spots jumping in one week, him and his boys was like McDonalds on the first on welfare day. They even took new bitches there and got their fuck on! They were having a ball and the time of their life. Money was flowing and so was the pussy. Low was tripping off Pep when he had Cindy, the most popular girl in their school give him some pussy and skull. Roe and Nut had their dope spots off the chain, there was always a freak hoe walking around butt booty naked, cleaning and offering sex. They had all the nigga's under them slanging their work 24/7. Puncho had gotten real cool with them. They even got tight with Big Dawg big crazy ass too. When Low went over Poncho's crib in La-La Land where there was alot of Ricans who stayed, he saw so many Ricans all in one house that he thought he was at a festival. It was like a party was going on every time he went over his house. Low's crib on Truedale was already were alot of Latino's lived. It was so many kid's in one house all the time that he thought the floor would cave in. The first time Low went over there, Poncho's Mom told him to stay and eat and wouldn't take no for an answer. So he sat down with the whole family and smashed some Rican food. Puncho had a good Moms, and it made Low miss his. He found out everybody didn't stay there, and his Moms had seven kid's that gave her alot of grandbabies, and this was their hang out all the time.

Low little brothers were doing good at their new school. They made new friends there and in the neighborhood, so Low was glad.

One day Low was at McDonald's on the South side on Market Street with Rat and two female's they had knocked off after school from their school, South High. They were eating their grub (food) in the parking lot there. It was crowded up there all the time after school like now. Low was eating a double cheeseburger when he felt something odd. When he glanced up he noticed people on the side of Rat's ride staring and moving the hell out the way. "Pull out man!" He yelled to Rat cause he was driving, as he reached for his burner. Rat jumped from Low's yell and went to put the car in drive as bullets entered the car and rang out.

Dirty and Tito were just leaving out the school parking lot of South High when they saw Rat and Low on the other side of the street, talking to some girl's after school. Tito was driving his Cutlass that was the same year as Dirty's but a whole different color, So Rat and Low didn't pay them no attention because they wasn't hip to Tito's whip,

"That's them hoe ass buster's Rat and Low there!" Dirty said pointing hyped.

"Sho is them bitches!" Tito confirmed.

Dirty reached under the car seat and pulled out a Glock 380 and cocked one into the chamber, "Pull up on them hoes!" He told Tito grinning.

They had to wait because it was too much traffic out after school and they got blocked in. When they were about to ride down on Low and Rat, the two girl's got into their car and they drove off.

Dirty yelled, "Fuck that, follow them bitches!"

They watched them go into McDonalds a couple cars ahead of them and drove up in there two cars behind. They drove past them as they went through the drive thru, so they stopped and backed up parking backwards, so they could watch them come out the drive thru, so they could blast them. But Rat came out and parked his car three down from them.

"Fuck that!" Dirty uttered heated, ready to get them. "Get ready to get ghost," he told Tito, as he opened the car door and slid out ducking. He was crawling behind car's and people were getting the fuck outta the way when they saw who it was and he was carrying a gun in his hand, Mostly all school kids were there and they all knew Dirty and his crew. They knew Dirty had murdered plenty people before and didn't give a fuck who got hit in the process when he started blasting. Dirty was a car away from Low and Rat when he heard one of them yell out "PULL OUT," so he jumped up and cut loose firing on the driver's side as the car peeled out burning rubber. Low hopped on the passenger door sitting down busting back as they hit the intersection. The girl's in the back were screaming and crying for their life. Rat took a bullet in the arm but it went straight through. Rat made it out onto the street with Low and Dirty still firing at each other as people screamed, yelled, and stuck to the ground like cement.

Tito drove up on Dirty yelling, "Come'on, come on nigga!" Dirty jumped into the whip and they sped off.

Rat had went through two red lights and bent a corner and stopped to check his arm. "You alright?" Low asked, looking back to make sure the girls were alright too. "Y'all cool?"

"Yeah, I'm straight. It went through an shit!" Rat told him looking at his arm.

The girls were in the back holding each other tight shook. They nodded their heads yeah, looking at him like he was crazy.

Rat drove out and turned his sounds up. "Damn, I got's to get these holes in my shit fixed," he said, shaking his head.

Low had seen who it was. "Them bitches think they did something," he was thinking to himself, as he leaned back in his seat gripping his pistol that was still hot.

"Yeah I got's to see them lames. But not in front of these hoes right now," Low was thinking. "Hit the drive thru so we can get some drinks nigga." He turned to the girl's in back, "What y'all drink?"

They smiled and said, "Madd Dog."

Low said, "Alright, get two gallons of that shit." He sat back and thought, "Yup, these hookers some straight up wine heads. Bucket head hoes," and smiled to himself.

When they drove up at the crib on Republic, the gang was out there and asked, "What the fuck happened to yo car Rat and your arm?"

Moose was there and was salty. "Let's roll on whoever!"

Rat told'em what went down as Low took the girl's in the house.

Moose told'em, "That nigga Dirty then took shit to another level! That nigga Lowdown ain't playin out this bitch! He then fucked up!"

Rat put something on his bullet hole and covered it up. Now him and Low were in the crib freaking the two chick's. Pep showed up and wanted to know what happened, but Low told'em we gon holla later as he finger fucked the girl on the couch.

Pep replied, "Cool," and got ghost. He didn't see the car parked up the street watching the trap house (dope house) with people in it.

Low and Rat was walking the girl's out to the ride so Moose could drop them off. Wanda drove up with her girl Linda. Low had his arm around girly as he walked her to the car, and Wanda just stared at him as he walked the girl to Moose ride and she got in, and then Low walked over to Wanda in her car.

"What's up?" Low said, leaning down looking at Wanda and her friend.

"I see you keep yo thang wet, huh?" Wanda told him, eyeing him up and down like she could see traces of him having sex just now.

Low brushed her comment off like he didn't even hear it. "What y'all up to?"

"Nothing, just headed to the Mall and stopped to check on you player. But I see you good," Wanda said being sarcastic.

"I try to stay good," Low shot back.

"Call me later." Wanda kissed him on the cheek and left. "Slick ass nigga," Wanda stated to her girl.

"You know how these dope boy's and nigga's is guurrll, straight up nasty dick as hell!"

Mary, Jay's girlfriend, didn't dig or feel Jay checking out other girl's and stood up mad and said, "Nigga take me home!" She had peeped him staring at Alvin's girl's ass and her the whole time they been there.

Jay yelled, "Bitch sit down!"

Mary replied, "Fuck you punk!"

Jay hopped off the couch and slapped the spit outta her mouth. She fell down and got back up dazed and he sucker punched the shit out of her in the stomach. "Told yo ass to sit the fuck down!"

Alvin jumped up and grabbed him. "Man chill out!"

Jay hollered, "Get the fuck off me nigga!" and pushed him. They began to fight right there in the living room, until Pep broke up

"Man take this girl home!" Pep told Alvin.

"Yeah hoe, kick dust!" Jay shouted. When they left, Jay told Low and Pep, "Fuck that hoe!" Jay had been messing with Mary about six months and he had strong feelings for her, but just didn't know how to express them or show her. She was a boss freak and had him wide open the first time she set the goods out to him.

Alvin dropped his girl off first since she lived the closes, then he went to the drive thru and got Mary a six pack of beer and some wine coolers since she asked for it before he took her home.

On the way to her house, she told Alvin he was different, and not like the rest. "You so sweet an cute."

Alvin was dark skinned, short, ugly, and looked like a for real chip monkey. She had him blushing up a storm. He didn't have alot of girl's till he got in the game and started making money and driving nice rides. Plus, being one of Low's dude's was a extra bonus.

She slid closer to him. "I like your car. Put Keith Sweat in," she told him. Alvin leaned over at a red light to change his CD player to put in Keith Sweat in and she started rubbing his back.

Alvin started sweating. Him and Jay had grew up together and always fought, but nothing serious, or messing with each other's girl. Alvin pulled from the red light and made it to Mary's house.

"Here you go," Alvin told Mary, hoping she would hurry up and get out the car. On the ride there her mini skirt had rode up her yellow thighs and he could see her white lace panties and had boned up.

She put her hand on his thigh and started rubbing it, telling him thanks for saving me, and bringing me home, you so sweet.

Alvin started studdering saying, "Aw, it wasn't noth...noth...nothing," she slid her hand to his dick and Alvin jumped, almost nutting on himself when this pretty red bone touched his dick rubbing it.

"Oohh, Alvin you so hard, let me take care of this fo you baby. Come on in, my Moms at work."

"I...I...can't, "he groaned, trying to fight the sensation.

"Alvin let me take care of you," she whined, pulling his wood out rubbing the pre-cum around the head. Alvin couldn't take it no more and leaned back. She started jacking him off right there. "Don't cum yet baby," she purred, "Come'on, let's go inside."

Alvin let his dick beat him out and went in and fucked her. Pussy power won out on friendship, like it does with every weak person with no morals and loyalty.

Tina had missed her period this month and was worried. She had only been with one boy in her life, and that was Low. She knew she was pregnant, and was wondering and praying this would finally make Low act right like she wanted him to be when they first got together. Low had bought her a car to get around in and she got in it to go tell him the good news.

Low was still at the crib on Republic with Jay and Pep when this Vet fiend they called Boss head came over. She was 38 yrs. old, brown skinned and thick as fuck! But it was her oral game that got her name.

"Hey y'all pretty dick nigga's," she said as she strutted in smacking on some bubble gum. Pep was in the back with some girl.

"What's up Boss head?" Low hollered.

"Boy you know what's up. Can a bitch get som'em for some of this boss ass head or what?" She told'em, licking her fat pretty lips she had.

Low replied, "Hoe, you right on time! I got some build up in my balls like a muthafucka!" Low squeezed his joint.

Jay laughed. "Shhiitt! Bitch let's see what that head bout today." Jay stripped right there to his brown skinny ass.

"You ain't said nothing," Boss head told him, and dropped down slobbing on his knob. Low pulled her shorts off and started hittin her from the back as she sucked Jay off while he sat on the couch.

Some fiends knocked on the door and Low pulled his strap out, and told them to come on in. The door was opened and you could see in through the screen door. Low grabbed a plate full of rocks (crack) on the table and served them butt naked with a wet boner. When the third fiend came in, it was this freak hoe Liz who didn't even look like a clucker (fiend) cause she was fine ass hell and looked young. When she saw Low's shit boned up she got nasty with him.

"Uumm, that look good. Can I taste it?" Liz asked licking her wet pink lips.

Low said, "Do babies shit on their self?"

After she gave Low some dome, he went in raw with no jimmy on. Her pussy juices were all over his pipe.

Tina drove up in front of the house on Republic and got out her car. She got up on the door and saw it was opened. She was about to knock when she heard moans and shit like someone was fucking right there. So she peaked in and saw her man Low fucking someone doggy style and Jay on top of somebody else fuckin. She almost threw up seeing her man ramming his dick in another. She snatched the screen open and ran in there heart hurting beating outta her chest and jumped on Low's back, punching him all over screaming and hollering like a crazy person,

"Dirty muthafucka! Hell naw nigga, I'ma kill yo ass!" Tina swung on him. Low yanked his dick out Liz and rolled over with his dick still hard and soaking wet in the air. That really triggered some emotions and hate in

Tina and she went extra loco on-his ass, swinging and screaming, "Fucker, bitch, fucker, I'ma kill you!"

Low grabbed her, "Whoa Bitch, chill out!"

"FUCK YOU!" She yelled trying to bite him.

Low palmed her face stopping her from biting him. "Hoe, if you was suckin a nigga shit and freaky with a nigga, I wouldn't be fuckin shit!"

Tears rolled down Tina's face as she screamed, "Let me go nasty muthafucka!" Low pushed her away from him, and Tina stared at him with such hate, then she stormed out of the house slamming the door, and peeling out.

Jay was cracking up on the floor butt naked. Pep had came out the back when he heard the screaming and saw Tina swinging on Low, he had thought some trouble was popping off and had bought his pistol out running.

"Man you blew it with her," Pep told him,

The freak Liz was trying to suck Low's dick, as he was coming down off the shock of his girl Tina knocking him.

"Fuck that square ass hoe! Bitch don't even suck dick!" said Low.

"Damn, that's fucked up," Jay remarked.

"You hoes finish y'all biz," Low told the two fiends, upset for real about Tina.

Tina had to stop her car and get her thoughts together. She had almost wrecked two times already. "Fuck that bitch!" She uttered to herself on the side of the road. "I'll never let him know about the baby now! Ooohh I hate him. Hate his stankin guts!' She screamed, gripping the steering wheel so tight her knuckles turned white.

Later on that day, Low picked up Wanda and they went to the movies. He was a little fucked up about Tina catching him. But she was always complaining about what he was doing, or what she heard, and that was annoying his young ass. She was jealous all the time and he wasn't on that shit. Fuck her! He thought to himself.

Smoke was in the bathroom when his rappie Hank knocked on the door and told him it was a weight sale out there.

"Yeah, yeah, I'll be out there in a second nigga," Smoke told him slurring, high as a cloud. When he came out there he saw Joe and lil Rob.

Joe said, "Man Smoke, we want nine of them thangs O.G."

Smoke turned around and went upstairs and came back with a plastic zip lock baggie. "Here, this seven of them. I'll give ya the rest later, alright?" Smoke told'em. This was the second time Smoke did this shit to them and never gave them their product that they paid for, shorting them. Joe and lil Rob frowned their faces up.

"Man, I'ma keep two grand, bet?" Joe asked.

Smoke glared at him with them blood shot frogeyes and said, "Nigga, you want this or what?"

Joe knew he couldn't get work from nobody else, cause Smoke would find out and he didn't allow it out there. Only his and Nate's product was sold out there. "Yeah, Smoke man I know you got me," he replied not wanting to make him mad at him. So they took it and left. When him and lil Rob got outside he said, "Man that nigga tryin' to play me and you like some hoes! If he don't give us our shit I'ma serve that old ass nigga some slugs! Fuck who he is, and what he then done before!"

Lil Rob added. "Hell yeah...That nigga slippin anyway, I caught him sleeping in his car the other night high, like he untouchable an shit! If that old ugly ass nigga don't give us our shit from them two times, we got's to do som'em!" Joe nodded agreeing.

The next day after school, Dirty and Tito were headed to the West side to check out the girl's there after school, as they drove through Mill Creek Park. Dirty had Randy, Keith, and T.J. in the car with him. Tito had Eric, Joint, and Bernard in his Cutlass. They were cruising through the park to get to the West side, when they spotted this thick ass, brown complexion, Serena Williams built honey, jogging in some spandex shorts that looked like skin glued to her magnificent body, super doper fat ole ass, and halter top with headphones on with her sandy brown hair in a long ponytail.

"Gawd damn that ass fat as fuck!" Keith hollered next to Dirty, seeing the chick jogging. They started acting a fool seeing how stacked and sexy she was. Dirty slowed down and Keith yelled out the window.

She turned around and they saw she had on some dark glasses and some juicy lips. She glanced at both cars full of young thugs and kept jogging, ass bouncing like two beach balls.

"Punk bitch, "Keith shouted out to her, mad she wasn't paying him no mind.

Tito was behind Dirty and everybody in his car was lusting at her and saying, "Fuck she thick as hell!"

Dirty said, "Oh, that bitch think she all that cause she got a fat ass!" He drove a head of her and parked. He got out and so did the dudes with him in the car. Tito parked behind him and they all got out to and sat on his car.

When she got by their cars, she stopped cause they were trying to block her way. She took her headphones off. "Is there a problem?" She asked, as she glanced at all of them in the eyes.

"Yeah hoe," said Dirty.

Keith stepped to her. "Bitch, when you being called by players, you stop and listen."

She glared at him through her shades and replied, "Nigga, you got me bent the fuck up!"

Keith went to slap her and she ducked it and came back up with a solid right fist that floored him, surprising all of them. Eric charged her from the back and she kicked out hitting him in his nuts smashing his balls like tomato's, he screamed out holding his shit in pain. Dirty threw a punch at her and it landed making her staggered back. He went to throw another at the same time she did and their punches landed at the same time knocking Dirty off balance some. They started going blow for blow, when Tito hit her over the head with his pistol and she collapsed to the cement, then him and Dirty started kicking her. Dirty bent down and ripped her shirt off and her melon size tits sprang out like chocolate treats, making them nigga's mouths water. Keith and Eric started feeling all over her and yanked her thin fabric shorts down. She tried to fight them, but they punched her everywhere they could like wild animals when they saw her goodies. Her sandy brown pussy hairs were glistening from jogging and fighting them sweating.

Dirty boned straight up. "She fine as hell! Look at this hoes pussy!" He said lusting. "Get her ass in the car!" They drug her to the back seat and began to rape her.

Joint, Bernard, and T.J. wasn't on no foul as rape shit, so they stayed in the car smoking weed tripping off them nasty, foul, trifling ass nigga's. When they were finish raping her, Dirty kicked her body out the car to the side of the rode, and they drove off.

The rape girl laid there unconscious for two hours. Then she woke up shivering and crawled to the road, and got enough strength to stand up and walked until some folks driving in a car coming by stopped, seeing her naked bloody body and pulled over to help. The black man and his wife got out their car and helped her in their car, covering her up and took her to the hospital. She was admitted, and pronounced beaten severely with broken ribs, wrist, and fingers. She had black eyes and bruises everywhere. She remembered who raped her faces like a photo picture fresh in her mind. She locked the license plates in her membrane like her birth date. When the police asked her did she know or remember anything, she told them, "No, I can't recall anything." Now she laid in the hospital bed sore in pain rethinking the events and faces in her head, as she balled her fist up and slammed them on the bed as tears ran down her face.

Low tried to talk to Tina but she acted all funny and told him he had changed. So he said, "Fuck her" and left her alone. She started messing with Bobby, the cat Low had smacked in school about her before. She knew Low didn't like Bobby and said the nigga always was peeking at him, and that Bobby didn't care for Low but kept his feelings about him to himself, but Tina knew how he felt. She thought messing with Bobby would hurt Low, but it just made him pay her less attention, and that really pissed her off more.

Two weeks had passed since the incident at McDonalds and Low had shot at Dirty and Tito a few times trying to get them but missed hitting others instead that worked for them and they messed with in the process.

Chapter 17
Power, Money, Pussy
That's the root of all evil, or should I say, Heart of a Goon…

Rat was driving this girl's hooptie (not so clean car) down the street that their trap house on Truedale was and the car cut off on him. He got out the hooptie salty and started walking down the street to their spot. When he got close to their trap spot, he noticed two white men parked on the street watching their crib a few houses up. He walked up to the car and tried to look in but they had spotted him and drove off. Rat knew it was Narc's and ran to tell Lowdown and everybody. Low was gone but Pep, Moose, and Alvin was there.

Rat busted in shouting, "Man the Narc's was just watching the fuckin house up the street!" He was breathing all hard sweating. "They drove away when I saw them!" They started cleaning up snatching things noided.

"I'ma page Low an let him know! "Pep said going to the phone. "Yeah we got's to close up fo a minute."

Low called back when he saw the code in his pager. Pep had tried his celly but it was off. "What's crackin?" Low asked when Pep answered while he laid in the bed with Sandy thick Mocha chocolate ass on Republic.

"Nigga we've been gettin watched by the Narc's, Rat saw them up the street watching the crib just now!" Pep told him hyped.

"What?" Low responded, rolling out the bed to peek out the window. "Yup, I see them up the street in a car! Man close up shop now!" Low told him and hung up fast. "Get yo clothes on," he told Sandy. Then he went to tell Jay and his little cousin Shawn to shut down. Jay was in there with Mary yellow ass and Shawn was serving a fiend at the door when Low came out in his boxers. Mary's eyes went straight to his pee hole in his boxers looking for his wood. "Shut this bitch down right now, we're being watched right now!" Low yelled. They looked at him scared, but the fiend didn't give a fuck who was watching.

"This the biggest one you got?" The fiend asked, examining the crack rock in his hand like it was a human heart he was about to need to live.

Low picked another rock off the plate real fast and handed it to the fiend. "Here, this on the house. Now get the fuck outta here slim." He took that stone smiling happy and jetted. Jay and Shawn got to cleaning up and tightening up. Low went back to the room to put his clothes on. "You straight?" he asked Sandy.

"Uh huh, I'm dressed," she replied.

Low told lil Shawn to take the bag of guns, dope, and other shit and run out the back door and go over Rat's girl house Reeka in the Kimmel Brook projects and wait. He ran out the back door and Low told Jay not to sell shit, and make sure wasn't nothing else in the house. "Come'on," he told Sandy. They went outside to her car and drove off.

She was driving as Low watched the rearview mirror and saw a car following them as they turned a corner.

"Yeah, I see y'all chumps," Low mumbled to himself. Low got on his celly and called Roe and Nut. Nut answered and Low heard loud music in the background."

"Who this?" Nut hollered over the music.

"Man cut that shit down!" Low told him raising his voice.

"Hold up," Nut yelled, turning the music down, "Yeah who this?"

"Man my spot being watched by Narc's, so I know y'all got to be too! So clean y'all shit up quick!"

Nut replied, "Got cha killa," and hung up quick to handle his biz. Him and Roe shut down and went to the Jets (projects) to chill. But in them projects things stayed cracking as usual and people out there wasn't going to stop getting money and high because it was hot out and the Task Force were out raiding spots. So Nut and Roe got in where they been fitting in there whole life. Money and activity never ceased in the ghetto. Even the roaches had to eat and made it known.

They had closed down for a week and a half, and cranked back up after they ain't see nobody watching the traps no more. Low drove into the Victory banging Boogie Down Productions in his Vette. You could hear him coming before he turned the corner into the Vic. Bobby and Tina was on her front porch when they heard the music coming and then saw him driving up. His whip was so clean it made Bobby hate even more, and envy him at the same time. Little cats were on the block that slanged for him and his crew and all greeted him with respect. Many of them didn't have no fathers living with them, or in their life like most kids in the projects, so Low was looked upon as a ghetto role model. And the ones who did have fathers were mostly dope fiends. Low always gave money out to the little kids out there, and they ran to see him every time he came out there or was around. When they rushed Low today, Bobby mumbled under his breath.

"Bama ass nigga," Bobby said, and Tina heard him. They both hated him, but for different reasons.

Low was passing out money to all the kid's when Bo sister walked up on him with her cute tight tummy showing in a halter top, tiny shorts, and sandals showing her pretty white painted toes.

"Hey Lowdown," she spoke smiling, showing nice even white teeth.

"What's up girl?" Low replied, taking all of her in and liking it all.

"You," she flirted.

Low eyed her up and down real slowly and said "fuck it" to himself, he was going to shoot his shot. She was 19 years old and he had always wanted to fuck her, but she never paid him no mind because he was young. Shit then changed now.

"Oh yeah, how can I tell?" Low shot back.

She put her little hands with the polished white nails on her hips. "Booyy, can I get a ride to the sto (store)? Then maybe I'll show you later on."

"Shhiitt, let's roll baby," Low replied, not waiting a second to pass a shot at her up.

Tina just looked at them with hate in her heart as Pattie got into Low's whip and drove off. She wanted to pick up a brick and bust his fuckin window out. She rubbed her belly thinking about the baby that was his.

Low went straight to the drive thru and got himself a Strawberry Boones Farm. Nut and Roe had hipped him on it and he took a real liken to it. Pattie wanted some Gin with some Orange juice. So Low got a 5th of that, cups, and ice. Then Low cruised around for a half hour while they sipped. He drove to the crib on Republic and parked in the back. "Come'on, this my spot," Low told Pattie and they got out and went inside.

"This a nice house," Pattie commented, liking the crib she had heard about.

Pep was in the living room with some Rican girl from LaLa Land on the couch chilling as customers came thru. They spoke and Low took Pattie in the back room where they had air conditioning and it felt good as fuck. Pep's mouth had dropped when he saw Bo's sister with Low.

Low went into a drawer and took out some light green weed and tossed it to Pattie. "Roll som'em up."

Pattie held the bag up inspecting it. "Boy you tryin' to get me all high an shit, so you can get some, you ain't slick nigga."

Low gazed at her and replied, "If I got's to get you high to get some, then you got me twisted."

She liked his confidence and responded, "Nah baby, I like you fo real and you cute as hell...You can get some cause I'm feeling yo crazy ass too!" She lit the weed inhaling, and gave it to him. While he was puffing she was coming out her clothes. Low boned up looking at her perky little orange size titties poking out. She got down to her white lace panties and rolled them down her slim pretty hips. She had a tight body with a little bush around her vagina. She started taking Low's shoes off and other clothes, when she got his boxers and pulled them down, his dick smacked his belly making her laugh. "Oh my, you holding lil nigga," she gasped with her fingers wrapped around his pipe measuring him.

"Nah, you mean big nigga," Low said, and she laughed and got in bed with him. She took the joint and hit it again as Low put his mouth on her titties and started suckin and lickin as he fingered her pussy.

"Uumm...uumm...oohh..," she panted and grinded her pelvis against his hand. "Sshheeiitt!" she screamed, climaxing all over his two fingers he had up her tight wet pussy. Low took his fingers out and they were shining like he dipped them in baby oil, and even smelled like it her pussy was so fresh.

"Now let me see what this pussy like," Low told her, climbing on top of her as she reached down and guided his dick in. His dick head was so fat he had to push it in.

"Oohh shhiitt, yo dick thick," she moaned when he entered her. Low took it easy for a minute til she loosened up some, and then he beat it up like a drum set. Her ponana was so tight around his swipe. Low almost busted when he first started humping, and it was wet as fuck! Low had to think of som'em else before he skeeted (Climaxed) to fast. He had waited too long to blow it now on a quick nut. He wanted to soak his shit in her as long as he could.

"Daammmm...Loowww... fuck...this pussy...Fuck me baby!" Pattie hollered like she had the holy ghost in her and pumped back cumming for the third time.

They fucked for a good solid hour, and Low busted in her two times. Now they were laying in bed catching some rest laughing.

"So, how was it? You animal!" Pattie asked.

"You alriigghhtt," Low told her playing.

She hit him. "What?"

"Nah, I'm just playing. You got some good ass tight hot pussy fo real real!"

"It should be...I ain't had no sex in like a year something."

"Oh yeah...Well let me get some more of this bomb ass wet-wet again," Low said, and she laughed. "Shiit I ain't playin gurl." They fucked again and Low took his time this session.

Smoke didn't give Joe and lil Rob what he owed them so they sat in lil Rob's spot with their nigga Will talking shit about it. "Man fuck that dope fien ass nigga. I say let's do that fien muthafucka in!" lil Rob told'em.

"Let's go!" Joe replied getting up. They snatched their guns, while Will stayed back to make some sells.

In this game if you slip, you slip hard, and most times you don't come back from it. Nigga's don't give a flying fuck about what you did in your past. Especially if they feel disrespected, played, and feel they got som'em to prove to themselves and others. Most times nigga's with rep's are the prey, they the prey because nigga's hate and want to do you in just to show their more of a killer then you. So you got's to stay on top in this game 24/7. It's a thinking game, and a whoever bomb first game.

Lil Rob and Joe spotted Smoke on the block drinking some Irish Rose with Hank and two other old heads.

"Smoke, what's up? You got that other work you owe us?" Joe asked, with his hand behind his back gripping a Nine Milla.

"Lil nigga, didn't I tell yo ass I got cha when it comes thru an shit?" Smoke barked at him like he was a chump.

Lil Rob up piped and said, "Fuck that Smoke! You owe us nigga, so pull that shit outta yo pockets!" He was waving the gun at his chest.

Smoke busted out laughing and said, "All you little chumps wanna rob me, huh? Well...." BOOM! The gun went off. Joe had shot Smoke cause he was reaching for his gun tucked under his shirt.

The blast staggered him as he fell backwards from the shot to the chest.

Smoke looked up at Joe and got mad as hell. "Bitch, you really then fucked up now!" He went for his gun again and Joe got even scareder by that statement, and shot him two more times so Smoke couldn't make good on his threat and that he was dead for sure.

Then lil Rob stood over him and went in his pockets. "That's what you get beating us fo ours old nigga!"

The other old heads had ran, but Hank stood there in shock. He couldn't believe his nigga, a stone cold killer, had just got killed by some young punks. "Hell naw, y'all ain't just kill Smoke!" He cried going to his body after lil Rob went in his pockets and took his dope and money out.

"Where the keys to the crib at?" Joe asked Hank, pointing his gun at him. Hank threw him the key. Joe and lil Rob went straight to Smoke's spot and took all they could. They came up on a half brick of powder and some cash.

Hank mourned and cried over Smoke's body for like 10 minutes until someone got him off. Then he walked straight up to the house on Delaware looking for Nate to tell him what happened to Smoke. He wasn't there so he told Body bag, who couldn't believe what he was hearing, so he called Nate and told him. Nate told him he would be there in a second.

Nate had already got wind that Smoke had been killed as he entered the house, and the look on his face wasn't nice. Hank told him what happened, and Nate wanted to know why they did it. Hank told him why.

"Al'ight, take care of him," he told Body Bag, "Let's go," Nate told his two girl's and left. When they get outside he went in sat in the back seat of his Benz for 10 minutes, as his women sat up front waiting to comply with whatever he said. He was fucked up about his partners demise. No matter how hard of a killer you are, you felt it when someone close to you dies.

"Shoot to the house on Fairmont," Nate said. It was right down the street from where they were and closer to the projects. When they got there inside Nate said, "Now listen...," he told Rena and Jessica.

Joe, Will, and lil Rob was chilling at his spot rocking the work up they just took off Smoke. "Man that nigga wasn't all that!" Joe boasted, "Did you see how I did that old suppose to be killa, nigga? Fucked his old ass straight up! Fuck'em!"

Someone knocked on the door startling them. Will asked who is it?"

"Do ya got a eight ball?" a girl voice asked.

"Yeah, hold up," Will replied, opening the door.

Two ski masked girl's bum rushed in screaming forcing the door to hit Will in the cheek dazing him. "Lay the fuck down!" They hit the floor quick when they saw them in all black pointing 44 Bulldogs.

The one ski masked girl stood over Joe and pressed the burner to his noggin hard, and whispered, "Where the dope an shit you dummies took off Smoke?"

Joe really started shaking and worried, cause he knew Nate had sent these two gun totting gangstress, that was his two women he seen him with all the time and had witness put in work plenty times.

Studdering Joe said, "On...on...the...ta...table."

The one with the pistol pressed against Joe's dome let their partner retrieve the stuff bagging it up. "Y'all suckers strip the fuck naked now!" The one holding the pistol to Joe demanded. When they were done stripping, the one holding the bagged stuff nodded to her partner. "This fo Smoke lame, never fuck with Nate's partner's!" BOOM! The shot split his head to the white meat and two more busted his heart.

The one holding the bag said, "That was personal. We still in business." And they walked out til they got around the building, and then started running all the way until they got to a house on Fairmont, and went in catching their breath. Nate was sitting on the couch listening to Bootsy Collins. The two masked women pulled their mask off and put the duffel bag on the table in front of Nate smiling.

"There it is daddy," Jess said with a big grin.

"It all went well, and I let them know were still in business as you told us," Rena told him, happy to have accomplished what he had sent them to do and take care of.

"Put that shit in the bag, y'all know what to do," Nate told them. They got to stripping their clothes and putting them in a garbage bag, then got dressed and took the garbage bag up the street to Body Bag, who disposed of all incriminating evidence. That's the main reason they called him Body Bag, murder scenes was his expertise.

Low had drove to West Lake and saw his auntie on the porch, so he stopped to holla at her. "What's up auntie? What you smoking on?" He asked, knowing something went down out there by the vibe.

"Booyy, nothing. You got som'em?"

"Naw, but take this money and get ya some," Low handed her some ends.

"Thank you baby. Boy it's a hot mess out here. Smoke then got murdered wit his crazy ass. And just now that young boy...uuhh, uuhh...what's his name? Joe, got killed they say."

Her friend came out the door and said, "Yeah, that's his name honey child. They say he the one who killed Smoke fo owing them. So, Nate had him smoked."

Low was messed up hearing that Smoke had got murk (murdered). He hopped up. "I'll be back, gotta go check on my cat's," Low told'em, hurrying up so he could go find out what was happening.

Low's aunt looked at the money he gave her in her hand. "Uuhh, I can buy me a ounce of funk to smoke and some wine coolers. Hell...some of that fried chicken from Kentucky Fried Chicken."

"I know that's right honey. Your treat, so I'm driving. Let's get the chicken first cause we gone have the munchies after some good green," her friend Marsha said.

Low walked to the pad (apartment) Smoke had out there, and saw Roe and Nut hanging with some other home boy's and a couple of chick's drinking.

"What's the deal?" Low asked, already seeing the solemnly faces on most of them. Roe told him what happened to Smoke, and Nut spoke up heated, cause Nate told them not to fuck with Will and lil Rob because they didn't pull the trigger and he had biz with them,

"Fuck them bitch ass muthafucka's! Ah nigga kill both them hoes off rip!" Nut grumbled.

"What?" Low said, not believing Nate said that.

"He said that was the way of the jungle. Like I was suppose to know what the fuck that meant!" Roe stated shaking his head. "And you know Nut taking this shit kinda hard, cause him an Smoke was tight. He already went looking for lil Rob and Will but couldn't find'em."

Low stayed there with them for about a hour when Pep drove up. Low told them he was going to go holla at Nate, and left. He called Nate and told him he was on his way to holla at him and Nate told him he would be at his music shop. Low drove into the back of the store like Nate told him to and parked. He got out and knocked on the door, and was buzzed in. Nate was in his office laying down on the sofa listening to Marvin Gaye. Low sat down and could see Nate was in deep thought, so he didn't say nothing.

When the song went off, Nate said, "Yeah lil brah, my nigga got got. He was slipping in this jungle and it got him....Got too relaxed, like he was untouchable an shit. I seen it coming and told his hardheaded ass. But he always had his own mind and was bullheaded," Nate sighed. "All over a punk ass couple ounces he owed." It was like Nate was talking to himself.

Low replied, "Well, what's up with them other two nigga's?"

Nate turned his head and looked at him. "It was business when Smoke didn't pay them lil nigga's what he owes them, but when those lil niggas killed him, it became business with some personal shit to me! I can't blame them lil muthafucker's cause they wanted what was due to them by a nigga who they looked up to for years. But, when he kept playin them like hoes, punks, and bitches, there pride was hurt and made them react.

Low thought about what he just said for five minutes, trying come to terms with how Nate was handling this and what he said.

Low said, "Yeah, I feel that."

"Nut and Roe can handle the Lake now. I'll talk to them later about it but I'm sure they already know what's up."

"Well. I'm outta here." Low got up to leave.

Nate called him when he was about to walk out the door. Low turned to him. "Low, never mix your emotions with yo biz. When do, it's like mixing gas to fire."

Low knew what he was saying, then walked out saying "later."

Up the street from the dope house on Truedale, Homicide Detectives Malley and Jackson sat with a team from Narcotics Division.

"These little thugs are making alot of money," Malley stated, watching the constant drug and money transaction at the house.

"Sure is. We got 'em selling to undercover's, but we don't got that punk y'all really want and after," the drug task force cop told Malley and Jackson.

Jackson replied, "Can't we bug somebody and make a big buy? I'm telling you guy's this thug is a murderer, and I want his ass off the fuckin streets!"

The task cop looked at Jackson and could see the intense hate, and wanting to get this young drug dealer off the street,

"Well, we can try," he stated.

Malley said, "Well let's do it damn 'it!"

Pep and Moose were at Moose Moms house in the Victory, when they saw Cathy with Brenda and Kim. Cathy was almost due and her stomach was big as hell.

"Hey y'all," Cathy spoke, as she walked to her car with Kim and Brenda. "Oh, Bo told me to tell y'all thanks fo the money and pictures y'all sent yesterday too. I bet it was pictures of some nasty bitches to," Cathy said smacking her gums and frowning at them.

"Naw Cathy, it was some cool pictures," Moose lied knowing he sent some naked shots of a few fiends and young chicks.

"Yeah right nigga. And I see yo ass don't come over and visit no more! Got a little money now and you acting all funky."

Moose was about to say something when Pep yelled, "What you stank hoes smiling an looking at? Huh?" Pep asked Kim and Brenda, who were giving him the goggly sexy eyes. Pep pulled out a 38 snub nose. "Y'all bitches got alot of shit started. Nigga's dead an shit cause of y'all hoes fo real!"

The one Pep use to mess with, Kim, said, "Baby we---" SMACK!

She didn't finish what she was going to say, cause Pep slapped her upside the head with the 38 and she fell down with a gash on forehead. "You hoes ain't allowed out here no more!"

Cathy dropped down to help Kim. "Boy why you trippin?! You didn't have to hit her! Let's get her up Brenda."

"Hoe's I ain't playin," Pep barked, then shot by Brenda's feet making her jump and Kim hop up.

"Ok...ok we won't come out here no more!" Brenda and Kim screamed. Pep and Moose walked away.

"Come'on y'all, don't pay him no attention. Let's go get ya cleaned up," Cathy said.

"Gurl get me the fuck outta here, fuck dat! Them nigga's killing people child!" Kim pleaded, trying to get out of there dizzy as hell.

Chapter 18
Karma can haunt you in life. Even kill you.

Low had a nice piece of change saved up. He was getting two birds and was only 15 years old. He had told his aunt Cookie he was going to move her out of the Westlake projects, but she refused. Saying she loved where she stayed and wasn't no excitement in other upper scale hoods. She called ever neighborhood the ghetto, saying no matter where you lived it was the people that made the place you lived at. But, he kept at it and she finally agreed to it. He gave her the money for it and to furnish the crib she chose on the South side, out in Boardman. She loved it. Pep had gotten his Mom a house out their where Cookie stayed at. Everything was going smooth and sweet for their crew. But, in this Goon life, when shit hit you, it hits you from all angles like a ton of bricks.

Dirty, Eric, and Keith was in Dirty's whip heading to the fast food spot Rally's on Market street, they had just left their trap house on Glen Haven, and was bumping (playing) some Too Short music (City Of Dope) when they drove into Rally's.

"Park this bitch, I got's to piss like a mug," Eric said in the back seat holding a bottle of Heineken between his thighs. Dirty parked and they got out. Eric went straight to the restroom, while they ordered some grub. They didn't know that someone had followed them up there from the trap house.

Eric was taking a piss at the stall when someone came in, and said, "Hey little dick."

He heard a girl's voice say close behind him and turned around seeing a girl with shades and a baseball cap on. He glanced down and saw she was holding a big ass 45 in her right hand. "What you want bitch, some dick?" He asked still pissing.

She took her glasses off with her left hand, and Eric squinted his eyes trying to remember her or see if he knew her while he was finishing pissing, and turned around to zip his pants up.

"Naw nigga, keep it out since you like stickin it where it ain't wanted anyways!" she told him.

Eric turned around with his dick in his hand and said, "Damn, if this what you want, then suck it an get it over with!"

"Naw hoe ass nigga, I'm that girl y'all raped in the park, remember? I want something else."

Eric stared at her and it hit him who it was. "Hoe I…" BOOM! The gun went off blowing his dick straight off! He screamed worser then a pregnant woman in labor grabbing what was left of his member, trying to stop the blood squirting out and pain. "Oohh my lord! Please help me!"

She stepped over him. "Now I want yo life!" and shot him dead in the center of his head, blowing the back of his shit out! Brains splattered on the wall and pisser as he hit the ground dead as last year. His bowels had let loose, giving the restroom a strong, deathly stinky odor. She put her shades back on and pulled the baseball cap down tight and ran out the restroom bumping into people who had heard the shots and were trying to get out of there scared.

Dirty and Keith were in the car waiting on Eric, eating their food when they saw everyone running. "Fuck this fool at?" Dirty said getting out the car to go check seeing all the commotion. A cop pulled up and he turned around knowing he was strapped. He got back in the car putting his burner under the seat. "Man I don't know what's goin on." They got out the car seeing more police and an ambulance come.

They saw the paramedics bring Eric out covered up on a stretcher. They knew it was him, because of his shoes and Nike socks he was wearing that day.

"What happened to him?" Dirty asked the police shocked.

"Why, do you know him?"

"Yeah, what the fuck happened?"

"Give us his name and I'll tell you."

Ten minutes later Dirty was driving away from Rally's with Keith fucked up about Eric. He couldn't believe somebody had just killed his nigga like that! And inside Rally's at that!

After she had ran out the restaurant, she jumped into the hottie and drove to the house on Warren, on the South side that was near the park she was raped at. She parked the car behind her house and covered it up, and went inside. She took all her clothes off and left them right there on the floor, then laid the gun on the dresser and stood there in front of a 5ft mirror butt naked. "Got one," she mumbled to herself, then she went in got in the shower. Her body was so tight and cut with muscles, with a nice big ole fat ass. She worked out 6 days a week. Took kickboxing, lifted weights, and ran. She had always stayed fit and in shape, but the rape that had occurred had her so fucked up, that she worked out so hard that she would collapse from fatigue. She went to college for Criminal Law to be an attorney or prosecutor in the morning at Y.S.U., but the rape had changed her inside.

Low never went to see or visit his family on his father's side, because they didn't acknowledge him. They blamed his father's death on him, his brothers, and his mother. He had heard his father's side of the family say it was his father's greed to take care of them that had caused his death. The way he died was always hushed up when he came around. So, when his father's brother saw him doing good, he decided to stop over at the house on Republic he heard Low was pumping (selling) out of.

Low saw him drive up and park across the street and didn't give him a second thought, as he stood in the driveway with Pep and customers came through. But when he started walking his way with a fake smile plastered on his face, Low knew he was acting.

"Hey nephew what's good?" he said to Low with a weak smile that Low saw through like a window.

"Shit," Low replied, then asked, "What's up wit you?"

"Ahh nothing much. Just thought I'd come see how your doing," he said, watching Pep make a transaction, stuffing the money into a leather bag that was over flowing with dead presidents. He had got wind that Low had bought his aunt and brothers a house, and wanted to slid in under him to get a piece of his change.

"Well, you see. So pull the fuck out now!" Low told him. He put a hurt look on his face, so Low screwed his face up on him and said, "Punk bitch I ain't playin! Kick mud!" His uncle Bart practically broke his neck running from there.

Laughing, Pep said, "Man you crazy!"

"Fuck that lame. Wouldn't even let me and my brothers come spend the night over his crib, cause he lived with some high class hoe in a big house when he had a good job and money. Use to dog us and not even claim us."

"Yeah, fuck him. Check though. Man these vet honeys tryin' to get at us nigga. I met them yesterday at this college party, and they hip to you. Talkin bout they heard all kinds of stuff bout yo ass."

"Oh yeah, where they at fool?"

"Nigga they throwin a party at the Union hall tonight."

"Shhiitt, let me throw some gear on then," Low told'em, going into the back room to put some clothes on. When he came back out he had a red suede Nike jogging suit on, red trimmed in white Nike Cortez shoes, and hat. He was letting his hair grow so he had a baby afro that was lined up all around sharp. Pep always rocked Adidas, so he had on an all-silk one, shoes and all.

"Let's bounce nigga, got some honeys with brains waiting on us," Low said smiling. They got in Pep's Lac and hit the party.

When they got there it was jam packed with cars and people outside kicking it. Low looked around at all the good looking fine women all around and to be his first time going to a grown folks college party, he didn't feel out of place at all.

"Let's get our party on with these square old chicks," Pep told Low as they got out the car to go inside. They had to pay $5 at the door. It was all kinds women inside there, white, black, mixed, and all kinds of nationalities. Pep spotted Donna, the college chick who had invited him. She was light brown, 5'7", slim, with a little bubble butt and cute. She was at a table with the girl who wanted to holla at Low and some other good looking women.

"Come on, there they go. The one in the yellow is the one who wanna holla at cha," Pep yelled to him over the music.

Low saw who he was talking bout and thought she was pretty. Donna saw them coming and told her girlfriends, "Here comes that little goon boy I was telling you guy's about, with his friend everybody keep talking about."

"Oh, they cute," the two of them said.

"What's up Donna, ladies?" Pep spoke greeting them. "This my homie...Lowdown."

Low nodded his head saying, "what's up?"

"Hi Pep, and did you say Lowdown?" The one named Penny asked.

"Yeah," Low answered her. "But they call me Low." They all hollered at Low, already hip to his name and him ringing.

"You guy's sit down an join us," Donna told'em. "This my girl Carla, Low," she said introducing them.

Carla reached out to shake his hand with her high yellow butt, and Low saw she was cute as hell. But, there was this brown sugary complexion sister sitting there with the sexiest face he had seen, and stunning brown eyes that made him stop and stare at her longer than usual. Him and Pep sat down and began to conversate with the two females they came to see and with the others too. Low kept staring at the brown-skinned one on the sly, and found out her name was Shakira, but everyone called her Kira.

Some college dudes came over to their table and asked Kira and Penny to dance. Penny jumped up and said, "Come on girl, let's get our groove on."

"I'm cool, gon' head," Kira told her. But their other friends told her to loosen up and encouraged her to get up and dance, so she said, "Okay, just one song." When she stood up the one piece body outfit fit her like skin, and Low's eyes nearly got stuck roaming her bodacious thick as a Snicker bar curvy body.

Pep shook his head like, "Damn."

The girl Donna was like, "What you shaking your head like that for?"

"Ah, nothing," Pep lied.

Kira ass was so fat, that nigga's on the floor had stopped and gazed when they were dancing with their girl's. Low and Pep got back into their conversation when all of a sudden they heard some female yell out, "Nigga get outta my face!" when the music stopped. They turned around and saw it was Kira yelling with a frown on her face at the dude she had went to dance with.

She started walking back when he grabbed her arm and shouted at her, "Bitch! Where..." BAM! Kira hit him so quick and hard to the nose that blood flew out as he stumbled and fell back into a table. His partner that was dancing with Penny went to help his buddy up. Kira came back and sat down puffing looking mad.

"Damn girl, I need to learn some of that karate stuff," Donna and Carla both said.

"I know that's right!" Penny implied.

"You alright?" Low asked.

She looked at him and held his stare, then said, "Yeah, I'm fine. Thank you."

The dude that helped him up came over to their table with the one Kira beat up lagging behind holding his bleeding nose. "A hoe!" He pointed to Kira.

Low jumped up so fast hitting him with a two piece and pulling his burner out that dude didn't even have enough time to regain his balance when Low slapped him up side his dome with the 9.M.M., He fell back into some people smearing blood all over their clothes. Pep started kicking him and the girl's screamed for him to stop and grabbed him off as security came. Dudes partner had bounced as soon as he saw the gat in Low's hand. The girl's told security what happened, and since it was their party, they escorted the beat up dudes out. The party started back up and Kira thanked Low.

"Wasn't nothing," Low replied.

"I told you heifers they were some goons," Donna square ass said, all over Pep. "Let's go dance baby," she told him.

When they went to the floor Kira said, "Well, I'm about to leave y'all," and got up.

"Hold up, let me walk you out to yo car just in case them lames out there hanging around," Low told her getting up.

"All ain't that sweet of him," Carla commented, looking at Low like she wanted to give him some butt right now.

"I'll be right back," Low told Carla.

Low and Shakira walked outside, and when they got to her car after walking in silence there, Low said, "Nice ride," when she went to an all-black 86 Grand National. She didn't comment and begin to look for the key to unlock the door. "Dang, it's nice out," Low said, trying to make conversation and not knowing what else to say feeling a little awkward, because she was so bad. "You got a good punch, where you learn that at?" Low asked, as he tried not to peek at all that junk in her trunk as she turned around finding the key opening the door.

She turned back around and looked at him. "Thanks for walking me out here to my car. Tell my girl's I said that I'll see them at school and to call me later, bye."

Low stared at her and said, "Alright...Bye," as she got in her car and drove off.

Kira watched him in her rear view mirror as she drove away. It was something about that young boy and his eyes she couldn't put a finger on. She knew he was young and that he was a goon. And she didn't like Goons one bit. But he seemed real nice and concerned about her well-being she thought as she got on the freeway.

Low couldn't believe how bad Kira was as he walked back inside. She was all woman indeed, with class and mass ass, he thought to self, as he got back to the table and sat down next to Carla.

"Did she make it out okay?" Carla asked looking at him cause he looked like he was somewhere else.

"Yeah, she cool," Low replied putting his arm around Carla and leaning back closer to her whispering in her ear.

Carla giggled. "Let's dance." They got up as Keith Sweat was playing, and Low grinded the shit outta her on the dance floor. Carla felt the size of his joint against her muffin and got wet. After the party, Low and Pep followed them to their apartment up in Liberty.

"Girl...we about to get some young goon dick! I told ya they were cute, didn't I?" Donna asked Carla, smiling up some shit.

"They are cute, and fun to play around with, but nothing to take home to the family. Plus, they suppose to be dangerous?" Carla asked, looking at her girl with a funny expression.

"Honey don't worry, we just going to see what's up with these drug dealing boy's. We never messed with none before, so it isn't nothing but testing the other side, okay?"

Carla nodded her head and said, "Alright," thinking about how hard and big Low's pipe was when he was grinding on her.

Liberty was a white section mostly, that was on the North side. They drove into this security apartment complex and parked right next to them under this long garage that a line of cars was under. Donna and Carla got out Carla's Camaro and told them, "Come on, we stay right there." Low glanced around as he held his gun, then tucked it in his waist. Pep just shook his head at him and followed them inside.

Their apartment inside was nice. You could tell it was a young females residents because it had a feminine touch.

"Want something to drink you guys?" Carla asked all proper, as she took her little jacket off.

"Yeah, you got some wine?" Low asked, having some taste for a Strawberry Boones Farm.

"We got some coolers, Millers beer and Seagram's Gin. Which one you want?" she asked him as she shay shaded into the kitchen.

"Let me get some Gin shit. You got some orange juice I can mix it?" Low asked.

"Yeah!"

"Me too and a beer." Pep yelled to her in the kitchen. Low took out a bottle of V's (valiums) and shook some out, then passed them to Pep.

"What's that?" Donna asked, looking at them like they were on some dope fiend shit. Carla came back with their drinks.

"Valiums," Pep told her.

"That stuff for nerves," Donna said, really looking at them weird now.

"Yeah, that's what they say. You want some?" Pep handed the bottle to her.

"Uhuh, I'm cool baby." These fools crazy, and they on prescription drugs, she was thinking, checking them out.

Pep washed the pills down with his drink. "Uurr..."

"Low, come with me in the back," Carla said. They got in the back to her bedroom and Carla shut the door and turned on some music. En vogue's slow cut came on and Carla started taking her clothes off, leaving her blue lace panties and bra on. Low stared at her little cute red bone ass and got hard as a brick.

"What you lookin at?" she asked, playing in her sexy voice.

Low put his drink down swallowing two V's and said, "Something sweet."

The smile on her face got wider. "Take them shoes off boy!"

Low sat on the bed and leaned back and said, "Help me out."

She walked over to him and saw his dick print, "Oh, you got a girl working, huh?"

"Nah, not yet," Low replied, staring at her little fat pie between her legs.

She took all his clothes off and got to his boxers and saw his dick sticking out the pee hole, like a thick long summer sausage and gasped, not believing this little nigga had a pipe like this.

Low grabbed his dick standing it straight up and said, "Think you can fuck with this?" He had saw the look on her face when she saw his dick, that's why he asked her that.

Carla gazed at his joint and said, "Umm, I don't know," she got on the bed on her knees and went straight to his dick, wrapping her hand around it and licking it like a blow pop, getting it ready to put it in her mouth.

"Uumm," she moaned as she licked and sucked it all over, then put it in her hot mouth.

"Damn, that's it girl, suck it," Low groaned, her tight mouth felt real good, being she had a little mouth anyway. "Shhiitt...damn you suckin this dick!" Low started pumping into her mouth feeling his nut build up.

She couldn't take it all but she worked it as best she could and it felt damn great to Low. He hollered out cumming all in her little mouth. It was so much she choked on it.

"Dang baby, you trying to drown me," she coughed, lips wet and glistening with his juices and her saliva. She gazed at his wet dick seeing it was still semi hard, and stroked it a couple times and it came alive getting hard again. She purred and climbed on top of him and guided his dick inside her, stretching her pussy to the max, trying to take him all in but couldn't, so she didn't go all the way down at first. "Oohh...fuck...your dick...so...so…fuckin big!" Low grabbed her hips and slammed her down on his pole, making her scream out. "Aahh shit! Fuck this alot of dick! Ssshhiit-teedd!" Low had his fuck face on and was giving her a goon fuckin! He beat the pussy up so good that she was sore as hell for three days and loved his goon lovin.

Pep had sexed Donna good to, so good she was on his dick now. That play toy shit they had in mind for them had back fired, and they became the play toys cause they fell in love with their Goon passion, Goon fuckin! Not them, just the dick whipping. To them, they were showpieces to brag to their girl's about…they thought and thought wrong.

Chapter 19
Revenge quenches my spirit...

Roe and Nut started making alot more money since they took over Smoke's position, and alot of people that wasn't eating (getting theirs) before was doing good, because Roe and Nut showed alot of love and gave out deals. Only ones hating was Will, and lil Rob. Nate had told Roe, and especially Nut to leave them alone about Smoke. Nut didn't appreciate being told that and let Nate know it. He told Nate he would just stay away from them, and hoped they did the same. Nut had started taking alot of Tuss (syrup). That stuff be having you mello, scratching, drowsy and nodding. It was like a lightweight form of Heroin.

"Man what's crackin?" Roe said to Nut as he sat in his car high with his main girl, Shawn thick black ass.

Nut looked up at him and said, "Shit killa. Just laid back, bout to take her to the sto (store) an shit," he was slurring like a muthafucka.

"Can't tell, boy we've been here a fuckin hour and ain't went no damn where! And you sho ain't driving me nowhere all fucked up like that!" Shawn expressed heated. "Got me bent!"

Nut rolled his red eyes her way. "Shut the fuck up!"

"Make me nigga!"

Roe jumped in knowing how they could beef and seeing his Ace fucked up. "Man let her drive fool, you too high nigga!"

"Sho is, and her smart ass still ain't driving," Nut replied scratching his neck.

Roe told'em, "Fuck it, get in the back and I'll drive then." Nut didn't say shit and just climbed over the seat to the back and laid down, while Roe took the wheel to drive. "A Shawn, come here," Nut said.

"Yeah right Nut, I ain't fuckin with yo high ass!"

"Fuck it then, turn my music up." The sounds of 2 Live Crew filled the car.

Roe backed out the projects parking lot and drove to the store on the

East side Shawn wanted to go to. When they got there Roe saw Pep's ride parked, so he parked next to him and they got out and went in. Nut was walking cool as fuck, madd dogging (looking at folks crazy or with a mean look) people. They saw Pep and Low with Wanda and her girl Linda.

"What's poppin nigga's?" Roe hollered to them.

Shawn just made a funny noise and rolled her eyes at them and walked off to the shoe section. She wasn't on seeing her girl's men with other chick's.

Nut said, "What's up Wanda?" but was staring at Linda's titties, that were busting out of her halter top with her nipples hard poking out.

"What y'all up too?" Pep said, laughing at Nut thirsty ass.

Roe replied, "Shit, just came to take this fool here girl to the store since his ass to high."

"I know that's right," Linda commented, seeing how he was drooling at the mouth, and switched her behind off.

"Hi y'all," Wanda said, and went to catch up with Linda.

"Damn, them freaks got some junk nigga," Nut stated, rubbing himself.

"You wanna fuck nigga, gone' and shoot yo shot. That ain't my piece," Pep told him.

"Hell yeah killa, you ain't said shit!" Nut gave him some dap and went to find Linda. They all busted out laughing, saying that nigga crazy.

Nut caught up to Linda and Wanda, and got all up on Linda not giving a fuck pressing his groin against her.

"Boy you better back up! You know your woman in here retarded." Linda said pushing him back off her feeling his hardness on her ass cheeks.

"Fuck that, you know you want some of this shit," he told her grabbing his dick. "Stop acting like you don't, fronting an shit!"

She looked down. "That little thing-thing, boy please," she said rolling her eyes and smacking her lips.

"Oh yeah," Nut responded, and zipped his pants down and yanked his dick out.

Astounded, Linda gazed down and said, "Boy you so crazy," but kept her eyes locked on his pipe licking her pink lips as she sized him up.

Wanda was peeking over her shoulder getting herself a good hard view.

"Gurl come'on for that nut get us in trouble." They walked off and Linda kept glancing back checking him out and winked at him.

"Yeah, you gon' head hoe!" Nut yelled.

Linda stopped and turned around. "Hoe huh?"

"You heard me, hoe bitch," Nut replied, eyeing her down and staring at her pussy like he could see through her tight shorts.

"I'll be that, but only to you," she stated, and strutted off shaking her nice brown ass.

Nut zipped his pants up puzzled by what she just said. Then walked off, catching his girl looking at some shorts and coming up behind her squeezing her big ole ass.

"Stop Nut! What, you got horny looking at them trashy tramps yo boy's got?" Shawn spat. Nut didn't pay her no attention and wrapped his arms around her kissing on her neck. "Yuk, stop Nut!" she said, but really enjoyed it. She had been with Nut since they were 12 years old and loved his dirty drawers.

A party was being thrown on the South side and Moose and Rat was there. They were on the dance floor getting there groove on when Dirty, Joint, Randy, and Keith walked in. They were too busy dancing to notice them enter, but Dirty spotted them and hit his partners nodding towards them.

"We got beef up in this bitch with them East side hoes!" Dirty yelled over the music to them. His partners knew Dirty didn't give a fuck about popping who ever, where ever, when ever!

Moose didn't know what hit him as he went to the ground and felt kicks. Rat had saw Dirty coming through the crowd and glanced around for Moose and didn't see him where he just was dancing at, so he went the other way from Dirty so he could go get his gun he left in the car. When he turned around someone smashed a 40oz bottle upside his head and started punching him, he was a big dude so he wasn't as fazed and ducked some then grabbed the first person he could and took them down with him throwing blows to their face and where ever they landed. Keith covered up as best he could as Rat's blows rained down on him fucking him up with solid shit. Dirty hit Rat in the head with his pistol and they started kicking him like they did Moose who was out cold on the floor. People bum rushed out the basement. The girl who threw the party and her cousins tried to break it up, and when they finally did Moose was still out. Rat was fucked up but still ready to fight some more. Dirty and his rappies had bounced and went to this other party that was being thrown three streets up since they crashed this one. Rat got Moose up and outta there and called Low.

Low, Pep, Nut, Roe and some workers were chilling at the dope house on the North side when Low's celly rung and he answered it. "Who this? What? Where you at?" Low was hyped. "Them hoe ass Bitches!" Low hung up and told them what happened.

"Let's go see them bitches!" Nut told them all high and ready to body someone.

Dirty and his rappies were hanging outside at the other party drinking, laughing and talking shit to some girl's that had left the other party and knew what they had just done there, for some reason bad boys, Goons, and hustlers attracted women like flies on dodo.

Low and them had stole a car and was now cruising down the street Dirty and his crew was now at outside. "Yeah, it's on an poppin," Roe uttered in the front seat next to Pep. "That's them there!"

The rape girl had been following Dirty and them since they went the first party but couldn't get close enough. She parked down the street and was watching them hang outside. She got out the car in all black with dark shades and a hoodie on even though it was dark, and started walking towards them with her head down. She was 5ft away when a car drove up and some nigga's jumped out blasting at Dirty and his crew. Dirty ducked down taking cover and busted back with his crew.

"What's up now nigga's?" Low shouted, ski-masked up during the gun firing. "Fuckin wit my niggas, it's on bitches!" BUCK, BUCK, BUCK! The 45 sounded like a cannon as flames shot out.

The hooded rape girl jumped behind a tree when the shooting started, she was mad as hell! They were close as hell and I probably could of had gotten at least three that raped me, but naw, this bullshit jumping off, she was thinking, as gun shots rung out and screams polluted the quiet night. She peeked around the tree she was behind and saw one of them shooting with his back turned to her, so she ran at him busting her 380 with the hollow point bullets at him, catching him in the shoulder making him drop his weapon. Dirty saw his nigga Keith getting shot at and shot, and started clapping on the hooded person who shot him. She dropped and rolled over when Dirty was shooting at her and returned fire.

Low and his crew had saw someone come out of nowhere shooting at who they were blasting on and popping one of them, making Dirty clap at them. So Low ran at Dirty shooting catching him in a cross fire between him and whoever the other person was. Dirty saw what was up and made a run for it with Joint and Randy tailing behind.

"Oh hell naw!" Low muttered to himself, and took off after them.

While Low had been busting on Dirty, the hooded person in all black had ran up on Keith and shot him full of lead, making him look like a rag doll that had been through hell. Then she saw the same person who was shooting at the same people she was, go after the one she wanted dead the most! She thought. So she took off behind him chasing Dirty and them.

Dirty and them stopped running and turned around and saw dude with the ski mask on their ass, so they unleashed some lead.

Low dove behind a house, and shot back. He yelled, bitches!" as he fired back. Sweat was dripping into his eyes. He lifted the ski mask up wiping sweat from his eyes.

The hooded girl had caught up with them and hid behind a trash can trying figure out how to sneak up on Dirty and his boy's as they shot it out with the other person, when she saw Low raise his ski-mask up to wipe his face.

"A you!" Pep yelled to the girl, catching up to them seeing the hooded person behind the car.

She turned around pointing her 380 at him, and Pep had his out on her. Low had heard Pep and turned around and saw them pointing guns at each other. The hooded person switched her eyes from Pep to Low but kept her pistol on Pep. Dirty and them jumped a fence when they saw them pointing gats at each other stalling. She saw them and took a chance and ran after them giving Pep a chance to shoot her in the back. Low saw the hooded person go after them over the fence and said, "Fuck it!" and went after them. Pep shook his head not really wanting to, but didn't want to leave Low to himself so he followed him. They heard gunfire a house down and ran that way. Low and Pep peeked around the house they were at and saw the hooded person blasting at Dirty and them as they were busting back hard! Low ran from behind the house bucking (shooting) at Dirty and them. The hooded person saw him and joined firing at Dirty and them.

"Ahhhhh fuck!" Someone hollered out on Dirty's side, then they saw him fall from behind the tree on his side. Dirty and Joint took off leaving Randy bleeding and crying from a gunshot to the kidney.

Low, Pep, and the hooded person ran up on Randy as he thrashed on the ground crying.

"Remember that girl y'all slimy fucks raped in the park?" The hooded girl uttered to Randy, standing over him clutching her gat tightly. Low and Pep was fucked up when they heard her speak knowing it was a girl under that hoodie, dark shades, and all black baggy clothes. "This for fuckin with the wrong one!" BOOM, BOOM! She shot him in the chest. "Fucker!" BOOM! Then in the neck. Low cut loose with his 45 hitting him in the chest opening him up like a orange as blood splattered his stomach down. Still releasing anger, the girl shot him four more times in the face, making him unrecognizable even for his mother.

"Yo! Let's get the fuck outta here!" Pep yelled to Low hearing the police sirens around. Low turned around to tell the girl to come on and she was gone. "Let's go!" Pep yelled to him again, seeing the girl was gone to.

Them two murders had made Low and his crew hot because everybody knew about the incident with Moose and Rat at the party. That made Detective Malley and Jackson put more pressure on the Tasks Force more to help them get Low and his partners off the street.

Three days later, Low was hanging with his two little brother's and Sandy at Dairy Queen on the East side. Sandy short dark chocolate thick ass was licking on her ice cream cone and Kevin was like, "Ooohh baby, you sure know how to lick that mug." Sandy looked at him frowning, as Otis busted out giggling. Low just shook his head grinning.

Sandy smiled, showing her evenly spaced pretty white teeth. "Ooh, little nasty boy."

Low just leaned back in the car seat enjoying the moment. It wasn't often he smiled and felt good like he did at that moment. But being and seeing his two little brother's happy made him feel like he did right now. Then thoughts of their mother penetrated and flashed in his mind, making pain shoot through him like pins were being poked in his flesh.

"You want anything else Low baby?" Sandy asked, bringing him out of the zone, getting out of the car.

"Umm…yeah. Get me a banana cone," Low replied, turning away and looking out the window, remembering a time him, his mother, and brothers were last here.

"Baby got back!" said Kevin, watching Sandy booty bounce away. Low busted out laughing. Times like this is what he needed to stay sane and keep tight.

Mary, Jay girl, had skipped school so she could kick it with Alvin. Alvin never went to school. They were at the Mall about to go to go see a movie showing there, when they bumped into Bobo sister Pattie and his woman Cathy. Alvin was stuck, and knew he was busted. He knew they knew this was Jay's girl, and the look on their faces showed it. His didn't hid his guilt either. "Hey Alvin," Cathy spoke, walking towards them grinning.

Pattie said, "Hey girl, what you two doing here? Where Jay an them?" She asked, already seeing the busted look on both their faces.

Alvin replied studdering, "They...they...around."

"Oh," Pattie responded, "Well y'all take care."

"Don't do nothing me and Bo would be doing," Cathy told them being funny, walking off laughing her and Pattie.

When Cathy and Pattie got away some from them, Pattie said, "Oooowwee, Alvin dipping in his niggas cookie jar."

"That's messed up. His ugly ass got a little money now he fuckin his best friends girl. Damn shame!" Cathy expressed shaking her head smacking her gums.

Chapter 20
Money can't buy love, but it can get you some pussy, and fake friends. But when it's not there, they sure ain't either!

Pep and Low went to check out their college chicks at their apartment in Liberty. When they got there and went inside, Shakira was there sitting down with Donna.

"Hey you two, y'all remember Kira don't y'all?" Donna asked.

"Yeah, how could a nigga not," Low replied staring at her as their eyes locked for second.

"Carla isn't here Low. She went to visit her parents," Donna informed him.

Low just nodding his head, letting her know he heard her and sat down across from Kira and gazed at her thick legs she was showing in some shorts.

Feeling his stare, Kira said, "Well, let me be on my way. I got a class to go to," she stood up, "Can't miss my work out."

Donna stood up. "Honey your fine, you don't need to exercise so much!" Donna told her giving her a hug.

Low stood up and said, "Let me see you out. Never know…them dudes might be out there from last time."

The girl's laughed, while Pep just shook his head, knowing what Low was up to, as he followed behind Kira close staring at her fat as rump. Pep licked his lips wondering if all that butt and body was good.

Low walked out the door with her watching her ass jump like dope boys when the police hit the block. He looked at her calves and noticed the muscle definition. "So you work out, huh?"

"Got's to have it," she answered, knowing he was checking her out.

"Yeah, I've been planning on starting myself," Low said, still checking out her ass.

She looked at him. "Um, yeah you need a little weight on them bones." and laughed.

Low smiled. "Oh yeah, I see you got jokes."

She got to her car and got in. "Well nice talking to you. And thanks for the protection to my car again," she said smiling.

"Yeah, nice seeing you again," Low replied, wanting to say more but was stuck. She started her car, then waved, and pulled off and her car stopped. She tried to start it again and it wouldn't start. Low walked to her car grinning.

"I see you find this amusing," Kira told him seeing him grinning.

He was still smiling because he had gotten another chance to talk to her and thanked the game god for it. "Nah, but I find yo hooptie amusing."

"Oh, I see you got jokes I see too."

"Pop your hood and let me see what's up," she did and Low looked under it at the engine, not knowing a damn thing about cars. He fucked with the battery and told her to try to start it now. She did and nothing happened.

"Shit!" she hit the steering wheel frustrated. "This is crazy!"

"Let's push it back out the way and I'll give you a lift where you want to go," Low told her. She looked at him like "yeah right nigga!" Low nodded his head towards his whip. "That's my ride right there…the black one."

She looked to the ride he was indicating, and saw the flyest Corvette she ever seen. "Okay," she agreed. "Let me grab my bag and purse. Then we can push it."

After they pushed the car back, Low said, "Hold up, let me go tell Pep I'll be right back, cause I'm givin you a ride." He ran back into the apartment and told Pep what was up. When he came back out Kira was leaning on her car ready. "Come on," Low told her, hitting the button on his key chain and his car alarm beeped deactivating. They got to his ride and she stopped at the passenger door as Low walked to his side and got in. "It's open," he yelled.

She blew her breath and got in shutting the door. "Thanks for opening the door for me, your such a gentleman," she said sarcastically.

Low started his whip and replied, "Shit, for what? You got more muscle then me. Shit'ed, you should be opening it fo me. Miss all in shape and things."

She couldn't do nothing but laugh. He turned his music on and hit the volume. Guy banged out the woofers vibrating Kira's big ole booty. She couldn't take the loud music and went to turn it down pushing the wrong buttons.

Low didn't know what she was doing, so he turned it down. "What's up?"

"Boy that almost blew my eardrum out!" She told him holding her ears, frowning her face at him.

Low laughed. "My bad, old lady," she laughed.

When they got to the gym she told him to take her to, Kira said, "I'll get a ride back...thanks."

"Hold up, I'm here now. I might as well see if I can start my work out program now. Especially since you crackin on me!" Low was serious about working out, but wanted the benefit of getting to know her too in the process.

"Okay...come'on Mr. Mouth. I'm sure your welcome." They went in and there were people in there boxing and being trained by coaches. It was only two in there kickboxing. "Let me go change," she told him.

The name of the club was the Buckeye Elks, and there was a bar attached to it that belonged to it too, that Low was hip to. Low watched a guy hit the mitts as he talked to a coach there.

"I see you with Kira," the coach said.

"Yeah."

"She one fast an hard hitter for a girl," he told Low. "Had to get her off a few of my boys a few times she was whipping them so bad," he giggled.

Low stayed there and watched her train as he got some training in himself. Afterwards, they went to Wendy's and she let him take her home. Low had her laughing the whole time. She didn't have that much fun with a guy in a long time. The incident that occurred to her had her guards up fully with men. She just didn't trust them. He drove up in front of her home.

"Alright, I'll see you at the gym," Low told her.

"Bet, and thanks for the ride and food. Talk to you later, bye."

Low had a feeling she was different than any other girl he then met, as he watched her go into her house, that was near Mill Creek Park. "Damn she fine as fuck!" He mumbled to himself driving off.

He drove to LaLa land and went over Poncho's crib. Puncho and Big dawg was outside with some other Ricans and females drinking Redbull beer and smoking trees. Low thought about how every time he came over here there was alot of people and they were kickin it. He got out greeting everybody, and started kicking it with them.

3 Weeks later

Pep was in a fiends ride coming from his stash house with a few ounces he had gotten fronted with from Low. He was on his way to the trap house on Truedale to break his product down and front his workers and sell the rest to his regular customers. When he got there he started breaking his work down, weighing and rocking it up. Rat and Jay was there selling their work, with some chicks they had over. This one white fiend that be coming through buying weight came over. He was a regular to Pep and Low now because he always bought ounces when he came. Rat called up stairs to Pep cause he was there customer and only wanted to buy off Low, but would get from Pep if Low wasn't there. He only got from them if Low and Pep wasn't there.

"Pep! Oscar down here!" Rat yelled up stairs.

Pep came down stairs, and said, "What's up O?"

"Nothing much my dude, just tryin to get 5 ounces," he stated.

Pep told him, "Hold up O, I got cha," and ran back up the steps. He came back with 5 ounces of powder in a clear zip lock baggie and Oscar paid him $5,500. They always taxed him $1,100 an ounce, knowing he could get it cheaper or buy four an a half.

Oscar drove around the corner when he left and parked behind an old looking van that was parked on the street. He got out and got in the van. "Y'all get it all?" he asked, throwing the 5 ounces to a white man in a Task Force jacket, sitting with two others.

"Yup, good work partner," the narc cheesed replying.

Oscar drove off and headed to the house on Republic. Low had just got back from working out with Kira. They had become real close and sometimes went out to eat together. Low didn't hit the pussy yet and showed her respect for not throwing it at him.

He really liked her alot, but she told him, because he was like a little brother to her. Low had responded not to let his age trick her. When Low drove up in his car on Republic and went in, Oscar drove up right behind him.

"What's crackin Oscar?" Low asked.

Moose and Alvin said, "What's up" to him.

"Hey, what's up buddies?" Oscar replied. "Man I need 5 ounces. You got it Low buddy?" Oscar made sure he said Low's name, so it was clear who he was buying from.

Low answered, "Yeah, you know it. Let me go get it," and headed to the back room to the little safe he kept in his room. Nate had told him not to keep too much work in the same house he sold out of, and to never keep money with it, cause the police can keep it if they found it during a raid with dope. So Low had never kept alot of money where he had dope, but he had started getting to relaxed and that can be your downfall. He only kept like ten oz at the most at the house, but that was enough for a good bust to the Task Force.

Oscar bought the 5 ounces and went straight to this abandoned house around the corner and went in. It was six Task Force cops, and detectives Malley and Jackson inside. Oscar took his shirt off and he was wired up.

"We got'em," the Task Force guy said all happy.

Malley and Jackson cheesed big time. "Can we go get there sorry little asses right now?" asked Jackson, wanting to see the look on Low's face when they arrested him.

"Let me go get the warrants and everything solid. So today or tomorrow if our boss ain't there," the task cop told them.

Later that day in the Victories, Low saw Cathy coming from Bobo's moms apartment with his sister Pattie. It was getting cold out and it was the end of October, so they had on short leather jackets.

"Hey how you Lowdown?" Cathy spoke.

"What's up big mama?" Low replied, cause she was still pregnant.

"I'm due in two months, so I won't be no big mama then nigga!"

Pattie said, "I thought yo ass was coming over to get me last night?"

Low looked at her cute red bone ass, and replied, "I was busy an got caught up."

"Umm huh, probably with some hoe," Pattie responded with attitude. It was Saturday, so kids were outside playing.

"You heard from Bo?" Low asked, trying to ignore Pattie's sassiness.

"He ain't called me in like a week or so," Pattie said, not mentioning Bo had cussed her out about her fuckin with Low.

"He called me this morning. Don't be sendin him no fuckin nasty pictures of them skanks either!" Cathy said twisting her lips up.

Low smirked. "I hear ya Cathy. Tell him I said send us some visiting forms so we can come see'em."

"I just saw him two days ago. I'll tell him when he call. Gotta go, later Lowdown."

"Go ahead Cathy girl, this nigga ain't getting away from me today!" stated Pattie, hands on her hips, "Call me later gurl."

Low laughed, and said, "Girl you crazy."

"No you crazy nigga! Got me all dressed up and ready to go an yo ass ain't show up! Fuck that!"

"Well since I'm being bullied. You wanna go grab som'em from Staples to eat?" Staples BBQ sauce fucked with your taste buds if you haven't had it in a while, it made you fein for some.

"Hell yeah," Pattie answered, thinking about their BBQ breast shrimp dinner had her mouthwatering.

On their way there in his Vette, he saw Jay coming from Gino's drive thru with Mary in the car with him. Low stopped and told Jay about the police he saw parked by the Victories. "So watch going that way."

Jay said, "Good lookin," and Low drove off.

"Uumm..," Pattie mumbled shaking her head.

"What's that all bout?" Low inquired.

"Just trippin off that sleazy hoe," she answered.

Low asked, "who?" frowning his face up, not knowing who she was talking about.

"Boy, that hoe Mary pretending like she Miss Goodie Too Shoes and she fuck'in his friend Alvin behind-his back."

"Girl you tripping," Low said, hitting the freeway.

"Honey I'm telling you they fuck'in, bet that! Me an Cathy saw them creeping together, lookin like love birds."

Low didn't reply, and just thought about it as they got their meal and stopped over one of his cousin's houses to finish eating. 'That's some foul ass shit, and I'ma holla at that nigga Alvin when I see his ass!' Low was thinking as he grubbed. When they got done smashing their food, he drove to Westlake and pulled into the parking lot. Nigga's were always out no matter what time of the year it was there. Low saw one of Roe's main workers and asked him where Nut and Roe was at?

"At the spot on Broadway," he told him.

Low pulled from there and saw Sandy driving down the street in her car coming towards him. She slowed down trying to stop him so Low stopped, knowing it would look real funny to both girls' if he just kept going. Plus, didn't none of them have claims on him. 'So fuck it!' he told himself. Sandy was looking at Pattie all crazy when Low stopped and rolled down his dark tinted windows and said, "What's up?"

"Um...I wanted to know if you was going to be busy tonight, cause I wanted to holla at you about something?" she told him, eyeing Pattie. "You going to be in the Jets tonight?"

"Yeah, I'll be here later on tonight. Al'ight," Low replied, and drove off, leaving her there looking stuck. She loved Low and knew he messed with other females. She grew up in the hood and watched goon nigga's interact her whole life since she was knee high. So it wasn't nothing new to her that they spreaded their loving like water in the summer time. She felt for him and would never flip on him about little things, she just prayed one day when they got more into each other that his infidelity would cease. Stop.

Low drove up in front of the dope house and some young hard leg nigga's were on the porch. He got out and they greeted him and spoke as he went into the crib, leaving Pattie in the ride...Roe and Nut was in there watching TV with some other soldiers with a pile of weed on the table in front of them.

"What's up killa?" Nut said to Low. "You fuck'in that now, I see," he said, talking about Pattie he saw in the car.

Low grinned a little. "Man you was right. She wanted to fuck with a nigga. Yo man, they throwing a party tonight on the East side. Y'all wanna hit it up?"

Nut replied, "Hell yeah killa. New freaks too! I'm wit that!"

"Yeah, we'll be thru. Where you gone be at tonight?" Roe asked.

"Deep in that!" Low said nodding to Pattie outside. "I'll be at the spot on Republic."

Low got back in the car handing Pattie a baggie   full of weed. "Roll one up," she took the baggie and rolled up a fat boy. "Blaze that bitch," Low told her when she tried to give it to him. Low smelt the aroma of the weed inhaling as she puffed on it.

Low made it to the house on Republic and him and Pattie went inside high as a kite, and fucked like wild dogs. When they came out the back room Low was about to drop Pattie off, then he saw Alvin in the living room with Moose breaking some stones down. The thing about him fucking his man's chick entered his mind.

"Yo Alvin, let me holla at cha," Low told'em, and lead him out the back door. It was dark and wasn't any lights in the back yard. "Man what's up with you and yo nigga girl Mary?"

Alvin looked down and you could see the guilt written all over his face. "Low man, that girl came on to me. And I don't know... It just happened."

"Check, that's yo nigga!" Low exclaimed, getting hype. "That shit ain't cool! Now you need to tell him bout that hooker!" Low walked away into the backyard by the trees. Alvin just put his head down feeling ashamed and went back into the house. Low was salty that Alvin let a chick get to him over his nigga. He believed two friends bonds was more solid and pure then a female who oblivious didn't have any morals, and love for the person she was suppose to be with. Low heard some cars pull up fast skidding in front of the house, and saw one coming up the driveway fast and ducked behind the tree. He was reaching behind for his gun, but had left it in the house on the table, so he ducked down and crawled to the neighbors then got behind their car in the driveway so he could see what was up. He saw a narc car and police hopping out with the Task Force on their jackets as four of them hit the back door. He peeked around the neighbor's house and saw the front full of police.

Moose and Pattie were in the living room when Alvin came back in shaking his head looking at Pattie, knowing she had told on him, when the front door busted down scaring them and the Task Force came in screaming and waving weapons.

"Lay the fuck down! This a raid!" They had shotguns and pistols pointing at them as they hit the floor and got kneed in their backs and cuffed.

Pattie was yelling, "Get the fuck off me bitches!"

Malley and Jackson were looking under beds and in the closets screaming, "We seen him come in here! Where the fuck did he go?" They came and stood over Pattie and asked, "Where did your man go?"

She looked up from the floor she was laying on and shouted at them. "Muthafuckin pigs, do you think I would tell y'all! Y'all got me fucked up!"

"Okay little slut, have it your way," Jackson told her spit flying out his mouth he was so mad. "Take her whoring ass down with them two punks!"

They put them in the cop cars and went through the whole house finding dope, guns, and close to $7,000 there. The Task force guy told them. "Yup, the other raid went well and they apprehended the suspects." He was on the celly getting all this information.

The undercover narc Oscar had helped raid the house on Truedale, when Pep and them saw him they started cussing his ass out, trying to get him.

"I got your ass boy!" Oscar said standing over Pep smiling and shit, like he just had the best sex in his life.

Pep yelled, "Fuck you bitch!" Oscar turned red, and put his boot in Pep's back and stood on him with his 260 pounds. "That's all you got fat bitch!" Pep grunted. The other cops broke it up and put them all in the paddy wagon and took them downtown to the County jail.

Low ran to Moose's cousin house, heart and adrenalin pumping to tell the guy's at the house on Truedale, and Nut and Roe to watch out cause he just got raided. A white man answered the house phone on Truedale.

"Yo, what you need?" The Task cop asked.

Low hung up knowing it was the police. He called Nut and Roe breathing so hard and talking fast that Nut got hyped just listening to him.

"Nigga they just raided my spot and the one on Truedale! They got everybody!" Low was pacing the floor all fast and Moose girl cousin Londa was getting scared and nervous.

"Man we bout to get the fuck outta here! You know where to find us, you need a ride nigga?" Nut asked, as he told everybody at the house he was at what was happening to Low.

"Nah!" Low told him and hung up. Low sat down contemplating about the sudden events and situation. "Fuck happened?" He said to himself getting back up to leave.

"You need a ride?" Londa asked.

"Yeah. Good lookin."

He got dropped off in the Vic's and told Bo's mom the cops had arrested Pattie for nothing, and she started cussing the cops out, like they were right there and they wasn't nowhere in sight.

"Don't worry Ms. Brown my Lawyer gon' have her out real quick! She didn't do nothing!" Low assured her. He stayed over there 20 minutes and then went over Cathy's spot. She was in the Kitchen playing cards with some girl's from out there, and they all had already heard and got word about the raids at his two trap houses. Everybody stopped talking when he first came in when they saw it was him.

"What's up?" Cathy asked.

"Hey Low," the other females spoke, some eyeing him down like fresh meat because he was getting it (getting money) out there. Some just wanted a goon like him in their world to knock their boots.

"Can I use yo phone right quick?" Low asked Cathy, in a rush.

"Go head. It's in the back."

It was already around 10PM at night, so Low called his lawyers home. Cathy, being nosey got her pregnant ass up from the card game and went in the back to ease drop on Low on the phone.

"Yeah, they all got arrested. I need them all out as quick as you can do it!" Low told his lawyer Sammie, pacing the floor sweating like crazy. "The girl ain't do nothing! Pattie Brown, yeah that's her name."

Cathy's mouth dropped when she heard Bo's sister was locked up. She had already told him Low was messing with Pattie, and he had went off. He even called his sister calling her hoes and shit. Now he was going to really flip.

The police had already been out in the Vic's looking for Low and asking have anybody seen him. Bobby had got asked where Low was too while he was out hanging on the block by Malley and Jackson. He had seen Low go into Cathy's apartment not too long ago. He went home and got out the little card Malley had given him and got on the phone. "Hello, is this Detective Malley or Jackson? Who is looking for Lenny, the one they call Lowdown?" he asked the person who answered the phone as he peeked out his window, keeping an eye on Cathy's front door that Low had went in.

"Well tell them this is Bobby and I know where Low is right now."

"Yeah, call one of them." Bobby was put on hold, and then heard a phone ringing.

"Detective Jackson here, can I help you?"

"This Bobby from the Victory, you just came out here asking where Low was at and gave me your card. I know where Low is at."

Jackson nearly jumped through the phone hearing that, and asked, "Where he at son?"

"He over this girl's apartment...1310."

"Thanks son, I owe you one," Jackson hung up and told his partner. They had been riding around going crazy searching for Low. When they got that call and information, then flew over there calling the Task force to let them know they found him.

Low hung up the phone and went to go tell his crews family about what happened and that he had his lawyer on it, and if they called, tell them to call him. He went out Cathy's back door and had just got to Moose moms door when he saw the narc's rolling up the street fast! Moose mom's door opened and he flew in shutting the door.

"Lenny baby, what you doing running in here all noided?" Moose mother asked, looking at Low as he peeked out the window.

"They raided our spots and got Moose and some others, and now they out there looking for me right now over Cathy's house!"

"You hard headed boy's ain't gon learn until they lock y'all asses up and throw away the key, or death come knocking on your door fo yo ass.

Darn kids these days!"

The Detectives and Task Force hit Cathy's apartment busting her door down running in with their weapons drawn waving them and yelling to hit the floor! Cathy was so scared and shocked she went into early labor from being frightened. The cops came out mad, while Cathy was rushed to the hospital.

Bobby was standing outside like everybody else watching, but he had a little grin on his face. When the police came out salty without Low, Bobby's grin turned upside down. "Fuck he go?" he asked himself, as he glanced around.

Tina was on her front porch with Kelly when they raided Cathy's place, and saw the expression on Bobby's face before and after the raid.

Low had called Nate on his celly, and told him the deal. Nate told him to cut through the woods and he'll met him behind East high school. As Low walked through the dark woods, the cold air hit his face making his nose and ears numb up. It felt good cause he was sweating a few minutes ago. He was thinking at that moment how could this of happened? What he was going to do? Was everybody alright? How was Pattie? He was mad, shocked, and wondering what the fuck he could do about this shit? He got to the end of the path and hid behind a tree leaning on it. 10 minutes later a car came up the street but kept going. Another one came and stopped by the path he was at, and the car window rolled down.

"Yo! What's up lil Brah?" Nate yelled.

Low stuck his head out and looked. Nate was in a different car that he had never seen before. Low ran to the car and got in. Nate two girls were sitting up front driving the old school Park Ave.

Low leaned in the seat breathing in the weed smoke and the tree car air freshener as the car pulled off.

"So what happened?" Nate asked, already knowing about the raids from his scanner and people on the street. Low told him what went down as they drove to the North side.

Jess drove up the driveway and they all got out and went in. Nate told Low what he thought, and Low had his mind together that night. He was still young and this was his first raid and seeing all his rappies get arrested, he was use to just himself being arrested. After hearing what Nate had said, there was only a few options to choose from and make. Nate told him to spend the night there, get some rest, and think on things.

The next day, Low woke up and called his lawyer from Nate's crib. His lawyer told him that he would handle all the people in court today, and that the girl, Pattie would be released today, and to call him back so he could tell him what he was facing cause they had some undercover buys made from him from a narc. Low heard that and was tripping, mad, and wondering who the undercover Narc was. He told Nate, and Nate said he would check with his inside source for him.

"I just got word, that they had a white undercover cop buy from you a couple times," Nate told him a hour later. "His code name was Oscar."

Low shook his head drunk, thinking he should of knew better. "Muthafuck!"

Chapter 21

In this game you embrace the sweet, but refrain from the bitter. But they go together...

Pep, Moose, Alvin, Jay, and Rat were all questioned, and asked to snitch on Low. They were told they would be cut loose and that they only wanted Lenny Trevor, A.K.A. Lowdown, for four murders and drug trafficking. Pep had did time and the deal sounded sweet to him, but he knew he wouldn't do no long time. Plus telling wasn't him or his skeelow. But who knows, when things come falling apart, most fall apart like leaves in the Fall time.

Low called his Lawyer hours later, and he told Low that they wanted him really bad, and are offering his boy's a deal to tell on him about all kinds of things that would plant him in prison for the rest of his life! He said he would work out a sweet deal with the judge for him and the rest, but he better hope the feds didn't pick up the case, because it would be hard then, but he was young, so it shouldn't be so bad.

Low was thinking any time is bad to himself when his lawyer said that. What the fuck wrong with this honkey? "Man just see what you can do!"

"Alright. The girl was released about an hour ago too. I made sure of that and watched her drive out of the parking lot myself."

"Good. I'll talk to you later." Low hung up and called Sandy to come pick him up on the corner of Fairmont. He knew Nate didn't want nobody knowing where one of his cribs were.

Sandy had heard what had happened and had been worried sick about him. Calling him getting no reply, so she stayed home waiting for him to call, because Nut and Roe had told her he didn't get caught in the raid and was still out. So when he did finally call she was happy as hell!

Sandy pulled up in her car that Low had bought her with the biggest smile as Low got in the ride. She started kissing him all over his face, saying how worried she was and missed him.

Low couldn't help but grin feeling her love for him. "Dang gurl chill. I ain't went nowhere! Stop at a store," she drove off happy her man was alright.

She stopped at an Arab store up the street and Low go out and went inside to buy a cold bottle of Strawberry Boones Farm. He got back in the car and used Sandy's cell phone to call his aunt Paula.

"What's happening auntie?"

"Boy, you tell me! The cops been at all the family houses looking fo yo butt. They must don't know about this new house yet cause they ain't been here yet. Ma said they been parked outside her house all day. You know how she is, she been watching them more then they suppose to be watching here."

"It's cool auntie. Listen, I need you to go to the bank for me and take out ten thousand, and give it to my lawyer for me today."

"Okay, but are you alright?"

"Yeah I'm alright. Thanks auntie. Love you."

"Love you to boy." They hung up.

"Drive to the Jets," Low told Sandy.

When Sandy drove into the parking lot, Low was sipping his cold Boones farm and smoking a joint. Low hopped out the ride and asked one of Roe and Nut's worker's where they were at?" He told Low over Smokes old crib. Sandy got out and followed Low over there. When they got there five young cats were hanging out in front slanging, shooting dice, and getting toasted.

"What's good Low, Sandy?" They all spoke.

"Shit, what's up?" Low replied going inside the apartment with Sandy. Roe was on the couch with Rhonda counting money, and Nut was dancing off Too Short with Shawn.

"What's poppin killa?" Nut hollered over the music, smiling as he held a pint of Maddawg 20/20.

"Evading the poe-poe, that's what's up!" Low replied, sitting down. "Bitches sweatin the shit outta a nigga!"

Roe said, "Here," and threw him a bottle of V's on the 10 side. Ten meaning they had a number on them stating what degree and how strong they were. "Fuck them bama's! Let's kick it!" They got smokey for an hour.

"Let me call my lawyer," Low told'em getting up to use the phone and taking it to the bathroom cause the music was too loud. He sat on the tub and called. His secretary answered and Low asked for Sammie, and she put him right through.

"Lenny I've been waiting on your call. Listen, I got a sweet deal considering the feds might take this case on you. The Judge and prosecutor will give you two years. But we can get you shocked probation with the programs you gots to take there. Now, would you do a year or two considering all the charges they have on you, and what their trying to do with theses unsolved murders? This is a sweet deal Lenny," Sammie told him, trying to make him take the deal.

Low nearly flipped on him. He never did no time before, and a year or two seemed long to him. "Man that's the best you can do?" Low asked, with aggression. "Didn't my aunt bring you that money an shit? Plus what I gave you already!"

"Yes, I've received it, but these Task Force guy's and these two Detectives are on your ass! You got alot of heat on you, all because of the accusations about them murders at the High school, and they have you on tape red handed selling to an undercover. The best thing to do is to turn yourself in, and take the deal while it's on the table, especially since you never know what one of your buddies might do."

Low knew he was right. The talk with Nate had assured him on what might come. "Alright, I'll take the deal. I'll call you tomorrow and let you know when I'ma turn myself in," Low told him and hung up. He sat down on the toilet feeling like he had lost everything. He got up, went back out in the living room, and turned the music down. Everybody looked at him. "I got's to go do some time, a year or two my lawyer just told me," Low told them, grabbing a 40 ounce and tipping it up taking it to the head guzzling it down.

"Man killa, that shit ain't nothing. A year or two ain't shit! Fuck it…let's kick it til you bounce then my nigga!" Nut said, giving him a goon hug. Sandy hugged him and was crying.

"Hoe, fuck all that crying bullshit!" Roe told her, turning the sounds back up. "My nigga gon' be al'ight."

Cathy had a baby girl at the hospital that day her apartment got rushed by the poe-poe. Bo didn't know til the next day when he called and no one answered, so he called his moms and she told him about Cathy and his sister. He slammed the phone down mad as fuck! Then walked to his cell at Mansfield prison and got in the bed.

His bunky was an old school nigga who been down a minute, noticed how he came into the cell and got in bed. "You alright youngblood up there?" he asked Bo up on the top bunk.

"This little punk ass nigga, I gave the game to, then got my sister arrested, and had the Task Force running up in my pregnant bitch crib and she went into labor! That lil nigga then lost his fuckin mind! Fuck his little hoe ass up!"

"That's messed up young blood," his old school bunky told him getting up, and leaving the cell. He wasn't on all that drama stuff. "Fuck   these young crazy ass fools these days!" He mumbled to himself as he went into the TV room to watch his Soap Operas.

Wanda had drove over to Low's spot on Republic, and saw the signs the police had up on the door after she heard what happened, and had been calling his cell and pager like crazy. Some white man kept answering his cell phone asking her what she needed. She knew it was the police cause she was hip to the dope game. She hit (went) the Victory up and asked some dudes she saw out there, because she didn't see her cousin.

"They all got arrested," Moose little brother, Fatcat told her. "But Low still out here somewhere."

Lil Danny knew Low was messing with Wanda and said, "I think he in Westlake."

"Oh, okay. Thanks y'all. Tell him Wanda lookin for him," she drove to Westlake projects looking for Roe and Nut. When she drove up in her red Iroc, nigga's were all over, flocking to her whip.

"What's poppin baby? Nice ride, what you want to rent it? What you need baby? I got cha boo! They were all asking her.

This little one around 12 yrs old shoved some rocks at her through her car window. "You lookin fo some stones or somethin?"

Wanda wanted to bust out laughing, but saw the serious look on the little boy's face. "Nah little hustler, I'm looking for Roe or Nut player. You know where they at?"

"Hell yeah, them my niggas," the little boy replied, fucking Wanda up with his foul lil mouth, talking like he was grown. "What's yo name, so I can go tell'em."

"Tell'em it's Wanda, Low's girlfriend."

"I got cha," he said, "Y'all back the fuck up! This Low's chick here!" Niggas backed up, but kept looking.

The little boy name lil Man ran to the apartment they were at, and was let in by one of the worker's outside that had the door today.

"What's crackin lil Man?" Roe asked him.

"There's a girl out here name Wanda lookin fo y'all." He saw Sandy and knew not to say it was Low's girlfriend, being wise for his age.

Low got up and tucked his gat in his waist that was on the table, put his Oakland starter jacket on, and stepped outside. Sandy just looked at him. Low walked to Wanda's ride and got in.

"What's good?" Low said.

"Ah baby, what's going on? Did you get raided?" She questioned, looking worried.

"Yeah, but it's cool now," he replied, knowing he wasn't feeling like it was. He wasn't feeling doing no time right now.

"Well what's going to happen? Are you going to get locked up? What?"

"I'll probably go do like a year or two my lawyer say."

Wanda just stared at him a second, then said, "Oh baby, I 'ma miss you," but inside her head she was already making plans for the next dope boy and nigga out there getting it to take his place. "Let's go to my place," she told him, trying to get some dick before he got locked up. "Damn, I 'ma miss this dick!" she was thinking.

"Not right now. I got some shit I gotta take care of, but I'll be thru tonight or tomorrow. Alright?"

"Okay," she kissed him, salty he was putting the pipe on hold from her. Low got out and she drove off. It wasn't that she didn't care for Low. She was just use to having a man around that was in the game. Being raised by her father that was in the game had gotten her proned to that life.

Low spent the night with Sandy at the trap spot there in the Lake. Now he was in the car with Roe, Nut, and their worker City. They had just came from Burger King and was in the ride getting smokey, drinking beer and Boones on they way back to the projects, when Low said, "Man drop me off on the East side over Wanda's crib."

Wanda heard a car drive up into her driveway as she hung up the phone. She was just talking with some new dope boy her girl had hooked her up with from the North side, that was 32 yrs old. She didn't waste no time.

Low saw the long t-shirt Wanda had on as she let him into the house. Low smelled weed smoke in the air as he entered and sat on the couch. The TV was on and Low grabbed the remote and changed the channel.

"Boy I was watching that!" Wanda said.

"I can't tell," Low told her laughing. She tried to grab the remote and ended up wrestling. Her t-shirt came up and Low noticed she was butt naked underneath. Low boned straight up on her and she felt his pipe poking her.

"Damn baby, let me see what's up with him," she said, taking his pants off and boxers off. Low was hitting her doggy style 20 minutes later, and rolled over afterwards after he busted one.

"I'ma go cut the shower on," Wanda said getting up ass wet from their juices, as her phone rung and she answered it. "Hello. what's up? Can you call me back? I'm busy."

Dirty was looking at the phone screwing his face up. "Busy! Bitch I'm busy!" he spat, hanging up. "Punk hoe think she all fly an what not!" Tito laughed at him as he called another chick up. "Nigga fuck you think funny?"

"You nigga. What's up wit that bitch?"

"Hoe acting funny, that's what! I bet it's a chump over there. I should go over there in beat both they ass!"

"Man fuck that cunt!"

Pep was wondering why he didn't get out yet, and was getting noided and salty. The lawyer Sammie had came to see him and the rest of the crew and told them to just be cool and let him handle things. But, Pep was now tripping because he haven't heard nothing from Low yet, and he had left messages through people in all for Low.

Low's pager went off again like it had been all day, but this time he saw it was his grandma's number. He didn't call no-body that paged him yet. He got the phone and called his grandma to see what was up. "This Lenny grandma, everything alright?"

"Yeah baby, everything alright. Where you at? This sweet girl over here Kira lookin fo you. Said she'd been calling yo butt all darn day, worried about yo mannish behind."

"Tell her I'ma holla at her later."

"No, you tell her yourself Chile," she handed Kira the phone.

"Low, what's up with you not calling me back?" Kira asked.

"My bad, alot of stuff going on. But let me call you back in like a hour, bet?"

She replied, "Alright, do that. Later."

"Make sure you driving right when you leave here cause them police still watching my house," grandma Faye told her peeking out the curtains. "You don't got no weed on ya do ya?"

Kira giggled. "No man. What they watching your house for?" Kira pecked around thinking grandma might be slanging.

"They after Lenny butt."

"Oh."

Rican Puncho and Big Dawg went to the Vic's and hollered at everybody they knew that was cool with Low to see if him and the rest of the crew was alright cause they had love for them. They had heard what went down, and that Low had gotten away. Then Pep had called and confirmed it, so they were out there looking for Low.

Low had gotten Wanda's hooptie and pulled out calling Kira and telling her to meet him at McDonalds across from Y.S.U. campus. He parked on the side after he ordered a Big Mac an Fries, sipping on a cold Strawberry Boones Farm, high as a kite from taking 4 Valium tens a hour ago. Kira drove up on the side of him, and got out her car and into his. Low couldn't help but admire how good and thick she looked. "Sheit, she might feel sorry fo a nigga an give me some going away pussy," Low was thinking, and chuckled.

"What's good gurl?" Low said, with mayo all over his lips grinning at her.

"Boy, you know what's up! Why didn't you call me back and let me know you were alright? Got me all worried about yo ass and you sitting here smiling like something funny!" She punched him in the shoulder, and Low busted out laughing spitting food out his mouth. "Low tell me what's going on," Low told her everything that happened and went down.

"Well, from what I hear, you got a nice deal going on. You know I'm studying Law, so I know a little somethin' somethin," Kira told him.

"Wish you were my lawyer then. I don't trust them muthafucka's fo real. Well, guess I'll get this time out the way then. But, before I do let's go kick it right now. Shoot, I'm bout to be gone in a second so I might as well go have a lil fun right quick!"

"I hear that! Oh yeah, Pep been calling lookin for you too. Donna said to call over her house if I saw you."

"Let me see yo phone."

"Hold up, it's in my car," she told him getting out to go get it, and coming back handing it to him. "Here you go crazy."

"What's her number?" She gave it to him and Low called. "This Low what's up Donna?"

"Dang, you could ask how I'm doing?" said Donna. "Pep been calling me trying to contact you. He said to tell you to leave a number when I talked to you, so he could call you on a three-way when he called me."

"Alright, is he cool?"

"Just worried it sounds. Wanted to know what's going on, and to tell you he would be calling me every hour."

"Call Kira phone when he calls, cause I'll be with her for a minute."

Donna wanted to ask what was up with that? "Okay, Carla been asking and going nuts worried about you too. She at work right now, but make sure you call her."

"I'll call her later on. Good lookin." (click) "Let's go drop this car off over my nigga's spot so we can go kick it. They got a good movie showing at the Mall I want to see."

Kira said, "Bet," laughing at the little boy in Low.

Low really like Kira as a friend and cool female. He didn't even get no sex from her so their relationship was more than just a sexual thing. She showed him that not all women gave up the goods like that and carried themselves with class and respect.

Pep and them were all on the same range in the County jail even though they were all under 18yrs old. Jay had just got off the phone with Mary.

"Let me get that Jay," Alvin told Jay, seeing him hanging it up. Jay handed him the phone and walked away.

Alvin dialed his number and it got accepted. "What you doing?"

"Thinking about you boo," Mary cooed. "Let's have phone sex, my pussy wet baby."

Alvin glanced over at his partner and said, "Can't dude here."

"He can't hear this pussy listen," she put the phone down to her snatch and Alvin could hear it making smacking noise as she played with herself, and boned up. Her freaky ass had him pussy whipped, and he didn't have no kind of control over himself. Alot of men sold their souls for a piece of ass. Even friendships.

Chapter 22
**Just because I'm caged don't mean I'ma change my mentality.
My spirit is still free to roam and execute all my next moves...**

Low kicked it with Kira til 2.a.m. and she dropped him back off at Nut and Roe's spot to get Wanda's car. He drove back to Wanda's house and spent the night there with her. The next day he went to holla at Nate and he told Low to put his money up so he'll be straight when he got out. So, Low went to handle his business first at his stash spots over his two family houses, then at the bank. His mother had left him the money she had been saving up from her taxes over the years and some checks from work. Plus, the life insurance money after she was killed was in the bank. He went to say his last good byes to a few, got Sandy and took her to his house in Campbell to get his fuck on, and spend some time with his brothers.

"Why you leaving?" His youngest brother Otis asked, tears coming down his little eight year old brown face.

"I'll be back, plus you can come visit me all the time," Low told him.

Little Kevin said, "He ain't leaving us like Ma," trying to be strong for his little brother, but he wasn't feeling his big brother being locked up away from them.

This was killing Low inside. They had always been close, their mother made sure of that, and that they showed each other respect and love for one another. Low said his last good byes and called his lawyer Sammie to be there when he turned himself in. Low knew this was just the start of his new life that was to come when he was released from the confines that he was willing turning himself into. He knew this was just the beginning of the after-math that was to follow.

When Low got downtown to the County jail and went in, he told them his name and was immediately hand cuffed and put in a holding cell. Sammie came to speak with him and make sure he was fine. When Sammie left, Low was escorted up-stairs and put on the range, as they took the handcuffs off through the bars. Low glanced around at all the faces that were staring at him. Some were sizing him up, seeing if they knew him, and who was he. Low stepped more in the range wearing the big ass orange jumpsuit, that was dragging at the bottom. Low knew he had made it big time when they put him on the murder range with all the older dudes. He knew it was the murder range because he saw two dudes that were on TV for it. At first he was noided, but everybody there heard of him when someone called his name out. Plus there was a couple old heads and fiends that he served there, so he got respect off rip. He looked to who was calling him and saw Moose.

"Low! What the fuck is up my nigga!" Moose yelled rushing to him, giving him some dap. The rest of the crew heard Low's name and came out their cells. Alvin and Jay were on the side with Low. Moose, Rat and Pep were on the other, but they could talk and see each other through the bars that separated them. There was one phone on each range, and a little black and white TV that was so small you could probably put it in your pocket. All Low's affiliates were there and they were all at the bars chopping it up about their situation, when two Deputies came to the bar doors calling Low's name. Low went to see what they wanted, and they told him to turn around and cuff up because he had some visitors.

Detective Jackson and Malley zoomed to the County jail when they got a call informing them that Low had turned his self in. They had him bought down stairs into the small interrogation room.

When Low stepped in the small room and saw it was the two rollers that been on his ass, his whole expression changed as he mean mugged them. And you could tell it wasn't no love between them because the Detectives were staring at him like he was the scum of the earth, rat shit!

"What the fuck you clowns want?" Low asked them all angry like.

"You little punk kid!" Malley screamed, and grabbed Low by his jumpsuit shoving him against the wall, yelling in his face, calling him punks and telling him he wasn't shit! Jackson came up on the side of him and punched him in the kidney. Then Malley kneed him in the nuts, making Low grunt and go down in crucial pain balling up.

"Now tell us about these murders you did before we beat you some more!" Jackson yelled at Low, stepping on his chest.

"Fuck off me fat pig...muthafucka!" Low uttered, glaring at him with nothing but hate.

"We'll be back to give your ass some more, you fuckin bastard!" Malley spat, bending down with his hands wrapped around Low's neck, then he laughed in his ear and stood up. "We'll be back."

Low was taken back to the range in pain from the beating he just encountered. His partners came to the bars gathering up, and he told them who had just came to whoop his ass. Some of them got scared, hoping they wouldn't receive the same and get called out next.

The cops had all the real evidence on Pep and Low, so they were looking at all the time. But, they really wanted Low. Sammie made a deal with the prosecutor, and everybody got only 6 months, except Low, and would be on paper (probation) when they got released. They all ended up going to Tico's Juvenile prison together. Low received two years, but with good time and programing he could be released in a year. Everybody took their time on the chin. Some of their girl's rode with them for a minute, but most of them went about their biz like they never existed. Most women don't got the stamina to roll with a man when he on lockdown. Most think and view a relationship as all physical and can't stay true without it. When it's more mentally and spiritual the glue that holds the two foundation together no matter what the situation, distance, obstacle and hate through in their mix. Real love always prevails.

Wanda started acting all funny towards Low four months into his bit, so he said, "Fuck her!" Sandy was rolling strong and his home girl Kira stayed in touch. Nate sent him pictures and he called him all the time. Low didn't want no visits, but Roe and Nut bought Sandy up anyway with balloons of weed and V's for him.

The college girl Donna, that Pep use to fuck with changed her number, and he didn't hear from her no more. The girl Amy came to see him one time with Sandy, but she wasn't really feeling Pep like that so that ceased. Pep was salty about how things went down and blamed it all on Low. It was all good when Low was putting him on, and he was getting cake and fuckin honey's. Now when the chicks wasn't fucking with him and he wasn't riding around in his whip free, he had an attitude, and blamed being there on Low.

"This dumb ass nigga Low bought all this stupid heat on us and got us all locked up," he was thinking to himself, as they all sat on the yard smoking green talking shit chopping (talking) it up.

"Man, I can't wait to bounce outta this bitch in two months. This spot got a nigga losing weight an shit," Moose stated, rubbing his big belly. The spot they were at held you until you were 21yrs old at the most.

"Nigga you bigger then you was before you came in here, fuck you talkin bout," Rat said, telling the truth, making them laugh.

"Yeah man. I'm going out there to chill, fuck this shit!" Pep expressed, passing the joint. "Can't be doing this time shit no'moe!"

"Fuck that, I'm going out there to get paid, and fuck hoes! This shit don't stop here, it's just beginning nigga. Hoes out there wanna fuck a goon nigga! And there's money to stack!" Low told them, and they could see in his eyes he meant every bit of it.

Pep was looking at Low like he was a monster, and said," Man I'm going out there to chill. You talkin crazy!"

"Nah nigga, you crazy! Acting all scary an shit! Fuck that, I know where I'm at. This shit ain't change me!" Low said. "This didn't turn me into butter, so I could melt."

Pep said, "Man, you retarded? Yo ass the reason we here now, bringing all that heat down on us and you still ain't gon'chill?"

Low jumped up and swung on Pep, hitting him in the jaw. Pep rolled over, cause Low was swinging again and he was sitting down when Low stole him.

"Get up pussy ass nigga!" Low shouted, letting him up.

Pep stood up and they knuckled up. Pep threw a right hand that landed, busting Low's lip. Low spit some blood out and threw three punches connecting with two of them, using a combination he had learned at the gym with Kira, staggering him, then rushing Pep slamming him on his back by taking both his legs from under him, and getting on top of him beating his face in with crisp blows, cutting him over the eye, making blood fly and his fist change colors. Jay and Moose grabbed Low off of Pep and Low kicked him in the ribs. Pep's face was bloody as fuck when he got up dizzy and was trying to get at Low but they held him back because the C.O.'s came running and cuffed both of them up and took them to the hole for 10 days.

That night in the hole, Low woke up out of a nightmare. The sight of seeing his mother's bloody death,-and life pour out her had him sweating and tense. He wiped the sweat off his face with his fore-arm, and got up in the one man cell to use the bathroom and drink some water cause his mouth was dry. He sat down sipping his water, and heard niggas talking and laughing about the street, kicking war stories. This one nigga named Red who been down since he was 16 and was now 20 was from his side of town in Youngstown, and was talking about how he got into it with some busters at this party and took their car. He was a silly nigga, you could tell by the way he was telling the stories and had everybody cracking up some shit in the hole. Low sat on the bed listening, and started laughing off some of the stuff Red was saying.

The next day, they called rec for them to go out for an hour to get some fresh air, work out, and talk. When they stepped out, Red's cell was right in front of Low's.

Red nodded his head and said, "What's up?" to Low.

Low nodded back and replied, "What's up nigga?"

"Damn nigga, I seen you come in yesterday and didn't know if you were still alive over there you were so quiet an shit. You al'ight?" Red said to Low.

"No doubt, just resting an shit," Low told him.

"Let's move it!" The guards told them, and they all started walking out in a line.

"Where you from?" Red asked as he walked in front of Low.

"Youngstown, like you."

"Oh yeah," Red said all happy to have a homie back in the hole with him and down there period. "Nigga we gon kick it. What's your name player?"

"They call me Lowdown."

"What? You Lowdown...Low, from the East side? That little crazy nigga I've been hearing bout?" Red asked, looking at him to see if he was bullshitting, and just fronting using a niggas name.

"I guess," Low answered, nonchalantly. To Low he was still the little dude no one really paid attention to. The one who always felt different and stuck to himself. A person hearing of him locked up still didn't faze him or give him the big head like it would do most.

They went out on the yard and chopped it up. Low liked Red. They hollered when they went back to their cells, all day and night. Red was getting released in 4mths and would be 21yrs old. His moms and his brother were the only ones that rode his whole bit with him from start, and stayed on the East side in Plaza View, not far at all from Low's hood. This girl Tracy had started back hollering at him his last two years that he use to fuck with before he got locked up. Red was 5 "7" with short reddish hair. They became tight in that hole and clicked good from jump. Behind them walls you can become tighter with a muthafucka then on them streets. They stayed up all night telling war stories, but nothing to get them some cases over. They chopped it up about some girl's and freaks. Red had been in the hole for two months for busting somebodies head with a combination lock, and was getting out the hole the day before Low. Low had sent word to his nigga's about Red through a kite (letter, message snuck out) and had them pay a clerk dude to have him moved to their unit (block) when he got out.

"Fuck that nigga, got me locked up!" Pep mumbled to himself in his cell. "That nigga think we gon be cool, he got me bent the fuck up!" Pep got moved to another unit so he wouldn't have to fuck with Low, but he still hollered at the homies.

The crew liked Red. They tried to get Pep and Low back cool, but Pep was like, "Naw, I'm straight." Low wasn't going to kiss his ass and couldn't believe the nigga was acting like that. Being behind them walls will make weak niggas scared and make them betray real friendships and bonds.

Low had his girl Sandy pick Red's chick up every time she came to visit. Red didn't have no money and all, but by being down so long, he had accumulated all he needed and more. Low still had a thousand dollars put on his books for him to do whatever with.

Red was fucked up on that. He never had nobody show him love like that before, and it hit him solid in the heart like a 45 slug up close.

"Nigga you going to be straight when you bounce out this muthafucka, watch!" Low always told him. "I got cha my nigga!"

Red knew he did to. This little nigga was all the way real, and a true partna, so he knew they were going to be all the way tight like a Jew in his money...

Chapter 23

Out of sight...out of mind, that's how most see it and live it. But true niggas and broads roll through it all, rain, snow, and bullets. But time beats out most. That's when the real shines...real niggas...real love...real friends.

The day before Moose, Rat, Alvin, and Jay were to be released, they threw a little party. Pep was getting cut loose to, but he didn't come to the party til the end. It was April 12th, 1991.

They all showed love to Low the day they were being released. Pep even gave him a hug. They all told Low they had him.

Their girls were all out there waiting for them in three rides. Moose girl Sofia was driving and had Rat's girl Pam with her. Alvin had his girl Ricka drive up with Jay's chick Mary. And Kelly came to pick Pep up with Tina, who's belly was big as hell. Moose fat ass was so happy he ran to the car sweating and kissing all over his girl's face.

Boy stop slobbing all on my face!" Sofia told him, wiping the saliva off her face.

They all got in their cars and drove off after they waved at Low and Red inside the fence. Red and Low waved back from the yard and watched as they drove off blowing their horns.

Low felt something, but didn't know what it was. It was love for his niggas.

Tina couldn't help what she felt when she saw Low at the fence. She wanted to tell him about the baby, and she wanted to hate him at the same time. So she let her pain and how she couldn't get over seeing him fucking another on her over-ride telling him about his baby she was carrying.

The hood, Victories took their homecoming like a big party and celebration, and threw a get together. Free food and drinks were giving out courtesy of Low. He had told his auntie to get all the stuff for their homecoming and their girl's will help her set everything up. They were all shocked and surprised when they got there. Everybody had a good time.

Pattie was asking Low's dudes about Low. "Tell him to call me! He ain't wrote me or nothing since he been gone!" She kept saying and complaining.

A week before their release, Dirty, Tito, Joint, and T.J. was on their way over these broads house in Tito's new Regal he just purchased, and was about to turn down Glenwood street when a car pulled up on them and opened fire. Tito ducked and slammed on the gas peeling out as glass sprayed everywhere and bullets penetrated the Regal. The person that was busting just kept shooting until Tito car crashed. Dirty drew his gun as the Regal smashed the pole, and jumped out blasting back on the shooter as they speeded off. Everybody got out the wrecked car.

"Who the fuck was that?" Tito yelled, mad as fuck cause someone busted on them and made him wreck his new whip.

"Nigga get yo scary ass up!" Dirty told TJ in the back seat. He went to grab him. "Nigga! AWW SHIT! HE SHOT!" Tito hopped back in the car, and pulled it off the pole and rushed T.J. to the hospital, but it was too late, half his head had gotten blown off!

A hour later at their trap house, everybody was wondering who just shot at them and killed T.J.

"Man who the fuck was that punk ass bitch?" Dirty hollered. "Hoe ass bitch muthafucka!" Dirty had done so much dirt and foul shit to people, that he knew it could be anybody wanting payback. He was use to beefing and getting shot at, him and Tito.

Moose and them had been out a week and had started balling again. They were getting their work from Nut and Roe. Pep had chilled out and moved in with Kelly and her Moms, out there in the Vic's.

Red and Low had started working out real hard on the steel weights, and running getting their gas and stamina up. Red was a work out freak, and was a cut up little nigga. Low had gotten taller since he was still growing, and gained some bulk on his frame. His birthday was next month and he would be 16yrs old.

Roe and Nut was out there taking care of their business. They b-days were coming up too. Roe's was on July 26th, and Nut's was August 13th. They would be eighteen and out of school.

"Nigga...I'ma bout to break wit a new whip on they ass out this mug!"

Roe told Nut and Moose, as they sat in his ride in Westlake parking lot while Nut counted Moose re-up money. "Nigga's let's go check some rides out."

"I'm wit that killa," Nut replied, high as hell. He had started fucking with that Tuss alot more. His girl Shawn was about to have their baby in September. Detective Malley and Jackson was glad Low had gotten locked up even if it wasn't for a long time. They had been keeping an eye on his crew, and tried to watch Roe and Nut too, but it was too hard in them projects, so they didn't stay on them long.

Low was sitting with Red chopping it when he bought up Pattie, Bo's sister. "Man, I'm tellin you she a fine muthafucker. And the pussy is off the chain."

"Nigga call her, I wouldn't fuck that up. The way you say that pussy poppin, I would be seeing what's up wit that!" Red told him.

"Yeah, you right. Let me call her ass," Low said, getting up to go call her, taking his little phone book out his pocket as he got on the phone and dialed her number. Low heard Pattie answer the phone.

She took his call and asked, "Is this Low? My baby?"

"Why? You fuck with that nigga?" Low said, playing with her.

"Like fiends fuck with crack, I fucks with that fine nigga!"

"Yeah this me, what's up wit ya? Long time no hear from?"

"Booyy, you just now calling me! Didn't your boy's tell you I said to call me?"

"They told me, but I thought you were all busy an shit, you know?"

"Fuck that! You still acting funny I see, an you locked up. Give me yo info so I can send you some pictures and write you. Let me get a pen an paper, hold on boo," she got off the phone for a second, and Low signaled Red to come over. "Nigguh, I still got it," Low told him smiling, cause it felt good that Pattie was still feeling him. Niggas be needing that on lock, cause it really does lift the spirit.

Red said, "Ask her do she got a girlfriend yo nigga can holla at?"

Low nodded his head. "Al'ight, I got cha. Thirsty ass."

She came back and he gave her his info. "You know I miss you like crazy Low. You put it on a bitch like that boo."

Low laughed. "Oh yeah, you ain't seen shit yet then," they both laughed.

"Bring it on then baby, cause I'm waiting on you. These lames ain't got shit on you out here, fo real!"

"So who you mess with now?" Low asked.

"Some sorry nothing, he ain't shit just something to do. But fuck him right now! Just tell me you wanna holla at me and whoever can get ghost like smoke."

"You know a nigga want yo pretty ass, and coming to holla at cha when I step out this bitch!" Pattie smiled ear to ear. "Check doe, my nigga Red here need a girl to holla at. Call one of your home girls right now on the three way so he can talk to her."

"Alright boo, hold on," Pattie clicked over and came back on line and you could hear a phone ringing.

"Hello," some girl answered.

Pattie said, "What's up Gina? My boo Low on the phone that I've told you all about, and he got his boy locked up down there with him who lookin for someone to talk to. So I called you cause you my gurl and I know you cool, and ain't ugly."

"Girl, if he that nigga Low's partner, then let me talk to him," she knew Low was about his business on them streets, and heard all about him through Pattie and others. She saw him drive by in his fly ass whip herself one time. So she jumped at a chance to get on his team.

Low put Red on the hook (phone) and they talked for an hour. He got her number and called her back. She told him to send her some visiting forms so she could come see him when Pattie came up. He told her they were already on the way.

Low was really feeling Sandy thick as Nicki Minaj ass rolling strong with him, showing her loyalty and commitment to be number one and his woman. She went and got his little brothers and took them places, that really gave her points. She was a good girl to him and Low said, "she was the only one who showed him true love to the fullest on being his woman an all, out of all them broads and hookers out there." The little things a woman does for a man while on lock goes a long way to him. You can win a man's heart by the actions you display while he's on lock.

Jay, and Rat was riding in Rat's new Chevy Caprice that was Midnight blue on blue, banging Ice Cube's "No Vaseline" coming down Oak street on the East side about to get on the freeway, when they saw Dirty in his Cutlass coming off the freeway they were turning to get onto, with Wanda on his side that use to mess with Low. Dirty had looked them straight in their eyes madd doggin them banging Scarface music.

Rat hollered, "Punk bitch!" Rat tried to turn the car around but couldn't. "That hoe ain't shit!" Rat stated, punching the dashboard as he stopped the car on the side of the freeway.

"Let's go nigga...we'll catch that soft ass nigga later!" Jay told him, not really trying to fuck with Dirty on that level of the game, cause he knew Dirty stayed strapped and would body their ass if they wasn't ready for him. Plus, he was trying to get back to Mary. "Wait til Low hear about this hooker," Jay told Rat, glad they were back going where they were headed to in the first place.

The day of Roe's birthday, Nut took him to pick his ride up from Classic Coach, who did it all except music. Roe drove out the garage and Nut was like "Damn!" Roe had flipped a 90 S-10 truck with a bowling ball flip-flop paint job, that had his truck changing colors at different angles money green, purple, and blue. It had gold deep dish Dayton's, and ground effects. His whip was raw as fuck!

"Playa I'ma catch you at the spot on Broadway," Roe told Nut. Talking about the house they had bought together and laid out, cause Nate had told them it was time for them to start investing their chips and putting it into good use. They had bought their people homes to. Nut called his aunt Toot his moms, cause his real mother had died when he was young of cancer. Roe had gotten his mother a house right next to Nut's aunt Toot, in a nice neighborhood in Boardman. They both never had a father in their life.

Roe drove through the North side on Elm street and everybody was staring like, "Who the fuck clean ass truck is that?" Honey's poked their asses out and gave him sexy looks. Roe hit the switches on his shit and made the truck dance on their ass! Niggas were hating and admiring his whip. If they wasn't hip to Roe busting his heat, the haters would of shot his truck or did some type of hating shit. He drove through scandal Crandal hollering at some honeys, and then to the Lake. Girls were jocking his whip, and on his dick like crabs. Then he shot up to Nate's music store calling him to step outside.

Nate was already out there waiting when Roe drove up and parked. "Player, I like this," Nate told him, inspecting the truck as he walked around it. "You did alright on this here. Sho nuff. Now check, I got some rap for you." Nate lead him into his office, "I want you and Nut to invest in some other things, feel me?"

Roe nodded his head agreeing. "That's what I've been thinking about since you told me last time."

"And tell Nut to lay off that Tuss mess," Nate told him, staring at him serious as hell. Nut had been trippin lately and Nate wasn't feeling it.

"I'll tell'em," Roe replied. He stayed there a half hour and left heading for the crib on Broadway. When he got there he saw Nut's ride and his girl Rhonda's parked in the driveway. He pulled on the side on them and got out, and went in through the back door. Nut, his girl, and their workers K.K. and Joker were in the kitchen cutting up dope, smoking weed. Roe said, "What's up?" to them, and they spoke back, as he glanced at Nut on the couch with a bottle of Tuss in his hand high.

"Killa, what's crackin?" Nut slurred.

"Sheit," Roe replied, looking at his girl. "What you doing over here?" Roe asked her with a mean mug on his face, cause she knew he told her not to be coming to none of the houses period without him telling her to.

"Nut told me you were on your way, so I waited. Let me go look at your truck and get outta here, because you trippin I see!" She was getting up rolling her green eyes at him. "Happy Birthday Daddy."

"Let me holla at cha," Roe told Nut, as he watched him scratching himself. "Man my nigga, you got's to lay off that syrup shit! That shit ain't cool."

Nut raised his head looking at him. "Nigga this shit ain't nothing. You fuck with it to!"

"Man I ain't had none of that mess in so long dog. I'm trying to stay on top of these lames out here and get this paper, feel me?"

"Nigga I stay on top of these busters! These niggas know what it is! This shit ain't got me unfocused. I stay on point killa."

"Nut you my muthafuckin nigga. Just lay off that bullshit!" Roe told him heated and getting up going outside. "Don't give my nigga no'moe of that Tuss shit!" he told K.K. and Joker, and walked outside to his truck. Rhonda was sitting inside. Roe just got in and drove off.

Rhonda knew something was on Roe's mind, so she didn't say nothing. She been with him long enough to know when something was heavy on his mind and bothering him. He would tell her about it when he felt like it, and she knew that. She loved him to death.

The next day Low got some mail from Kira. When he opened it some pictures fell out. He looked at them and saw she was with her girl's from Y.S.U. campus. "Yo Red, this the babe Pep use to fuck with." Low called for Red, to come look at the picture.

"Damn, she alright. I got's to try an tap that ass when I get out," Red said.

"Nigga you got that coming. We gon' fuck mass hoes when we step, bet that," Low told him, giving him some dap. "Let me call the crib."

Red walked to the phone with him, and got on the other one, saying, "Ain't none of them colder and thicker then Kira still."

"Fo sho," Low agreed, calling Sandy. "But my baby up there toe to toe with her on the ass an thick side nigga," Low told him, talking about Sandy.

"Yeah, she is stack more then a Big Mac," he agreed.

Sandy took his call, and he had her call Moose on his celly and he answered. "What you eating on fat boy?"

Moose answered smacking on some pork chops. "Funny. Man you ain't going to believe what Rat and Jay told me. Who on the horn with you that called?"

"Sandy."

"Hit me back at my girl Sofia house. I'm bout to step in right now." Moose hung up.

"Ah baby, I'ma call you right back."

"Better," Sandy replied.

Low called Moose right back and he accepted the call. "What's the deal?" Low asked getting amped.

"Dog, yo old flame Wanda, she fuckin wit that buster Dirty punk ass! Rat and Jay saw her rolling in his ride together."

"Oh yeah...she fuckin wit the enemies huh? Punk bitch!" Low felt like he was being played. After all him and Wanda been through with both their parents getting slain together, and him murder'in them two Jamaicans for her. Plus them fuckin, he thought she would at least respect him and not fuck with the enemy. Which she knew damn well was his arch nemesis. He wanted to kill her at that moment.

Moose could tell Low wasn't feeling this shit, and knew he was gone be tripping and would smoke someone without a care right now. He had witness it with his own eyes, so he feared Low in some ways.

"Man I'ma get back at cha later," Low told him hanging up.

Red had heard him on the other phone going off and knew something wasn't right. "Nigga you cool? What's up?"

"Holla at me when you get off the horn," Low told him, walking away. Low was seething, thinking about killing both they asses right now as he went outside for some fresh air and sat on a bench by himself. "That bitch Dirty gon feel me when I step outta this bitch!" He told himself. Red walked up on him and broke him from his murderous trance. Low was feeling like he was getting played.

"What's poppin home boy? Everything cool or what?" Red asked, looking concerned. Low told him the deal, and they sat and plotted together about what they were going to do when they surfaced on the bricks.

On Low's birthday, he got a visit from his grandma, aunt Paula, his brothers, and Sandy. That day, after the visit, him and Red got high and drunk on some hooch (homemade wine), getting toasted. Red was getting out next month in August, on the 28th, and Low was going to miss his silly ass. Low had told Red he was gone be straight when he bounced, and that they were going to get major money together when he stepped.

Tina had a little boy in April. He looked just like Low. The day she went into labor, she got even madder at Low because he wasn't there, and she didn't get a chance to tell him, and made her resent Low even more. Bobby had stayed up there with her, her brother Dino and her mother when she had their baby.

On Low's birthday, Tina sat on her porch holding their baby boy she named Montel, that was the spittin image of his father. Everybody thought the baby was Bobby's, but he knew deep down who's baby it was. Him despising and loathing Low made him keep what he knew to himself. Her mother knew, but Tina made her promise not to say or tell nobody. Especially Low.

(Two days later)

Moose was cool with Bobo, and always had been. They had grew up together. So Moose could tell Bo wasn't digging Low to much as he spoke to him over the phone.

"So my sister still fuckin wit that little nigga, huh?" Bo asked, after Cathy told him she was.

"Yeah, her and her girlfriend went up to see him and this cat Red. They cool," Moose said, and added, to try to calm Bobo down some, cause he didn't want to see them beefing. Bo was a down ass nigga and he loved him. But Low was, and is, a stone cold-hearted muthafuckin killer! And wouldn't hesitate to smoke Bo's ass like some good weed. So he was trying to keep the peace, and make Bo leave Low the fuck alone. Low wasn't the same little cat he use to be. HE WAS A FUCKIN BEAST ON THESE STREETS! A MONSTER!

Chapter 24
"Shit don't change...I'ma Goon fo life!"

The day of Red's release, him and Low smoked a fat one and chopped it up before he left. "No homo, but I'ma miss yo ass my nigga!" Red told Low. "You a real nigga."

"Yeah my nigga, no homo I'ma miss yo silly ass to," they both laughed at each other. "Let's go nigga, it's yo time to shine player." They walked to the front, to the building you had to go in to get released at, and stopped.

"Man call me at my Moms spot tonight. I should be there. If not, I'm deep in my girl's guts," they both laughed.

"Pound it fo me too my nigga. Now go on before they keep yo ass here, al'ight I'll try in call ya later." They hugged, and Red went in the building door. Low stared at the door for a second after Red went in. Then he walked to the rec yard so he could see him off. He had gotten Nut and Roe to come an get him and look out for him. They told Low, no doubt, and would be there. So Low went to the fence to make sure. As he got on the yard he saw a crowd of niggas by the fence where they could see the parking lot and heard bass from somebodies car. He knew it was his rap dawgs as he got closer and saw a clean ass white Blazer with a metal flake paint job, sitting on gold Dayton's, shining as the sun beamed on it. Roe and Nut was leaning on it draped in gold, looking like big time rappers an shit. They saw Low coming and waved. Low felt good seeing his two road dawgs out there sitting pretty on them thangs coming to get his new road dawg, that their just meeting on the strength of him.

Nut got in the Blazer and changed the music to Dear Dairy, and Scarface pumped out the woofers making cats on the yard go bananas, talking about "that's my shit! Man yo nigga's out there doing it! They saw Red come out walking towards the blazer and everybody yelled for him. Red pumped his fist at them, feeling good to be outside of the fence.

Red walked to Roe and Nut and they gave him some goon love, dapping him and giving him a hard hug, while shaking his hand roughly.

"Let's be out killa," Nut told Red.

Red looked through the fence at Low, and they threw up their fist. Nut and Roe did the same and they all got in the ride. Nut put it in gear and drove off blowing his musical horn.

They took Red to the Mall and bought him mass clothes, shoes, and other things so he   would be fresh to death. Red was hollering at every girl he saw. With no restraints on biting your tongue for so long, a nigga would say some crazy things to a female. Red called his Moms on his new celly they got him and told her he would be there in a little while. Red was happy as fuck! He was high and drunk as hell! When they got in the Blazer from coming out the Mall, Nut asked Red, "Nigga you fuck wit these?" and threw him a fresh bottle of valiums.

Red looked at them and saw they were the blue 10's, and said, "Hell yeah," opening the bottle and popping four off rip. "Niggas let's roll."

A hour later, smacking on some Staples Red craved for, they pulled up at the trap house on Broadway and told Red to come on. Joker, K.K., and two other niggas with some honeys were in there.

They took Red to the back. "Low told me to give ya something. Hold up, let me have my bitch bring it through," Roe told Red, as he dialed on the celly. "Ah Kat, bring that on Broadway right quick." Kat was Rhonda's nickname he called her Kitty Kat, Kit Kat or just Kat because of her eyes.

Red was talking boss shit to two of the girl's high, when Rhonda drove up and came in. She handed Roe a duffel bag. "Good lookin. I'll see ya later," said Roe, slapping her on her nice yellow plump behind. "Let's go in the back," he told Red and Nut. They went into the back and sat down. Roe opened up the duffel bag and pulled out 12,000, nine ounces of fish scale (cocaine), and a Tec nine, and said, "This you playboy."

Red was stuck. He never had so much dope and money at one time before in his life. "Damn, my nigga looked out fo me!"

"He told me to tell you this ain't shit, and that he just wanna see what you do with this first," Nut told him. "Check killa," Nut said taking two keys off his key chain and throwing them to him. "This on us killa, that silver Nine Eight outside for you." Red had seen the clean 8 ball (car) when they drove up in front, sitting on chrome deep dish Dayton's with a black ragtop, and power hold. "Get paid nigga!"

Red stayed there another hour with them, then got into his 8 ball and pearled out feeling good as fuck, banging "Straight outta Compton." Twenty minutes later, he pulled in front of his mother's apartment in Plaza View on the East side, not far from the Vic's, shaking her windows with the four "12"inch woofers in the trunk.

His mother looked out the window seeing someone parked in front of her place vibrating her windows, having a feeling it was her son and came outside with his brother and girlfriend Tracy. Seeing his reddish hair from the inside car light, they knew it was him. Red was leaning all the way back sideways, and looked up smiling at them. They rushed to the car opening the door. Tracy got on his lap hugging him as she sat on his lap kissing him all over.

"Girl, let him out that car so I can get me a hug," his mother Fancy complained.

Red laughed, lifting Tracy up and getting out the car hugging his Moms. "Hey Ma."

"Boy it's bout time you got here. Who's car is this?"

"My dudes an Low looked out for me," Red told her.

She was already hip to Low because of them murders on the news, gossip, and what she heard. She knew him and Low had become friends while incarcerated, and Low had looked out for him. She didn't like him messing with a person with a rep like what was being said. But she knew her son was a goon to and could handle himself. But this Low boy had killed alot of people they claimed, she was thinking at that moment looking at him seriously. "Just be careful, that's all I ask."

Red knew his mother didn't want him back in them streets. And saw the look she gave him when he told her Low and them looked out for him with the car. "I will Ma."

"Boy you high? Come'on in, I cooked yo food. Been waiting in the micro wave fo yo butt all day."

They started walking towards the crib and Red palmed his girl's fat soft ass as they walked in squeezing it. "You know what it is later," he whispered in her ear. She giggled, knowing she was going to get a raw ass

Goon fuckin!

Red was chilling still at his Moms house an hour later when they all heard some loud music from some ones ride in front of the apartment. Red looked out the window and saw Moose, Jay, Alvin, and Rat's big ass leaning on two clean whips. He told his Moms and them it was for him, and stepped outside. They all gave him some love, welcoming him home.

"Nigga let's go kick it!" Moose told him.

"I got's to chill wit my family right now for a while, then go fuck my girl real good after that," Red told'em, and they all laughed, agreeing on that one.

"Well come holla at us later or tomorrow. You know where to find us," Moose said handing him a card with every bodies number on it. "Peace my nigga," they all said later and left.

Red took Tracy to Wagon Wheel motel, because Low use to tell him how he took his females there to fuck in their Jacuzzi suite. Red fucked Tracy so good and long that night, she was bowlegged and soar for two days. He gave her $1,000 and told her to go find them a nice crib out the way somewhere. He had talked to Low that night over his Moms crib.

Two weeks on the street later, Red had opened his own trap house on the East side on Garland, and it was bopping hard. He was out there handling his business. His girl had found a nice house that nobody knew about like he told her, by the Lake on the east side. He told his mother he was going to buy her a house when his money got up. He was on McGuffey with Jay in his Lac mackin to some chicks, when some niggas riding deep in a Coupe Deville pulled up in front of them and gangstered their ride cutting them off. Red snatched his 32 shot Nine milla and jacked one into the chamber, as the niggas got out the Coupe.

One of the girls remarked, "Aaww shoot, here come yo crazy ass man gurl!"

"What the fuck!" Red said putting his ride in reverse pulling back an parking, and hopping out clutching his burner with Jay following.

Dude that was driving the Coupe had approached one of the girls that was suppose to be his woman. "Hoe you out here fuckin wit these chumps on me? Bitch get yo funky ass in the car!" He hollered to the pretty brown petite female then glanced at Red and Jay coming his way.

"Check player, don't ever roll down on me like that again!' Better yet, you bitch ass niggas hit the ground!" Red gritted, raising the gat and shooting by their heads two times, making them hit the ground as if they were trying to blend in it. Red stepped to them and kicked the driver in his side, making him groan out, then walked to his ride and leaned on it looking at the girl inside. "So what's up baby girl, you wit this lame?" He asked the girl that was suppose to be dudes with the Coupe.

She looked at Red all calm, leaning inside staring at her like he didn't just bust his gun, and heard about him out there getting money with Low's crew and pushing a fly whip the first day he got out, so she wanted to jump ship to a better one, and said, "No!"

"Well go get in my car," Red told her. She got out and got in Red's whip.

Jay was just looking at Red, but was still holding his gun on the niggas Red had on the ground, and said "fuck it to himself!" and looked at the other girl's with her. "Y'all wanna roll to or what?"

All three of them said, "Hell yeah!" and hopped in the back seat.

Red shot dude's car tire and went in his car, coming back out with a hand full of tapes. "Nigga get a CD changer, broke ass nigga!" He muttered, walking to his ride with a bag of weed he got out dude's car. Red and Jay got in the ride and drove off as Red was flipping tapes out the window he didn't like, going down the street.

The nigga's on the ground got up cussing like a muthafucka! The driver, Richard, was going crazy. "Who the fuck was that chump nigga with Jay?" He shouted, staring at Red's tail of the car. They all knew Jay.

"Man…" one of them spoke, "That's Red…he fucks with Low an his nigga's," he said all scared like. The other cats there were all telling him to let the shit ride! They knew they wasn't on what Low was on, at all!

But, Richard was like, "Fuck Low and his niggas! He locked up anyway. That bitch got me fucked up, thinkin he can play me like that and take my bitch! Yeah right."

His partners just shook their heads, not wanting no parts of Low and his click. NONE!

Red had got in the back with all three girl's and was talking boss shit, rubbing all on them clowning and making them giggle as they smoked Dro and drunk. "Go to my spot on Garland," he told Jay, who was driving now.

When they got there, three of his workers were on the porch, Bill, Demon, and his cousin Dollar. Jay drove up the driveway and they all got out. "Hey, what's good here?" Dollar, tall, skinny narrow ass said, with a 40 ounce of Old English in his hand eyeing the females all thirsty.

"Nigga sit yo freak ass down!" Red told him, going into the house with the females behind him.

Dollar was like, "Uumm," to the girl's following behind them licking his lips. Red knew his workers since they were young, and had been doing dirt together since they could walk.

Dollar got freaky with them on the girl's. They had the three chicks naked in less then an hour running trains on them. When they were finished, Dollar had Billy drop them back off. When he drove in front of the house to drop them off, someone started shooting at them. Billy stepped on the gas speeding off with the door wide open. The girls were just about to get out the ride when the gunshots came. The girls were screaming up some shit! The person shooting was behind them in a Coupe Deville. Billy's back window shattered and the girl next to him was screaming, making him even madder.

"Hoe shut the fuck up! Shut up and hand me my gun under that seat!" She gave it to him shaking, and he yelled, "All you hoes lay down!" as he pointed his gat out the back window and busted back. BUC! BUC! BUC! The Deville pulled back and the girl in the front seat sat up and looked back at who was shooting at them.

"That nigga Richard stupid! I don't know why I fucked with his dumb ass in the first place!" The girl in the front seat said, sighing.

"Oh you know that buster shooting at us?" Billy asked heated.

"Yeah I know the punk!" she replied. "That's the boy Red pulled his gun out on today, I use to mess with."

Billy drove back to the trap house pulling in the driveway, and Dollar saw his ride with the girl's still with him. Him and Demon jumped off the porch. "Nigga what the fuck happen?" Dollar asked heated. As he was telling them, Red and Jay came out the house.

"Oh yeah," Red said, "Londa, let me holla at cha," he told the girl that messed with Richard, and lead her in the back room for 20 minutes and came back out saying, "Let's roll. Bill you can drop them off over the other girl's house, "he told him pointing to the other girl. "Jay, Dollar, let's bounce!" They got in Jay's ride he had parked there and Red told him to drive to the Plaza in the Lincoln Knolls? When they got there, Red got out with a screwdriver and told Jay to meet him behind East High school. "Come'on Dollar."

Red saw a Sunbird and peeled it burning rubber off. They meet Jay behind, the school. "Drop yo shit off in the Vic's nigga, we gon' follow you," he told Jay and they parked up the street while he parked, so no one could see them. Jay came running back and Red told him to drive and go past his Moms right quick. Jay did, and Red told him to park around the corner. Being inside for years had made him more caution about what dirt he did. Hearing and knowing others mistakes had put him on point when doing things that could have him behind bars for life. Red came back 15 minutes later with a gym bag. "Now let's go see what's up wit this bitch!" Red told them putting his black leather gloves on. "That bitch nigga stay on Kimmel," he told Jay.

When they got there, they saw Richard's car, and Red told Jay to drive on past and park up the street, four houses from Rich crib. It was like 11 p.m., so it was dark out.

"Cut the sounds up a little nigga, cause you breathing hard as fuck. You cool dog?" Dollar asked Jay, as he smoked a cigarette in the back seat.

Jay ain't never did no premeditated killer shit before for real. He had shot at others though, when wit his crew. He was tripping off how Red was talking on his celly all calm.

"Yeah, I'm cool."

They sat there for a hour just waiting. Nigga, where this busta at?" Dollar murmured, getting impatient. As soon as he said that, Rich came outside and got in his car.

"There he go," Red mumbled, cutting his celly off not even telling who-ever he was talking to bye. Red had told the girl Londa to call Richard and get him to come pick her up.

Dollar sat up and put his cigarette out. "Bout time, damn."

Jay got all nervous and started the car pulling off after him all fast.

Red looked at him and said, "Slow down nigga! We ain't tryin to hip him onto us fool!" They followed him down McGuffey and got right behind him at a red light.

"Put y'all ski-mask on now!" Red hollered. "Now pull on the side of this chump bitch!" Jay did, and the car was still moving as Red jumped out the door shoving the 44 magnum in Rich face yelling. "Don't move nuguh! Put this bitch in park! NOW! Now get yo bitch ass out!" Red dragged him to the ride and Dollar put his Clock to Rich head as Red pushed him inside and hopped in the back with him. "Let's go!" he yelled to Jay, who had the car stopped looking all shocked. "Go by the lake!" he told Jay. "So you wanna play gangsta, huh nigga?" Red hollered smacking Rich in the face with his burner busting his noggin open, making blood gush out.

"Oh, you gangsta!" Dollar grunted, and started punching and kicking him. Rich was balled up on the back floor screaming like a wild pig.

Jay got to the lake and Red directed him to this dirt road to drive up. "This cool right here, park this muthafucka!" Jay parked and Red got out then grabbed Rich by his ankles, dragging his crying pleading ass out the car. Dollar had to pry his hands off the car seat he had in a death grip. Jay wasn't feeling this ordeal as he stood watching.

"Nigga, don't play with real niggas without being real with this shit here!" Red shouted, talking about gun play waving the gun in Rich face. "Nigga this fo my dogs ride!" BUC! He shot him in the leg, making Rich howl like a Wolf. Then, Red walked over to Jay handing him the gun. "Nigga get some!"

Jay's eyes got big as boiled eggs. He took the gun and walked over to Rich crying bloody ass and shot, and missed, hands shaking like crazy.

Dollar said, "Nigga," pushing him out the way, "This how you shoot a bitch!" and shot Rich in the same leg. Rich jumped up from the dirt road screaming for his life, and Red hit him over the ear with the pistol dropping him like a sack of potatoes.

Red said, "Man pop him in the head!" He told Jay. Jay was stalling to long, so Red took another gun out his waist and pointed it to Jay's dome. "Nigga pop him in the head!"

Jay closed his eyes and squeezed the trigger. BOOM! He opened his eyes and watched Rich eyes get big, as he started jerking on the ground then went silent. Jay felt sick.

"Let's bounce," Red said, and got in the driver's side and drove off. He went back to the trap spot and cleaned any prints and evidence out the car, and got rid of the murder weapons. And went back to business as usual.

Chapter 25
**Just cause we broke bread, got money,
and banged females together, don't mean I love you...**

Jay was sick as fuck that night and threw up two times. He laid in the bed with Mary talking, feeling nauseated. The smell of gun sulfur still stinging his nostrils, as the sight of Richard's soul left his flesh was fucking with him.

"That nigga crazy, pulling his gun on me! Fuck Red!" exclaimed Jay.

Mary asked, "Why he do that baby? Y'all got into it?"

Jay looked at her, and answered, "Fo nothin, that's why! Hating on a nigga."

Low called Red the next day. "How you living my nigga? You all good?"

"Yeah man...had to take care of some light weight shit last night. Wasn't nothing doe. That nigga Jay soft brah. Straight up pussy boy, I'm tellin ya." Red and Low had made up some codes to let one another know what they were actually saying, without saying it while on lock together. So "light weight" meant murder.

Low replied, "Oh, fo real? Well do what you gotta do to stay on solid ground. Feel me my nigga?"

"No doubt. You still want me to send them roses to that raw ass big booty honey fo ya?" Red asked. "Wit yo soft ass."

Low chuckled. "Yeah silly ass nigga. Do that fo me, it's her birthday today."

"I got cha partna. Hit me up later."

"Al'ight, good lookin. Later my nigga." (click)

Red drove over to holla at Roe and Nut at their house, but they wasn't there. So he went to the flower shop and got the roses and candy for Low, and had it sent to Kira at her job like Low asked. He didn't blame his nigga for doing whatever for Kira. She was definitely a dime piece with her head on tight.

Two hours later, Kira got her gifts at work and just smiled and blushed as her co-workers teased her. It felt good getting the gifts. She never had a man be so thoughtful and sweet. She really loved Low like a brother and knew he wanted more from her. She just wasn't ready for no intimate relationship right now.

It was October, and Low was short to getting out and couldn't wait. All he thought about was what he was going to do when he surfaced. All being there did was make him even more determined and eager to hit the street and get money, holla an fuck with honeys, and live that Goon life to the max!

Pep sat on the porch in the Vic's broke as hell, pockets hurting. He saw Red drive up in his 8 Ball and get out to holla at Moose and Rat, while they were rolling dice. Pep still had his Lac and it was still clean as hell. His girl Kelly was pregnant with his child and he needed some ends. So he was thinking about getting back in the game.

Jay drove up and got out and came over to the dice game. He looked at Red kinda strange and Red picked up on it.

"What's up Jay? You cool nigga?" Red mugged him asking.

Jay responded, "I'm straight Red."

Moose glanced up from the game at them cause he felt some tension between them. He saw the frown Red was giving Jay, and that Jay didn't want no problem, so he continued playing dice.

Alvin Picked up Jay's girl Mary at her aunt's house, and they were on their way to the Hotel when Alvin celly went off. "Hey Ma, what's going on?" he answered. "Alright, I'll be there in a minute or two," he said, and hung up. "I gotta drop my Mom off some money right quick," he told Mary, turning the ride around.

Jay had left the dice game to go see what was up with his nigga, so they could get their high on because he needed it right now, his nerves were bad. The incident and Red just glaring at him all crazy had him paranoid and uneasy.

Alvin had just got to his mother's house and told Mary to "hold up" as he went in. Mary was bobbing her head to the music when Jay drove up behind Alvin's car, and got out walking to Alvin's car seeing someone in it. When he looked in he froze for a quick second, and Mary just looked at him with her mouth opened.

"What the fuck you doing in my nigga's car?"

Mary studdered, trying to come up with a lie. "I...I was...lookin fo you and he seen me walking."

"Bitch what's wrong with yo car?" asked Jay opening the car door where she was. "Hoe, you fuckin my nigga?" he grabbed her by her t-shirt, yanking her out the car. "Huh?"

"Get the fuck off me Jay!" Mary screamed swinging wild hitting him in the face, igniting his anger even more of catching her with his best friend.

"Ah hoe!" Jay yelled and punched her in the face two times busting her nose.

Alvin came out an saw them fighting and ran and grabbed Jay off Mary. "Chill my nigga!"

Jay swirled around and shouted, "Nigga, you fuckin my bitch?"

Alvin couldn't lie, or say shit, he let his head drop and Jay stole on him, knocking him on his ass. Jay went back to yanking Mary out the car, because she had hopped back in, and she was screaming even louder then before. "Bitch shut the fuck up! Jay yelled as he dragged her to his car.

Alvin had ran to his car and reached under the driver's seat, pulling his gat out. "Jay let her go!" He shouted.

Jay turned and looked at his suppose to be nigga, friend, and saw he had his gun out on him. But when your heart and dick in a fucked up situation like this, your not thinking to clearly cause your mind isn't the one leading the issue at hand.

"Fuck you nigga!" Jay shouted, opening his car door to put Mary inside.

Alvin squeezed the trigger and the bullet struck Jay in the shoulder, spinning him around and down the side of the car. Alvin kept his gun out pointing it at Jay as Mary ran to him.

Jay couldn't believe he just got shot by Alvin, his best friend over his girlfriend, and his heart still over ruled his sense of thinking. "Bitch nigga, you shot me! Nigga it's beef now!" He yelled, going inside his car looking for his gun. Alvin was scared now, so he started shooting at him busting his front window out and a bullet hitting him again in the back. Jay dropped when the bullet struck him in the back this time. Alvin ran to Jay's car, and saw him lying in his front seat bleeding, and it hit him what he just did to his best friend who he grew up with. Then Mary called his name, putting him back in the darkness he was already in about her scandalous ass.

"Alvin baby let's go!" Mary screamed, as she pulled on his arm trying to pull him away from his dying friend Jay.

Alvin's mother came outside screaming, standing there shocked at what her son had just did to his best friend. "Boy what the hell you just do?! You done lost your fuckin mind?"

"Ma I didn't mean it," Alvin pleaded, looking stupid.

"Let me go call the ambulance, and you better get yo ass outta here before the cops come! You hear me? Go boy, Go!" His mother yelled.

Alvin looked at Jay, and got in his car with Mary as she drove off. He was drunk, discombobulated, and tripping glancing at Mary thinking, damn, all over her.

Mary parked in front of her home and looked at Alvin. "Baby, it's going to be okay. Just go hide out until you find out what happened to him," she kissed him and got out the car going in the house.

Alvin sat there a few minutes like a zombie, then drove off heading to the Victory. He drove up right where Moose, Rat, and Red was at playing dice with some others and just sat there.

Red had peeped him coming and had kept his eyes his way. Then he noticed Alvin was just sitting there staring ahead, looking at nothing. Red glanced at Rat and Moose getting their attention, and nodded towards Alvin sitting in his car. They stopped playing dice and went to see what was up with him.

"Alvin, what's going on?" Moose asked, while Rat and Red bent down looking at him inside the car.

Red peeped Alvin's gun on the passenger seat and the dry blood on his mouth, and asked, "What's up nigga, somebody fuckin wit you?"

Alvin turned his head looking at Red, and said, "I just shot Jay," like he was in a trance or something.

Red asked, "Is he alright?" Really not giving a fuck, hoping he was dead.

"Nigga is you crazy? What happened?" Moose hollered, not believing this. Them two nigga's he had watched grow up thick as thieves.

"He caught me with Mary."

Red had heard from Low while on lockdown that he was just checking Alvin about fuckin his dudes broad when the raid jumped off. Low told him that Alvin told him he wasn't going to fuck with her no more when they were on lockdown together. So he never told Jay about his partner fuckin his piece.

Red said, "Man you shot yo nigga Jay over that hoe? You trippin nigga, fo real!" Red shook his head disgusted with him.

Alvin replied, "He sucker punched me first!"

"Nigga you still don't suppose to shoot yo nigga bout no tramp ass bitch!" Moose stated, "I got's to go see if he al'ight!" Moose rushed off and Rat caught up with him hopping in his car leaving.

Red took Alvin's gun off the seat and told him to go chill out until later.

"Al'ight," Alvin replied, and drove off.

Red walked over Pattie's house cause Gina was over there. Gina was the girl Low had Pattie plug him up with while on lock. They were on the porch with Rat's chick Pam, drinking coolers and blowing green. "Hey Red, what's up?" They all said when they seen him. Cathy came out the apartment door with a plate of food, saying hi to Red.

"Nothing but the grind'he replied. "Ah, if Low call ya tell him to call me, it's important," he told Pattie.

"He just hung up on me a minute ago. He mad at me or somethin."

"Why you didn't call me back when I paged you earlier?" Gina asked Red.

"I've been at the dice game, you should've put yo code behind it if it was important," Red told her, staring at her big shining juicy lips.

"Well, can you take me home? I got's to get dressed cause we going out tonight."

Red said, "Let's go then," and walked off.

Gina huffed. "Damn!" and got up telling the girl's she would see them later, and caught up with Red.

Nut's girl Shawn had their baby a week ago, and him and Roe had just walked into K-Mart cause Nut was looking to buy his new born baby boy some more toy's and stuff when they bumped into Linda, Wanda's friend that Nut been at and trying to fuck for the longest, She was with some skinny pretty brown skinned girl looking at some cups and glasses.

Linda saw Nut coming and said, "Oh boy, here comes this fool boy again," remembering the last time she saw him in a store when he up piped on her showing her his man hood right in the store not giving a fuck.

Nut walked right up on her and spoke, "How you fine ladies doing today?" He eyed Linda all up on her.

"How y'all doing?" Roe added.

"Hi Roe," Linda said, and smacked her lips making a noise when she looked at Nut, not even speaking to him.

Linda's friend said, "Hello gentlemen."

"At least someone got manners," Nut told Linda, then put his hands out introducing his self to her girl. "My name Nut, and this my roadie here…Roe." Roe and Nut were wearing some black Dickie's sagging, hoodies, and black Timberland boots with big dookie gold chains on that had their names as emblems.

"Don't let him trick you honey, this the crazy one here," Linda told her friend pointing to Nut, "and he the nice one," talking about Roe.

"Gurl stop acting like that. You know you like a nigga. You saw my jewels, (private, Johnson, for you slow mutha's) now you acting funny, huh?"

"Nigga, you must be joking. That thang was tinny tiny," Linda replied, laughing.

Her girl went, "Uumm," and laughed with her.

"You can't handle it with yo scary ass. Been duckin a killa cause you know I'll knock yo back the fuck out!" Nut told her grabbing his dick.

"What? Nigga please, I'll drown yo lil bitty dick ass!" Linda retorted.

"Well page me tonight, here go my info," Nut told her writing his hook down.

Her girl said, "My name Jamie," to Roe, while Nut was writing his info down.

"You going to be wit yo girl later?" Roe asked her, wanting to see if her ass had some deep good pussy.

"Probably but call me anyway," she went in her purse and came out with a business card, proclaiming her profession in doing hair.

"Hope your not like your buddy," she said playing.

"I wouldn't know about him, but I'm handling."

"I hope so," she told him looking down at his dick.

Nut was trying to give Linda his number, but she was acting all funny. "Nigga I'm straight."

Nut said, "Fuck you, fake hoe!"

Her girl Jamie said, "Take it gurl, you said he small." Edging her on, cause she really wanted to get with Roe fine ass, cause she knew about him out there stackin his paper and rep.

Linda looked at her friend and said, "Alright boy," and took it. "And I ain't on no freaky mess boy," she rolled her eyes at Nut.

Nut laughed. "Chill out, I ain't going to hurt you," and walked off grinning, knowing he was going to beat the pussy up if she let him fuck.

"Girrrll, see what you did. That boy crazy!" said Linda.

"Shit, they got money doe honey child, don't they?" They laughed together, and said together "I know that's right!" Giggling, thinking they came up.

Red drove up into Gina's driveway on Bruce street in LaLa land and she invited him in. Red had things to do, but them juicy lips with the burgundy lip stick on her made him get out the car and go in. He sat on the couch looking around her living room that was nice, then he picked up her phone and called some of his pager numbers back, and missed calls on his celly. Gina came out from the bedroom in a all yellow lace pantie and bra set, and bent over seductively turning on some music. Red saw all ass and pussy sticking out, and forgot what he was saying on the phone to someone.

Still bent over, Gina turned around and asked, "You want something to eat?" real sexy like, making sure she got his attention.

"Umm…bring me a beer," Red answered, enjoying the view. She switched to the kitchen and came back with a cold glass of beer for him and handed it to him, sitting down right next to him. Her perfume invaded his senses. Red started drinking his beer.

"I don't know why you haven't been over since you've been out. You act like you don't even like me," Gina pouted.

"Gurl, you know it ain't even like that. Nigga been trying to get this paper, that's all. With lips like that, how the fuck a nigga gon pass you up," Red said, not bullshitting, joint hard as steel gazing at her lips.

"Uumm…let me see then," Gina cooed, as she went to his zipper and got his dick out, seeing he was hard. "Mmm…," she moaned and licked around his joint. Red sat back, and let her lap his shit up like a melting ice cream cone in the 90 degree weather. She took him in her mouth and the heat from her around his dick felt so good. Red peered down and saw them big juicy lips going down with the sensation and tried his best to hold back from cumming, but them pretty lips and boss ass head game she had was taking him there. She was moaning suckin his shit real good. 20 minutes later. Red blew his load down her throat, and she swallowed it getting every drop.

"Damn gurl, you tryin to suck the blood outta nigga dick," Red groaned, stopping her cause she was still suckin on his dick. She came up smiling, lips wet with cum and spit.

"Whateva boy, you liked it."

"Sho did. Now let a nigga see what that pussy like."

Chapter 26

Alot of times we think on the physical aspect only.
Not what detrimentally could destroy us and what we have...

Moose and Rat was told at the hospital that Jay would be fine. They wasn't allowed to see him at the moment so they left.

Mary had gotten on the phone running her mouth about how Alvin had shot his best friend over her, cause Jay caught them creeping. So word spreaded quickly.

Low had called Pattie and she had told him what she heard, and that Red said to call him as soon as he could. So he had Pattie call Red for him on the three. Red told him to call over his moms spot in like ten minutes cause he was about to pull up in the Plaza right now. Low told Pattie he would call her right back.

Red went into his moms apartment and she was on the couch watching her show. "Hey Ma."

"Boy, your girlfriend called here looking for you."

"Alright Ma, I'll call her in a minute." Red picked up the phone when it rung and accepted Low's call walking into his old bedroom. "Yeah man, that bullshit true, cause I know you heard."

"Man what the fuck wrong with them fools? They on some weak ass shit like that?" Low was furious.

"Yup my nig. Jay a hoe nigga for real. And Alvin got a weak mind. What's up, you want me to take care of this light weight shit or what?"

"Nah, fuck them with that girly shit! Let them handle it themselves. Alvin told me he wasn't going to fuck with that stank hoe, but I see he whipped."

They talked for a half hour, and Red told him he just hit Gina and how raw her skull was. "She do got a set of dick suckers on her yellow ass," said Low, thinking of her making Red laugh.

Red left his moms and headed to see if he could catch up with Nut and Roe again, to let them know he would be re-uping tomorrow. They wasn't there, so he drove up to Broadway and saw them hanging outside with their two workers and some females in the yard.

Nut had gotten a gang of toys, and his girl Shawn had caught him coming back from K-Mart, as she was riding with her friends, Rhonda, Roe girl, Pep old use to be flame Amy, and Low's chick Sandy. So they were outside listening to Shawn cuss Nut out about all the stuff he kept buying their baby. Joker was trying to get on Amy, but she wasn't with it. They didn't have enough money and clout for her. Red hopped out of his whip.

"Killa, what's crackin my nigga?" Nut hollered.

Red replied, "Nothing but this money my nigga."

"I heard that," Roe commented.

"Why you buying all this stuff for Kemond, Nut?" Shawn asked Nut, seeing he was trying to get out of what she was stressing. "You know he to young fo them video games right now!" She had one hand on her thick hips glaring at him, waiting on an answer.

"That's my son, and he gonna have all the muthafuckin shit I didn't have! Bet that!"

Red sat on the steps, and Amy got up and handed him a can of beer.

"Here Red," she said, and sat next to him.

"Oh, okay. I see my money ain't long enough," said K.K., and they busted out laughing.

Later that day, Red had Amy in his whip as he pulled up in the Vic's to make a quick stop to pick up some money. He had fronted some little cat out there and he had paged Red telling him he needed some work. When Red got out the ride and the car light came on and Pep saw Amy in his ride.

Pep walked up to Red's car. "Ah, what's up Amy?" he said, but she couldn't hear him because the music in the car was so loud, but she noticed him saying something to her by the car. She turned the sounds down.

"Hey Pep, how you doing?"

"I'm cool. I see you doing good," Pep stated all sarcastic.

"Yeah I'm okay," she felt kinda awkward cause he was acting all funny staring at her with his face frowned up. "Glad you out, huh?"

Pep didn't reply cause Red had came back. "What's good Pep?" Red spoke getting in the whip, feeling the vibe from Pep.

"Whud up?"

Red turned his sounds up and drove off. When he got two blocks up he stopped at a stop sign and turned his music down, and asked Amy, "What's the deal with that nigga?"

She pretended she didn't know who he was talking about. "Who Red?"

Red knew she was fronting like she didn't know who he was talking about. "Pep, that's who. Why you acting like you don't know who?"

"Oh him? We use to talk before he went to jail. That's all."

Low had started hanging by himself since all his road dawgs were gone. He worked out some times with his little crew, but for the most part he kept to himself. He was getting out in like 2 months. December was the month of his release and he couldn't wait. It's on like a muthafucka! Was all he kept saying to himself. He had let his hair grow into braids and had beefed up. "Them hoes gon feel me when I step out this bitch! Yeah," he thought, as he jogged the yard with his Walkman on.

Dirty and Tito had just dropped Brenda and Kim off, and was driving past the Victory when they saw Moose coming out the Arab store on McGuffey. "Yo, you see that bitch?" Dirty asked Tito. Dirty got that feeling he got whenever he was about to murder someone.

"Nah, who was it?"

"That fat bitch Moose nigga! Turn this mug around!" Dirty told him, placing the sawed off shot gun in his lap.

Moose had just came out the Arab store with a big bag of Cheese Curls with a 40 ounce of Old English, and stopped to talk to some old heads hanging outside flat foot hustling for change. "You got something on ya?" One of them asked Moose.

"Come'on man, you know I don't fuck wit that small shit no moe. But follow me to the Vic and I'll have one of my people hook ya up proper," Moose told him, as he was opening his car door he heard a car coming and turned around to see who it was, and saw Dirty leaning out the window with a sawed off pointing his way, and his heart stopped as he lost the grip on the bag in his hand. As soon as the 40 ounce busted on the ground, the shot gun went off spraying pellets everywhere, hitting Moose and others around him. Moose slid down the driver's door with blood leaking out from the pellets that tore his flesh.

"Nigga, you see how we did that fat pig bitch? That's what I'm talkin bout! Laying these hoes down that fuck with us!" Dirty hollered all japed, as they got on the freeway heading to the South side.

Moose had survived and was put in the same room as Jay cause Rat had come up there with his family and had them demand it. Red showed up and found out who did it and was heated as fuck! He knew all about Low's beef with them nigga's Dirty and Tito, cause Low had told him about their war stories.

"Let's be out!" Red told Rat at the hospital. Red stole a car and they swooped by one of Tito's and Dirty's trap spots looking for them that night and didn't see them, so Red shot up their two trap houses, and two workers hanging outside, and pearled.

One week later

Rican Puncho had just got off the phone with Low, and him, and Big Dawg went to see Red. They pulled up at his house on Garland, beating some Rican rap. Dollar heard them and came outside.

"Whuz up wit y'all? You got some of that funk ya had last time?" Dollar wanted to know.

Big Dawg nodded his head yeah, and Puncho got out the car saying, "Ah essay, you like that leaf, huh? Good eh?"

"Hell yeah! Sell me some of that shit."

"Hold up essay, we smoke wit cha, eh? Come on Big Dawg, and bring thee funk wit cha." Big Dawg got out with a big bag of light green weed and they went in the house.

"Roll that shit up," Dollar said, throwing Dawg some blunt wraps. Demon and Bill was in there to. A half hour later it was smokey as hell in there. Red drove up and came in with Rat.

"Damn, y'all nigga's in this bitch getting toasted as fuck! I thought the house was on fire," Rat told'em, sitting down next to Demon who was knocked out high on the couch.

"Eh essay, I've been waiting on ya. I got's that fo ya. The thing Low said you wanted. Come'on, "Puncho told Red, getting up with Big Dawg following them outside. Dollar tried to get up and sat back down he was so fuckin high.

"Man what y'all put in that weed an shit?" Dollar hollered, they just laughed at him as they walked out the door.

Puncho opened the trunk of the hooptie. and it was mass weed in garbage bags back there. "Give me $15,000 fo all three bags essay, deal ah?"

Red jumped on it. "You got a deal partna."

Chapter 27

Behind them walls can make you or break you…change you or make you worse! Them walls change lives, make lives, and take lives. So, some Goon halfway, while very few Goon for life…

(Friday, December 13th 1991)

The day of Lowdown's release, he sat on the cold bench outside for a hour just letting his mind wonder and drift. "These walls and fences held me in here like a fuckin' animal, punk bitch mu'fucker's," he thought to himself.

"Young brother, I see it's your day to rise out of the belly of the beast." this tall dark skinned brother said to Low, standing looking down at him.

Low glanced up to see who was invading his last quiet time there, and noticed the dude he always saw reading books all the time and talking about issues that Low never thought of before.

"Yeah man, I'm outta this bitch. This shit fo the birds," Low replied, getting up about to leave.

"True. And for brothers who slipped and got caught up. I hope you got your head on tight brother, and have formulated a blueprint to succeed out there in the jungle. There's alot of legit things you can do out there besides run them streets."

Low stopped and stared him in the eyes and said, "Yeah, I know some real legit shit I'ma about to do, get money brah."

"Young brother, I can tell you have alot of anger inside you, but you can take it and revitalize it to your advantage, and use it to the best of your ability. I know your smart, cause I've observed you while you've been here."

Low glance away for a minute then turned back and said, "Yeah I hear ya, but I gotta be in them streets. But good lookin out on the advice," and walked off to get his things he was taking with him, which was nothing but certain photos and letters. The rest he just gave away. As he got to the building, he said his last good byes to the cat's that walked with him. He saw that tall dark skinned brother behind them staring at him and he nodded his head. Low nodded back and was about to walk off, but turned around and went to the tall brother. "What's your whole name brah?"

"My slave name is Cecil Wallace. Why do you ask?"

"Just wanted to know," Low told him. Dude put his hand out to shake Low's, and he shook it, then left.

When he got to the front desk and they gave him his money he had on his books in a check for $7,593, he thought it would be in cash. Then they gave him his release money $75 Dollars in cash.

Low walked to the front building where visitors come in at and leave, and was greeted by the two Detectives Malley and Jackson. Low's whole demeanor shifted.

"So Lenny...what you going to do since you on your way out?" Jackson asked, standing up with his badge flashing on his suit jacket as if he polished it.

"Hoe, I'm bout to get paid and handle my muthafuckin business! What the fuck you thought! Fuck y'all!" Low muttered, madd dogging them walking past heading for the door.

"Lenny!" Malley yelled, walking towards Low who stopped when he called him. His face was red from being frustrated cause he couldn't keep him there or put his hands on him. He got in Low's face, "You'll be back, you punks always do!" he gritted.

Low glared at him, then spit on the ground by his shoe. "Suck my dick," Low told him, and walked off.

"Little fucker, I'm going to kick your ass! You watch an see!" Malley shouted, making a scene. Low heard the sounds from somebody ride as he stepped out building into the parking lot. He glanced around the parking lot and saw Nut and them hop out a Candy Apple Red Chevy Blazer tricked out in gold. Red got out the driver's side grinning up a storm, Rat, Moose, and Dollar got out a white Chevy Caprice on Gold Daytons. Low walked towards them and everybody gave him a goon hug, even Dollar.

"Shoot nigga, as much as my cousin Red talk about you, I miss you to!" Dollar said, making everybody crack up. They all got in their rides and drove off. Alvin didn't come cause Low told them he didn't want to see that nigga right now.

Low was in Red's ride with Nut and Roe looking back. "Man them buster ass cops was waiting on me when I got to the front. Hope y'all don't got nothing in this car, cause they might try an pull us over or have the Highway Patrol do it," Low told'em.

"Shiieetted, we all strapped in this bitch," Nut stated. "Pull this bitch over so we can ditch our heat."

"Fuck that!" Roe stated. "Put y'all heaters in this bag and I'll run if they do. Fuck them hoes!"

Red said, "That sounds good to me," reaching under his car seat taking out a big black 45 automatic. "Here dawg...now crack them drinks and let's celebrate this niggas home coming."

Low was taken around and shown the new trap spots and all. They kicked it for three hours getting lifted then Low told them, "Man I got's to go see my family and get some pussy."

"Here, take my keys to the whip," Red told him, handing him his Blazer keys. They were at the crib on Broadway.

"Good lookin. I'll get at y'all later." Low hopped in Red's whip and headed to Westlake projects to pick up Sandy. He turned up D.J. Quick on the CD player and the woofers pounded. Nigga's and honey's were checking him out as he drove. He drove up in Sandy's parking lot and parked. He could see her apartment and saw someone peeking out the curtains. He knew it was Sandy, and that she had been waiting all day for him. He turned off the car and was about to get out, when he saw Amy coming as he shut the car door.

"Oh…Hi Lowdown. I thought you were Red. I heard you were getting out today. I know your glad," Amy said. It was cold out so she was rocking (wearing) a pink short fur coat, tight jeans, and pink leather boots. Looking Damn good.

Low noticed she had got thicker and still wore gold on all her fingers. "Fo real. I see you still lookin fly an thangs."

She smiled. "You think so? Thanks," she replied. "I know my girl happy her man out."

Low heard a door open and close, and turned and saw Sandy coming out her spot in a short tight mini, legs thick and shining from baby oil, looking like two tasty fresh out the stove turkey drum sticks. When it came to looking good, some women didn't care how the weather was outside.

"Hey baby," Low said, "Come give yo nigga a big hug an kiss." Sandy looked at Amy beaming with joy, and gave Low a big wet kiss. Low had picked up 25 pounds and had got taller. He had his hair braided to the back. He looked older and better then ever. He palmed Sandy's big soft booty, and slid his tongue in her mouth. Sandy sucked his tongue like a Starburst candy.

Amy said, "Tell Red I'm looking for him, and it's good to see you out Lowdown. Holla at you later gurl, cause I know you overdue," Amy laughed walking off.

"I'll tell'em," Low told Amy. Him and Sandy got in the ride and drove off. "I got's to stop at the gravesite. You want something from the sto?"

"No baby, I'm cool."

Low bent down at his mother's tombstone talking to her for about 20 minutes. "I'm out that spot now Ma. It wasn't what I thought it would be. I know not to sell nothing to these busters I don't know no more, and to let my partners handle it. Otis and Kev are doing good too. Getting big, like me," Low flexed on the sly and chuckled. "Sorry I ain't been up here in a while, but I had Sandy bring you some flowers for me. Well, let me go now, got's to go see the boys and family. Low poured some of the Boones Farm he was drinking on the ground. "Love you." He walked back to the ride getting in thinking. When they got on the freeway, Sandy had slid close to him and had started playing with his Johnson. She took it out stroking Low.

"Dang baby, it done got bigger and fatter." Sandy panted and put her tongue to work licking the precum and head, then taking him in her mouth suckin the skin off his dick. Low tried to think of something else but she was putting in work like she was thirsty to get his nut to quench her thirst. Low came all in her hot mouth, grunting out, trying not to wreck Red's ride.

"Gawd damn gurl, you know I got's to hit that pussy now," Low told her breathing hard, getting off the freeway.

Sandy leaned back against the door saying, "Uuumm, that was yummy daddy," and opened her smooth thick chocolate legs throwing one over the seat revealing a panty less crotch.

All Low saw was a fat, hairy, pussy glistening, then she used two fingers and opened it up, and it was bright pink. He boned right the fuck back up! He bent a corner and pulled on a dark street, and dove right in the pussy head first. He was never a pussy eater, but being away for a minute and Sandy proving she was on his team made it worth it. She held it opened a second while Low licked her clit, and all around her vulva lips.

"Ooohhh...damn daddy...that...that feels gooood!" Sandy wailed in ecstasy. Low opened her pussy up with one hand, and started licking her so good that Sandy started wiggling and grinding his mouth. "Fuck daddy, you...you...got me…cu…cumming! Ooohhhwwwee!" she howled, shaking and shivering.

"Turn that ass over," Low told her, still shivering and trying to recover from climaxing so hard, Sandy got on her knees panting. Low squeezed her ass cheeks with both hands and spread her open, and entered her pink wet pussy with one good slow stroke, making her gasp in pleasure and pain. Low beat that ass up for 15 minutes, and nutted so much in her it was running out.

"Dang daddy you tore this pussy up," Sandy told him, as he drove off grinning. "I'ma need more Kleenex," she said wiping her coochie. "Uumm."

30 minutes later, Low and Sandy was at his house with his two brothers and aunt Paula chilling. Paula had cooked his favorite meal for him, and Sandy spent the night there. Sandy was the first girl he ever spent time with and let get close to his family. He loved Sandy, and never felt like he did with another.

The next day Low woke up feeling funny because he had slept on a real mattress after being on a thin stuffed mat for a year. He took his Vette out the garage and had Sandy drive it following him to Red's trap spot to give him his ride back. After he did that, he dropped Sandy off and told her to find them a house since she was about to graduate.

"Fo real baby?" asked Sandy, happy as hell!

"Yeah. Get one out the way too."

Sandy started kissing him all over his face. "Okay. Love you."

Low had called Nate, and he told Low to meet him at his crib on the North side on Crandall. Low got there and was let in by big tittie Renee. "Come'on in cutie," she said giving Low a hug, smothering his face with her chest. "Nate waiting on you. It's good to see you out cutie pie, been dead around here with-out all your drama," she laughed.

Low followed her to the back room where Nate was at, counting money with Jess. It was stacks everywhere in piles. Nate got up smiling, seeing Low. "My lil nigga, I'm glad you out," Nate said hugging Low. "Had my dawg all up in that kiddy camp. It's time to do some real muthafuckin business out this bitch now! Sit down. Go get Lowdown some of that good stuff we got baby," Nate said to Jessica. "Man listen here, it's time to step yo game up player. "Fuck that little shit, ya hear me? I got faith in you, so I'll tell you what. I'ma throw you five bricks of that China White shit! Can ya fuck with that?" Nate looked at him to see what would he say after just being released. Most cats would fall back, scared.

Low's blood was pumping like a gas pump on the first of the month. Five birds was what he knew he could get some big ends with.

"Hell yeah I can fuck wit that! Brah I can make love wit that there!"

Nate smiled. He knew for real now that Low was fully into this Goon life! "Cool lil nigga, cause if you do alright with this, which I know you will. We going to do some other big things." He wanted to tell him that he was thinking about giving him, Nut, and Roe the connect when he got out the game. They sat and chopped it up for a while, drinking some expensive wine that had Low fucked up like never before, feeling good and mello as hell. When Low left there, he drove up to his mother's grave site and chilled a hour out in the December cold. He sat on the ground with his back on the tomb stone talking.

"Yup Ma, they tried to bury me. But, I'm even smarter then before. Watch, I'ma do some things out here." Low sat there a while longer, then got back in his Vette and went to meet Sporty. He called Sandy and told her to be home cause he needed to use her car.

As he was driving Sandy's car he was thinking, "Damn, I need my own spot. As soon as I give Nate this $75,000 off these bricks, I'm getting me a chilling crib."

Low drove up at Dairy Queen on McGuffey on the East side and parked for ten minutes, then this car drove up in the back of him and a dude in it waved his hand, indicating to follow me. Low saw it was Sporty in the color car he said he would be in, and followed him. Sporty drove three blocks up and drove into this driveway and got out, and waved to Low to do the same thing. Sporty opened the house door with Low by him and they stepped in. Low smelled food cooking and some old music by the Whispers playing, reminding him of his moms.

"Is that you baby?" Some woman yelled out coming into the living room. "Oh, I thought I heard someone," she said. "Are you staying to eat baby? Hello," she spoke to Low.

"How you doing ma'am," Low replied. His mother always taught him good manners.

Sporty answered, "Uh huh, I ain't going nowhere. Come on," he told Low, and they went in the basement. "Stay right here." Low sat down on the couch chair, 5 minutes went by then Sporty came back with a brown grocery bag. 'Here you go playboy."

Low glanced at him like "Damn, that's it?" And got up and picked the bag up feeling it had some weight to it. "Good lookin man," Low told him feeling just a little anxious, thinking ahead on his next moves with all the dope he had in his arms.

"You cool with that?" Sporty asked, knowing how he felt his first time he held alot of work in his possession.

"I'm straight," Low replied, like he was offended.

Sporty knew he was cool then. This little nigga thought I was going to take it back or something, Sporty grinned thinking. "Let me walk you out." Sporty had heard about the murders that Low had suppose to have done, and could sense it in him, and in his eyes he saw what he had seen in many killers before. Depthness of the souls he took. No remorse.

Low drove over Red's house, because it was close and he trusted Red. Tracy answered the door and Low walked in with the brown bag.

"Hi Low," Tracy said.

"Red here?" Low asked, sitting the bag on the living room table.

"Nope. He left about an hour ago."

"Let me use yo phone to call him right quick," Low told her.

She knew how Red felt about Low, so she knew he wouldn't mind her letting him in and using the phone. "It's right there," she told him, going into the kitchen. "You want something to drink or to snack on?"

"You got any Boones and some chicken?"

Tracy had to laugh cause it was funny to see and know this big money ass, suppose to be killer was drinking Boones Farm. "Red keeps some in here for you and sips it now an then."

Low got Red on the horn and told him that he was at his house waiting on him. Tracy bought him his Boones and some chicken she warmed up. "Thanks Trace, he on his way."

Red showed up and Low showed him the product. "Damn nigga! I ain't never seen so much white!" Red stated.

They sat in Red's Crib and broke two of them down, and Low fronted Red one for $22,000. Low had his girl Sandy hold some and stashed the rest over his uncle Pete's house.

Later that day, him and Kira sat in Denny's eating. "Boy, you just coming to see me and you've been out? Don't make me fuck your butt up!" Kira told him, putting her fist up.

"Ain't no thang, had to take care of some biz."

"I see you've put on alot of weight and let your nappy hair grow. You look handsome."

"Handsome enough to get some play now, huh?" Low asked, looking at her smirking.

"Boy, you know how I feel about yo butt. You like a little brother to me…plus you too young."

"Oh yeah, don't let the age trick yo juicy ass. It's fooled alot already!" Low stated, getting a little heated.

"I hear that. So tell me, what you got planned since you out now? You got your shit and head together?"

"Hell yeah, I'm tight. It's all bout this paper chase to stack fo me."

"Low, can't you get a job and chill out? Or go to school?"

"This is my job. And I'm in school, you didn't know! You got to stay on your toes and stay on point out here in these streets. Shit ain't no joke!" Low wasn't trying to hear that stuff Kira was stressing. He had love for her, but his heart was into this GOON LIFE shit to deep right now! "You ready to pearl?" he asked her.

"Yup," she replied, knowing he was a little salty cause she was trying to get him out the game and streets.

Low drove up Kira's driveway and parked. "Well call me later when you can," Kira told him, leaning over giving him a kiss on the cheek. Low turned around and they stared at each other for a second.

"Be careful out here," she said, and got out the car.

"No doubt," Low replied, and watched her big ole ass bounce away. "Damn, one day I'm going to be all up in that!" he thought. "Bet that!"

Jay had got out the hospital and was back with his home boys. But him and Alvin made it a point not to be around each other. That night when Low left Kira's house he called everybody to come over Moose house.

"Man I'm tired of this hoe shit!" Low shouted at Jay. Red and Moose was there playing a game on the TV, and Rat and Dollar were on their cells talking to some chicks.Everybody was watching and listening to Low as he got hyper and hyper. "Where this nigga Alvin at?" Low asked, going to the window to look out. "Y'all niggas know better! All over some stank hoe and all this pussy out here! Shit crazy!" Low shook his head, digusted.

They heard a car drive up and Moose went to get the door, hoping it was Alvin cause Low was going off and he didn't want him to flip on him. "It's Alvin," Moose sighed, relieved.

Low yelled, "Let that nigga in!"

Moose opened the door and Alvin walked in and saw Jay, and turned around to leave.

"Sit yo black ass down!" Low hollered at him walking up on him. Alvin saw the look on Low's face and knew he was dead serious, so he sat down. "Now you nigga's got beef with each other, over some stankin ass hoe, huh?" Low walked over to Jay and stood over him.

"Man that trick ass nigga shot me over my bitch!" Jay shouted pointing at Alvin.

Low walked over to Alvin. "So you in love with this hoe, nigga? Yo nigga hoe?"

Alvin studdered, "Ma…ma…Man...it ai...ai…ain't like tha…that Low!"

"Nigga tell me what it's like then, since you fuckin wit yo nigga's bitch! And you told me you wasn't! HUH?"

"Man Lo...Low...tha...that nig...nigga trip...trippin," Alvin studdered.

"Nah you trippin nigga!" Low replied yelling.

"Man, I di...didn't mean to...to...sho...shoot him, it just hap...happened an shi...sheit!"

Low went off, "Muthafucka you ain't shit! You shot yo nigga over some tramp bitch!"

Alvin jump up and said, "Man she cool!" all loud like catching feelings trying to defend her.

Low snatched his burner out his waist and slapped Alvin up side his dome and he fell back on the couch. Blood was leaking from the gash over his eye, and he was dizzy trying to get his senses back in focus.

Jay jumped out his seat trying to get at Alvin, but Red held him. "Let me get at this dirty ass nigga! Soft ass bitch! Let me get his hoe ass Red! Get off me!" He shouted.

Low turned around and yelled, "Sit the fuck down! Now you, get the fuck outta my face!" He told Alvin.

Alvin got up stumbling, wiping his bloody face with his shirt as he went out the door.

"Man, who got the weed around here? All this drama got me ready for some good ass smoke an shit," Red said, joking around easing the tension, making everybody laugh.

That night Alvin laid in bed with Mary. "Fuck all them muthafucker's. I can get money by my damn self!"

"Sure you can boo," Mary added, japping his ego up rubbing his balls. "They need you, you don't need them."

Three hours later they were all feeling good. They had smoked some Hydro weed and drunk some Gin.

"Nigga's, let's go out," Red told them.

"Where at?" asked Low.

"Nigga the Clubs, Bars, and see what's up!"

Low had never been to the Bars and Clubs before. He wasn't even eighteen yet. "I'm wit that!" Low said. "Just get me in them muthafucker's."

Red said, "No problem player. Let's go get fresh to death on these bitches and clowns."

Chapter 28

**Advanced in that Goon life you step the game up, moving up to the
adult life, doing adult things, like Bars and Clubs…Picking up speed.
Once you surpass that, you're on your own, straight GOONING...
Ahead of the game....**

Low had bought a all blue Nike jogging suit he had gotten at K&P, this
store that sold all kinds of stuff in McGuffey Plaza. You could catch all
kinds of honeys there too, because they sold weaves, wigs, purses, women
and men's clothes, shoes and all.

Low was in his room getting dressed with his little brothers talking.
"Man that's a clean outfit," Kevin said laying on the bed.

"I'll buy you one tomorrow if you want one," Low told him.

"Me too," Otis spoke up, raising his hand like he was in school.

"Man stop copying my style," Kevin told Otis.

"I'ma get both y'all different colors then. Is that cool?"

"Cool with me," Kevin replied, and Otis nodded his head yeah.

Low got in his Vette and met Red and them down in the Vic's. It was
like 9:30 P.M. when he drove up and saw them all out by this girl's
apartment Rat was sneaking with on the sly.

Low rolled his window down and asked, "Yo, y'all ready or what?"

"Nigga we been ready…been waitin on yo slow ass, let's roll!" Red told
him, and they all got in their own rides and drove off tailing Red. It was Jay,
Rat big goofy looking ass, Moose fat butt, and Dollar skinny silly narrow
behind with them.

Tina had seen all of them all dressed up and had watched from her
upstairs window. She had heard Low was out and figured they would be
hooking up, that's why they were all dressed up. So she wanted to see how
he looked since he been gone. In deep down she really missed him. Even
though she hated how he treated her love for him. When Low drove up in
his Vette her heart fluttered. He didn't get out the car, but knowing he was
there was enough to stir up emotions.

When Low and them drove into the Bar called Jitso's, it was jam packed. They had to find parking spaces near each other. Red, Moose, and Rat always came here and too other spot's, Jay only been there a few times. Red parked by the door on the side. Low was a new comer, so when they got to the door Red had to vouch for Low cause they were checking I.D.'s. Red gave dude working the door a $50 bill.

"I don't want no trouble outta him," Dude working the door told them. "You look familiar dog, what's yo name?" he asked Low, thinking he had seen him there before and he had caused some trouble.

"Lowdown player," Low told him, eyeing him down to see if he was going to react in some kinda way like he had beef, feeling his heat in his back tucked.

"Ooh yeah, I'm hip to you. Ah man, I'm trying to get some money and I know your the one to holla at."

"Holla at me later on then," Low told him, knowing he would send him somewhere else, because he didn't know him like that.

"Cool, y'all gon' right on in. Ain't no need to pat y'all down," he said, winking at them.

The smell of alcohol, perfume, and smoke hit Low's nostrils as he inhaled it in and glanced around at all the women of different shapes and sizes, dancing and laughing. It was more women then men there.

"Come on!" Red yelled over the music that was thumping hard as hell by T.L.C. (Creep) leading the way to a table some people had just left and was putting their coats on to leave at. They sat down and a waitress came to their table.

"What's it going to be fella's?" she asked.

Moose and Rat said Rum and Coke.

Red said, "Bring two bottles of Gin with some orange juice, and 40 pieces of chicken out this bitch! A 24 pack of Colt 45 and a cold bottle of Dom P. Here, this fo you sexy," Red said handing her a crisp $100 bill. "And keep this table flooded with whateva we run out of."

Moose told'em, "I'm bout to go get my fat ass on the dance floor with these broads," and got up and started shaking it up. To be big, he knew how to move and dance.

They cracked up when Moose started dancing with these two females who were putting it on him. "Look at that fat nigga sweating, he going to pass out!" Red hollered, making everybody bust out laughing.

"Man let me go grab one of these honeys up," Jay told'em, and walked to a group of ladies and talking to them. They looked over at Low and them at their table, and a minute later they all came over.

"These my homies, this here is Rat, Red, and Low," Jay pointed out introducing everyone.

"How you fine gentlemen doing?" One of them spoke. "I heard of you Low, a couple times," the tall slim pretty one said.

Low saw she was a sexy foxy chick. She had her haircut short in a sexy little cut, highlighted with blond streaks. She had long legs that went on for days in some high heeled boots that made her look taller, showing her lovely legs in a leather mini skirt.

Low replied, "Hope it was all good."

She smiled. "Some of it."

The rest of the girl's spoke introducing themselves.

"Sit down an join us ladies," Red told them, making room for them.

The tall honey sat next to Low and her mini skirt road up her pretty caramel thighs. Low glanced down and saw purple trimmed in white panties.

She saw him looking, and said, "You kinda young to be looking down there baby. How old are you?"

Look stared her in the eye and responded, "Old enough to tame that cat, bet that."

"Oh, okay. Well you old enough in my book then sweetie. My name Irene...if you didn't hear it the first time over the music," she said extending her hand out. Low took it seeing her nails were nicely done and her hands were soft, as he smelled her perfume.

Moose came back to the tables all sweaty. "Al'ight, y'all cool I see. I'm bout to go holla at the girl's I just burnt on the dance floor. Had to show they ass a big boy had moves an shit!"

Red said, "Yeah right. They had yo ass holding up the walls like you were about to die an shit nigga, stop playin," they all laughed, including the females. Everybody started getting their drink on and their table stayed flooded with alcohol.

"Let's go dance," Irene told Low pulling his arm. Low didn't think he was a good dancer until he hit the floor and the beat took over and he lost control. Being locked down for so long and never getting to get his groove on, made all that come out. Red and them were shocked for a second and laughed. But five minutes later, their asses were out there jamming too. Low was all up on her tall pretty brown ass when Humpty Hump came on by Digital Underground, and she jacked that soft little fat booty up on him throwing it. Low had his dick right between the crack of her ass, boned up. After the song went off, they sat back down and she was rubbing his pipe under the table. She 'whispered in his ear.

"Ah y'all, I'll be right back," Low told them.

Irene took Low by the hand and led him outside. Low hit the alarm on his Vette and they got in. "I'm about to blow your top off," the Vet (older) told Low in a sexy voice. Low glanced around and put his gun on his side, then pulled his pants down enough off his ass so his dick was out and nothing would get on his clothes. She gasped when she saw the size of him. "I see you working with a little monster there. I'm bout to rock your world young buck."

"You sho do alot of talking, instead of proving," Low told her holding his joint. She bent down kissing his shit all over softly, and Low turned his sounds up and Eazy E's "She Swallowed It" came on. The vet had some mean cap, she had Low toes curling up.

"Damn, suck this...dick! Fuck girl!" Low grunted. She took his dick all the way in her mouth, deep throating him. Low couldn't hold back no more and hollered out gripping the seat with one hand and her ass cheek with the other, cumming hard as she took it down her throat, "Aaahhh...ssshhheeeiittt! Gaaawwddd!"

"Ooohh baby, you got some sweet juices," Irene purred, still suckin his dick. Slurp...slurp...Irene kissed his dick and came up. "You going to have to get this pussy one day."

Low said, "One day, fuck you talkin bout? Hop on this muthafuckin dick an ride it. Later!" Low responded looking at her like you got me fucked up.

She looked down and saw he was hard as a brick already and hurried up taken her panties off and raising her mini up over her waist, and jumped on Low's lap like her ass was on fire and his dick was cold water, sitting down with her back to him she guided his dick into her. "Ooohhh…uumm…," she panted, feeling him stretch her as she eased down on him. "Uumm...mmuhuh…"

Low felt the tightness of her pussy walls wrap around his wood, and it felt good. "Uugghh…" She started riding him backwards. "Yeah ride this dick! Urrhh!" People walked by and could only see through the front window, because the sides were tinted, and saw Irene hopping up in down in pure ecstasy moaning.

"Ohhwwee…damn this...dick ggoooddd!" She screamed out, bucking and fuckin Low bouncing like crazy. You could hear her ass cheeks slap down on Low. SMACK! SMACK! SMACK! Irene came three times soaking Low's dick, balls, and thighs. Low busted again filling her up. She got off him and a sloppy popping sound issued. She went in her purse panting and took out some Kleenex, and wiped both of them off smiling.

"Umm, that's some good ole young dick. Let me give you my number," she told him. "I got's to get some more of that there dick." Her face was glowing from the good fuck.

Low was back in the Bar 15 minutes later on the dance floor, kicking it with some other honeys.

Alvin was in such shambles, that he couldn't even think straight. Someone knocked on the door of Alvin's house.

"I'll get it, you stay there boo," Mary told Alvin as he held the ice pack over his wound. Mary opened the door and Alvin's main girl Cocoa barged in shoving her out the way. Mary's eyes got big as fuck!

"Bitch you gotta alot of nerve, now you answering the fuckin door at my man's house! Bitch you got all this mess started wit yo whoring ass!"

Alvin heard all the commotion and forgot about his girl coming over. That slap to the dome had his mind on some other things. He rushed out.

"Hoe take care of your business then, and I wouldn't be!" Mary spat.

"Whoa, y'all chill out! Mary my girl here, so I'll holler at you later."

Alvin said.

Cocoa slapped Alvin and walked off. "Fuck you punk, ugly ass bitch!" She screamed going out the door. "Hope you get yo ugly ass kicked again bitch!"

She had slapped him right were Low had cracked him, opening the gash right back up and blood leaked down his face. "Damn!" Alvin cried, rushing to the sink in the kitchen.

Mary shut the door and went after him. "Fuck that stankin hoe and them niggas boo," she told Alvin rubbing his back, putting him back into the darkness to what was real.

Low and them left Jitso's and drove to the after hour gambling spot at the end of Campbell, that the Mob had their hands in. It was crowded as hell too. "Let's hit the dice game up in the basement," Moose told'em.

It was white Mob dudes down there rolling dice with the blacks. When they got into the smokey air basement, there were people gambling around in groups making bets. They called this hole in the wall Cow's.

"Nigga bet $500," this skinny kid with alot of gold hollered to this fat brown skinned dude.

Fat dude replied, "Bet!" He licked. "Bet a "G" back nigga!"

Skinny dude said, "Bet," and craped out. "It's on!"

Fat dude told'em, "Bet $5,000 little nigga!"

Skinny replied, "I'm cool."

"Yeah I know," fat dude told him, and walked away with the cash in his fat palms. "Broke nigga."

Someone yelled out to fat dude, "Vic you a mu'fucka!" as he walked off.

"Big bank take lil bank clowns!" Vic hollered back, as he bumped into Low. "My bad little nigga," he said looking at Low as he kept walking. DAMN, THAT NIGGA LOOK FAMILIAR, Vic thought. His two soldiers were following him, as they got to the stairs to go up, Vic stopped. "Man find out who that lil cat is in the blue suede Nike jogging suit," Vic told them.

They both looked to see who he was talking about, and one of them said, "Man that's that fool young nigga Lowdown from the east side with his home boy's," Vic's face changed, and he went up the steps.

Low and them got in the dice game for a second, and then Rat said,

"Yo, let's hit Jeff & Butch shit up." That was another gambling joint out there.

As soon as they drove off from Cow's, Dirty, Tito and their gang pulled into the back and parked. Vic got out a car he was in outside parked, and walked over to them. Dirty had a AK on his lap when the passenger window came down and Vic leaned in.

"Fuck took you niggas so long? They gone now!" Vic told'em.

"Damn!" Dirty uttered mad." Al'ight we'll catch'em later."

Moose had marks from the shot gun pellets on his face, that made it look like he just got over the chicken pocks.

Low and his road dawgs lost like $4,000 that night. They meet some vet women and took them to the Telly that night. Low was really starting to like that old school ponana.

Chapter 29
A crushed heart can keep something valuable away from you...

The next day Low drove into the Victory with Red and parked his Vette.

It was 4pm and the kids were out of school, so they ran over to Low when they seen him to get some money like always. Low gave them some money and him and Red were turning the building on their way over Rat's crib when they bumped into Tina carrying her baby boy Montel.

"Hey what's up Tina?" Low said, stopping and standing in front of her staring at the baby in her arms.

Tina was caught off guard when Low appeared in front of her out the blue. This was the closest he ever been to the baby since she had him and her nerves were jumping. "Nothing Low," she replied trying to get pass him.

"Let me see this little soldier, "Low told her reaching to take the blanket away from his face.

Tina's heart stopped and she couldn't move. DAMN, HE GON' KNOW IT'S HIS SON WHEN HE SEE HIM, she was thinking.

Low looked at him, and Red peeked over his shoulder, having heard about Tina while they were in the joint from Low.

"Damn, he lucky he don't look shit like ugly ass Bobby," Low stated.

When he said that, Tina's temperature heated up. "Thank goodness he looks like me!" She slapped Low's hand away and stomped off.

"Damn my nigga, that hoe still salty at yo ass," Red told him laughing.

"Fuck that bitch wit her crazy ass!" Low said, and they walked off. FUCK HER PROBLEM? Low thought, still feeling for her. After all she was his first real girl and had showed him love.

Tina got in her car and put Montel in his car seat. She was mumbling heated to herself. "Fuck that punk ass nigga, we don't need him or shit from him," she started the car and was about to drive off but broke down crying. "I hate that boy!"

Rican Puncho and Big Dawg met Low and Red over Rat's crib and they got smokey as all out. "Man essay, I tell ya...I got bomb weed connect... bomb essay. Get you shit loads of skunk," Puncho was telling Low. "Just let me know when."

"Bring that killa on then. I can sell the shit around the way." They hooked it up, and a hour later Low told them he had to pearl.

"Go ahead, I'll get a ride," Red told him.

Low kept thinking about Tina as he stepped outside. He saw lil Danny and Doe Boy. "Yo lil Danny comere."

"What's good big brother?" Lil Danny said, with a smile on his dark Hershey colored face.

"Do me a favor and make sure Tina and her lil boy al'ight fo me," Low told him.

"I got cha," Low gave him and Doe dap and left.

In his Vette he called Kira. "Yo, what's up?"

"This appetite, just got in and was waiting to see if we're still going out to eat, cause my butt is starving like Marvin right now."

"I'll be there in like 10 minutes," Low told her.

"Boy you better hurry up before I start chewing on this couch, shoot."

Low pulled up in front of her house on the South side and blew the horn. He called her number and she answered. "How that couch taste?" Low asked playing.

"Boy whatever. I heard you outside. Let me grab my purse," she came out in some skin tight black jeans and short leather jacket.

Low gazed at her thighs as she walked to the car, and thought, Damn she thick as fuck! She got in the car and her perfume assaulted his nose. "I see you smelling good, looking good," he told her checking her out, not caring if she knew.

She glanced at him and smiled, showing them pretty straight white teeth. "Boy, don't I always? Stop flirting and let's go!"

Low really was digging Kira. She was his friend, and he never had a real one that was a female before. He wanted more with her, but she treated him like a little brother. They went to Bob Evans and smashed. While there Sandy called, and he told her he would be there later on. He hadn't saw

Wanda, but she had been around looking for him. He wasn't trying to fuck with her since he heard she was fucking with Dirty. He was still human, so he was feeling some type of way about that discovery.

"You know their throwing a party at the Union Hall tonight, don't you? My girl giving it," Kira told Low.

"Oh...one of them college ones huh? All preppie cats up in there," Low said playing.

"Boy if you want to come, then come. Shoot, you can be my protection again," she laughed.

"Sheit, how can a nigga not come now. I got's to protect all that!" They both laughed.

"Funny Low. Well, let me go get dressed. You ready?"

"Yeah, I'm full." Low dropped her off and went over Nut and Roe's crib. Nut was in there fucked up on Tuss.

"Man let's hit this college party up tonight! It's going to be mass bitches there," Low told them. "I'm telling you niggas, it's going to be some freaks in that bitch!"

"Killa, I hate them high class snotty nose hoochie hoes. But I'm wit it," Nut agreed.

"Let me call Red and see if he wanna roll," Low said, hitting him up asking him. "He said cool."

As they all got together later on heading to the Union Hall party, Low said, "I'm tired of this two seater, I got's to get me another ride." They were in Roe's steel grey Park Ave with the deep dish chrome Dayton's. They stopped at the store to get some drinks before they hit the Union Hall. When they finally got there, Red was parked, sitting on his car with his cousin Dollar talking to some honeys. Roe drove up banging "Ice Cube" and parked right next to him.

"Wuz poppin niggas?" They all greeted each other as they approached Red and dollar.

Nut said, "I see y'all got some fly ass ladies here, how y'all beautiful creatures doing?"

"We fine," they all answered smiling, checking out his Goons swagger.

"I know that's right, y'all sho is," Red commented, making them all blush.

"I'm bout to go in," Low told them.

"I'll get at y'all sweet things later on," Red told the girl's.

Nut said, "Me to!" and the females giggled as he walked off like he was a big dude that weighed 200 plus and only weighed 160.

They got to the door and had to pay $5 to get in. When they all stepped inside, Big Daddy Kane old school song was on (Ain't no half stepping) and the floor was pack with some bad broads. Nut and Roe took off to the dance floor, and started getting their groove and freak on. You could tell they were straight goons and project niggas out there the way they were dancing and all on the females. Low just looked at his two road dawgs grinning. Them niggas wasn't shy at all.

"Player's let's get us a table while we can," Red yelled to Low and Dollar.

As they were headed to a table, Kira called Low's name. She was sitting with Donna, the girl Pep use to mess with, Carla, the one Low use to bone, their friend Penny, some white girl, and this brown sugar skinned chick who was sexy as hell, with sandy brown hair that was in a ponytail. Roe and Nut showed up grinning.

"You guys can sit with us, just grab some chairs," Kira told them. Red and Dollar was staring at how fuckin stacked Kira was when she got up to make room for them.

"Alright," Low said all cool like.

"Who your friends?" Kira asked. "Introduce them to us with your funny acting self."

Carla was staring at Low, wondering why he wasn't speaking and acting like he didn't know her. "Dang, you can speak," she rolled her eyes with attitude at Low saying.

"I see you, what's up?" he responded lamely.

Low introduced them, and Red got straight on Donna like he said he would when they were on lock down. She was smiling and flirting right back with him.

"Want to dance?" Roe asked the brown skin cute one.

"Alright, I'll dance with you for a second," she replied, and stood up in them light blue color jeans, her ass was on swole. Looked like two gallons jugs of juice. Low had to take a second glimpse real hard himself her booty was so fat and round. He thought Kira had a fat ole ass, but this had to be her twin sister cause they were running neck and neck like a mu'fucka!

"That shit crazy!" Nut remarked, talking about her ass.

The girl's looked at him, and asked, "What is?"

"What you talking about?" Penny asked.

"All that donkey on girlie, damn!" Nut told'em, trying to look around someone in the way of his view of the dance floor from getting another look.

"You sure is nasty and don't got no manners," Penny told him, twisting her cute little light skinned face up at him.

"Shit'ed, her ass is fat too," Nut said, pointing at Kira coming back with a plate of food. "Let me see yours."

Low just shook his head, while the rest of them all cracked up.

Roe liked girly when he first saw her. But when he saw them thighs and smile, he wanted her. "What's yo name again, I didn't catch it?" he asked her as they walked to the dance floor.

"My name Shelly but everybody call me Sha Sha." As soon as they hit the dance floor another song came on by Color Me Bad (Sex you up).

They got to dancing and Roe looked into her brown eyes. "You sho is pretty," he whispered in her ear.

She blushed, and told him, "Thanks."

When she turned around Roe saw her fat ole derriere, and was like "Gawddamn" to himself. I got's to have this stallion for real! When the song ended, they were walking back to their friends and Roe asked her was she in college?

"Yup. I'm taking up Law. So what do you do for a living?"

Roe was stuck for a second, so he replied, "Street sales."

Shasha giggled. "I bet you do. How old are you?"

"Eighteen," he answered. "What about you?"

"I'm 22 and building," she replied. They got to their table and chilled. Dollar had gotten all on the white girl and she was laughing at everything he said and it wasn't all that funny.

Low felt someone staring at him and turned around and saw Shasha all in his grill. He saw something in her eyes, then she turned away.

"Y'all know New Year's in two days, and we're having a party, well a block party like. All y'all can come if you want too," Donna told'em.

"Where at? Red asked. "Cause I'm there fo sho."

She wrote down the address and gave it to him. "My number on there to, if you interested," she said batting her eye lashes.

"Fo sho, I'ma call ya," Red told her licking his pink lips.

Roe tried to get Sha number in all but she told him she was with someone.

Low took Carla out on the dance floor because she kept asking him. "Why you didn't come see me since you've been out Low?" Carla asked him while they were dancing.

"Been busy, just like you were when I was locked up." Low let her know why, and that he didn't forget how she forgot about him when he was locked up. He wasn't really trying to fuck with her like before. Her loyalty to him had showed him she wasn't worth his time, or even to fuck! He wasn't giving away no free pipe to her and she didn't appreciate it. Low danced with Kira after he got rid of Carla right quick.

That night, Red went home went Donna and fucked her brains out. Dollar fucked the white girl at her crib in Poland, banging her back out, making tears run out her eyes. Penny played like she didn't like Nut but slid to the hotel with him like a two dollar whore, and got treated just like one. Low and Roe just went home to their main girl's and laid back.

Low woke up the next day smelling breakfast as he laid in Sandy's bed in the Westlake projects. She came in with his plate 5 minutes later all smiling as she handed it to him, and sat down.

"What you smiling at?" Low asked, crunching on a piece of bacon off his plate.

"I'm pregnant," was all Sandy said.

A piece of bacon dropped out of Low's mouth, as he looked at her stunned. "What? You having a baby? My Baby?"

"You heard what I said boy. I'm having yo baby. I'm just two weeks over my period, but I'm sure I'm pregnant cause I took the test."

"Comere," Low told her, giving her a hug tightly. His world had changed some now. "A baby, me! I can't believe this shit!"

"Are you happy Low? Cause we could have an abortion."

"Fuck yeah I'm happy, don't be saying that bullshit!" Low had a serious look on his face.

"Okay," Sandy smiled happy. "I found us a nice house yesterday too. It's on the East side on the Sharon Line. Ain't no other houses near it but some woods, it's nice and out the way baby. I hope you like it."

"Then get it. Just let me know how much, alright?"

She was so happy and hugged him real tight, not wanting to let go, and kissed him all over his face.

Low thought about this baby coming into his life and mumbled. "I wish you were here Ma."

Sandy heard him as she held him, and her eyes watered. She had meet his mother before she was murdered, and she was real cool and treated her nice. She had noticed the harden of Low's way when she departed. But he always showed her love. Some times when Low wasn't aware of her around, she would see in his eyes something so intense, that it made her body temperature heat up. Even his dreams were wild and crazy. But she had gotten use to them….him…his ways. Or was it that she just adapted. Love makes almost anything bearable.

Chapter 30

Just cause we made money together don't mean I won't take from you...even kill you... fuck you thought! This shit deeper than me and you...

Joint drove up the driveway and parked, while Dirty was bending down picking up a sack of weed he had dropped. "Nigga, ain't shit else down there!" Joint told him as he was getting out the car, heading for the front door. When he went in, he went to the kitchen, and was about to cut the light on when he heard a woman voice say.

"Bitch don't move a mu'fuckin inch!" she hissed.

He turned around and saw a 380 pistol at his head, and knew this wasn't no game. The deathly tone she used made him realized that.

"Now drop down nigga, before I put you down!" She demanded, and he got on his knees.

Shaking, Joint said, "What's up? You want some money? Dope?"

"Shut yo bitch ass up! Where yo gun at, huh? Take it out and lay it on the floor!"

Joint did as she told him, shaking up some shit.

Dirty got the last of the weed buds he could find and got out the car. When he got to the screen door and was about to go in, he heard a girl yell "Drop down nigga, before I put you down!" and reached for his gun in his waist and peeked in and saw Joint on his knees with a pistol to his head from the girl.

"Now bitch, you wanna rape women, huh? Sick bastard! Well I'ma bout to rape you back!" she screamed.

Dirty went to turn the screen door knob and pushed it open, and it creaked, making noise.

The rape girl heard it and swirled seeing Dirty and aimed her gun his way firing, then swung it back towards Joint who was trying to roll out the way and shot Joint, and hit the back door as Dirty returned fire. The bullet went into Joint's left eye and came out the side of his head. Dirty got up after she ran out the back door and saw Joint leaking from the head, shaking on the floor and ran for the door. He saw the girl run through the yard next door and fired at her as she leaped over a fence missing.

"Bitch!" he shouted, and went after her but she was gone.

Dirty dialed 911 and the ambulance and police came. Joint was still living, which was a miracle. Dirty sat over his big brother house 30 minutes later, and told him it was a girl that did it, and been doing this! "I heard her an saw her my fuckin self!"

Vic couldn't believe it, but after Dirty kept stressing it, he knew he was telling the truth.

"Man what fuckin hoe y'all done raped?" Vic asked Dirty and Tito, not feeling that news. "Think back you foul mu'fucka's!"

Alvin and Pep sat in Pep's Lac talking. "Man, that nigga Low think he the shit. He slapped me with a pistol like I'ma bitch or som'em," Alvin explained to Pep. "He think I'm sweet, but he don't know me! I'll kill that buster ass chump!"

"Me and him use to be real close, you know that. But he then took shit too far out here. He going to get what's coming to him, watch in see," Pep stated, thinking about how Low got out on him when they fought. "What you working with on the "D" side?" Pep asked, wanting to know how much work he had.

Alvin replied, "I got nine of them thangs, but I owe Rat this 10 G's I'm holding fo him."

"Fuck that lame! Keep it so we can get something together, feel me? Let me get back with you in a minute, I got's to do something," Pep told him, getting out his ride, trying to think on how he could come up on some money to add with Alvin so he could get back on his feet.

"Al'ight, just holla at me." Alvin got out his car and left.

Pep went to his crib where he stayed with Kelly, who just had his little girl. He went in the bathroom and sat on the toilet taking a shit, thinking about how he could get the money to get back on his feet. It's hard when you get use to having money and things, then all of a sudden you don't got it like that no more. A thirsty nigga will stoop to anything on your ass if given the chance and opportunity.

Pep thought about all the dudes out there he could rob. "Damn, that's it!" he said to himself. "I know these lames got work and money I can take out here! Rat keep shit over his girl's pad," he thought saying. He got up after he wiped his ass, not even washing his hands, and went in the bedroom to the dresser drawer taking out a ski mask and his gat. "I got's to get this paper." He went out the back door and put his ski-mask on over his face. He got to the back of Rat's apartment and knocked on the door and no one answered. So he knocked two more times, and still no answer. He tried the door and it was locked. Then he tried the window and it raised up. He glanced around inside, then climbed in. He started searching all over for money and work, and found $6,000 under the mattress up stairs and was happy with that and bounced.

He didn't notice the girl across from Rat's spot peeking out her window at him the whole time. He had his ski mask on but took it off when he got to the end of the apartment building, and she saw him. "Ooohhh," she said and called the girl who apartment Pep just broke into.

When Rat's girl Pam called him and told him what just happened, and Pep did it, he was threw the fuck back! And didn't believe it. He flew to his crib and saw it was real, so he called Low and Red.

"Nigga get the fuck outta here! I'm on my way!" Low was smoking mad. After all the things they then did, he couldn't understand why Pep would do this foul ass shit! Stealing from the niggas you done broke bread with, did time with together, fucked honeys with, got paper with and bodied chumps with. You never know a person morally until their pockets are hurting. My grandma always told me this in many ways." People can become undignified and unjustly when money is involved, or their stomach is touching their back.

"Hoe ass nigga!" Low commented to himself, flying over to Rat's crib cutting corners.

When he got there, Red was already outside with Rat and two of their dudes, Doe Boy and lil Danny. They all stepped inside and Low asked how much did he take?

"Just $6,000," Rat answered. "He missed the work I had in the coach."

"Let's go see this chump ass nigga!" Low told'em heated.

Pep had went and met up with Alvin. "Nigga we going to blow up out this mug!" He told Alvin all happy and japed, as they sat in Alvin's house not too far from the Victory. "Let's buy a half brick. Hold the money and we'll handle this business tomorrow, I'm bout to head back home."

"Right dawg," Alvin replied, as he let him out. "It's on now."

Low, Red, lil Danny, Doe Boy, and Rat got to Pep's apartment and knocked on the door. His girl Kelly answered opening the door and Low and Red bum rushed inside with their guns out knocking her down as they searched every room. "Where the fuck Pep at?" Low shouted to Kelly.

She was so scared she couldn't catch her breath, crying and shit, "I don't know, he…he left in his car."

"Tell that nigga, we know he did it so give it back!" Low told her with a scowl, and they stormed out the door.

Pep was just driving up in the parking lot and his head lights hit Low and them coming out his apartment with their guns out. He slammed on the brakes and threw his car in reverse as bullets struck his ride cracking the front window. "FUCK!" Pep shouted as he bent down backing the car up.

As soon as they stepped out of Pep's spot he was pulling up. They spotted him as his head lights flashed on them and he stopped his car. Low raised his burner and Red followed suit as Low blasted first. "BOOM! BOOM! BOOM! BUC! BUC! Pep started backing the car up faster as bullets pinged. He side swiped two cars as he got out the lot and slammed his ride in drive peeling out reaching for his heater that had fell on the floor as he got ghost out the Vic's.

Low and them ran to Rat's car to go after him seeing him turn down a street, and lost him.

"Man when I catch that snake bitch I'ma fold his ass up!" Low gritted.

Pep went back over Alvin's house and got the money and bounced.

The next day Red and Low was riding in his ride, and Low was still tripping off that nigga Pep. They were on their way to the car lot so Low could buy something slick. They got out at the Cadillac dealership on Market Street in Boardman, and saw some clean ass rides up there. A white man came out and showed them around, not believing they actually had any funds to afford one of the newer vehicles, so he took them to the back where the use cheaper cars were.

"I see what I liked in the front," Low told him, knowing what he was thinking and doing.

The white dealer looked at Low like Yeah right.

"Okay, let's step back up front gentlemen. But these automobiles here are alot cheaper."

When they got up front Low walked to what he was talking about. "This bitch here raw!" Low stated, talking about a 90 Burgundy Fleetwood. "This the one I want right here," he told the white man, who was looking like he was tired. The Fleetwood was gleaming so hard you could see yourself in the paint.

The white dealer stared at Low, and asked, "Are you sure?" not believing the balls and nerve of this young black goon looking boy.

Low took the duffel bag off his shoulder opening it, and dumped knots of money on the hood of the car he wanted that had rubber bands around each one and a piece of paper on top indicating how much it was wrote on it. "Sure as a mu'fucka," said Low smirking at him, loving the dumbfound expression on his face.

"No problem young man. We can work something out. Shoot, we can keep dealing if you coming like that buddy," the dealer said with a shit eating grin.

Low made the deal under the table with the white man and paid him close to $16,000. Low wanted to pay the whole thing off but the dealer warned him that it wouldn't be a smart decision, and look right on paper. Low had to call his uncle Pete to put it in his name. He signed some papers stating he would be paying car notes on it every month. Low drove out of there feeling like new money fresh off the press. Red tagged behind him as he stopped at Classic Coaches where they hooked your ride up. Low told them he wanted the gold package, and added his own taste to it to. He had them order certain things they didn't have. Gold button seats, Gold Truce and Vogues, burgundy rag top with the gold trimmings with three humps, snotty nose gold grill, and he had to have Sound Choices put the eight "12"inch woofers in the trunk. He heard Too Short rapping about having eight woofers on his demo and had to have it. He wanted his whip to be ready for when he started school in two weeks. They told him the car system would take a little longer then two weeks. He paid ten-thousand for the loudest car system they could install.

(New Year's Eve 1992)

Low kicked it in Westlake projects with Sandy and his rappies. They were going to that college party later, that was suppose to be a block party over Penny's house. They had been hoping Pep would appear but he was laying low somewhere. When they did hear he was spotted somewhere, he would get ghost, never staying in one spot for more then two minutes.

The college party was packed with females everywhere when they got there. It was chilly out so they went in the house. Kira was on the floor dancing with some muscle bound football player from their college when they entered. Low and them leaned on the wall and scoped out the scene. It was Moose, Jay, Rat, Roe, Nut, and Lowdown.

"There go Shasha, let me see what's up wit her thick ass," Roe told'em, walking towards her.

Shasha had on brown tight jeans, a short tan leather coat, with knee high leather brown boots. Low was like "Damn she got a big ole butt." Kira was thick as a chocolate chip milk shake, but she didn't show her ass off as much.

Shasha saw Roe coming and sipped her drink. She glanced behind him as she was drinking out her plastic cup and spotted Low, and they locked eyes for a split faction of time and something stirred in her groin.

"Hey what's up? I see you're getting yo drink on early," Roe said to Shasha. She laughed, showing the prettiest white teeth, with red lip stick on her juicy soft looking lips. Made Roe want to french kiss her.

"Mm huh, I'm trying to bring this year in differently from the last one," she said as she dazed off looking like she was thinking about it. "I didn't kick it or have much fun last year."

"Oh yeah, that's messed up. Well hang with me and we'll see what we can do about this year. Believe me, we'll have a ball."

"Damn, who that?" Rat, Jay, and Moose asked, talking about Shasha, when they saw Roe talking to her and they peeped her profile from the side and back.

Low answered, "That's Kira's friend."

Kira spotted Low and came over, making nigga's freeze what they were doing to take in her voluptuousness. Rat and them spotted her and all said, "That's crazy she that thick like that! And you talkin bout y'all just friends!" Low looked at them with a serious grill.

"Lighten up partna, we just joking wit ya," Rat told him.

"Hey Low, hi y'all," Kira yelled over the music, with red brick lips and a tight Guess jean outfit on.

"Whud up Kira, you sho lookin good as fuck tonight gurl," Nut told her.

"Oh boy shut up. What you guy's gon do, hold the wall up?" She asked them because they were posted with their backs against the wall chilling. "Let's go dance Low!"

Low got on the floor and started dancing right by Shasha and Roe. He felt some kind of vibe with Shasha but couldn't put his finger on it. Roe hollered switch during a song, and they traded partners and Low had to dance with Shasha. They eyed each other and started dancing.

"I see you got some moves," Shasha commented. "Didn't think you hard core gangsta cats knew how to dance."

"Oh, you got me bent," Low took it down to the floor on her and she cracked up, breaking the tension or whatever it was.

"You silly."

The song went off and Low asked her did she have a table or seat? she was about to reply, when Roe appeared and hugged her.

"Let's find you a seat," Roe told her, and they all walked and sat by the wall where Rat and them had gotten them a table and chairs. They all had a ball that night. Low went back and laid up with Sandy, listening to her talk about the baby and the house on the Sharon Line.

Kira was driving Shasha home from the party, when she asked her what was up with her and that Low boy?

"Oh, he just my little friend. Why, you like him?" Kira asked, gazing at her real quick while driving.

"Just asking honey, he cute though," she replied, changing the subject right after. "That party was live tonight girlfriend."

"Um huh, it was off the chain. I see Roe was all up on you to," Kira threw out there laughing.

"Shoot, I couldn't go nowhere without that fool following me. Did you see him honey? He alright, but he isn't my type."

Low woke up dripping with sweat from a nightmare. In this dream he saw masked men coming after him with guns and knives, and he was running because he wasn't strapped. He heard his mother calling him. So he turned around and saw her being surrounded by the masked men, and ran to help her. When he was about to grab her, the ski-masked dudes started shooting at him and shot her, making her explode, flying blood and matter everywhere, soaking him with her flesh and blood. That's when he snapped awoke drenched in sweat. He had jerked up so abruptly from his sleep that he had awoke Sandy.

"What's wrong baby?" she asked, touching his back feeling all the sweat on it. "Dang, you soak in wet boo. Let me go get you a cold towel," she came back and when she touched Low he jumped, scaring her for a second. He had zoned out for a minute.

"My bad," Low told her. She wiped him off, and he laid back down, still awake for another hour before he fell back to sleep. Sandy was use to his nightmares, but they still puzzled her and kept her a little scared for him, not herself.

Chapter 31

Love is pain, when your constantly trying to make it work with your mate. But when you grow up with pain as your mate, it's hard to tell who's really your partner...

Nut was so high on Tuss that his girl was cussing him out, because he was suppose to take her and their little boy Kemond, over his aunt's house hours ago because she was having a little family get together at the house Nut had bought her in Boardman.

"I'm so tired of you fuckin wit that bullshit Nut! Tired of it! You hear me?" They were in their plush house with the two car garage, swimming pool in the back, and big yard out back.

"Gurl I ain't tryin to hear that dumb shit. You drive then," Nut slurred, throwing her the keys.

"You need to stay yo high ass here, going over there all fuck up like that!" hissed Shawn, shaking her head at him.

"Bitch, I told you to stay outta my business! You coming or what?" Nut got up staggering.

"Don't call me no more bitches nigga!" she spat, looking at him all crazy as she put the baby coat on. "And I'm driving, dumb ass mu'fucka! You remind me of Smoke old ass."

That there hit a nerve in Nut. "You better watch what the fuck you say Shawn!" He stood over her swaying, eyes blood shot red.

"Nigga get outta my face an go brush yo funky ass breath so we can go. Damn yo shit leaping!" Shawn told him frowning her face up.

Nut couldn't help but crack a smile. He bent down and kissed her. "You love it." Which was true.

Low was riding with Moose down McGuffey, when they spotted Wanda coming out of the Arab store with some nigga rocking alot of gold on.

"Pull over there where that hoe at," Low told Moose.

Moose saw who he was indicating and didn't like it one bit. He saw

Low take his burner out. "Man chill."

"Fuck that chill shit nigga!" Grunted Low.

Wanda saw Moose car and looked on the passenger side and saw Low. Her heart jumped.

Moose parked by her as she opened her car door and Low hopped out. "What's up?" Low said, gripping his heat.

"Hey Low, I see you haven't been to see me since you've been out." Low was looking even better then ever, Wanda noticed taking all of him in.

Low asked, "Who this hoe ass nigga wit you?" with his screw face on leering at dude.

Dude looked at Low over the car, but didn't see the gat Low had in his hand cause the passenger side was next to her driver side. "Nigga who the fuck you think you talkin bout?" he yelled over the hood.

"Bitch I'm talkin bout yo hoe ass!" Low gritted as he raised his burner over the hood. Dude saw it and ducked fast, as Low busted at him. Dude ran in the store crunched down low.

Wanda was stunned at what Low was doing, acting like he was stone crazy and didn't give a fuck. "Please stop Low!" She screamed. "Please!"

Low took off after him in the store not even paying Wanda no mind. Dude was in the back of the store trying to find a back door to get out of, when Low entered and started clapping, making him duck down behind the old canned goods. The Arab running the store yelled for Low to stop or he would call the police, not really wanting to cause he knew Low since he was a baby. Moose ran in shouting at Low to "come on!"

Low yelled out, "Buster I'll see you later, pussy!" Low turned around and looked at the Arab taking out a wad of money and put it on the counter. "Sorry, Almil," he told the Arab, and him and Moose walked out.

Wanda was still standing there shocked. "Boy you tripping. Did you kill him? Why you do that? I can't believe you just did that crazy shit!"

Low leaned on her car and said, "So what's been up wit you?" Like he didn't do nothing.

Moose yelled, "Come'on man before the poe-poe get here!"

"I'll be to holla at cha tonight," Low told Wanda, and got in the car.

"Whatever Low," she huffed, and went in the store to see if dude was shot or alive. The Arab was trying to get dude from behind the freezer when Wanda came in. She saw dude was scared shitless. "Come'on, for we can get outta here," she told him. He didn't move a muscle.

"He gone?" he asked, shaking like a butt naked bitch in the winter time.

"Yeah he gone," Wanda nodded her head saying. Not believing this clown was talking and acting like a stone killer and goon not long ago. Now he acting like somebodies bitch in prison.

That night, Low stopped at Wanda's house, but only stayed for like 10 minutes. She was tripping about how he was acting. He didn't even fuck her, he just stopped by and asked her about Dirty. Which she admitted to hollering at before, but wasn't messing with no more. Low just walked out her crib.

Two weeks later

Low went to pick up his Burgundy 1990 Fleetwood with the crush velvet guts (seats) with the gold button in them, gold trimmings inside, burgundy rag top with the three humps in it, Moon sun roof, dark tinted windows, eight "12'inch Punch woofers, gold all on the outside with the snotty nose grill, Gold Truce and Vogues. Wasn't nothing on the street fuckin with his whip. His girl Sandy had gotten the house on the Sharon Line, so all was looking good for him. Red had took him to get his ride out the shop and when he backed that baby out the garage, and the sun hit it! It gleamed and sparkled like a mirror.

"I got's to come with something new now. Damn my nigga flossing to fuckin hard!" Red said in admiration.

Low turned his music up, and it set off car alarms on rides around there his shit was hitting and banging so hard. The bass made Red's jogging pants wave and move as he stood outside by the Lac. Low was playing K.R.S. (Criminal minded). Red got in the passenger seat bobbing his head to the sounds like hell yeah nigga.

Low turned his music down after he flipped through a few songs to see what he liked, and asked Red, "What you bout to do?"

"I know you about to show off fo a minute, so meet me at my spot on

Garland in a hour or so."

"It's on," Low replied, giving each other some dap.

"This bitch killin'em out here dawg, Yo hog hurting these lames out here!"

"This bitch raw, huh?" Low asked smiling.

"Like a mu'fucka!"

Low felt good as hell as he pushed his hog through the streets making niggas hate, admire, respect, and envious. Hoes and honeys were like "Oooohhh, who is that in that pretty ass car with the banging system?" Niggas saw their girl's staring with lust in their eyes flirting when Low glided past beating. It was like they wanted to fuck his car.

Low was banging so hard as he came down this crowded and popular street on the South side called Hillman, that he didn't notice the rollers turn the corner coming his way. When he looked in his rear view mirror he saw them, he bent a corner real fast tossing his Tec Nine out the window. The cops put their flashers on and turned the corner after him. Low stopped and the two black cops got out of their cruiser. One went to the driver's side and the other on the passenger side.

"Wow young man. You sure got alot of sounds up in this pretty Caddy. Let me see your driver's license, you look real familiar too," the cop on his driver's side spoke.

Low reached for his license and showed it.

"Okay...so you that young drug dealing killer huh? This that kid from the East side they call Low or Lowdown," he told his partner.

"Oh yeah," he replied, taking a good look at Low, hearing all the tales and stories.

"Get out the car so we can search it, and you. You got any money on you baller?" The one on the driver side asked.

Low got out and he patted him down while his partner went through the car. He took a knot of money out of Low's pocket.

"Damn young baller, I see you out here clocking an things," he told Low flicking through the money.

Low told him, "That's hoe money pimp juice."

The cops laughed, and said, "Real cute...real cute baller. So you wouldn't mind if we took a couple of these," and peeled off $400 dollars.

Low replied, "If it makes you feel better, you pigs can take that whole thing and get the fuck outta my face."

"Much better," they said, pocketing the money.

"And since y'all cool now, let me go get my shit I threw out the window." Low took his hands off the hood and started walking down the street. The cops just shrugged their shoulders at each other watching Low. Low picked up his gat and came back with it in his hands. "We done here, right?"

The cops looked at each and replied, "Yeah, just keep this quiet," thinking this young cat is off the hook.

Low drove off banging his sounds. "Fuck you hoes," he thought to himself. He drove around for a minute hollering at chicks he saw. Then he visited his moms grave site. When he left there he stopped on Garland and kicked it with Red and them for a while.

"Man let me get ghost, gotta go to school in the morn. So I'll holla at you niggas later," Low told them, and everybody said alright. Low went to the crib Sandy was hooking up for them and chilled. The crib was coming along nice, and Low felt good about the location she chose. Low stared at Sandy's belly as she slept, thinking about the baby she was carrying.

The next day, Low tried to get in school, but they told him it was too late to get admitted. Not really wanting him to enroll there because of the three homicides that took place at their school that he was accused of. They had gotten the security to escort him back to his vehicle. Everybody was staring at him in awe. His name was becoming notorious, infamous.

Ben and Rick were outside cruising around the school in the morning like everybody else do. They had graduated and was attending the police academy to become officers of the law. The death of their two best friends Roy and Sam still lingered in their minds and weighed on their hearts, and took a toll on their spirits. It was their murders that prompted them to become police. They couldn't understand how Low was still on the street, and acting like he didn't kill their friends. They nearly peed in their pants when they saw him banging his music in a clean ass Fleetwood, as he cruised pass them looking them dead in their eyes, as he drove into the schools parking lot. They watched him park, eyes big as apples, and go inside.

"What the fuck! Man we got's to get that punk for Roy and Sam for real!" Rick stressed to Ben, who's mouth was still hanging open stunned, staring at the door Low had entered like he seen a ghost or monster.

"I hear you man," Ben uttered. "We'll get him."

Low called his aunt and told her what happened at school.

"They can't do that mess. Call your lawyer!" She griped. "I'm so sick of these folks picking on you with this dumb stuff!"

"Al'ight, I'ma call him right now." Low hung up and called, and the secretary told him that Sammie was busy, and would call him right back when he got a chance, cause he was at court at the moment.

Low drove to his house he had with Sandy thick chocolate ass and went inside and laid down. It was still early for a hustler so he fell to sleep in their king size bed. Sandy was at Rayen at the moment finishing up her last year, and was going to attend Y.S.U. college to take Business Management.

Bobby had seen Low drive into the school that morning. He was salty at first, but got happy when he found out they wasn't going to let him attend and kicked him out. Now he sat at the table at lunch time with Tina and them, as Pep's girl Kelly ran her mouth.

"I'm glad they didn't let his retarded crazy ass back in our school. I hate his dumb ass! Pep ain't been home or spent the night ever since that night Low and his little homies were shooting at him!" Tina expressed, heated.

Moose brother Fatcat was like, "Low my nigga. Pep foul ass robbed from one of his own niggah's. Fuck Pep!"

"That mess ain't true, and you don't know what the fuck you talkin about, wit yo fat ass!" Kelly spat mad as hell.

Fatcat replied, "Yeah I'm fat, and sho is my pockets, skinny ass hoe. And everybody knows what yo baby daddy trifling ass did! Get his dick outta yo mouth."

"Fuck you!" Kelly shouted and pushed her food tray at Fatcat spilling some on him as she stomped away furious.

"Fuck!" Fatcat hopped up yelling wiping milk off himself. "Dumb ass dyke!"

Lil Danny and Doe Boy was at another table cracking up. "Nigga you know you wanna eat that shit off the table fronting," Lil Danny cracked on Fatcat, making them bust out laughing.

Dirty was 19 years old and never finish school. When he did go, it was because he was trying to come up on another chick there. Tito just never went and he was smart. They were sitting at their trap house getting high as hell talking about females when Dirty got on the subject of the broad that killed Joint he heard and saw.

"Man, I'm telling you it was a bitch that did Joint fam. I heard the hooker say he raped her. The only bitch I can remember we all fucked was that big booty one in the park a while ago, you remember her?" Dirty asked.

"Hell yeah I remember that ass and tight pussy! But ain't no hoe got the heart to be at us like that. Do you actually believe that shit?"

"Nigga I'm telling yo ass it was a bitch! She the one that's been doing this shit and killing our nigga's and I'ma smoke that bitch like a joint when I catch her ass!" Dirty hollered heated, pushing the girl that was on his lap off of him on the couch onto the floor hard scaring her and going outside on the porch. "Hoe bitch, I'm going to get yo ass, watch," he said to himself. Lately, every girl he met he was noided of. He even shook them down for weapons. And really the fat ass butt ones thoroughly.

The rape girl just watched Dirty from across the street in a yard. "Yeah punk, I'm on your ass. Soon you will die like the rest of your raping ass friends," she whispered to herself, "Soon bitch!"

Chapter 32
**Money bring bitches, and bitches bring lives, muthafucka's
getting jealous and mu'fucka's die...
(2Pac) 1992 Feb, 7**

Bobo stepped out from the gates and out the door from Mansfield
Prison. It was like 75 pounds of weight had just fell off his shoulders. He
heard some bass from a car and glanced around the parking lot, and saw
Low get out a clean ass burgundy Fleetwood that he had heard about from
everybody. He started walking towards them with a big grin on his face.
Everybody gave him a hug and goon love. It was Rat, Moose, and Low that
came to get him.

"Nigga, I see you on swole now," Rat told Bo, noticing he had put on
some weight.

"Nigga you know I've been pounding that steel in that mug. Damn, this
ride bad Low!" exclaimed Bo, checking out the car and then Low, seeing a
change and aura about him. He wasn't the same little cat he knew from
before, and he had gotten bigger too. But his eyes held some shit in them.
Bo couldn't believe Low had killed all the people that he had heard. "Boy
you've then got big."

"Yeah, I'm still growing an drinking my milk," Low told him, smiling
at his rappie.

"Let's get the fuck outta here, this place gives me the creeps," Moose
told them getting in the car, shaking his body like he was cold.

"We know you wanna go get some pussy player, but before we drop
you off over Cathy's, we got something fo you," Low told Bo, as they drove
into the Victory hours later.

Bo looked at his hood feeling good to be back. He had told himself that
when he came home he was going to be the top dawg and in control   of
the hood like it should always be. Wasn't nothing like coming home after
being gone for a while.

They went over Rat's crib and his girl was there so he told her to go upstairs cause they had some business to take care of.

"Dang, can't I atleast say hi to Bo, dang!" His girl Pam huffed. "Hi Bo… glad to see you out. I know Cathy happy."

"Hey Pam, thanks," Bo replied.

Pam rolled her eyes at Rat and stuck her big double D's out, then marched up-stairs switching her yellow behind with attitude.

Rat went up behind her, and came back down with a suitcase while they were talking. "Here," he told Bo, handing him the suit case.

Bo looked at it, then laid it on the dining table and opened it. It had half a brick in it, a pound of light green weed, $10,000 and three guns. Bo's mouth dropped to the floor it looked like.

"Low gave you most of it, but we all threw in," Moose told him, chewing on a piece of chicken he got out the microwave.

"Hell yeah!" Bo said excited, giving all of them some dap smiling up some shit. "Man you nigga's showed me love."

"Dog, you showed me love, so I'm showing love back, "Low stated, meaning it.

Later on, Bo went over his main chicks crib Cathy, after going over his moms. His sister was there, but she had moved out and stayed with Low somewhere, Bo had heard. He was salty at her but she was blood. So he gave her a hug. "Shit, she grown now," he said to himself, thinking about how Low just looked out for him.

What Low just gave him really was the only reason he was feeling like that at the moment. When some folks get a little something, they brush everything else aside.

"Hey sis, how's my little lady? I see yo boney ass has picked up some weight," Bo told his sister Pattie, thoughts of Low hitting that ass flashed in his head.

"Brother how long you've been here?" Pattie asked, checking her brother out. He had been doing Juvie bits all his life, and this was his first time going to an adult prison. He looked good, she thought.

"Ah, about a hour now," he answered.

"Boy I should punch you in yo nose fo that. You know better then that! Ma and Cathy been at her place waiting on yo ass all this time and you been here!" Pattie put a fist in his face, "I'm calling Cathy on yo ass!"

Bo stayed there with his mom and sister for a minute, but Cathy kept calling, and came over there to get him, so he left with her a hour later. When they got back to their place, Cathy told her baby sitter Tye she could leave now. Cathy was all over Bo when Tye shut the door.

"Where the baby?" Bo asked, as Cathy took his shirt off.

"In the back sleep," she told him, as Bo went in the back she locked the door, and went after him. Bo was watching his baby in the play pin sleep. "Be still while I take these pants off," she told him. "I need some dick," she purred, not having no sex since he been gone, keeping it gangsta with him. Cathy took his dick out, and started licking and sucking the skin off his shit. Bo just laid back enjoying the brain, and started thinking, "Now what the fuck I'ma do with all this work I got?"

Low had just dropped Moose off at his crib around the corner from the Vic's he shared with Sofia. When Moose put the key in the door he heard someone utter, "Nigga don't move to fast. You know what I came fo, so don't act funny! Let's get inside!" Moose opened the door and Pep muttered, "Where the goods at fat boy?"

Moose turned in saw Pep. "Man Pep, why you doing this? We go back to far fo this! All you got's to do is ask and you know we'll all look out fo ya."

"Al'ight, show me where the shit at then nigga!" Pep shouted.

"Moose, what's going on in there?" Moose girl Sofia asked from the other room.

"Tell that bitch to get her ass in here," Pep whispered, with the pistol to his head.

"Nothing, comere," Moose told her. Pep pushed him inside the living room and Sofia stood there shocked seeing Pep with a gun out waving it at them.

"Get yo stankin ass on the floor!" Pep yelled at her, and she dropped to her knees crying.

Low glanced at his pager going off on his side vibrating and saw Moose number. "I just dropped him off, what the heck he want now? Low thought, picking up his cell phone and turned his music down calling him. "What?"

Low asked, as he slowed down pulling the car to the side of the street. "Nigga you bullshitting? I'm on my way!" Low whipped the hog around in the middle of the street and headed back Moose way seeing nothing but red and thinking murder! He pulled up in front of Moose house, and Moose was outside with Sofia. Low jumped out his ride clutching his heat in his hand.

"Man that lame ass chump done fuckin lost his mind!" Low stated, with his face screwed up. It made him madder, cause Pep use to be their partner, now he was taking from them like they wasn't nothing to him. Like they were bitches!

"That shiesty mu'fucka then took a bird and $17,000 from me," said Moose, sick as fuck!

"What?" Low exclaimed, not wanting to hear this. "Hell nah, fuck that!" Low muttered, and hopped back in his car. Moose tried to catch him and get in, but Low was zoned the fuck out!

"Hold up, hold up!" Moose hollered, but Low peeled out leaving him. Moose got on his phone and called Rat and them and told them what just happened as he got in his car.

Low drove straight over Kelly's apartment (Pep's baby mama) and knocked on the door. She opened it and Low bum rushed in like before, but this time he was waving a big shiny 357 Mag. Kelly was in there playing cards with Bobby, Tina, Kelly and cousin Misha who stayed out there, and was always fighting. They all looked at Lowdown shocked and scared when they saw him waving that big ass gun, with flames in his eyes.

"Where the fuck Pep ass at bitch?!" Low demanded, all crazy to Kelly.

"I don't…" She didn't get to finish what she was about to say cause Low shoved the burner to her temple.

Bobby was scared to death, but Tina got up and shouted in Low's face, "Lenny get that damn gun out her face! Fuck wrong with you!"

"Sit yo ass down, I ain't playin! Now where the fuck he at?" Low demanded again shouting louder, pressing the gun to her cheek now.

"Oh my god Lenny, please!" Tina begged.

Kelly was studdering and crying. "I…I…think…he…he over…Alvin's …hou..house…I..I…think."

Moose had just drove up, and Rat had ran over there from his apartment. They both ran to Kelly's apartment seeing Low's car and her front door wide opened. They ran inside and saw Low with a pistol to Kelly's face, and Moose pleaded.

"Low, be cool, we want Pep. Just come'on partner," Moose said, trying to get Low not to kill Kelly.

"I know where he at now!" Low told'em. "Y'all hold them here while I go see what's up!" Low told Moose and Rat. Rat and Moose looked at him crazy.

"What?" Moose asked, not on holding people hostage, especially them because he knew them from the their hood.

"Nigga hold them here fo she won't call Pep ass and let him know!" Low gritted at Moose handing him the other gun out his waist.

Moose didn't want to look like no scary ass muthafucker and nodded his head, taking the gun. "Al'ight," Moose agreed not really on it forreal.

Bobo had ran over after Moose had called him telling him what happened. Bo entered Kelly's house seeing Low with the gun to Kelly's face after he gave Moose the other gun.

"What the fuck is going on?" Bo asked seeing the scary look on Kelly's face. Moose told him as Low hit the door.

"Hold them here, I'm rolling wit Low," Bo told Rat and Moose. Bo got in the car with Low as he started it. "Let's roll nigga," he told Low like a killa.

Low didn't even give a fuck he was in his own car, he just wanted at Pep for being sleazy and grimy. Low parked down the street from. Alvin's house and checked his gun, not saying shit. Bo just looked at him and followed when he got out the car with his 380. Low ducked behind two house from the back, and got behind Alvin's. He glanced in Alvin's window and saw Pep and Alvin weighing up dope on a triple beam, where he always did his thing.

"Yeah that bitch nigga in there," Low murmured to Bo. "Let's handle this shit and get the fuck outta here."

"Man you should of seen the look on that fat bitch! I took all his shit, fuck them niggas man, we bout to blow up out this mu'fucka nigga!" Pep bragged to Alvin, all hyped still from the lick (robbery) he just did.

"We should rob all them bama ass niggas forreal! I know Low got a grip somewhere," Alvin told him. "We can lock this shit down dawg!"

Low tried the door on the side and it opened, he slid in with Bo behind him. Low ran right in on them laughing about what they planned on doing to him, when they saw Low brandishing that big ass chrome 357 it got church quiet. Their faces changed as if they were attending a funeral.

Low stared at Pep, the nigga he broke bread with, had love for before, and didn't feel nothing but betrayal, hate, and death. "So it's like that now?" Low growled face screwed up, death lurking in his eyes.

"Man Low, I ain't have shit to do with it," Alvin cried.

"Shut the fuck up!" Bo told him.

"Grab the work and shit," Low told Bo. "is this all of it?" he asked Pep.

"Yeah man. Low you like a brother to me. I was just fucked up and needed some money, I wasn't tryin to play ya or nothing," Pep pleaded.

Low felt something stir in his stomach and come up through his chest. He thought it was hurt from this being his nigga, and that he was going to be sick or something. But it came through his throat and out his mouth. "Burp," it was a burp from the beer and food he had just drunk and ate. A sinister smile appeared on his face, and then he shot Pep in the middle of his face blowing the back of his dome out, painting the wall behind him a dark red as he crumbled to the floor, and Low stood over him and shot him two more times in the face, making parts of his face, brain matter, and skin flew everywhere shattering his skull.

Bobo was stuck, stunned, and couldn't move and believe what he just witnessed Low do. Then Low swirled around and blasted Alvin right in the left eye blowing his noodles all over the couch making it look like grandma's spaghetti, as he shot him two more times in the chest in the heart. Low snatched Bo's gun cause he was just standing there froze, and ran through the house making sure nobody else was in there and came back. Bo was still standing there like a statue.

"Nigga let's get this and go!" Low shouted, as he was grabbing the stuff shoving it in a duffel bag cause Bo was acting all dazed and slow. Bo started helping Low. "Let's bounce!" Low told him, and they ran out the side door. Low called Moose when they got in the street. "You can let them go now!" And hung up.

Kelly flew to the phone to call Pep after Moose and Rat left and got no answer. "Take me over Alvin's House!" She told Tina, with a worried scared look and tone. So they all got in Tina's car and drove over there. Bobby wasn't trying to get any more involved then he already was.

Kelly ran to the front door and knocked when they got there, and no one answered. She saw the hooptie Pep been using, so she walked to the side of the house and saw the door opened and went in. "Pep, Alvin!" she yelled out.

Tina got out the car looking at Bobby scary ass still sitting there in the car. "I got's to go make sure she alright," Tina told him. Bobby puffed and got out the car. They started walking up the grass and heard a scream. "Fuck!" Tina mumbled, and hurried up to see about her girl.

Bobby said, "Fuck that, I ain't on this!" But Tina kept going, so he went after her a couple seconds later. When he went in the side Tina went in he heard crying, and then saw Tina trying to drag Kelly off of Pep's bloody body. The only reason he knew it was Pep was because Kelly was hysterical, screaming and crying over his faceless corpse.

"Wake up Pep, wake up baby! Oh gawd no! Please gawd no!" Kelly wailed with Pep's blood soaked all over her. Tina couldn't help it and vomited. Bobby saw all the blood and mangled bodies and flew out of there woozy sick, and called the police.

Low drove to the North side and got cleaned up over Sandy's mom apartment while she was at work. Bo was tripping on how calm Low was, all laughing and shit. He knew then for sure that Low was not that same little cat he was before, he was a stone cold muthafuckin murderer! But he still felt like the bigger of the two on things, the hardest. Low was just crazy and sick in the head," Bo thought, as he glanced at Low nodding his head to "Above The Law" music (Black Super Man).

Low had gotten rid of the murder weapon, and had told Sandy to pick that work up he left at her mom's crib in the projects. Low drove up and parked at Roe and Nut's chill house on the North side on "Fairmont, an told Bo, "Come on nigga, let's go get high." Bo just shook his head to himself, "Yeah, this fool nut's," as he went in with him.

The heart of men change when certain circumstances occur in their lives. Sometimes it brings out the positive inside, and sometimes it brings out the darkside. One thing for sure it does change, is inwardly how we view and see things.

The cops Malley and Jackson were at the murder scene asking Kelly what happened? She was about to tell them until Tina told her if she wanted to live for her baby she better be quiet. Tina secretly thought she was doing it for Kelly or because of the baby she shared with Low.

Bobby had told Jackson and his partner on the sly that it was Lowdown. Now Jackson and his partner sat in their unmarked cruiser talking about Low.

"We both knew he would kill some more, but his own buddies!" Jackson said astonished. "He's like a fuckin Charles Mason. We got's to stop this little fuck!"

"Un huh, I'm with that all the way pal," Malley replied.

Low's lawyer called him the next day and told him he could go back to school. "Cool, you always come through for me," Low told him. He got dressed and drove to school.

Moose, Rat, Jay, and Bo sat over Bo's spot he had with Cathy blowing tree's, discussing yesterday's incident.

"Man, I told you that lil nigga off the hook," Moose told Bo.

"Yeah, he fuckin' retarded. But he ain't all that!" Bo replied. "I just got out and this mu'fucka murder two nigga's with me with him! That's some bullshit there. Nigga know I just got out too!"

Moose had a feeling Bobo still had some kind of hate towards Low, and he just wanted him to leave it alone and get money. Low was a heartless muthafuckin' killa for real, and he knew Bobo couldn't touch Low cause he wasn't ruthless and heartless enough, or thought like him. Low was an animal!

"I'm glad that bitch gone," Jay stated, talking about Alvin. "I was going to murder his ass myself!"

Everybody looked at him like "Yeah right!"

Red came through and met Bobo for the first time. Bo had heard about Red through the crew. It was something about Bo that didn't fit right with

Red after 20 minutes being in his presence. But he just brushed it off as it being their first time meeting, being street niggas, cause some dudes just have this vibe and aura when you first meet them, or arrogance.

Tina sat watching Montel playing. "You not going to be nothing like your father," she mumbled to him. She thought back to the grotesque murder scene she witnessed. "I can't believe Lenny has turned into such a monster, he used to be my baby," she thought back to their time together and tears rolls down her pretty little cinnamon brown face. Montel was starting to look more and more like his father.

To be continued: Read series two "MY PAIN, MY LIFE"

About The Author

The author/CEO: Danny Trevathan is a native of Youngstown, Ohio. He is currently completing his college courses in business and hospitality, while finishing his many novels and building his Publishing Company Underground Elite.

We Help You Self-Publish Your Book

The Big Flex Teaser $799.00
70 page books or less ONLY
    NO Exceptions!
1 free proof of novel before print, 1 Book Cover,
1 Year Free Subscription to Mink Magazine,100
Books, 2 month Ad in Mink / 1 CD with novel
set in word & PDF format. **Order our Self-Publishing Guide On a Value Meal Budget Today for $11.95**

Best Wishes,

Crystal Perkins-Stell, MHR
Essence Magazine Bestseller
CEO/ Founder Crystell Publications
No One Can Beat Our Prices!
PO BOX 8044 / Edmond – OK 73083
(405) 414-3991

New Big Flex Anthology Plans -$300.00 For Each Author 4-5 per book.
60 pgs only – Scan Typeset, 1 Proof, Book Cover Ad in Mink
Big Flex E-Book – 695.00
Scan Typeset, 1 Proof, Book Cover CD file, E-Book Upload, Ad in Mink

Option A $1399.00	Option B $1299.00	Option C $1199.00
2 Proofs –CP & Printer	2 Proofs –CP & Printer	2 Proofs –CP & Printer
Book Cover/	Book Cover	Book Cover
ISBN #	ISBN #	ISBN #
100 Books	100 Books	100 Books
Regenerate E-File Typeset/ 8 hrs Consultation	Regenerate E-File Typeset/ 8hrs Consultation	Regenerate E-File Typeset / 8hrs Consultation
1 CD with novel in Word & PDF format	1 CD with novel in Word & PDF format	1 CD with novel in Word & PDF format
Correspondence	Correspondence	Correspondence
1 Year Subscription to Mink Magazine	1 Year Subscription to Mink Magazine	1 Year Subscription to Mink Magazine

We're Killing The Game.

No more paying Vanity Presses $8 to $10 per book! We Give You Books @ Cost.
For An Extra Fee, We Offer Editing- If Waved, We Print What You Submit!
These titles are done by self-published authors. They are not published by nor signed to Crystell Publications.

Underground Elite Publishing
ORDER FORM

Name_____

Registration#_____ (If incarcerated)

Address_____

City_____ State_____ Zip_____

Phone_____ Email_____

Contact information_____

All Books are $15.00 Please include $4.00 for shipping & handling.

Please add $2 more for each additional book.

_____ Heart Of A Goon (Series one) Released from cage.

_____ Heart Of A Goon - "My Pain, My Life" (Series two), Caged until Oct/Nov 2012

_____ Heart Of A Goon - "Immortal Don" (Series three), Caged until 2013

_____ Heart Of A Goon - "New Era" (Series four), Caged until 2013

_____ Dope Fiends Son, Will be released soon

_____ Hood Psycho, Will be released soon

_____ Was Always You (love story), Will be released soon

_____ Taste (short erotic stories), Will be released Soon

Any questions concerning orders or to leave feedback, please call 304-997-4577.

Email us at: underground_elite@yahoo.com.

Visit me on Facebook at: Danny UndergroundElite Trevathan.

Website coming soon: underground_elite_pub.com

My finished book will appear on e-book and of course in paper back, before my birthday April 30th. So, I'm giving my FB friends the first opportunity to order in advance your own copy or copies of one of the most realistic novels, books, and literature ever! Let this be your next read, "FRESH OFF THE PRESS!

To place your order, make checks or money orders payable to,

Jeanne Thomas
c/o Danny Trevathan/UnderGround Elite
P.O.Box 2122
Bristol, TN 37620

For any questions concerning orders, call (304)997-4577. Leave message if no answer and someone will surely get back to you. First book, "HEART OF A GOON" (Series one) is $15.00 plus shipping. Please add $4.00 for shipping and handling. All together for one book and shipping and handling is $19.00. Please allow 3-4 weeks for delivery. UnderGround Elite Publishing appreciates your services, so we give you good reading and stories. Take care and enjoy reading.

Email me at : d.treva99@yahoo.com